Ravens
Rebirth

Sojourners 6

Catherine Gruben Smith

Illustrated by Emilie Gruben

Sola Deo Gloria

Scan for a curated playlist!

"For when we were yet without strength, in due time Christ died for the ungodly." - Romans 5:6

For Patrick:

My hero and protector. With each movement and breath, you scatter diamond love in every direction. I will love you forever, on beyond death.

Contents

Chapter 1: Toast

"I am thine, save me; for I have sought thy precepts."
Psalm 119:94

The dust swirled around Naqi and he held back a cough. He risked a glance around the cloaking lens, three interlocking sheets of glass and mirrors that deflected anyone's searching gaze. He couldn't see into the FFs' headquarters. Not being able to see made it harder to guess what Atif and the rest of Naqi's team were doing, somewhere inside that complex of buildings. His eyes darted to the thin circle in the ground cutting around the buildings and the acres of green garden. Somewhere down there two vast giants of metal sunk into the ground, just waiting to be called up and form a massive shell over the whole complex. An ingenious method of keeping anyone from entering. Or leaving. A shudder ran over the techy's spine and he sent a prayer up for his team to hurry.

They should have already exited the buildings, he should be able to see them marching through the gardens. What had happened in there?

Naqi turned his attention back to his cords and wires, plugged into the joint of the metal shield resting underground. Everything stayed connected, ready to be flipped on at a moment's notice. Unless the FFs tried to raise their shield again, Naqi's job here was done. He fiddled with the connections, and a little whistle slid through his teeth. Then he stopped trying to pretend to be busy and distract himself with other things, and spun to the frizzy-haired Sojourner hiding with him.

"So, besides rescuing the Bible, what do you do in your spare time?" Naqi asked, grinning at Mariah Perry.

"You mean besides being flirted with by weird little geeky men?" she asked pointedly. Her arms stayed wrapped around the black tool bag hiding its precious cargo. Her fingers tingled, as if they could feel the ancient leather and crackling pages even through the black bag. She held the only copy of God's word in her arms. Her kingdom's charter for life, the

11

Sojourner's one chance to resurrect from the invader's ashes. The lifeblood of her religion. The wonder of it made her stomach clench.

"Yes, besides that," Naqi grinned back. His mandible vibrated as a voice broke over his bone plant, and Naqi grimaced.

"Keep the shield open!" Atif hissed, the intensity of his words vibrating Naqi's jaw uncomfortably.

"I am, boss, there's nothing happening here, you don't have to–"

"It will happen, suddenly," Atif hissed back. He was trying to be quiet, Naqi realized. Otherwise his boss would be shouting at him. "As soon as Nehemiah shows up, the shield will close. They want him, Naqi."

"How is he coming?" Naqi demanded, slapping a pair of goggles over his eyes and scanning the circle of their horizon. "There is no sign of approach."

"I don't know. But–" Atif broke off, and for a second before the vibration went still, Naqi could hear someone else on the other end, a peremptory voice barking a question. Then it all went quiet and he was by himself in the dust with Mariah Perry. Naqi spun to his instruments, rechecking everything. He paused and glanced around the empty landscape. The horizon could be seen for miles in each direction. Surely he would have a second's warning, nothing he knew of could bring someone instantaneously into a place this open... If he started his gadgets working, it was unlikely the enemy would detect them. Right now the FFs were focused on resetting security, busy running their normal checks. But he could be noticed if he started interfering. With his gadgets off, he stayed invisible. Better to wait till the last possible second to start the system. But...

His hand went to his jaw and absently rubbed it, remembering the intensity in his boss's words. And the continued absence of his team, that told him something was already wrong. Naqi reached out and pushed his gadgets on. Mariah's eyes widened as she watched the thick collection of wires running to the massive joint of the shield. The whole mass shivered, hummed, and began to vibrate, hard enough to disturb the dust around it. A

Brunhiem laser dropped in her lap.

"I really hope you won't need that," Naqi said. The wispy little man held a pair of copper laser goggles out to her. "But just in case something starts happening, I'll feel better knowing you're armed. Do you know how to fire that thing?" Her hand ran up the rifle, fingering the sleek black material, and one finger pressed the primer. She could feel the heat growing as the rifle primed.

"I know how to use it," she said, in her best of-course-I-know-all-about-the-next-lesson-and-wouldn't-be-staying-up-to-learn-it-just-before-you-do teacher voice, the one she had to use too often for the young adults. Inside she desperately tried to remember the instructional courses on lasers from her days becoming certified as a Sojourner teacher. Naqi grinned at her again, with that frank admiration that flustered her into almost liking the weirdo. Then he turned back to his gadgets, checking levels, resetting connections, and watching to be sure they weren't shut down by the enemy. On one small screen he pulled up a map of the complex and pinpointed their four men. No, make that five; Atif had the mute. But there were a lot of people standing in front of them right now.

A fireball of orange flames rent through the quiet, rising above where the cloaking lens blocked out their view of the complex. A wave of dust and detritus swirled over them as a vast bang and heat rolled past. Naqi and Mariah pulled behind the shield, their backs banging into each other as they coughed and blinked against the heat and dust. *Distraction 1 employed,* Naqi thought. His heart hammered in fear for his team. He knew the plan; only use the distractions in a desperate case.

A whining, ringing hum bubbled over the two crouched behind the lens.

It pulsed inside them and seemed to knead their mind with an intolerably high-pitched power. The desert heat suddenly became eclipsed by a frigid cold that sucked with a fierce wind, plucking at their clothes like a living monster. Through his ringing ears, Naqi heard the lenses crack and glass beginning to shatter. The heavy cloaking device shook like a sheet of paper,

and suddenly shot off in pieces, drawn toward the sucking cold. Naqi darted forward, flinging himself on his gadgets and connections, trying desperately to hold them in place. From the corner of his eye he saw Mariah, her hair crackling around her head, roll onto the mass of wires and slam her hands down on the connections, physically holding them in place against the plucking wind. Naqi looked up, trying to comprehend what was happening.

A ball of terrifying, inky, shifting black stood five yards in front of them in the garden. White bolts shot over it like snakes made of light. For an instant he saw it there, grass clods, flowers, glass shards, dust clouds, drawn toward it as it hummed and sucked and hissed. Then it disappeared, mushrooming up and seeming to swallow itself. Naqi and Mariah panted on the ground staring at four men in full tactical gear, one of them dwarfing the others. Nothing could be seen of their faces, copper masks fitted with laser goggles and gas filters made them seem some sort of inhuman insects. The dragon-skin vests completed the feeling, giving them black plates instead of skin. But Naqi recognized the broad shoulders and black curls of Nehemiah.

The great joint of the shield creaked and whined. Mariah Perry gasped and pulled back and Naqi's gaze flew to his wires. Sparks spurted from the connections. A murmured prayer slid from him and he jerked on a pair of heavy rubber gloves, the strange men forgotten. It looked like he got to do his job after all.

"The prisoner is required in room D2."

The voice came loud, demanding, and smug. Taban skittered to a halt. Atif swung his hand down from his jaw to cut off communication with Naqi, and studied the situation. There were fifteen of them. Black-clad, perfectly drilled soldiers, they stood in files blocking the hallway in front of the team. Their commander, a tall woman with pounds of makeup smeared

over her face, stared at him with her hands on her hips and an ugly smile on her face. The "prisoner" in Atif's arms twitched, and he felt the raspy effort it took for the mute to draw in a gasp; either this woman or room D2 was known and hated by the mute. Atif didn't wait to hear what else the woman had to order. His hand slid into his pocket, clasped the detonator, and his thumb slammed down on the first button.

A massive bang erupted from the garden. The window beside the woman shattered, spraying glass onto the soldiers. Their line wavered as the fireball outside shook the hallway and washed over them with nauseating sound and heat. Hands shot up to cover their faces from flying glass and the drilled lines broke.

Atif whirled and sprinted back the way they had come. Otar thundered in front of him, the big man's hammers out in his hands, swinging back and forth. It cleared a path better than any show of lasers would have done. Shareef dropped back a step to run beside his boss, his laser ready since Atif's hands were full. Taban took up the rear, and Atif could hear his grim laughter as the fighter ran backward, firing behind them. Shouts as Otar barreled forward, screams as windows shattered and the walls shook, yells from the officers trying to bring order, the vast roar of the fireball consuming the hill in the garden; it rang around the team in a cacophony of chaos as they bolted over the marble.

A green countdown began flashing in Atif's contact. The hour was up. Nehemiah would be here, if he stayed true to his promised timing. A doorway loomed on their left, with natural sunlight spilling out, and a cool breeze wafting into the hallway.

"Out!" Atif roared, and slammed his shoulder into Shareef, driving him through the door. He glimpsed a wall of broken French windows, elegant white shelves, and a patio with overturned chairs and bloodstained tile. The mute in his arms jerked as Atif darted past the white shelves, and the weight in his arms changed. Atif couldn't spare the time to see what it meant. He focused on Shareef, watching him pull his shields out as he sprinted ahead of Atif through the windows.

1. Toast

Psalm 119:94

The supplier darted out with his shields up. Infrared laser beams stung the air around him, and Shareef's battle cry rang through the chaos as he skidded to a walk, muscles bulging at the force slamming into his shields. He strode forward, his laser firing in steady bursts. Atif followed on his heels, clutching the mute to his chest in an instinctive effort to keep the torn figure from as much shaking as possible in their mad run. He felt Otar catapult past him, so close he nearly overbalanced his boss. An animal bellow ripped from the big man as he shot forward to help Shareef, his hammers a blur in the afternoon light. Atif risked a glance behind him. Taban's lithe form came flying through the windows, his arms already whirling, sending throwing stars to lodge in their enemies. As the stars exploded, the screams and acrid smoke added to the chaos.

Another gasp wheezed from the mute. Atif eased his clutching hold and began to walk. The mute was their rescue mission; but he was also their shield. The Fat One did not want this man dead, he needed him alive to draw out Nehemiah. As long as Atif's men stayed near the mute, no mass death weapon could come against them.

Around him his men raged as FFs raced toward them. Enemies seemed to spring from hallways and doors and pathways. Through his contact Atif watched at least a hundred bodies moving toward them, swarming like ants on a dead carcass. But those in front held back. Taban, Shareef, even the big Otar attacked so ferociously the FFs wavered. Atif and his men were ahead of the crowd, on the edge of the mass of agents heading their way, if he could just get them back to Naqi they would make it. One boot followed the other, scrunching over the gravel, and their movement turned to a jog.

Their enemies came after them. Hesitantly, as though they awaited orders. But they came. Now the mass could be seen pouring into the garden, some in carefully drilled formations, some single entities darting toward them in a run, so many people out for their blood. The main army of agents waited for an order, praise the Lord of Hosts. The single entities waited for nothing; excitement and a lust to be the first to bring in the

infiltrators shone in their movements. But the singles got in each other's way. Those in the back pushed forward trying to get ahead, and the ones finally shoved to the front only had time to glimpse the threats they dealt with before one of Atif's men found him. Otar bellowed like a bull, keeping their path clear in front of them. Shareef screamed insults and curses beside them as he absorbed laser rays with the shields strapped to his arms. Taban's laughter seemed to encircle the little team. Foot by foot, they went through the garden, marching forward in a tight formation, wading through chaos and blood and screams.

A humming whine eclipsed every sound. It rang in their minds, swallowing everything in its high-pitched power. Every fight paused as that whining hum took over their brains. A sucking, freezing wind cut into their skin, with a stab of white light that pulsed from the corner of the garden. For two heart-beats, the cold, humming, all-encompassing wind eclipsed eve-rything. Then all of it pulled back into itself and disappeared with the suddenness of a nightmare. The FFs stood still, dazed, blinking at nothing. Only for a second, but it was enough. Atif's boots slammed into the ground as he kicked suddenly into a run, shifting the mute to one shoulder. Atif slammed into the few enemies in his way, and FFs went flying, flung through the air like toys. The garden paths opened to the team, and they ran, firing over their shoulders in a desperate attempt not to get shot in the back. As he bolted across the soft turf his contact zoomed in on Naqi's corner, and Atif's mouth tightened.

Four men stood in a patch of ripped up earth. The four de-ployed, scattering in a line over the grass. For a moment Atif gaped, wondering what they were doing. Then it landed.

A red pulse eclipsed the dusty afternoon light. A toaster beam, capable of taking out whole buildings and hundreds of troops with one shot, and it was aimed at those four men.

Naqi waited only yards behind them. Naqi, and their one chance of keeping that impenetrable shield open. Their one chance of escape lay in the path of a toaster beam, and Nehe-miah didn't know it.

Atif's contact flashed red, as warnings strobed in his vision.

1. Toast

The order from the Fat One had finally come through. The whole mass of agents at this base rushed toward Atif's team.

If they came out alive from this one, it would be God alone Who made it happen.

Freddy's belly jiggled as he hurried through the halls of his headquarters. A small package was tucked under his arm and his strafer laser hung on his belt, but nothing else seemed out of place with his movements. Agents and personnel pushed around him, each hurrying to their posts. Each assuming their boss headed toward the command center. The laser blasts and screams drifted through the walls in an incessant wail.

Two yards ahead of Freddy, Nicky stepped out of the command room. He stared at his boss, his dark eyes hard. Tarin towered behind him, her makeup smeared with ash and soot, a jagged cut on one cheek where a piece of flying glass had caught her. Nicky's hand lifted and he tapped his bone plant on.

"Orders, boss?" he said into the command feed, drifting to every active agent in the headquarters. "The shield won't lift, and we can't get a good shot at the group in the desert without taking out the mute and Hillson too." Freddy jiggled past him and his hand went to his jaw.

"Rush them," Freddy ordered into the same feed. His voice came steady, no hint of worry or distress in it. The tone carried an absolute faith in his men, a certainty in their winning today. "There are only a few of these people, and we have orders to nab the beasty and the young Hillson alive. Charge them at full speed, they can't keep you off for long."

Freddy tapped his feed off and kept moving. Nicky glanced at Tarin. They stepped out of the command center and trotted to catch up to that red hair shifting steadily toward the garage. The noise of the fight went on behind them. Something rumbled under their feet and the walls shook. Tarin cowered, her arm coming over her head as she looked up at the florescent lights shaking under the force.

"You know how many are already dead, right?" Nicky murmured in his boss's ear. "How many more will be dead in a few minutes with an order like that? These four people who just zapped in came prepared."

Freddy glanced at him. His face was sallow and sweaty, his jowls hanging loose in a face pinched with haunted fear. He paused as he reached the garage door and the bio-scanner started its work on his thumb.

"The shield won't close, the book is gone, and they have a SOLTD to leave whenever they're ready. We've failed the Wolf," he said, his voice flat. "Oh, the infiltrators and these new four will certainly die. A few may get out before our agents overwhelm them, it is possible. But the young Hillson isn't one to desert his own, he will die here helping the others get out, before we can take him alive. And that wasn't part of our orders. We've failed the Wolf. I gave our agents a quick way out. You two can choose your own way to die."

The door opened, Freddy Masterson slipped through, and the garage slid shut with a soft snap. Nicky slowly turned and stared up at the tall woman beside him. Tarin's red mouth pinched so tight her lipstick could hardly be seen.

"Let's get out," she murmured. "Quick."

Chapter 2: Ariel Shot

"For yet a little while, and the wicked shall not be: yea, thou shalt diligently consider his place, and it shall not be."
Psalm 37:10

The whirling, nauseating, cold wind zipped back into the SOLTD. Nehi lifted his head to see where they were, his military mask rushing his consciousness on. It took in the situation faster than his own vision and relayed it to the young man. He felt Peter, Tanzid, and Cobeau grouped around him and drew courage from their solid presence. Green living gardens, a complex of buildings, a line of burning ground and blackened walls, a mass of living men converging on one spot about a quarter mile ahead of them, and two living bodies just behind in the dust. It all registered in a moment. Then warning bells rang in his ears. His mask blossomed, metal plates unfolding and sliding into place to create a full helmet. A red warning flashed in his left eye, zooming in on one cube-shaped room standing on top the other square buildings. A twinkle reflected off white metal, and Nehi spotted the laser cannon.

"Toaster!" Tanzid yelled. The men scattered with precision and speed, each carefully dressed exactly alike, forcing the enemy to choose their target. Their arms swirled, clacking two pieces of shield together. Nehi felt the vibration run up his wrists as his atmospheric lens hummed and began to work. Lines of ionizing heat shot out in tight hexagonal shapes, till a honeycomb refracted, diffracted, and reflected the light three feet in front of him. Heat struck back, but Nehi hardly noticed. Through the Kerr atmospheric shield, he could see the scene in front of him as if through a magnifying glass.

FF agents raged, beginning to converge in a teeming mass that looked like ants trying to swarm an enemy. Through the mass, Nehi caught a glimpse of what ran just in front of the crowd. He saw Atif, and a bundle of rags and blood that could only be Joe.

The decimating whine as the carbon monoxide lasers shot

from the cannon filled the air, and Nehi forgot everything else as his heart thrilled with the fear. The toaster held twenty separate particle accelerator chambers; in essence, it was twenty separate lasers joined into one massive beam. If the toaster had the time to generate enough energy before firing, it could undermine a building with a prolonged shot. His palms were sweating as he held his Kerr shield steady. Because they fired the toaster immediately, it would be (for the massive gun) a weak shot. But still bad enough. A shrieking hiss sounded as the toaster beam hit, and Tanzid grunted and gasped over their headsets.

Nehi's helmet flashed a warning in his right eye, and it took a full second for him to realize it wasn't flashing for Tanzid's sake. Someone approached him from behind, fast.

Nehi shoved both halves of the shield to his left hand, spun on his heel, and faced backward. A thin wispy man raced toward him, from the arid dirt beyond this garden, shouting something that couldn't be heard over the chaos. Something looked vaguely familiar about him, and Abid sprang uncomfortably to mind. But Nehi didn't have time to think about that now.

He snatched the silver tube from his back and flung it at Peter. His friend's arm shot from around his shield, slammed a second tube onto Nehi's, and flung it again at the last man. Cobeau's massive fist caught the tubes and slapped them onto his end. The chimera rammed a mortar down the tube, pulled the assembled gun against his shoulder, and sent the shell flying toward the square room perched on the buildings. The operation was perfectly timed, and the mortar exceptionally aimed. The beam only had three seconds on Tanzid's shield before the shell landed, and one second to try and glimpse who fired it before Cobeau tucked the weapon out of sight.

A massive explosion rocked the base as the toaster went up in flames. Tanzid gasped again through the headsets; but it was intense relief, a breath dragged into burning lungs. Hope whipped into Nehi's hand and out to his full arm's length. The muzzle rammed into the man rushing up on him from behind. The wispy man stopped, rocking on his heels, his hands held up

as Hope pressed against his thin chest. Nehi retracted the helmet back to a mask, allowing him to hear this wispy character.

"They are after you, Nehemiah," the man said.

"The FFs?" Nehi asked. His voice sounded distorted and strange to his own ears as it drifted through his mask.

"Yes," the man nodded. His Adam's apple bobbed as he swallowed with an effort. "I am Naqi, Atif's man. He has your friend." The Compton's barrel traveled up Naqi's neck, and he flinched at the cold metal. The muzzle hooked the thin chain showing above the man's collar and pulled a small metal folk-art PP into the dusty light.

"May I?" Nehemiah murmured. The Compton's muzzle carefully jabbed the PP's screen and the familiar tinkle of metal on metal shifted as it morphed into the IDP cross. The laser stayed another second poised at Naqi's neck.

Nehi spun on his heel again. He snapped his shield off, clicked it on his belt, and swung Hope to bear on the mass of men around the complex of buildings. His silent, invisible laser began to strike down the threats his mask chose as the worst.

"You need to get out of here, you're the one they want!" Naqi almost wailed.

"I'm the one they won't kill," Nehi said. "They're convinced I have information they need. The other person out there with you, bring them here, we have to be together to leave."

"No, fall back to us," Naqi ordered. "And make it quick!" The man spun and ran back for where he came. Well, that was unarguable, he would have to be found now before they could go. But first Atif and his men were in trouble. Nehi began to walk forward slowly, waiting as his mind assessed all the information his mask dumped in his brain, looking for the right method of attack. Hope fired steadily, automatically picking out threats and helping clear a path for his allies. Through his mask's amplified eye he could see Atif and his three raging men, and the tattered bundle of Joe. The team was blotted from sight as FFs converged, blocking their way and swarming in a mass around Atif.

"Do you see our rescue?" Nehi asked, walking steadily

forward. A brilliant red beam pierced down from his right, and Peter gasped. They had another toaster up there.

"Saw them. Also heard the geek, and don't like it," Tanzid said. Nehi heard his voice in his natural hearing as well as his headset, and glanced to the right. Tanzid marched beside him, his blaster priming in his arms. As Nehi glimpsed him, the enormous gun bucked, and a blob of white power cut through the FFs ranks. A deadly whine shot over their heads as a second mortar took out the toaster. The enemy had guessed the wrong target, as Nehi had hoped when he gave Beau the weapon.

"Why aren't you on support fire with Pete, like I ordered?" Nehi growled.

"Take this," Tanzid said, and shoved the heavy blaster into Nehi's arms. "She'll do more good than that puny thing you're using." The dark-skinned agent jerked a grenade from his belt, flicked the pin out, and lobbed it at the crowd to the left of Atif's group. A cry rang from the area, then came the bang, more fire, more smoke. More screams. Out of the corner of his eye, Nehi saw a great form running. Cobeau raced for Joe. He would break through every barrier to hold and protect his little friend. Laser bursts lit his helmet and armored vest in a steady stream, lighting the chimera with a fearsome white glow. A roar of pure animal fury broke from him and a shudder crawled through Nehi as he gave Beau what cover he could.

A rumble came from the earth under their feet, as something underground exploded. A portion of the complex of buildings folded in on itself in a heap of dust and rubble and screams.

Cobeau smashed into the FFs. He went through the wall of men as if they were paper, smashing a hole five people dense in the crowd, to get to his chosen master. For an instant in the chaos, Nehi's mask showed Cobeau, towering over Atif. The chimera plucked up Joe, cradling him in one arm, and all six rushed through the hole the chimera had made and out onto the open grass. One red-haired one came half carried, leaning heavily on his teammates.

All was smoke and screams and raging warfare. Laser beams and projectiles were everywhere. Nehi's mask flashed

another warning, and through its enhanced vision he saw a netting gun priming on the complex. If that fired it would encapsulate them in the thick wires, leaving no way to fight back. And they had only been able to bring two mortars. Nehi's mind whirled, looking for their way out. Cobeau and Atif's men barreled past him, bleeding and burned, but still running. Atif swung neatly to Nehi's left side, his Healys bucking and whining.

Nehemiah started backing up, walking backward as the blaster bucked again and again in his arms. They had to be together to use the SOLTD and get out. But if they turned their backs and ran, they would be mown down by the suicidal crowd of FFs rushing down on them. The Kerr shield only worked if you stood still. And they couldn't stop now, not with these mad people rushing for them like mindless ants. This situation was completely untenable. On his right, Tanzid flung two more grenades into the oncoming rush, businesslike and steady. On his left Atif spun, grim and stately, firing with stunning rapidity into the onrushing ranks. Under his mask Nehi bit his lip searching for a way to extract them all alive. A laser beam slammed into his shoulder and he felt it burn under his vest. Nehi kept marching backward, steadily, swiftly, but his eyes were on a small spot under the grass. His mask had found one other thing for him.

In the right corner of this garden, only about ten yards away from them, eight massive generators were sunk into the ground. Nehi flung the blaster back at Tanzid and Hope sprang into his hand. Hope's beam focused on the buried wire to the generators. His finger pressed the trigger and held it, and he could feel the Compton pistol heating and beginning to shake under his hands. He forced the beam steady on his spot and picked it up to a trot.

A mottled shadow fell over Nehi, and for an instant the terror of certain capture took over his mind. The first shot from the netting gun rushed toward his head.

A dark hand shot up into his view, and a Kerr shield flew past him, its metallic oval glinting in the sunlight. The netting

curled around the metal. The weighted ends of the net slammed around the shield with a sickening crack. It smashed into the turf and bounced past Nehi's foot. The young man breathed again and kept moving backward. But his aim never wavered.

A pulsing whine and terrible tugging hit his joints. Cold stung him as if liquid nitrogen touched his skin. He felt his mask coating with ice. Hope sprung up in his hands as the force threw her aim off. He whirled toward the feeling and dug his shoes into the ground, trying to keep himself from dragging toward the pull, grasping for a reason a SOLTD would be activating now. Were they leaving without them?

Still too far away, he glimpsed Peter, Beau, and the others grouped in the desert around what looked like a huge black snake, firing incessantly at the FFs as a cover to Nehi and his little group. Not leaving, they weren't the type to desert their brothers.

But just behind him the black ball of a SOLTD pulsed.

Someone was coming.

Jill kicked her heels against the metal cot. The sound rang through the jail cell, bouncing off the metal walls. She growled and flung herself on the hard mattress, letting one trim arm drape over her face.

"Just wait, sweetheart," Bill's voice drifted from the cell across from her. "We won't stay here long, I'll get you out."

"No, we won't," Jill moaned. "The UPC have no reason to keep us here. They'll get tired of it soon." *And then what?* All three of the trio thought it. One name echoed through their minds like a death knell. *Wolf.*

"Remember that cave up in the KAM mountains?" Bill broke the silence.

"Yeah," Will's gravelly voice rumbled around the three. "I carried so much loot there for you two."

"We three, Will, we three," Bill purred. "When we get out of here—"

The air current changed as the door swung open, and Bill's words cut off into sudden silence. Jill's arm slowly came off her face. She couldn't hear anything. No squeaking hinges from the door. No footsteps in the hall. No priming lasers.

A harsh choking came from Will's cell. Jill slowly swiveled to sit on her cot. Every inch of her felt cold. The sound stopped. She stood, slowly, staring at the single metal grate in her door. Through that she could see into Bill's cell if she wanted to. Bill's voice broke the quiet. A sharp, terrified cry cut off quickly. Another choking sound. Jill's feet moved, almost unwillingly, taking her toward the door. She stood on her toes and looked out the grate.

A wolf's head stared back at her.

Jill's shrill scream echoed off the concrete walls.

Nehi caught a glimpse of the pulsing black ball, then the two black halves of the SOLTD mushroomed out and sucked into their copper balls, as the dark energy and matter pulled into their own z shielding cases. A woman in a shimmery scaled suit stood on the grass holding the SOLTD. A utility belt strapped around her hips bristled with weapons, and she rested a Krackmen against her shoulder. Her blond hair was pulled back in a long ponytail to keep it away from her face, a rock-hard image of perfection. Eight beefy, well-armed soldiers stood ranged behind her. As he glimpsed her, the red of her priming Krackmen lit her face. Ruby red lips pulled up in a tight smile.

"Come on, boys," she said, a dark enjoyment dancing on her voice, "let's eliminate these cretins and cripple a Wolf's paw." The men fanned out in perfect timing and perfect training, and grenades flew over Nehi's head like falling stars.

In a flash Nehi remembered Joe's hesitation to promise to alert him, the mute's caginess about his contacts and mysterious disappearances within kingdoms, and he knew who this was. It seems the crossed lover had access to Joe's distress signal. He had this one moment, and might never get another. He

fell back as she strode forward. They met on the torn, dirt-strewn ground of Freddy's ruined garden. Nehi clicked his Kerr shield together in front of them and pulled his mask off. It was a calculated action, showing enough trust in her as an ally he let her see his features. As the honeycombed shield cut them off from the furious fight, he opened negotiations.

"I know you. We have a common enemy. Let's work together and cripple more than one paw." Her eyes ran up and down him and settled on his face. Something twisted those perfect red lips but he couldn't define the expression. Around them lasers fired, the daylight obliterated by smoke and flashes of red and white laser blasts going off almost incessantly. Screams and battle shouts and grenades shook the ground. They could see the fight in vivid detail through the Kerr.

"Do we really?" she said. Nehi got the uncomfortable feeling something moved behind those words he didn't really under-stand. "Give the Raven a message. His facts are correct. Wolf is holding the cache over my head in an attempt to get me off his tail. I'm in."

Ariel Athenia spun around Nehi's shield and her hand shot to her belt. Cherry bombs equipped with mini drones shot from her hand and zipped off through the broken windows of the headquarters. More explosions lit up the air, more smoke curled into the sky.

"Stupid boys, fall back," she shouted, almost lazily. "Stop heading toward the enemy."

"Get to the desert," Atif shouted above the chaos. Ariel's bright eyes spun to him for an instant. She nodded, then went back to the fun.

Nehi fitted his mask on and let the metal plates slide back into its helmet, thankful to cut off a little of the noise and smell drifting around him. He clicked the Kerr back on his belt and moved again. A laser beam hit him in the chest and he felt it burn under his vest. Probably a random shot, but who could be sure? He jerked Hope up, aimed at the area under the grass again, and held her trigger down. His feet moved steadily back-ward toward his friends. Tanzid staggered beside him, a gasp

coming as his left arm went limp. But the agent kept moving, his Blaster bucking and steaming as it hung from his shoulder holster.

Ariel and her team moved a few yards to their left. They shifted steadily toward the desert, a little ahead of Nehi's small group. So many weapons of mass death shot from them into the FFs. A few of the enemy wavered, turning back to what safety might be found in the buildings' cover. But most just ran harder toward them, reaching for their own death-dealing weapons. He saw one of her agents drop and lie still. Then another. There were still too many FF agents rushing toward them in a suicidal fury.

A tendril of white smoke snaked off Hope's two copper balls, and his hands grew numb from the effort to control the shaking pistol. The connectors had never stayed open this long, the dark matter and energy heated to dangerous degrees in their excitement. But another tendril of smoke lifted into the air, this one from the sunken wire connecting all the generators to the complex of buildings.

Atif swung back and forth around Nehi, his Healy lasers whining and steaming as he protected the young man in his retreat. Atif worked without comment, but inside he felt miffed. This was a really bad extraction plan; they wouldn't even have the chance to use that magical glowing ball as things stood, the FFs would be on them in seconds, well before they could reach their companions at the end of this garden. Then Ariel's eyes flicked to the tendril of smoke rising off the ground from Nehi's work. A laugh split her perfect face.

Two deep earth grenades shot from her and landed on the tendril of smoke.

A blast of heat and yellow flames slammed into Atif. He was flung to the side and rammed into the powerful agent beside him. Tanzid's hand pushed into his shoulder, driving him back up as the two staggered. Another wall of flames and heat and smoke went up beside the first, then two more, and another in a line. Nehi's gloved hands latched onto his companions' shoulders, and he bolted for the desert, dragging them with him.

Another bang and roar, and Tanzid's consciousness reeled under the heat and power pressing down on him from the massed explosion. Black, acrid smoke filled the air and coughs began to rend his lungs. Nehi dragged them past the last of the burning generators, the heat lessened, and Atif and Tanzid found their senses again.

The three men flew over the ripped-up grass where the SOLTD had landed, making for the knot of allies standing just outside the circle of green. Everyone in that knot seemed to be firing something, providing some cover to keep Nehi and his men alive in their reckless dash, as the heat and smoke masked everything in confusion. They vaguely registered Ariel running like a deer to their left, her men in a clump around her; three of them corpses being carried out. The black smoke did its work, and Nehi and his group reeled and coughed uncontrollably as they stumbled over the last bit of green onto the dry dirt. Nehi felt Peter's arm dart around his chest, and his black-gloved hands tightened on Atif and Tanzid. Then the sickening, swirling cold of the SOLTD closed over the scene.

In the second the SOLTD gripped the ground they were standing on, it tore through everything near it. Nehi noticed a flurry of sparks as a mass of wires was shorn through. Two great hulking shields of metal rose from the ground just in front of their SOLTD, seeming to shoot out of the earth toward each other, forming a bowl. The last glimpse Nehi had of the FFs that had haunted his life for two years, was a scene of acrid smoke, burning, crumbling buildings, screaming masses of people beginning to fight each other in panic, and those two great shields enclosing it all in nightmarish blackness. It seemed like the hand of God closing the evil into itself, confining it in its own living hell to extinguish in smoke and fire.

Whirling, freezing wind and blackness took over the world. A sense of weightlessness, of being tugged, and frozen claimed him. His mind spun with sickening force as his stomach convulsed.

Soft, good earth slammed into the bottom of his boots, and Nehi's knees buckled. Every ache in his body woke and

screamed at him. The whirling fiend of cold wind hissed and shrieked back into its two balls, and he knelt coughing and gasping on a circle of acrid dusty land, splayed over the beautiful green of Doctor Harold Pablo's backyard. His helmet retracted into its mask with a steady click of metal plates. He pulled the mask off his face with a little gasp of relief and his own vision took over again.

A heavy thud sounded in front of him and Nehi looked up from smoke-stung eyes into the reddened, weeping eyes of the chimera. Beau leaned forward and laid a filthy, bleeding form in Nehi's arms. For a moment, as he automatically pulled the small body closer to keep him from rolling off, Nehi panicked, knowing he was dead, that they were too late, that he had failed Joe in the ultimate test.

The mute's chest expanded and fell. A wheezing sigh flew from his lips, and Nehi sagged in relief. Peace hovered on Joe's face. He lay blissfully insensible, but he knew even in his subconscious that a friend held him. Nehi looked up again into Cobeau's smudged face. The chimera beamed through his tears.

Chapter 3: Snapshots

"Open thou mine eyes, that I may behold wondrous things out of thy law." Psalm 119:18

"W hoa," Shareef breathed. The single word cut through the tension, and people began to unbend. Feet shifted off the arid patch of dirt to the springy green grass, shoulders rolled to ease tensed muscles. A few chuckles and groans sounded as the clump of people began to break into groups. Shareef slumped on the ground. He let his back rest against Taban's leg as Otar packed his wounds. The backdoor shoved open and Anna darted out with Harold Pablo and Daniel at her heels.

"Whoa," Shareef murmured again, in a very different tone. He quickly looked away from Anna and forced his eyebrows back to a normal position, noticing with amusement that the rest of his team were doing the same thing. Except Naqi. Naqi seemed to only notice the frizzy-haired one. The beauty and the doctor converged on Nehemiah and the rescued one, and conversations started up again.

"Stop saying, 'Whoa,' you sound like an idiot," Taban commented irritably. He finished winding a bandage around the hole burned in his arm and looked up with his cat-like smoothness at Peter. "Where are we and how did we get here?"

"Oh, and by the way," Shareef cut in, punching Taban in the leg as a reminder to be polite. "I am Shareef al Tahid, this is Otar Beliah, and the rude one is Taban Nameless as he has never told us more than his first name." He dug two fingers into the tub of anti burn gel Taban held out and rubbed some over the blistered crease on his scalp. Filings of scorched red hair tumbled off his fingers. "Thank you for pulling us out."

"You need not thank him for getting us out of a situation they put us in," Taban jeered. Peter laughed and held out his hand, beginning the introductions and explanations. But everyone kept glancing back to the little group kneeling on the circle of dirt. After a moment, the conversations died down, as everyone stopped pretending and just watched. Harry complained

steadily as he made his assessments of the mute's condition. Atif was surprised to hear the maledictions focus on the mute himself, not curses of vengeance on his attackers.

"I've told him, over and over and over," Harry muttered as he felt Joe's ankle, "he can't keep doing this to himself!"

"That isn't fair," Anna broke in. "He was after the most important game, and thought he could make it out all right."

"It's not his fault he failed to bring it home," Nehi agreed, his voice tired as he held the mute. His shoulders were slumped, and those watching had the feeling it came from more than just weariness. An uncomfortable idea they hadn't actually won began to settle into those milling about the grass.

"He didn't fail."

Every head turned. Mariah Perry stood apart from the others, her hair sticking out everywhere, freckled face smudged with smoke and dirt. Naqi walked toward her, his black bag in his arms.

"He gave it to me to get out, then let himself be caught to give me the chance I needed to break free," she said, and reached for the bag. The bird's song seemed out of place as Mariah Perry pulled an ancient, leather-bound book from the bag. Everyone stared, hushed and riveted on the beautiful volume. Only a handful had ever seen a book in person. Only three had ever seen this book, and had never thought to see it again. Their book. God's own words. The lifeblood of the Sojourners, the sword of every Christian warrior. The teacher hugged it to herself and looked at the company. Mariah began to walk toward the little group on the circle of desert ground. The men parted in front of her, goggling at the book, too awestruck to even draw near the precious tome.

"He told me to give it to only one person," Mariah Perry's sweet voice said, and every eye flicked to Nehi, before riveting back on the wonderful book. Mariah stopped before the little group and a smile twitched over her dirty face. "Are you Anna Hillson?" Anna nodded, a fog seeming to come over her. The thin arms unfolded, the great book stretched toward her, and Anna found a wonderful, incredible weight transferred into her

arms.

Old paper, ancient glue, and crumbling leather filled her senses. She ran a hand over the faded designs on the front of the book and fingered the worn lettering; *Holy Bible*. God's own words. Here, in her arms, in this yard, He waited to speak through the printed pages. So many words. So much wisdom and knowledge! Every breath hushed and every eye focused on the beautiful young lady, as she laid the ancient book on her lap and gently, so gently, opened it to the center. The delicious crackle of old paper and binding filled the air, and even the birds stopped singing as they listened. Her olive hand ran down the ancient page and stopped.

"'O praise the LORD, all ye nations: praise him, all ye people,'" Anna read. "'For His merciful kindness is great toward us: and the truth of the LORD endureth for ever. Praise ye the LORD[1].'"

No one said anything. Anna's eyes moved, devouring the words, and the others stared in awed silence. A wet cough spilled from the mute, and Nehi felt the thin body shake with the effort to breathe. Harry scooped up the mute and headed for his surgery, muttering again, Beau at his heels like a worried dog. The doctor's gaze flicked to the pale Shareef as he walked past, and he ordered the chimera to "bring that one too." It broke the spell in the yard, and everyone began to mill and murmur to each other. Nehi reached gently for the book, awe on his face as he brushed his fingers against the ancient paper. Anna yelped and slapped his hand away.

"You're full of smoke and dirt and I don't know what!" she accused. "Go wash up, then touch the two-hundred-year-old book!" Nehi grinned, and stood up slowly, achingly, his legs shaking and weak. He wondered if this was how septuagenarians felt as he headed inside to obey. But he paused as he noticed Atif and Tanzid. They stood alone, yards apart from the chatting groups as the men exchanged stories of the day, bandaging their burns and cuts in private, like battle-weary hounds licking

---

[1] Psalm 117

their wounds. Nehi grinned again and motioned to the two awkward, grim warriors. Atif and Tanzid tensed as they stepped toward him, waiting to hear what he needed now.

Nehi waited till the two men were near enough he could have whispered to them. Then he dropped a hand on each of their shoulders, bowed his head, and began a prayer of thanksgiving. Enoch Mickelson always ended his lessons, "If you come out of it alive, be sure to stop and give thanks." Nehi had taken him seriously and Peter was at ease with it as he stepped beside his friend and joined in. The rest of the men blinked, shuffled, and then bowed their heads, and guiltily wondered why it felt so awkward to come before their King with fellow brothers. Today, Nehi didn't prolong it. But his words were heartfelt and easy, and Atif and Tanzid both felt a pang of surprise at finding they were the main subjects of his thanks. An amen slid from him, and Nehi beamed at the two men.

"Atif, this is Tanzid, and the other way around," Nehi said quickly, "say something nice to each other, while I go wash up so my sister will let me look at the miracle we just helped rescue. Nice work today!" He gave one last enthusiastic pound to their shoulders and shuffled off into the house.

Tanzid and Atif stared at each other. They offered a respectful nod, and went back to cleaning their wounds.

Joe's eyelids fluttered. Someone shifted beside him, but nothing in him felt fear. Soft pillows propped him up, a warm comforter draped over his body, and through his cracked lids he could see sunlight playing over worn wooden floors. The pain and weakness were with him and as annoying as he expected. But the weakness let him out of comprehending the worst of it. The someone beside him leaned closer, Joe smelled spices, and a smile spread slowly over him.

"Do you want yogurt or soup?" Anna murmured. If his face didn't hurt so much, Joe would have laughed. Only Anna would have had such a perfect, practical greeting. He painfully closed

his fist, making an "S." Ten minutes later, Joe was propped on his bed upstairs in Harry's house, handing off his fourth emptied bowl of soup for Cobeau to cart away, and accepting a mug from Anna. Steam curled from the cup as he wrapped his eight un-broken fingers around the hot pottery and inhaled the scent of pumpkin, spices, and coffee. Every inch of him hurt. But he felt deliciously safe, warm, and cared for, and the pain hardly even registered in his mind. Joe slumped, and Anna deftly adjusted the pillow between him and the headboard. A sigh slid from the mute and he smiled a happy, painful, lazy thanks and turned to his coffee.

Anna settled in a chair beside him and picked up her drawing pad again. A sketch of running horses laid over the hard white pad in her book, but she kept half an eye on her friend as her pencil moved. In three minutes the mug tipped dangerously, as Joe's eyes fluttered closed. Beau's great hand clamped over the latte and gently pried Joe's fingers from the handle. Anna smiled to herself as she watched how hard Joe held on, even when asleep, and sat her drawing down as Beau disappeared with the cup. Impulsively she reached out and smoothed the blond hair away from Joe's closed eyes. He was so small, and looked so helpless lying there, bruised and bandaged. The biggest thing about him was the bulky cast on his ankle. But he looked happy. Anna smiled again, thanking God fervently that he lay here, alive. She had prayed that same prayer over and over these past three days. But seeing Joe open his eyes and smile and eat and sleep naturally...thanks filled her again. She let it spill over in praise as she began to stack the dishes and organize the medicines.

Anna's song spun with the sunlight out of the invalid's room, and the thud of Nehi's boots paused on the wooden stairs. A smile touched his face and smoothed the wrinkles from his brow. As he trotted up the old wooden stairs and turned into the little room, sunlight played at his feet, dust motes dancing lazily in the beams, and he fancied for a moment that the tiny specs spun to the rhythm of Anna's song. He leaned against the doorframe, watching Anna sing as she tidied the room. His eyes

went to the bed. Joe could hardly be seen under the big green comforter, and for a moment Nehi let himself believe his friend was just sleeping in. But the IV drip beside the bed gave a sharp reminder he wasn't just asleep.

Anna spun around at the sound of Nehemiah's sigh. He met her gaze and tried to put a smile on his worn face for her sake. She smirked at him, and let a hand go to her hip.

"You're as bad of an actor as Joe says, brother dear, stop trying," she ordered. Her smile left. "You've been talking to Harry. How bad is it?"

"The doctor says Joe's health is shattered," Nehi said. Anyone else in the house would have tried to cushion it for the beautiful young woman, and most had advocated not even telling her, afraid to make her cry. Nehi knew his sister better. "Joe will never get back to his old vivacity. It will probably take him months to even get out of bed."

"They hurt him that much?" Anna murmured, her eyes darting to the little curled form.

"Maybe. He certainly had a lot of blood loss and wound trauma from a pack of dogs attacking him. Harry seems to think it's more because Joe's never stopped, even when Joshua Noble gave him the chance, and the knocks to his health have just built and built till this pushed him over the edge. At least Shareef is already up and about, that's some good news." Another sigh slid from Nehi and his eyes went back to the small form on the bed. "I'm glad I don't have to tell him."

"Doofus, no one's going to tell him," Anna said with a twist to her lips, as she flicked a pillow at her brother. He deflected it automatically and looked at her, trying to guess what she was thinking. Even for Anna, she was taking this awfully well. She rolled her eyes and didn't make him guess. "I mean no one's going to tell him *like that*. Look, if you were laid up and bored and in pain what would be the best thing for you? Hope, of course, hope that you're getting better and it will all go away. Telling him it will take months and months and may never happen is not the right way to help an invalid. At least not in those words, you can almost always couch the truth in hope. And in this

instance, it may not even be true; he may defy Harry's prognos-tications out of stubborn pride." She snatched the pillow off the ground and went back to straightening, humming contentedly.

"That does sound like Joe," Nehi smiled. "I'll bring a bag of apples when he's awake enough to appreciate it."

"Ah, but does an apple a day really keep the doctor away?"

"Only if you aim high enough," Nehi commented, and grunted as his sister shoved the dirty dishes into his arms. Anna smiled after his retreating back and picked up her drawing again, glad she had given him a little hope. She silently prayed it might be a realized hope as her pencil flew over the drawing paper to tweak the horse's flowing mane.

"Finally," Daniel drawled as Anna tripped into the kitchen. "You've been upstairs for ten days now!"

"That is a twisting of the truth," Anna said in mock self-righteousness. "I've been downstairs often since Joe was res-cued, you're just never here when I am. Have you enjoyed your romps with Atif?"

"Spy games and rescue missions shouldn't be called 'romps.' The team needed someone who knows how to work a SOLTD," Daniel shrugged. His hand shot out, caught Anna's wrist, and he pulled her to the table. She slid obediently into the seat across from him, and looked up at his serious face. "For the first time in over a week we're alone, and now I want an honest answer from you. Why did Joe send you the Bible?"

To tell me he heard that I wanted him back; to show that he cared, but this is bigger than us, a way of explaining why he <u>*wasn't*</u> *coming back. A precious, priceless package to show he un-derstood,* she thought. Outside, Anna just smiled.

"Yeah...not an answer," Daniel drawled. "You've been hang-ing around that mute too long, you're picking up his conversa-tion tactics." Anna laughed and bounced up to get her tea.

"I don't really know why Joe sent it to me," she said truth-fully, refilling the tea kettle and using the action to hide her

face. "I might guess one or two reasons, but we'll just have to wait till Joe's a little stronger and can answer questions like that." She turned around and smiled at her brother. "If it was very important he could tell us now, you know. And he hasn't tried to sign a word, which means we don't have anything desperate to fix or worry over."

"Really," Daniel drawled. He shook his head and muttered into his coffee about people who put too much trust in people. Anna just smiled again and poured her tea.

"Now, tell me about your adventuring with Atif and his team," she ordered.

The sound of the old-fashioned doorbell clattered through the house, and Anna gave a happy squeal and reached for a second teacup. Only someone with the key to the front gate would make it to the porch to ring the doorbell, and (knowing who was already in the house) that meant Peter and Elizabeth.

"I've got it," Nehi called, as he trotted off the stairs into the entryway. The old hinges squealed as he pulled the door open, and he searched for a good tease for Peter.

Sunlight glinted off sandy hair and a gangly man with a huge grin on his face. Nehi's mouth dropped open.

"Paul!" he yelped. A laugh spilled from Paul Sireton, and Nehi joined it as he pounded him on the back and pulled his friend from KAM inside. "What are you doing here?" Nehi demanded as Peter and his family stepped in after him, grinning at Nehi's surprise.

"What kind of a greeting is that?" Paul pouted playfully. "It doesn't sound very happy to see me." The baby blew a raspberry at Nehi as she kicked in Elizabeth's arms, and lifted two chubby hands toward him. Nehi obeyed Martha's request as he demanded an answer, taking the baby and resting her in the crook of one arm. She started whacking Nehi's chest in excitment as she saw her face reflected in one of his buttons. One fist met his chin with good force, and he paused to blink. The party burst into a laugh as Nehi worked his jaw. Then Anna ran in among them, questions pouring from her. The conversation buzzed through the entryway, as everyone tried to hear over

everyone else. Harry leaned over the banister from the second story.

"Excuse me for interrupting, people," he said with mock politeness, "but there is an invalid up here I'm trying to keep asleep. Would you mind taking it to the den? Oh, hello Paul. Here so soon?" Paul pointed at the SOLTD Peter held and smiled up at Harry.

"These things are miraculous, you know that right?" Paul commented.

"Science, dear boy, just science," Harry corrected.

"Wait, you knew he was coming?" Nehi asked the doctor.

"Yes, now shush. I'm trying to take Joe's resting vitals and you lot are not helping with the resting bit." Harry disappeared from the banister and headed back toward Joe's room. Anna deftly stole the baby from Nehi and trotted toward the kitchen before he could claim her back. Elizabeth followed, and her husband tagged at her heels and pushed on through toward the shed to return the SOLTD to Quintus.

"We have a monthly hologram call setup for the IDP branch leaders," Paul finally answered Nehemiah, lowering his voice dutifully, and beginning to follow Anna toward the kitchen. Daniel fell in beside Nehi, listening with interest as he took stock of the newcomer. "To make sure we're all still alive, and give us the opportunity to gather prayer requests. The situation here with Joe's health needs and various refugees landing in Harry's house came up at the call last week. I passed the word through my branch, and they immediately put a collection together to help with expenses." Harry strode in and Paul paused to shake his hand. "Harry, my wife gave me leave to stay and be a refugee too for a couple of weeks. Can you take in another? I figured it's about time we renew some solid connections with our closest branch. And..." His eyes flitted to Nehi, his face working with a thinly veiled eagerness. His words failed him. Nehemiah blinked back at Paul, wondering what he was having such trouble saying. Daniel burst into a laugh.

"Come on," he said. "The book's in the upstairs dormitory, where it will be hardest for a thief to wander in without our no-

ticing, Beau's on guard up there right now. Though he's probably napping, as I tend to find him these days. Yes, you may look at it."

A shaky sigh sounded in the darkened room and Nehi lifted his head from his lantern. He kept the light tucked under his leather jacket so it didn't disturb the blackness of the room. He automatically tucked the photographs closer against himself, feeling a little like he had at eight years old when he borrowed a light and played with it under his covers for hours past his bedtime. He hadn't told anyone about the snapshots he took of the first fifty pages in the beautiful book they had rescued. Even among their small set here in Harry's house, Nehi wasn't sure it would be approved.

"I replaced your emergency energy rations," he said quietly. Silence hung for a moment, then came the slight rustling of fingers sliding under a pillow. Silence, then another sigh, this one pent up breath let out in a burst of relief. The old panic of a man who had experienced true starvation; knowing food lay within reach stilled it. Sheets rustled as Joe moved again, then a stilted, automated voice spoke. Joe had found his gloves beside the bed.

"Thank you. You do not have to sit in dark."

"I know," Nehi said, then decided to add a little more. "Headaches stink." Joe thought calling a migraine a headache was like comparing a knife wound to a splinter, but didn't take the effort to say it. "It's good to have you awake. Listen, Joe, the Wolf's spurned lover showed up at your rescue." Sudden stillness showed Joe had gone rigid. "Did you see her?"

"Yes." The single word told Nehi so little! "What did she tell you."

"'Give the Raven a message,'" Nehemiah quoted. "'His facts are correct. Wolf is holding the cache over my head in an attempt to get me off his tail. I'm in.' Do I get to know what it means?"

"Not yet," Joe signed, and Nehi bit his lip in the dark,

desperately wanting to push and beg and whine to get an answer. "Soon. I hope. Wish I could say, Knee-High. But too." Nehemiah waited, but the silence and stillness dragged on.

"Too what?" he finally prodded.

"Too dangerous."

"Why?" Nehi burst out. "We have the Bible back, Joe. The FFs are gone, their headquarters disintegrated and took hundreds of them with it. I guess there are probably a few scattered around still, but for practical purposes the FFs are gone. Who else would bother to pose a danger?"

"Wolf." Silence tingled in the room as Joe let the single word sink in. Another breath wheezed painfully out of him. "Have you told about her?"

"No," Nehi answered. "I think you're rubbing off on me. I've waited until I could talk to you first. I just told everyone she was a contact of yours, and that satisfied most. Daniel's not convinced that's the whole story, but I think the others are."

"Good. Don't tell anyone else about her, especially not her message. Anyone, Knee-High. Even Anna."

"Really?"

"Yes."

"I don't like keeping secrets, Joe."

"Me either."

Nehi's mouth closed and he listened to the wheezing breaths coming from the bed, each one tight and controlled. The silence ticked into a minute.

"I need your help, Knee-High. I cannot fight Wolf right now. He is. Dangerous. And very skilled. He has his own SOLTD, if he knew how much I know I would die. I thought I was already but God said no and now... I can't die yet, still have one job, still have to take Wolf down. After the Bible lets you bring back Sojourners, then... I can't die yet. Please."

"I'll keep it between just us," Nehi promised. But it curled in his belly and Daniel's suspicious face wouldn't leave his mind. The questions screamed at him; so many things hung unsaid in those brief sentences! Who was this enemy lurking in the shadows, that Joe even feared him in the comfort of his own

bedroom?

"Thank you," the gloves said.

The silence closed in, and dragged into long dark minutes. Nehi furiously ran over the past two years again, searching for any clues, anything that might give him an idea of who Joe dealt with. Who this enemy might be that could rise in the midst of a house filled with trained agents and kill someone in their bed. The mute lay still, trying not to focus on the pain that consumed his head. He failed. All he was right now was pain and infuriating weakness. He needed something outside himself, especially in this blackness.

"Sojourner's Kingdom is alive, Knee-High," Joe signed. He could hear the movement as Nehi sat up sharply, and a light glared as he shifted. Joe winced and the glow disappeared again quickly.

"What do you mean?" Nehi asked, his voice urgent, pleading for more.

"The IDP have a chapter there, we have almost since the beginning." Silence spoke between the gloves stilted words, as if Joe moved slowly. "Strong, hardy, accomplish good things. Sojourners live under destruction, a whole kingdom under the wrecked one. I met IDP branch leader while out. Nice old guy."

"Why haven't you mentioned it before?" Nehi asked.

"No reason," the gloves said. Nehi bit his lip, forcing himself not to press it. It must hurt to sign right now. But did he mean "no reason to tell you till now," or, "I had no reason not to tell you and just didn't"? If it was the first, why was Joe telling him today? The silence fell again and the darkness pressed in. Another sigh, laden with the effort of drawing a breath, came from the bed.

"Do you want to tell me what happened?" Nehi's voice drifted softly through the room.

"No," the automated voice said. Silence fell again, and Joe could almost see the look he felt Nehi give him in the dark. He took the effort and moved again. "I do not want to sign much. But." The sentence ended there, and the silence and darkness closed in again.

"But what?" Nehi prodded.

"You do not have to sit in the dark," Joe signed slowly. A soft chuckle came from Nehi. The cheerful sound diffused through the room and dissipated the heavy nightmares hovering in the blackness around the mute.

"It's ok, Joe, I'm not freaking out over this dark, it's…it's different, it's a healing kind of dark. I'm not going anywhere. Especially since Beau joined the party and ran off with Atif, Peter, Paul, and Daniel on the latest rescue mission and deserted his nursing duties. He hasn't said more than four words in this whole two and a half weeks since you got back, and with the way he's always been glued to you it's a surprise to see him downstairs so often. It's almost like he has something on his mind. You wouldn't happen to know what it is, would you?"

"Glue is his own man," Joe signed.

"True enough," Nehi said, silently storing away the mute's dodging answer as a curiosity. "Anyway, it's ok, I'm not going anywhere. I owe you for last month." Silence came again, but even to Joe, it didn't press as much. He let his mind run off on last month, the conversations and forced quiet moments with Nehi and pranks with Anna. And these days. Every time he could open his eyes, he found Anna, Nehi, Beau, or Harry; one of them sitting there waiting to give him a cheery hello and welcome him back to the world. Golly, it was good to have friends.

"Thank you," the automated voice said, and Nehi wished he could see Joe's expression. This felt like having half a conversation. "Will you tell me something?"

"What?" Nehi asked.

"Anything," Joe signed, too quickly, and a little gasp came. He went on before Nehi could stir to help. "Found Doctor's birthday gift?" Another chuckle came from Nehi.

"Sometimes, Joe, I think you're omniscient. Yes, Harry stored the camera you gave him last year in the upstairs dormitory and forgot about it. Yes, I found it. Yes, it had everything still untouched in it, and yes, the last time I was on guard duty for the Bible I did use it for what you think. I used all of it, I owe Harry more film now. These cameras really are a remarkable

invention." Movement came, and a sliver of a yellow glow appeared by the wall. Joe could just pick out Nehi's face, shining with a look of reverence and wonder as he stared at the photographs on his lap. Nehemiah's voice rolled across the room, soft and heavy with amazed joy as he began to read.

"'In the beginning God[2]...'"

---

[2] Genesis 1:1

Chapter 4: Moonlight Visitation

"Blessed is the man that trusteth in the LORD, and whose hope the LORD is." Jeremiah 17:7

Nehemiah and Joe poured over the first ten pages of the book, marveling and speculating on the stories found amidst the words. Gradually Nehi noticed Joe's signs grow fewer, then the mute's breathing pattern changed. Sleep claimed the invalid. Nehi tucked the photographs inside his pocket, turned off his light, and slipped quietly out of the room.

Nehemiah came downstairs yawning and rubbing his face to try and wake himself up. Beau quickly stood, his heaping plate in his hand, and trotted for the stairs. Anna looked up from her black leather case where she was working on a drawing at the table, smiled, and pointed at the plates piled with sandwich things on the counter. A low murmur of conversation came from the open door to the den, and Nehi amused himself by trying to decide who was there. Paul's laugh drifted out, and Tanzid's firm voice. Occasionally Shareef and Naqi chimed in, though he couldn't hear what the conversation was about as he gathered a plate of food. Harry's old recliner creaked as the doctor leaned forward to stick his head around the door into the kitchen.

"How is the patient?" he asked.

"Sleeping," Nehi said, and yawned again. "He chatted with me some tonight."

"Good, very good," Harry nodded. The chair creaked again as the doctor sank back with his pipe. A contented cloud of brown smoke hazed the doorway around him.

"He is such a bachelor," Anna whispered to Nehi as her brother settled at the table, and he stifled a laugh. Nehi leaned forward conspiratorially.

"Two and a half weeks ago, while the fellows and I were out getting Joe, did you and Dan...do anything?" he asked.

"Nail-biting," she whispered. "Is that a secret?"

"No, I meant... Dan seems convinced Harry is our Wolf,"

Nehemiah murmured. Anna sat up sharply and looked at the cloud of smoke, a troubled frown wrinkling her face. "And before Atif whisked them off on another mission, Naqi and Shareef told me about their end of the Joe business. The FFs knew I was coming. It could have just been an assumption that I would come to rescue Joe, I guess, but it seemed more certain than that."

"As if someone told them," Anna clarified. Nehemiah pursed his lips and nodded. "Before Joe ran off on his Bible rescue mission, he said the Wolf was near us, in Story Land?"

"Not necessarily in Story Land, he signed 'near,' and then very implicitly said it didn't have to be the same thing as 'here.' Did he mean this Wolf is a friend of ours, someone close? Or…" Nehi darted a glance over his shoulder at the brown cloud. "I like him, Anna! And Joe seems to trust him completely."

"Joe trusts him with his life, every time the doctor employs his skill for our little mute." Anna studied the door, her frown still on, and spoke slowly. "From when you left, till when you came rushing back, Harry was never out of my sight. I spent most of the time with him telling me about how he met Joe, about Joshua Noble, how glad he was that Joe and I were friends, and about how he chatters when he's nervous while I tend to clean kitchens."

"You do?" Nehi blinked, glancing around the messy black and white kitchen.

"Harry and I spent the time together," Anna brought him back to the point. "He could have sent a message by a gadget, I suppose. He would have only had a few seconds to do it, while my back was turned. But before you left, there was that hour we were all rushing around like madmen gathering things and getting you ready to go. Anyone could have slipped off during that chaos."

"Where's Daniel? Can we bring him in on this?"

"He zipped back with Paul and the grim young warrior about an hour ago, and disappeared into Quintus's shed," Anna said, using their nickname for Atif and closing her leather case. Nehemiah wondered what unfinished picture lay on the hard

white pad inside. "Come on, your sandwich will wait."

"Will my stomach?" Nehi muttered. But he followed his sister out the door toward the old shed Quintus had claimed as his inventing room and lab. Faded red paint peeled off the boards and the roof sagged, but Quintus didn't seem to mind. As they hopped out onto the grass, they could see Atif keeping a look out through the single smudged window. The door opened as the twins walked toward it, and Atif swung through, holding it politely. He offered Anna a little bow as she stepped in, and she smiled her thanks. Atif spun toward the back gate and strode off. Nehemiah let the shed door swing closed and trotted up beside Atif, matching him stride for stride.

"Hello," Nehi said. The grim young warrior stopped and looked at him, respectfully waiting for what he had to say. Nehemiah rocked on his heels and smiled. "I didn't have anything really to say except that. How did the mission go?"

"We came upon the UPC agents unawares and zipped out with seventeen of our brothers and sisters," Atif stated. "The SOLTD is of inestimable value to our work. Did you need something?"

"No. Look, Atif, I'm sorry if my being here is awkward for you," Nehemiah blurted out. He shrugged, a half smile on his face and his dark eyes holding Atif's. "I guess I just wanted you to know it's not awkward for me. You don't have to run off every time I show up. In fact, I would enjoy a visit one of these days, to learn more about a man who reminds me an awful lot of my friend upstairs."

"The mute?" Atif asked, one eyebrow raising.

"Yes, Joe's always rushing off to save somebody."

"I see. Well, as you say I am 'rushing off to save somebody.' Those we rescued today had word of another church in similar difficulties," Atif stated. "Perhaps when I return we will have more time." He nodded at Nehi and headed toward the gate again. Nehemiah gave a mental shrug and let him go. He turned back toward the shed and trotted into the musty, strange-scented old building. Daniel and Anna stood staring at Quintus with blank expressions as the old inventor droned on about

something. Nehi listened for a minute, decided he didn't get it either, and interrupted.

"It sounds fascinating, Quin, but Anna and I were hoping to have something of a family council. Do you mind if we steal Danny?"

"Don't call me that," Daniel growled under his breath, but Quintus drowned him out.

"Of course, my dear fellow! I was just telling him I would take his recommendations for the SOLTD into consideration. The answer is yes, now that I know the intricacies of this technology well, I ought to be able to make them quite a bit smaller."

"Perfect, thanks Quin," Nehi told him. Anna slid an arm through Daniel's, and the three headed for the pretty bench under the lilac bush in the corner of the yard. It was the only corner still pretty. Brown dirt and dying grass and flowers littered every other spot. Circular dots of different hued land lay scattered about the yard, each in a different state of decay. Anna's nose wrinkled as she dropped on the bench and surveyed the scene.

"Daniel, you're going to have to make Atif find a different spot to land his SOLTD," she ordered. "Poor Harry's yard was immaculate when we got here!"

"Nothing to worry over," Daniel said. "Harry told me he did some doctoring for a landscaping family and took service as a payment. He came out yesterday and commented it looked like the good old days. I'm glad you two called this meeting. Remember when we had that weird council on the beach? Well, now we have our Bible back. What bridge are we crossing to get home?"

"Did you find anything about the Wolf while we were out?" Nehi asked, plopping cross-legged in front of the bench as there wasn't room on it for three. Daniel looked at him for a moment, his scarred face inscrutable.

"I wandered a little and watched while you were out," he said. "I think I may know something about the Wolf's activities during that time. But I'd rather keep it to myself till I know for sure. You two mind? You have so many secrets with that little

mute, I figured it won't annoy you much."

"We don't keep secrets from you," Anna said, annoyance sharp. Daniel snorted and looked unconvinced. He just turned back to Nehemiah, watching as the young man absentmindedly shifted dirt from one pile to another.

"You're thinking about something," Daniel stated.

"Joe just told me there are Sojourners keeping the kingdom alive under the invaders. A thriving IDP branch is there, apparently. He said he met the leader."

"Another thing he didn't mention," Daniel muttered.

"Why did he wait till now to tell us?" Anna asked.

"I don't know," Nehi said slowly, plucking a piece of grass and pensively starting to chew it. "But I begin to have the idea we don't know anything about the situation in our old kingdom. I really don't want another mission like Joe's rescue, where we have no clue what we're headed toward and have to wing it and hope we survive. If we're to make an informed decision about what to do next, the IDP leader would be an ideal source for up-to-date knowledge, and our best ally for finding allies."

"That's actually really bright," Daniel said, and Nehemiah gave a good-natured laugh at the surprise in his brother's voice.

"It is, and I'll talk to Mariah while you're tracking down the IDP man, before Naqi takes her home tomorrow," Anna put in. "But in a way, this brings us back to the original question. If we're bringing in IDP leaders, and generally trying to make plans, who can we trust around us? We don't want enemies in our council chambers. We trust the Ravens," she added quickly, as Daniel moved to speak. He shut his mouth again. Nehemiah began ticking names off on his fingers.

"Atif and his men were nowhere near when Joe intimated the Wolf was close, including as friends; we still barely know them. So that's five. Tanzid and Quin weren't members of the flock until just a few weeks ago, so that lets them out too."

"Joe seems to trust Harry..." Anna said, letting the sentence hang.

"Someone betrayed Nehi to the FFs," Daniel stated. "We're meeting this IDP leader somewhere undisclosed, and not

bringing in anyone but those seven just mentioned by Nehi."

"And the Ravens," Anna and Nehi chorused. Daniel rolled his eyes but made no objection.

"First problem," Nehi said. "How do we find this IDP leader without Paul or Harry's help? They're the ones who would have that information."

"Joe," Anna said quickly. "When he wakes up again."

"And Atif," Daniel said. "Once Joe gives us a starting point, I'm sure the grim young warrior will go pick up someone with me."

"I bet Tanzid knows a good neutral, hidden location to meet," Nehemiah said. He threw his grass blade away and his back straightened. "Right. I think we've got a working plan to begin with." The three looked at each other for a moment. A wide smile spread over Daniel's face.

"The first step to getting our home back," he said, and his hands went behind his head with a contented sigh. A tingle went through the twins. Answering smiles spread over them, as they felt their heartbeats beginning to thunder. The reality of this meeting started to settle. *Home.* It seemed so long since they had been able to use that word.

Nehemiah's stomach rumbled and he hopped up to go find his sandwich. But as he trotted for the door, Joe's half finished sentences hung in his mind. *"After the Bible lets you bring back Sojourners, then..."* Then what? Nehi sighed as he pushed through into the kitchen, feeling achy and weary. Even if they managed the herculean task of ousting the invaders and re-starting their kingdom, the fighting wouldn't end there. At least not for Joe. And Nehi would be by his side, in whatever came next.

Joe barely held back a groan as he stirred and the pain hit him again. Three weeks. It ought to have been lessening a little by now, at least beginning to feel better. He did stay awake longer these days. Which wasn't always nice, he admitted rue-fully as he stared out the window and watched the dust motes

circling through the sunbeams. Oh, he hurt. And Nehi had run off with those photographs somewhere, he couldn't use them as a distraction today. Maybe he could sneak upstairs and read the book himself... Joe's eyes went to the bulky cast on his throbbing ankle. He sighed and slumped back, his head sinking deep into the pillow.

The door clicked open. Outside noise (voices and clinking lunch dishes) invaded Joe's sick room and his eyes darted to the door, letting his eagerness show. But it wasn't the chimera he expected.

Daniel strolled in, two plates in his hands, and a package under his arm. A glance showed him Joe's hunger for anything outside these four walls. He left the door open. Daniel dropped the package onto the bed and let it bounce. Joe glanced from it to Daniel and back again, his curiosity showing strong.

"When I went out for groceries this morning I ran across a street musician tired of his work," Daniel answered. "I figured you might like a violin again, even if it is a little cracked." Joe's face lit up and his hand shot for the package. A wince cut across his face, and his hand twitched. Daniel swept the package to the foot of the bed, dropped onto the chair beside Joe, plunked a plate of spaghetti next to the mute, and swept up his fork.

"Nope, not now. You eat first, and take your after lunch nap like a good invalid, then you can get into it. Anna wanted to send you up soup again," he commented. A smile twitched over Joe. He sat up slowly and moved the plate to his lap.

"Thank you," he signed, and Daniel acknowledged it with a nod; he had finally begun to recognize some of the simpler signs.

"Knew you would be sick and tired of the mushes by now," Daniel said. "A man needs meat, even if it is in tiny pellets buried inside tomato sauce." Joe laughed and tucked into the lunch. He didn't eat much of it, Daniel noticed. But at least he seemed to enjoy what he did get down. Daniel took the proffered plate back, sat it on top his empty one on the nightstand, and crossed his hands in front of him. "So what'll it be? I could lecture you about disappearing on your own and then having to be rescued

by people's younger brothers. That would probably amuse you. Or I could tell you a few of the less dirty jokes I've learned from Shareef and Otar recently. Or give you an update on the state of things as far as Atif and his business goes. Or I could tell you a story, and make it as rambling and boring as you like, so you can fall asleep in the middle and I can be offended."

Amusement danced over Joe's cut face as he slumped back down on his pillow. The mute held up four fingers. Daniel's hands slid behind his head, his legs stretched out in front of him, ankles crossed, and he launched into it.

"Once upon a time, a man named Binky decided he really needed another name. You might be surprised how much of an adventure such an innocent resolve took him on. It all started when..."

Guire Sumpleton slunk down the street, his breakfast tucked under his tattered coat and his eyes darting constantly around the wooden houses. They leaned over the muddy streets, seeming to leer at any who dared to move under their dark boards.

"Knew a man what died from a falling plank once," Guire muttered under his breath. Those who knew him grew used to his endless mutters. "Walking along and 'bam' plank fell from a house right on his head. Killed him dead. Happened."

A hand shot from a dark alleyway and latched onto Guire's neck. A strangled gurgle came from him as he was jerked into the dark. He felt fur and claws on the hand. Terror sparked through the man, his eyes bugging. His hoarded breakfast tumbled to the mud as he scrabbled at the hand around his throat. Gray fur filled his vision.

"I don't like your country, Guire." The Wolf's voice curled around him and Guire whimpered. "Walden is too muddy and too boring. And much too poor to interest me. Listen closely, so I can leave." The hand let go of Guire's throat. The man gasped and sagged, his knees going out. A gloved hand shoved against

his chest pushing him against the wooden planks of the build-
ing towering over them and holding him upright. The claws cut
through his shirt and pricked his flesh. "I'm looking for someone, Guire. I think you know where she is." The mask of the gray
wolf moved closer and he smelled the damp dog fur as the
whisper filled his mind. "Tell me where the mermaid lives."

Atif followed the hulking chimera through the moonlit alleyway, marveling at how lightly the big man moved. He
seemed to float over the weeds, and even the stray cats hardly
spared him a glance. The moonlight bounced off the high
wooden boards and concrete walls surrounding them. Almost
unconsciously Atif's hand rested on his Healy strapped to his
thigh. Cobeau had risen at his window at two this morning,
smiled a hello when Atif nearly took off the chimera's head in
his shock, and calmly rumbled that Joe wanted him. Atif's brow
creased as he walked behind the silent chimera, and wondered
again what had made him grab his greatcoat and leap out the
window to follow Cobeau into the night. The answer came to
him as soon as he posed it. Curiosity. Not just about what the
mute wanted from him in the middle of the night and why they
were taking back alleys, but about the mute himself. It had been
three weeks since he had seen the mute, but the tragic torn figure had seldom left his mind. Everyone in Harry's old house
seemed to paint a different picture of the GI in the upstairs bedroom. Daniel Hillson didn't trust him, Atif knew that.

A mangy tabby cat raced over his path, and Atif's fingers
brushed his gun's stock again. Cobeau stopped, gripped a familiar fence with one hand, and vaulted over. The lilac bush draped
elegantly over the wooden slats rustled and waved in the
moonlight, then settled. Atif gripped the wood and hoisted himself over, painfully aware the bush rattled and shook with his
movements. As his boots hit the soft grass behind Harry's
bench, the chimera glided off again. The big man stayed in the
deepest shadows and seemed only a deeper shadow himself as

he stole over the torn up yard. Atif followed on his heels, over the ground and on up the house front, gripping the siding and pulling himself toward the open bay window on the second story. His fingers scrabbled for a moment, then he pulled himself over, landing lightly on his toes, so no one downstairs would hear his entrance. His eyes darted to the bed, where the green comforter lay rumpled.

"The chimera says you wished to see me?" Atif asked, his voice pitched low. A cool breeze blew in from the window behind him and rustled the pages of a tattered black notebook that stood open on the night table. A low whistle came from his right, and Atif pivoted, one hand going to his thigh again. A pale figure huddled in a chair in the shadow by the window, one small foot encased in a ludicrously large cast. Atif's heart pounded; he could have been killed ten times over by the silent, still little man. But then the green eyes latched onto his. They twinkled, laughing at his shock and suspicion. Suddenly all Atif's distrust seemed silly, and he wondered if he blushed as his hand left his gun.

"You wished to see me?" Atif asked again. The amusement left the battered face. The two green eyes latched onto his again, but now his expression was hard and businesslike; the face of a fighter. A pale hand lifted, two of the fingers bandaged and splinted. A sheet of paper, covered in a tight, poorly written scrawl, crinkled as it slid into Atif's hand. He turned the page to the moonlight and began to read. After the first few lines he dropped suddenly into a chair on the opposite side of the window. He read through the page once, stared at the wall for a few moments, then read it again. Atif's eyes rose. Cobeau towered behind the mute's chair, his arms crossed as he silently waited. The GI sat with his chin resting on one knee, his cast on the ground, perfectly still, seeming almost asleep. But through those slitted eyes he watched Atif's every expression and movement. Joe's hands rose and moved elegantly and swiftly in the moonlight.

"You will want proof," his gloves said in their stilted, automated way. The sound had been turned to the lowest setting,

and Atif had to strain to hear it. Joe stuck his thumb over his shoulder, his eyes darting up at Cobeau. The gloves sputtered gibberish and the mute rolled his eyes. Beau reached out one long arm, swept up the black notebook, and dropped it in Atif's lap. A quarter of an hour passed slowly, as Atif paged through the papers, his face creased and his lips a tight line. Joe shivered, rose, drew the window closed and bolted it, then sank into his chair and waited again. Another five minutes passed in silence, even the stirring breeze gone.

Atif leaned back in his chair. One hand went to his face, as he blinked at the notebook open on his lap. His head shook once, as if he were trying to make himself accept something.

"This will change the shape of our world," Atif murmured.

"For the better," Joe's gloves said. Atif looked up and met the green eyes. He didn't bother to veil his doubt. He took the discussion on a different path.

"You have gathered your information carefully. But it is hardly proof," Atif said.

"I signed you would want it. I did not say I had it," the gloves said, and Joe's expressive face held the story of years of disappointed attempts. "I have tried. If it was there, I would have the proof, and would give it to you. But I know it to be true." Atif sat still, studying him.

"Without proof you cannot act," he said.

"I can force Wolf into the open. But not until we are strong enough, until after the Sojourners resurgence, or we will lose the prize," Joe signed. Atif's gaze automatically went to the papers on his lap.

"It is an incredible tale you weave," he muttered. "Why are you telling me this now? Does Nehemiah Hillson know?"

"Only you and one other, a –" the gloves stumbled over the words, and a computerized "a-a-a-a-a" came from them. Joe swept them off with a grimace and slapped them over the chair arm. He looked up at the towering chimera, and Beau's low rumble rolled over the little room as he began to translate. "You and a Shield-Bearer from Geatland alone know the full tale." He looked up at the grim, tall man across from him, each new cut

livid on his pale skin, the stiches holding them closed deep wells where the shadows gathered. "Wolf needs watched, there's greater danger to our brothers and sisters than I've told you yet. I am not capable of keeping up with Wolf right now." Joe motioned behind him at the chimera. "Glue can't do this work alone."

"You wish me to keep track of the Wolf, curtailing the danger without raising suspicion," Atif stated, watching the mute. Joe nodded.

"The twins help a lot, I don't think you'll have to do much."

"I thought you said you had not told them?"

"Do they have to know to help?" Joe signed, and that twinkle came back into his face for a moment. Atif realized he looked more like the young man he should be with that twinkle. Without it he was a shriveled, scarred, ageless thing...who had found out a villain most of the world didn't even know existed, and uncovered a secret that could change everything.

"How long have you known?" Atif asked, suddenly very curious. Joe slumped back in his chair and a sigh slid from him as he watched the moon outside the window.

"Too long. It's a burdensome secret. But you won't have to keep it long. The kingdom will be renewed, the Hillsons will return to their judgeship. Then we will be strong enough to hold Wolf," Joe signed, his pale hands making elegant shadows in the moonlight. Atif noticed the mute already assumed he accepted the task. The grim young warrior leaned back, running over the past, analyzing every look and conversation again.

"This Wolf is a sly one," Atif murmured. "But I see now, something in me did suspect."

"I know." The chimera's translating rumble seemed to fill the room, and a tingle ran through Atif as he stared at the small form curled in the chair. A little smile lifted the mute's mouth as he motioned out the window. "I chose this room years ago. I can see everything that goes on out there, and hear most of the conversations in the den when I want to. I noticed your hesitation."

"You are not as incapacitated as everyone thinks." Atif

studied the mute again for a moment, and made his choice. He would believe the one who held the Wazir's white card. It took a very smart and skilled man to gain that card, just the sort who could uncover something the rest of the world never suspected. But he was still curious.

"Why are you trusting me with this knowledge?"

"Because Knee-High called you in before anyone else, and put both our lives into your hands. I know he trusts too quickly and too much. But he's not an idiot." A smile hovered on the mute's face, and in it Atif could read a little of the tight comradeship between the two. It pleased him and put the last of his disquiet aside.

"You say there is more danger that you have not told?" Atif demanded. The mute's face hardened.

"Wolf has chosen the IDP as scapegoat for the book thieves. Once Wolf's last treasure is acquired, the IDP will be framed, and the world will erupt in a massive hunt for every Christian." Atif's knuckles turned white as he gripped the arms of his chair. "I know how Wolf is going to frame us, but not when, or where he is keeping the 'proof' against us. I also know he has it setup to automatically start if he disappears for a significant amount of time. We can't just kill him, and we can't let him roam. A-t-i-f, we must not let Wolf out of our sight until we are strong enough to act."

"Surely you are wrong. The Wolf would not be so vile to the people of the book!" Atif hissed, dropping into old Islamic terms in his agitation. Joe's lined face didn't change.

"Wolf betrayed Knee-High, remember? If you and your team hadn't been there (a surprise to everyone but Knee-High) I would be dead and he would be in FF hands. Yes, Wolf is capable of this. Will you help?"

"Of course," Atif murmured, his voice almost hoarse. He squared his slumped shoulders and looked back at Joe. "You need to deactivate your slaver plant." The mute's eyes went wide and alarm tightened every muscle in him.

"You know?" Joe signed, his hands a blur.

"We all know by now. I am surprised you have not realized

it." Atif pulled a thin, clear wire from his pocket. "I can deactivate it, though I fear it will not be comfortable for you."

"Fry it," Joe ordered.

"That is likely to kill you," Atif said slowly, staring into the green eyes.

"I would rather die now than have Wolf take it over," Joe signed, and something in the hardness in his face told Atif he only spoke the truth. He hesitated another moment, then pulled out his PP to reprogram the wire. Joe looked up at his big friend, hovering near the door.

"Glue?" he signed, and as he translated the chimera took a half step closer, his back straightening as he listened. "I told him to."

Atif didn't pause to let himself think about it, though he knew the mute had said that to keep the chimera from breaking his spine for what he was about to do. Atif drew in one deep breath, and slid the wire onto Joe's scarred jaw.

Chapter 5: Satyrs and Sick Beds

"I will bless the LORD, who hath given me counsel: my reins also instruct me in the night seasons." Psalm 16:7

The hissing wind of the SOLTD cut off into silence in its maddening way. Displaced pine needles, dirt, and twigs thundered down on Nehemiah's head, and his arm went up to shield his face. Tanzid grabbed his shoulder and jerked, flinging the young man backward. Nehi hit a bed of pine-needles and rolled over the spongy ground, just registering a massive shape creaking and cracking as it came at them from above. A great pine tree crashed into the ground five inches in front of him. A tremendous boom rang through the forest and the needles under Nehi jumped and shook as it fell. He lay still, shivering from the effects of the SOLTD, staring at the giant trunk inches from his face. A low whistle slid from him.

"We need a safer traveling method," Tanzid said. He shouldered his blaster and headed uphill through the pine forest. Bright sunlight gleamed around the tree trunks, hinting at a break in the forest. "The SOLTDs are fast, but they aren't safe."

"I don't think they were really meant to be used yet," Nehemiah breathed, his eyes riveted on the pine. He shook himself, hopped up, and trotted after Tanzid. His course took him beside the fallen trunk. It was a partially rotted goliath, and would have squashed Nehi like a toad if it had hit him. "I think Quin barely got them working, and those who found out about it got so excited at the idea they started using them before all the bugs have been completely worked out."

"Not a good idea," Tanzid said.

"Agreed! But they sure are useful in this type of business," Nehi grinned.

"Useful sure, but have you thought through this? These things can be dangerous, Nehi, and not just because they're untried."

"What do you mean?" Nehi asked as he followed Tanzid's broad back through the trees.

"Weapons. Messy, bad ones you can't guard against because they just pop up, tearing everything around them apart." A shiver ran over him. "I don't like it."

Before he could consider a reply, Nehi stepped through the trees into the sunlight. He stood at the tree line of a mountain range. Behind him the forest waved in the breeze, seeming like an army of dark giants. In front of him, a grassy pinnacle rose like a bald head, pillowed on a blue sky. A switch-back trail cut through the grass and snaked off over the peak and out of sight. Nehi breathed deep, overjoyed to be on a mountain, and ran to catch up to Tanzid as the agent toiled up the trail. He quickly realized he was really high up, as his breath left him and his mind threatened to go giddy.

"Where are we?" Nehi panted.

"Faerie," Tanzid panted back, and Nehemiah didn't feel so ashamed of having run out of breath so fast. "Careful wandering."

"Dangerous?"

"Sometimes. This is an out of the way spot where I've never had any trouble, but the people here insist on going adventuring, so you can never be sure. And the satyrs keep breeding in the forest. I haven't been here in a while, they may have made it this high."

"Why did you come here? I mean, was it your home, a mission one time...?"

"Camped here for a summer when I was sixteen and had a broken arm to heal. I liked it, and come back occasionally." Tanzid paused, panting more, and looked over his shoulder at the young man behind him. "If the hall still stands it's an ideal location for a secret council. But if Anna decides to tag along, never let her out alone."

"She can handle herself better than most–" Nehi started, but Tanzid's hand landed on his chest pushing him back. A brown finger was suddenly under his nose, emphasizing every word.

"Never let her wander alone in Faerie," Tanzid ordered. He swung around and started up the switch-back again.

"Ok," Nehi nodded, and trotted ahead to catch up. "Tell me

more."

"Don't you ever run out of curiosity? Or words?" Tanzid asked, looking over his shoulder again.

"Not yet," Nehi grinned. "What's something else about this place I should know?"

"Be nice to any old person you run across. Really nice. Especially if they're begging. I'm out of breath, if you want conversation, you make it." Tanzid kept moving, and Nehi smiled at his back, feeling triumphant. That chat had seemed like a friend to a friend, especially in the way it ended. He was making progress.

The trail led on, and Nehemiah's heart pounded with the effort of the climb as he finally topped the ridge and lifted his head again to see where he was. The green grass rolled off in a beautiful waving field, rising gently in a soft hill. On the top of the hill stood a square building of wooden planks and thatched roof, carved with delicate pictures and spirals.

It also had a flock of two legged animals hissing and yowling as they teemed through the doors and windows. Nehi's mouth fell open as he stared. The animals were as tall as him, mossy green and rich brown in color, with the crooked back legs of a goat and long clever claws on the end of their front paws. A lion-like tail swished and wound behind them as they pattered through the great front door.

"Darn it," Tanzid muttered. "Those things are worse than squirrels for infesting a place."

"I don't understand this relapse," Harry murmured, bending over Joe. The mute lay glassy-eyed in the little bed, shivering even with the green comforter over him. His face was pale as paper and strained, his breathing shallow and painful. Anna watched in silence, helping the doctor where she could. She had drifted naturally into the post of his nurse during their weeks in his house, and her gentle common sense made her very good at it.

But today she wished she could skip out on the job. It felt so hard to see her sweet friend like this. Harry worked quietly, easing what he could for the mute, and trying to decide the cause. The loudest sound in the room came from Beau's rumbling snores, where the big man slumped in a corner asleep. After about ten minutes, the doctor sighed and reached for his IV drip.

"I think the best we can do is let him rest. Let's knock him out for a day and see if it helps." Harry checked the system to make sure it was all working and comfortable for his patient, and stood up, his job done. But he paused, and for a moment the doctor melted into the friend as Joe's taught muscles slowly began to ease. Harry leaned down and drew the green comforter closer over the mute, tucking the edges in around the little form. Anna suddenly remembered wondering, that first night in the Sireton's basement, if anyone had ever tucked Joe lovingly into bed. Her heart went out in thankfulness to the doctor, as he turned and walked from the room to see about his eight o'clock appointment. Anna glanced down at Joe again, watching his breathing steadying as the drug took effect. She turned reluctantly to follow Harry.

Bony fingers clamped onto her wrist and pulled her to a stop. Anna looked back quickly. Joe stared at her, and she could see him trying to cling to consciousness for just another moment, his green eyes pleading with her from his tight face. She sank to her knees, gently unclasped his fingers, and shifted them till they slid comfortably between her own.

"I'll stay right here, Joe," she promised. Relief played over him. His eyes closed again, his head slumped, and he let himself drift into the drug. The blessed blankness of sleep took over. Anna sat on her heels and held his hand, Cobeau's snores the only sound in the still room.

"Satyrs?" Nehi asked, watching the animals teeming around the building.

"Yeah, and the smaller green ones are fawns," Tanzid answered. A deep-throated human roar rose over the animals' cacophony.

"It sounds like their occupation is contested," Nehi said.

"Begone with thee, vile monsters of the Night!" a voice echoed out of the building. Tanzid gave a groan. A wild caterwaul lifted from the satyrs, and a host of them swarmed out the door. Three catapulted over their packmate's heads and slammed into the grass. Nehemiah felt the thud of their landing even where he stood, and his eyebrows rose. He poked Tanzid and they started to move again, their hands on their lasers as they eyed the crowd of animals.

One spun on them. A long tongue stuck through sharp feline teeth in a hiss. The face was hideous; a round pumpkin of a thing with slit evil eyes and a bestial hatred. Two triangular ears peeked over its head till the tips almost touched each other. The animal hissed again and lurched toward the newcomers, its goat legs pounding into the soft ground. Tanzid jerked his blaster around, his pulse humming in his ears as the creature's claws flashed in the bright sunlight and its caterwaul filled the air. His blaster hummed as it primed; still four seconds from being able to fire. The clawed hands swiped for his throat and Tanzid leapt back. The satyr compensated with the lightning reflexes of a predator, faster than Tanzid. Claws and hissing mouth filled his world. For an instant the certainty of death flashed in front of the agent's eyes. The caterwaul stopped, silenced in mid-flow. A padded paw hit the side of Tanzid's face with a soft thump, limp and lifeless. The paw fell away as the creature thudded into the ground. A tendril of smoke curled from a hole burnt through the thing's face. Tanzid looked over his shoulder, his heartbeat still thundering. Nehi held Hope steady as he moved around his friend.

"Let the puny thing go first, at least until your battering ram finally manages to prime," Nehemiah commented, a teasing smile on his face. Hope fired into the crowd of creatures, picking off each one that spun their direction, and eating away at the fringes of the pack. A pulsing power sounded from the

building, and two more of the satyrs flew out over the heads of the pack. The creatures broke in panic. Wild howls and screeches filled the air as they pounded for the dark trees in a rush, their tails whipping around them.

A man stepped into the doorway as the animals retreated, and Nehi let Hope drop to study him. He stood at medium height, crooked nose, curly blond hair waving in the breeze, and blood red armor plates covering his body. He leaned on a long, thick pole and something very similar to Wiglaf's sword hung strapped on his waist. The man looked at the newcomers with a frank honesty that was both likeable and a little annoying; he looked unimpressed with their performance. As the last satyr disappeared hissing into the woods, he beamed and gave a low sweeping bow.

"Behold, I have redeemed thy hall for thy return, my lords," the stranger boomed.

"Thanks," Tanzid said, unenthusiastically.

"For this service I, Sir Cuthbert the Grandiose, have rendered to thee this day, I ask only that thou charitably make my name known at the castle upon this Micklemas Eve."

"We're not headed to the castle anytime soon," Tanzid said, and tossed his blaster to Nehi. "I've been here before, let's just jump to the point. I want to use this place, you already claimed it by chasing out those beasts, and I'm not going all the way to the castle just to stick your name on an overcrowded wall of glory. I'll wrestle you for the use of the hall." The man drew himself up and stared daggers at Tanzid.

"I know not who thou hast met here," Sir Cuthbert said, "but I do not deal so with strangers in the wild places. If thou hast a mind to use the hall, welcome. We each of us need shelter where it can be found, and largesse and mercy are prized by my lady as much as strength." He suddenly looked bashful and turned away, blushing to his blond roots. *He doesn't have a lady,* Nehi guessed from his sudden embarrassment, and grinned at Tanzid. The agent rolled his eyes and they headed inside to see how much damage the nesting satyrs had done.

The place smelled like a barn. No, it smelled a lot worse.

Carved, wooden furniture lay overturned and pushed into corners, most of it gnawed on. Sir Cuthbert dropped onto the only upright chair, next to an enormous, cold fireplace hearth. He didn't move to help. It took Nehi and Tanzid a full hour to sweep it out and get it reasonably clean. Tanzid strode out and came back dragging half a tree under one arm and a pile of brush under the other. Nehi reached for his flint and tinder. Soon a bright fire blazed in the hearth, and wood smoke and warmth began to permeate the hall, slowly overtaking the satyr smell.

Nehi chatted with the knight as he worked, getting the layout of the new country. He found himself highly intrigued by the fact the man occasionally used Christian catchphrases, and obviously had no idea what they meant. It would seem *The Faerie Queen*, their base, didn't do much explaining but had some ties to his own book. And a lot of weird things that didn't correspond to reality. Like ointments that could heal anything with a single drop, and magicians that could change their aspect or charm your senses to see things you didn't really. And Night personified as a person, such that this knight seemed to think there really was a giant up there glaring at them whenever the sun left.

But what Nehemiah actually fished for amongst the chatter eluded him. Sir Cuthbert was informative and polite, but said very little about himself. It wasn't very helpful in telling if he could be trusted or not. His conversation devolved into an animated explanation of honor, in all its glories, and its overarching importance in this world. He obviously meant the lecture for Tanzid's improvement, and Nehi had a hard time not chuckling at the two, as Sir Cuthbert lectured with angelic animation and Tanzid tended the fire and rolled his eyes. A lull finally came as Sir Cuthbert faltered over trying to find a worthy description of courage.

"So, Sir Cuthbert, you staying around long?" Tanzid broke the quiet. The knight gave a hearty laugh, and Nehi found himself smiling as it filled the hall and mixed with the bright crackle of the burning logs.

"I know I was not a welcome sight for thee, returning as

thou must have thought to thy empty hall," the man chuckled. He grimaced, reached down, and slowly drew his left leg forward. When he pulled his hands back fresh blood covered his palms. "But I fear I cannot leave thee to the silence of the woods this eve. My steed was slain by the vile satyrs ere I happed upon this place and I wast raked by their poisonous claws defending thy hall." Tanzid dropped to his knees and began to unscrew the armor plates. One eyebrow rose on the knight's face at his immediate reaction. Nehi swung his bag from his back and fished inside the soft black leather for his field medicine kit. But as he and Tanzid stripped off the armor, they found the blood already beginning to congeal. Three deep cuts ran down the man's leg, probably from an animal already slain and falling. They had missed anything vital, and seemed shallow enough not to be dangerous.

"Poisonous?" Nehi asked, looking at Tanzid.

"Typical Faerie dramatics," he said, shaking his head.

"Excuse me, recall I canst hear thy remarks," Cuthbert said. His voice didn't boom. Nehi glanced up at him and saw his face had paled, and sweat stood out on his skin.

"I think I'd better get some heavier antibiotics," he commented, and swung his bag around to use what he had now. "What are you doing way up here fighting satyrs on your own?" Nehi asked, as he doused bandages in alcohol. "I mean besides covering yourself in glory and blood." Cuthbert's face colored up to his fair hair.

"I wished to forget," he stated, looking away.

"Spurned, eh?" Tanzid pressed.

"Yes. Ah, but... I must be truthful, for it would betray my honor if I was not so." The man sighed then straightened up again and told it in a rush. "Not by a lady as you assume, but by the whole castle. I was striving to break the black stallion, but alas, it was more than my skill could manage. I was thrown, sprained my...lower end, and I could not bear the jeers. I shall not return until I have redeemed myself." Tanzid and Nehi glanced at each other, then back at the blood-soaked leg.

"We'll be long gone before he gets anywhere," Nehi

shrugged. Tanzid hesitated a moment, then nodded, swept up his blaster and marched out to make a check of the area. Nehemiah crossed his legs comfortably in front of the fire and pulled out his Grady. He pressed the communication button.

"God is for us, Atif, we've got our meeting place at the first try. The fire is awfully cozy here, and I have a premonition that a satyr haunch will taste pretty good with a smoky flavor," he said.

"Verily, thou speaks rightly," Sir Cuthbert commented, some of the boom back in his voice.

"There you go, I'm right," Nehi told the Grady. He took his finger off the communication button and waited.

"All is secure?" Atif barked. Nehemiah gave a little smile at his disdain for any chatter, and answered as stiffly as he could manage, wondering if the grim young warrior would get the hint.

"Secure. Prepare your operation. I am commencing stage two now and heading to retrieve your team's coordinates." He took his finger off again and waited. Nothing came over the set. Either Atif got the hint too well and was offended, or he just didn't consider an answer necessary. Nehi didn't bother to wonder, and headed out the door to find Tanzid. The agent knelt on the grass with a knife, busily skinning a satyr.

"Our Sir Cuthbert needs better antibiotics, stage two just started so we need Naqi, and a loaf of bread sounds great with meat," Nehi said.

"I'm not riding that SOLTD twice in one day. Who knows what it does to your insides," Tanzid said.

"Fair enough," Nehi nodded. He pulled out the wand, extended it, attached the two smaller balls carefully in the center, and began to program it. "I'll go get the stuff. I reported everything as secure, Atif and Dan should be readying to leave for the Sojourners now. Keep this place secure, please."

"Don't knock over any more trees."

"He doesn't look so bad now," Nehi murmured to his sister. He peeked through the cracked door, eyeing the mute curled on the bed. Dark patches lay deep under his eyes and he looked terribly small. But sunshine glittered over him, and Nehi could see the mute's fingers drumming softly against the covers, keeping the beat to some song playing in his head.

"He woke up after only six hours, of course, because he's Joe," Anna said, "and demanded food and ate like a champ. But just remember please that he isn't as strong as he looks, and don't excite him too much today."

"Ok," Nehemiah promised and walked in. His boots clumped on the hardwood floor and left bits of mountain mud with each step. "I hear your appetite's as big as Beau's and I may have to stay and do some shopping because of you," Nehi declared as he gave his friend a friendly punch in the shoulder. Anna's palm went to her face. But Joe grinned at Nehi, sat up slowly, and signed back with decent speed and no little heartbreaking hesitations.

"Is that s-a-t-y-r fur I see clinging to you? Oh look, blood too. You've been off having adventures without me."

"You started it," Nehi shrugged.

"Just because I have a bad habit doesn't mean you have to pick it up," Joe signed pretending to pout. Then he grinned and sank back against the headboard. "So why are you back again? Are you going to whisk my perfect nurse off to have adventures without me too?"

"Anna refused the fun," Nehi said, in a tone that clearly disapproved of her choice. Then he dropped into seriousness and lowered his voice to a murmur. "No, actually it's so you can take part in the adventure. Atif and Dan are downstairs forming a team to gather the Sojourner IDP leader you mentioned and whisk him off to a spot in Faerie Land that Tanzid and I have cleared. We're ready for a council of war. The thing is, none of us know who he is or how to find him." Joe swiveled and reached for the pad and pencil on his side table. His actions were slower than usual, and Nehi could see his mouth tighten and his eyes crinkle with the strain of moving. The mute started

scribbling. Nehemiah sat back and watched the light play over the floor, idly wondering where Beau had disappeared to. Two white notes pushed into his hand, and Nehi looked at the mute again.

"There's a few names and coordinates to start the hunt," Joe signed. "He was headed there a couple of weeks ago. When they do find him, the second note is so he knows they're from me. He might be more inclined to play along that way."

"Thanks Joe, you're a brick," Nehi commented, tucking the notes into his pocket. "I hope this IDP man is ok with sudden adventures. Do you want to come along? I can go deliver these to Daniel and then whisk you off to a bed in Faerie Land." He glanced over his shoulder to make sure no one was there and whispered conspiratorially. "We don't have to let Harry know till we get back."

"Thanks, but no, I'll stay here and let you young ones play. Although it might be fun to watch," Joe signed. A twinkle sparkled in the mute's eyes.

"You're enjoying a joke at my expense, aren't you? What don't I know?"

"Oh so much, my boy, so very much!" Joe laughed. "You'll find out this one soon enough. Make sure Frowner gets the note on the first page about the SOLTD I left in a pile of wood near Crosstown. That needs recovered. Go on now, run along and play." Joe made a condescending shooing motion toward the door, with a perfect imitation of a parent toward a pestering child. Nehi batted playfully at his head, and Joe dodged and laughed. Nehi grinned as he stood up and clumped toward the door. It was awfully good to see a happy Joe again.

The sound of Joe's violin followed him out. The notes didn't soar today, they swam gently through the room, a soft beauty to the slow melody. It sounded like a story, a sad story that moved into gentle peace. Nehi paused just outside the door, standing beside Anna. The twins listened as the song spun with the sunlight and died into a quiet silence.

"I think he's asleep again," Anna whispered. Nehemiah nodded. He didn't feel like breaking the silence of that dead song.

Something hung on those notes... It ended on a resolved major chord that spoke of joy, yes, but something underlay it that wasn't really at peace... His Grady vibrated in his jacket pocket as Atif requested his coordinates, and all the things he had to finish leapt back into Nehemiah's mind.

He trotted toward the stairs, fingering Joe's notes and headed to find their second team in this scheme. It was time for Atif and Daniel to go adventuring.

Freddy shivered in the little cave. A sneeze burst from him. A deep sullenness filled his soul as he pulled out his dirty handkerchief again, sniffling and huddling over his small fire. Only a few short weeks ago he had been surrounded by all the comforts he could want, with the ability to command anything that struck his fancy. And now look at him. Dirty and cold, hiding out in a sea cave on the Story Land coast.

His eyes darted to the package wrapped carefully in protective leather. He could find a buyer and start over with the funds from the sale. His day would come again.

If only he could be certain the Wolf was out of the picture. Freddy glanced around the cave convulsively, his face tightening in a fear that never left.

The shadows shifted and his gaze darted to the mouth of the cave.

A huge head blocked out what little sun drifted through the opening. Black hair bristled all over that head, and Freddy's eyes nearly bugged out of his face. The shadow deepened around him as a chimera followed the head into the cave. A red light melded with the shadow, overtaking any sunshine and covering Freddy. The light beamed from the snub nose of a specially made Brunhiem laser, primed and ready in the chimera's massive arm.

A hairy finger pointed at the package behind Freddy. His fat fingers scrabbled behind him, shaking so hard it took him a moment to grip the package. He held it out to the figure, still

goggling at the apparition.

"Unwrap it," the chimera rumbled.

"All right, all right," Freddy stuttered, his fingers fumbling at the leather strings binding it together. His mind screamed at him. *How did they find me?* The packaging fell away and a series of ancient documents glowed, the red light reflecting off their plastic sleeves. The chimera's massive hand closed over the journal pages and left the rest. He stepped back out of the cave. A sliver of sickly sunlight filtered through again, and Freddy sagged, his shaking hands on the cold stone ground. *How did they find me?!* If one person could find him, another could too.

The Wolf could track him even here.

The chimera paused, his brown eyes going to the shaking man in the little cave. His face creased in a frown.

"Not safe," he rumbled.

"What?" Freddy whispered. The chimera flicked a SOLTD from his belt, handling the heavy tool as if it were a matchstick.

"Not safe. Will be soon, but not yet. Take Jesus. Then you're always safe. And go here."

A paper fluttered to Freddy's feet. The cold of a SOLTD wrapped around the cave as the whine pierced through Freddy's brain. His finger shot out and clamped on the little paper as his fire sucked into the freezing darkness. The chimera, the pages, and what little life the fire's warmth offered disappeared. Freddy sat shivering and stunned.

The Raven's man had found him.

The Wolf could too.

A low moan came from Freddy and he folded slowly into a ball on the cold stones of the cave. His fingers shook as he lifted the piece of paper. The Black Raider's familiar scrawl swam into his focus.

934 Bleison Road, Walden. Bring her your information about the Wolf's package.

Chapter 6: Council of War

"The mouth of the righteous speaketh wisdom, and his tongue talketh of judgment." Psalm 37:3

The SOLTD pulsed and screamed its inhuman whistle. Nehi clutched Anna's fresh bread, and felt Naqi's hand clamping tighter on his shoulder. His boots slammed into earth, the whistling rose to its crazed pitch, and the SOLTD fell away from his vision. Nehi saw Tanzid leaning against the door of the house watching, and a glow of pleasure swept through him at having gotten so close to his destination. Tanzid straightened and walked off into the woods without a word. Naqi shivered and headed toward the house with his bag of heat sensors and security gadgets. Nehemiah followed him into the warm glow of the firelight to rebandage Sir Cuthbert's leg. But he glanced back at the dark woods, silently wondering where his agent had wandered off to.

Tanzid returned twenty minutes later with wild herbs and potatoes. They shoved the tubers under the glowing coals gathering steadily deeper as the fire burned. Their scent began to permeate the room as they roasted and the men waited. The meat sizzled and popped and Tanzid turned the spit. A simultaneous rumble came from four stomachs as they watched the cooking flesh.

Naqi glanced down as one of his gadgets vibrated.

"Atmospheric disruption, here they come," he reported. The pulsing whine of a SOLTD invaded the hall almost before the words were out. Cuthbert grunted and crossed himself, gripping his electric lance. Nehi stood up, dusted the dirt and ashes from his pants, and began to stroll for the door. He was the official team leader here, and a Hillson. He ought to be ready to meet the Sojourner IDP branch leader properly. The great hall doors shoved open, swirling in leaves and grass and the night breeze. A cheerful voice rode the cool air. It washed over Nehi and carried him back to boyhood; sitting in class with Anna, complaining over political tests, and laughing at the dinner

table with–

"Samuel!" The name yelped from Nehi. He sprang on the newcomer before the old man could get all the way through the door. His arms wrapped around him in a bear hug that lifted the white head four inches higher and turned the cheerful voice to a strangled gasp. Nehi found himself gripped by two strong bony hands and pushed back. Samuel Thomas stared at him with incredulous delight shining on his face.

"You're alive!" they both burst out, and laughter came, bashful and wet and incredibly happy. Nehi's mind spun and the next few minutes seemed to go by him in a blur as the mix of emotions collided and danced and wailed in him, drowning out everything else. The hole from his missing parents broke open and flooded him with the familiar black sorrow, mixing with delight and overwhelming relief at having his old teacher near... it was like he had suddenly found a spot to tie his rope. An anchor. That's what Samuel was. An anchor tied to Christ's wisdom, and to memories of long days spent with his parents. Nehi drew in a deep breath and closed his eyes for a moment to let the sorrow and joy mix and sink into him. He brought himself back to the present forcibly and looked back at the company.

Daniel held the conversation, outlining the eventful task of finding the IDP branch leader and getting him here. His sardonic manner leant itself to storytelling, and his audience sat laughing and enthralled. The adventure was a good one but he didn't prolong it. After a sketch of events he lifted a finger and pointed at the knight lounging on one elbow on his red cloak.

"If you had to take over the building, Nehi, why didn't you kill the owner outright?" he drawled. "Only dead men can be trusted not to tell secrets." Sir Cuthbert didn't bridle. He gave an indulgent smile, and Nehi knew he understood it as a tease. Nehi's opinion of him went up a notch. There were only a handful of people Nehemiah had met who recognized Daniel's caustic moods at the first meeting. Cuthbert also didn't try to explain himself, but let someone already trusted do it. This weird knight knew people.

"You wouldn't have me turn out someone clumsy enough to get wounded, would you? He might have been eaten by a moth or something," Nehi shrugged.

"Thou might not tease so if thou hadst met our moths," Cuthbert commented and Tanzid laughed. He knew about the giant treetop dwellers. The rest of the company accepted he was cleared and not a security issue, and got on with business. Which was dinner. For the next few minutes nothing was heard but eating and grunting and an occasional, "That's good." Samuel finally sat his de-meated bone down and leaned closer to Nehi.

"Will you tell me how you've been? About the scars, perhaps? Also, the note sent by the little blond-headed enigma, is he all right, or should I be concerned and try to get him out of a mess?" Nehi laid his potato down and launched into it in a quiet, confidential tone. He spoke fast, outlining the past two years with precision and holding nothing back. It was harder than he expected to talk about the days with Abid. A lot harder. He was a little surprised to find that after Abid's rooms faded, Joe immediately took center stage and held it; not the crazy events he and Anna had been through, the IDP, or finding Daniel again, but Joe. The little dancer flitted past as the savior, confusion, and friend that had made the past two years bearable. More than bearable, even enjoyable. Samuel listened, putting in a question to clarify a point here and there, but never really interrupting. Nehi made it to the hectic rescue, the reclamation of the Bible, and getting them all to this strange building in Faerie, and stopped. Samuel nodded slowly as he absorbed it all.

"I'm going to have to thank Joe heartily the next time we meet," he said. He laid a hand on Nehi's shoulder. "Thank you for telling me." His hand squeezed and gave Nehi a happy little shake. "I can't express how glad I am to have you beside me again!" Accepting the confidences, and letting the young man know it was all fine. For some reason he couldn't explain, Nehi needed that confirmation after telling about Abid and Simmons, that knowledge Samuel still looked on him the same. Maybe it exposed a nerve that would never fully heal, opened

him at his most vulnerable. Maybe somewhere in his soul, shame still clung to him after Abid's de-humanizing tactics. But whatever caused that bashfulness and insecurity to resurface, Samuel dispelled it in an instant.

Nehi sat tall and happy as Samuel cleared his throat and swept the gathered company with his smile, making it clear he was ready to include them. He shifted to his knees, folded his hands, and bowed his white-haired head. The munching around them stopped. Samuel Thomas accepted his role as the elder there without any hesitation or apologies. He opened the proceedings with a simple, heartfelt prayer for wisdom and gratefulness for the opportunity granted this company. Then he looked up, his blue eyes shining and a smile twitching over his face.

"I understand we have our book back. It is time for the Sojourners to retake their kingdom and let the light shine again," he said. Cuthbert's eyes widened and he looked around him with new interest. "Come brethren, let's begin. How are we going to force out the invaders and reclaim our own?"

"Harry says you should be sleeping," Anna commented. Joe glanced over at her from where he sat up in bed, idly playing an imaginary whistle. *"Oh?"* the look plainly said. "Yes," Anna nodded. "He's downstairs complaining about it to his patient."

"What do you think?" Joe signed, and morphed back into his playing. The splints had come off his fingers this morning and he seemed to be enjoying limbering them up. Anna paused her knitting, reached into the bag resting by her chair, and pulled out a recorder. Joe laughed, his eyes shining as he took the instrument and began to finger it lovingly.

"I think before your relapse, you were stronger than you made us all think. Why didn't you go with Nehi to the council?" Anna asked. "You had more of a reason than being in recovery." Joe hesitated, then began to sign slowly, staring at the comforter. Uncomfortable with looking at her while he spelled it

out, perhaps?

"When Frowner came for me and was carrying me out of the FF's place, and Knee-High and Blaster and the others all swept in, I realized something. As I just lay there and watched, I didn't feel like I had to do anything. I mean, I couldn't really have helped, not enough to count for anything. But...they were good men. In their souls and in their skills, they were capable of handling the situation without me. I've never really felt that, Beauty. I've always been the one who had to get others out of the mess, to understand the violent and be violent back to defend and rescue. This time, they were good. Knee-High and the others didn't need me. They don't need me. And that's really nice. To know that someone else can take care of the world, and I don't have to go rushing in to save it all...at least for a little while..." His face went distant, seeing something she couldn't. His eyes went to his fingers running up and down the recorder, and his expression became tired and a little worried.

"There's also the fact I'm not recovering like I should. I'm weak, Beauty. I need time to get stronger, after this resurgence you're all planning, I'll be needed again. For a little while. And I need to be strong enough to handle it."

"Handle what?" Anna asked, her knitting in her lap. Something hung behind the mask on Joe's face. Worry? Sorrow? She wasn't sure, but there was something... His mood flipped as if he hit a switch, an impish smile springing over his face as his eyes laughed at her. One eyebrow went up with a, *Wouldn't you like to know*? A reel in a minor key spun from the recorder, dancing, laughing, and mysterious all in one. Anna laughed, then hit him with a pillow. The recorder cut off with a sharp squeal.

"Stop being so mysterious with people you know you can trust," she ordered. "There's more hiding behind your mask, out with it, what is it?"

"Fine," Joe signed, and took on a playfully puffed-up manner, "the real reason I didn't tag along is I already know everything they'll decide." Anna hit him with the pillow again.

"And don't be a prideful fool, you've already fallen too often

recently," she said. Joe grinned, slid the pillow behind him, and sank back against it.

"There, you're unarmed. Why didn't you go with him?"

"Those SOLTDs make my stomach sick," Anna grimaced. Then she grinned. "And I knew you could tell me what they would decide." Joe laughed and let his eyes half close as he idly watched Anna's needles fly. A few minutes passed in quiet as Anna followed her pattern and Joe lay cradling his new recorder. Anna broke the silence.

"So what are they going to decide?"

"A carefully timed attack in the north and south, combined with an internal uprising. A smaller team will go in first, to cut off the leaders' command center. When communications are cut, the IDP-alerted Sojourners rise as a body and kick the invaders out, with our people in their midst adding fresh blood and good weapons. They'll have a third team ready to sweep in wherever trouble crops up. It will be the north that needs them."

"Do you think that will work?" Anna asked, surprised by its simplicity.

"Yes. With God's help. We will need a place to claim as our headquarters though, where people can meet and plan. Somewhere inside the kingdom, a spot the invaders don't know about, fairly accessible to allies coming and going. That's not going to be easy to find."

"Uncle Adam's cabin," Anna said promptly. Joe tipped his head at her, one eyebrow rising in surprise.

"You have an uncle? What cabin?"

"Had, unfortunately. He died when Nehi and I were six, I wish I had more memories of him. I know he and father were very close, and Daniel still feels the loss. But he had a cabin high in the forest on the edge of the kingdom. Daniel never really liked to visit it. Too many memories to make it a fun stay for him, he told me once. But Nehi and I often disappeared up there, especially in the winter when it was too cold to camp and we wanted to do some skiing. I don't think anyone knew of it except our family. And Peter, we took him with us once."

"Interesting," Joe signed, staring at his comforter again, his face blank as he considered it. "That should do. Yes, that sounds like it will do well. That makes us one step closer. With the Bible back and God's grace, I think this might work."

"That reminds me to ask. Why did you send the Bible to me, Joe?"

"Because you're the best one to bring it back to its pedestal and show the world it's returned. By giving it to you I officially appointed you Keeper of the Word," Joe signed. He lay indolently against the headboard, and Anna detected something fake in his attitude. It had a hint of the way he used to act toward the twins, before he trusted them, a shield pulled over him.

"That's quite a job," Anna commented mildly.

"You're perfect for it," Joe smiled.

"Is that the only reason, Joe?" Anna asked, watching him closely. She saw his hesitation and the infinitesimal color that went to his cheeks before he covered it all with his adopted lazy attitude.

"Should there be more?" he signed. A smile twitched over Anna's face. But she turned it away from the mute, wrestling her notebook out of her pocket.

"One nice thing about having to stick around the house because you need a nurse," Anna commented, "is that I've had the time to draw." Joe's hand closed over her notebook and he drew it onto the bed. "You might have asked first." He gave her an impish smile and flipped it open to see her newest artwork.

A cloud of white dust spurted up into his face. Joe sneezed. And sneezed. His head snapped back and forward in helpless rapidity, sneezing with explosive force. Harry's house-shoes pounded up the stairs, but Anna didn't notice. She was laughing too hard.

"You should see your face!" she gasped, almost doubled over. Joe sneezed, the whole bed shaking with the force of it, his green comforter covered in the white powder. Harry spun into the room and paused, taking in the scene. "You left your sneezing powder in the pocket of your pants, I found it in the

laundry!" Her arm snaked around her stomach as she guffawed. Joe sneezed, the bed creaking and jumping with it. But he laughed with Anna, between the bursts. Harry leaned against the doorframe and shook his head at the two ridiculous young people, a little smile creeping over his face.

"You're cleaning the bedclothes, young lady," he commented mildly, and moved forward to help Joe recover his breath and his dignity.

The sun broke over the horizon, sending its heat waves to kiss the bald head of the mountain top. Nehi yawned enormously as he stepped out of the hall to watch the sky turn gold. The council of war had taken all night, with plans propounded, rejected, accepted, and refined. Nehi felt as exhausted as if he had fought a war. In a way he had; a war with ideas, and he had won. Some of the others had put forth some pretty stupid, elaborate plans.

"How doth the ilk of the council please thee?" Sir Cuthbert's deep voice rolled over him, and Nehi turned toward the sound. The knight sat propped against the hall, watching the sun rise. He had limped outside fairly early in the proceedings, wanting sleep. The ground squished pleasantly under Nehemiah's boots as he walked over and sank down next to the knight.

"We decided on a concentrated surprise attack. One team from our ranks will go in early and, 'cut off the head of the snake,' as Atif puts it. Then the Sojourners rise up as a body. I think it will work, if God wills it and we don't die."

"That wast the plan first brought forward by thee, and amended by thy brother. I thought me it had a wise simplicity about it," Cuthbert smiled. Nehi wasn't sure what to answer. Cuthbert looked back at the sunrise, watching it slowly topping the trees. "Thou art a Sojourner. When thou arrived thou said thou camest from Story Land."

"We did. I've been living there for a bit."

"I thought me thou believed the rot about truth changing

and no real right or wrong."

"'Rot' is a pretty good word for it," Nehi just commented.

"It is an abominable falsehood, which has done much evil and will do more. I know not how a man could live in such a belief. To say thus would be to forfeit all chance at an honorable life, for honor itself is no longer stable. All becomes merely battles of strength, for no consideration of the right winning couldst enter in. Chaos, destruction, and violence are the inevitable end of the monster Evolution and its hellish brood of Moral Relativism."

"People have tried to put it into structures," Nehi said hesitantly. He agreed wholeheartedly, but curiosity begged him to egg on this sudden turn to the conversation. "The Battle Kingdom is already where you mention, but KAM and the People's Kingdom have both given it some kind of stability."

"It is a temporary stability. I have been told the world before ours stood for century upon century, and our book inclines me to believe it, for even the language is older than most. It must be a remnant from more years than we of this age comprehend. I think me our two hundred years of history are but a small trial, in which we may flex the muscles of our ideas and kingdom break lance against kingdom to see who shall stand."

"That's certainly possible," Nehi agreed guardedly, suddenly feeling out of his depth. Sir Cuthbert looked at him and burst into his hearty laugh.

"Thou art cudgeling thy wits over how such a one as I, from the small land of Faerie, spurned and jeered upon, has thought of such high matters!"

"I've been told I have a pretty open face," Nehi said, his head ducking as embarrassment climbed over him. Cuthbert laughed again and slammed a hand amiably into Nehi's shoulder.

"Nay, thy curiosity is admirable, and wilt be an asset to thee as the years march on. I was the king's squire for much of my life, and detailed often to deal with the business concerns of commerce over our borders. As such, I was once allowed to look upon our book, and read much of it. The duty fell to me to

learn of our neighbors and the world outside, such that it should taint our fair land as little as it might. For there is much to taint honor and true knighthood in the outer world."

"That's true enough. Is everyone here honorable?"

"Thou art striving too hard to be innocent, lad, and I read in thee a reason behind the questioning."

"Tanzid warned me not to let my sister wander, if she came this way," Nehi admitted, embarrassed again and hoping he wouldn't take offense. "I was just wondering if all the men here are...true knights, as you put it." Cuthbert's face fell and every line hardened to the warrior, leaving the genial companion somewhere deep inside him.

"There are the black knights. They are vile indeed and sprinkled throughout our land as pestilence upon a fair garden. Ever our king strives to drive them forth, but always those in our midst turn from honor into the blackness, stealing away a maiden for their own pleasure, or dealing death for wanton destruction or the mere desire of gain." Cuthbert looked at Nehi, and he felt the intensity behind the gaze. "It is partially for this reason I have ventured to speak to thee. I see wisdom in thy fair countenance, though thy years be scant. I have long since come to value the way of the Sojourners. There is much in your creed that cleaves to my soul and that I see reflected in the world around me. There is vileness in each man, though we strive to gainsay it. A battle rages daily inside my own soul, well I know, against honor. There is a fiend inside me which is only sated by a beast's wild urge to gluttony of the self. Yet I have met but one of thy people in my time. He was a meek, bespecktacled thing, ever cowering and ducking, and I cared not for his sacrilege of manhood. Thou and thy companions are of a very different sort. I wouldst thou couldst tell me more of thy Way."

"I would be delighted," Nehi smiled, and settled more comfortably on the grass. This looked like it was going to be a long discussion. Sir Cuthbert beamed at him, but interrupted before he could start.

"I have noted thy tendencies to prattle, so by thy leave I will say one thing more before I offer myself and the fountain of thy

tongue runs freely. Whether or not I agree fully with thy creed, I know my kingdom has sorely missed the Sojourner's strength. With thy kingdom fallen, we smaller lands have trembled, and many have dwindled as their people flee to stronger countries. Without thy armies to hire or thy voice in the marketplace of the kingdoms, we small lands become prey to others. The Battle Kingdom and eke the Prophet's Peace have had men vilely prowling about our borders of late. I hereby offer thee the aide of King Harold the Golden, knowing well I am his true mouthpiece. A contingent of knights is at thy service in this coming fight, wherever thou might find use for us."

Chapter 7: The Backer

"Let your conversation be without covetousness; and be content with such things as ye have: for he hath said, I will never leave thee, nor forsake thee." Hebrews 13:5

Concrete slammed into Samuel's shoes and he caught at Naqi's shoulder, shaking and groaning as the SOLTD hissed back into itself, like an evil demon squalling at having to leave.

"I'm too old to travel on those things," Samuel gasped, rubbing a hand over the lower end of his spine. His eye landed on the shoots of deep green creeping through the concrete under his feet, and he looked up quickly. Fronds swayed over them, enormous and intricately patterned. The scent of exotic flowers, mold, rot, and garbage filled his senses, and Samuel looked at the geeky man beside him. "Story Land?"

"Don't look at me," Naqi shrugged, "I'm just following orders from my boss. I assumed you knew the destination had been changed last moment." A low whistle came from their left, and the two men swung around, hands going to their weapons. A small blond-haired figure sat on a brick wall beside the roadway. His white cast thumped as he swung his legs like a little boy. A smile split his face, shifting his livid red cuts as he waved at them.

"Sorry, that was my request that brought you here," he signed.

"Creeps, you gave me the jumps," Naqi complained. "I don't know your language."

"He does," Joe signed, motioning to Samuel. "And he's the one I actually wanted." Samuel repeated the words for Naqi, studying Joe as the mute spun slowly, hung for a moment from his fingers, then landed on his good foot in front of them.

"Well, if he's the one you want," Naqi huffed, "I'm going to move along. Atif has a stack of things he wants me to do. Should I send someone to pick you up?" The tech man glanced meaningfully at the mute's cast as he said it. Joe grinned at him.

"No thank you. We're just a block from Doctor's. He and Beauty don't know I've been out, I'd appreciate their continued ignorance," the mute signed.

"I bet you would," Naqi grinned back. He gave a wave and trotted off. The two studied each other. Samuel was the first to break the silence.

"I heard about the past two years from Nehi. Thank you, Joe, from the depths of my soul. Thank you for taking care of the twins when no one else in the world could have done it." No sarcasm invaded the words, they came steady and frank. It lowered Joe's shields despite himself, making him feel decidedly bashful. "If ever I can do anything for you and Cobeau, believe me, I will try and do it with all of myself." Joe's eyes turned away and he felt flustered, unable to fashion his thoughts. People didn't thank him with that kind of fervent heat, as if he was really something special.

"Well, that makes me feel a little silly for what I was about to ask," Joe signed. Samuel's laugh boomed around them and his hand went out automatically to clap the mute on the shoulder. Joe dodged out of instinct, a cringe flashing over his face. Samuel covered the awkward moment with a ready grin.

"The way you signed that warns me I may not like it, but I meant what I said, and it includes the trivial. Come on, Joe, why did you send for me?" Samuel demanded. Joe noticed he diplomatically said "send for" and not "kidnapped" and liked him better than ever.

"Beauty (my name for A-n-n-a) and I have this war going on." A wily smile broke over the mute's face, but even through it Samuel could see the weary black splotches under the eyes. He silently sent up a prayer for healing for this little man; more than just bodily healing. The mute paused and tipped his head on one side.

"What's your sign name, by the way?" Joe asked. Samuel colored, and it was his turn to glance away.

"Well, you have to remember, it was my sister who named me," he said, in a rush, "and you know how sisters can be."

"I do, actually, a little now," Joe signed, his smile suddenly

warm. He made a, 'get on with it' motion and raised his eyebrows. Samuel crossed his arms with the palms facing his shoulders, and brought his fingers and thumbs in twice in quick succession, as if he was squeezing two imaginary oranges. Joe burst out laughing.

"It's not that funny," Samuel frowned.

"It fits! That's what's funny!" Joe signed as he laughed. He sucked in a dramatic breath, pretending to force himself back on topic, and Samuel rolled his eyes. Joe silently noticed it was easy, even natural, to tease this old gent. And Samuel got it, and laughed too. It had taken weeks before it felt natural even with the twins. He filed it away as another very nice oddity of Samuel Thomas and sidled a little closer conspiratorially. Samuel accepted it as an olive branch for the dodging-the-friendly-shoulder-slap episode earlier, and leaned in to complete it.

"Ok, Teddy Bear, here's the deal," Joe signed, "I've already warned Knee-High not to mention you to Beauty, and Doctor has an impressive sized pantry..."

"I'm glad we came back for dessert," Tanzid commented, sliding a cookie from Anna's cookie jar. He started weaving in a happy food dance as he bit into it. Anna gave a distracted "glad you like them" as she hurried around the kitchen getting lunch ready. Tanzid reached for more.

"I'm curious where Atif and his crew zipped off to again," Nehemiah commented from where he slouched in a kitchen chair.

"I hope he shows up soon so I don't have to keep his lunch warm," Anna said. She sprinkled salt over her brown rice, then moved to get the bread out of the pantry. She opened the door with one hand, her eyes on the bag of salt in her other hand as she tried to remember what else she needed it for. Then she looked up. A shriek tore from her and she staggered back, knocking against the table and dropping the salt bag, sending an explosion of white cascading over the kitchen. Tanzid and

Nehemiah whipped their lasers out and leapt for the pantry, Nehi's chair crashing back into the tile with a bang. Then they noticed Joe leaning against the kitchen door frame. Laughter shook the mute so hard he couldn't stand up straight. Nehemiah grinned and slid Hope back into her holster. Tanzid still moved cautiously as he opened the pantry, one hand on his primed laser. He blinked in surprise.

"Hello," the agent commented. A laughing answer drifted out. Nehemiah's grin stretched wider.

"That's why you told me not to say anything? You're an idiot, Joe," Nehi told the mute, as Joe tried to suck in a breath, his face strained and one arm holding his broken ribs as he laughed. Anna flew past Nehi, her arms going around Samuel in a crushing grip, a little sob sliding from her. But after a quick hug she pulled away and spun on Joe. The mute slid to the floor and sat helpless with silent laughter.

"Joe you little beast!" Anna lashed out, one trim foot stamping the tiled floor. "You nearly gave me a heart attack, and keeping poor Samuel in the pantry, what kind of a welcome is that after a long trip? And look, you made me spill the salt everywhere! You're not even supposed to be out of bed!" The mute held up a placatory hand and managed to get his merriment down to hiccupping giggles. Joe staggered up and grabbed the broom.

"I'll clean up the salt and buy you some more. Does that help?" he signed, trying to look apologetic and failing miserably. He started laughing again, leaning on the broom. "You should have seen your face Beauty, it was priceless! Do I get a point for the best surprise so far?" Anna smiled despite herself, hugging Samuel tight.

"All right, I'll grant you that one, it was the best surprise anyone could have! Samuel, what are you doing here? Are you the leader of the Sojourner's branch of the IDP?" Anna asked. Her hand went up to pause any reply and she spun to Joe, as he stood balancing on his good leg, using the broom for a crutch and panting through his giggles. "You, upstairs, now."

"Oh come on, I just–" Joe started, losing his laughter. But

Anna pointed upstairs, her mouth firm.

"Upstairs and back in bed, or I'll call Harry and he'll sedate you again."

"But I–" Joe tried, suddenly forlorn.

"I mean it!" Anna snapped. Joe sighed with heavy melodrama and began to shuffle-hop out of the room. Nehi smiled and followed him. Joe rested a hand on his friend's shoulder, using him as a living crutch to hop up the stairs, as the two commiserated silently over the gilded cage.

As Joe slumped back on his bed and the comforter floofed up around him, he could see Nehi chafing to get back down and visit with his old friend. The mute waved him away cheerily, declaring he wanted a nap. Nehi gave him a smile and slid out, and Joe leaned back against the pillow with a little sigh. His ribs hurt. To his own surprise, he found he actually did want a nap. Weariness clung to his bones, and his ankle throbbed with the shooting pain again. A niggle of worry crept through him, wondering how long this frailness would claim him. But Joe shut it out, focused on the comfort enfolding him, on being safe, and made himself relax. He drifted off slowly.

A fresh breeze blew over him, messing with his hair and getting up his nostrils. Instantly, Joe's hyper-alert system was awake, and aware he wasn't alone in the room. His eyes stayed closed, and he kept breathing easy, letting himself enjoy the comfort, the breeze, and the delicious fact he felt no fear. That meant whoever was in his room was a protector, a trusted one, a banisher of fear. It felt so very good to have friends. Joe amused himself by guessing who had sick duty today. Harry always smelled like disinfectant and pipe smoke, so no doctor. Beau would be humming, so it wasn't him. Anna had been cooking with garlic for lunch, and he couldn't smell that scent either. So the person blocking the light from the window and giving him that comfortable feeling of safety must be Nehi. Joe opened his eyes, ready to shoot out a tease about satyrs.

Samuel Thomas sat beside him, Nehi's Grady turning his white hair an eerie green.

Joe started, jerking away automatically. His back hit the wall

with a smack and stars flashed in his vision. Samuel looked up. He gave a gentle smile and didn't move. *Careful not to scare the scarred one,* Joe silently supplied, and hot annoyance rushed through him at his own reaction.

"I'm sorry I startled you. The twins let me take a turn sitting in the sick room for a while. Daniel is regaling the house with another tale of a daring rescue performed this afternoon, and Cobeau came in hungry then crashed for a nap. I didn't realize it would worry you."

"I'm fine," Joe signed in what would have been a snap if it were words, surprised by the heat behind it. And the knowledge he meant it. He hadn't been worried by this old gent's presence. And that was his subconscious talking, which had never lied to him yet. Samuel smiled again, a little more genuinely, and laid down the Grady with a businesslike air.

"Good. I volunteered for the service partially to let them have their fun, and partially in the hope you would wake up."

"The window?" Joe signed. Samuel chuckled, the winning sound filled the room, and Joe found himself smiling.

"You caught me, I thought it might wake you. Although it does feel nice," Samuel said. "Joe, I brought you something, and I have a proposition for you. Or perhaps a suggestion…maybe a little of both. But first the package…" Samuel leaned down and rummaged in a bag by his feet. Joe leaned back comfortably, weighing an idea of his own as he waited. Samuel straightened, and Joe saw black fabric lying over his arm. A sparkle of interest sprung into the mute's eyes. Samuel shook it out and Joe found himself looking at his old black jacket. A smile spread over the whole mute as he held out his hand. "I'm a little surprised you're not snatching," Samuel grinned as he handed it over and watched Joe almost petting the fabric. "We found it when searching the tunnel systems for Amran. I'm afraid I was the one who 'tipped them off' about your useful jacket, and I apologize for that slip of the tongue. I didn't realize how deep the treachery ran."

"Not everyone in that section's a traitor," Joe put in. "Mostly Amran, and a few he's taken with him. C-h-a-r-l-e-s is all right

as far as I know."

"I'm glad to hear it!" Samuel said, relief almost shining from him. "I couldn't be sure, but had no one else to leave in charge. And that leads us nicely into my proposition. I can see you are not as desperately ill as Anna or Harry think, and I personally have found the best way for an active person to heal is not by being suddenly relegated to 'useless invalid.' I don't like making decisions about my IDP flock without taking counsel first, and there are very few people I trust to give me informed, Christ-like advice." Samuel paused and regarded Joe. "Do you think we might help each other?"

"Am I one of the trusted?" Joe blinked, letting his incredulity show.

"Why, don't you trust yourself?" Samuel asked, without a smile.

"Not all the time," Joe signed cautiously.

"Good. Then I trust you even more than I did. No one should trust themselves, not completely. 'The heart is deceitful above all things, and desperately wicked: who can know it?[3]' The thing is, I trust you more than me. Or at least, I think your opinion on IDP matters is to be courted. Would you mind if I start up a messenger service with you and come visiting occasionally?"

"All right. But are you willing to do something for me?" Joe asked.

"I did say I would do anything I could to help…" Samuel answered, stressing the last two words and letting his sentence trail off.

"It's not illegal, Teddy Bear. At least your part isn't," Joe grinned at him.

"Why am I not comforted?"

"This revolution you're all planning is going to need funding. You can't create more SOLTDs or put weapons in an army's hands or feed hungry bellies on promises, and you all know it. Doctor has fit the bill like a champ, but he's running low even

---

[3] Jeremiah 17:9

7. The Backer
Hebrew 13:5

though he wouldn't say so. The IDPs have stepped in, but they all have their own problems too, and have already spared a lot on this."

"What's your solution?" Samuel asked, hesitation on his face. Joe twisted in the bed, slid his hand between the mattress and the wall, and came back up again with something wrapped in a pillowcase. With infinite care Joe sat the thing on the bed between them and let the pillowcase fall away.

A black marble statuette of a female in a toga gleamed in the afternoon light, her delicate features turned demurely to her feet. Samuel sank back in his chair, a whistle sliding through clamped teeth.

"That can't be an original?" Awe filled his voice. Joe's eyes didn't leave the statue, and the smile on his face was one of reverence. He just nodded. "How on earth did you get it?" The tone came suddenly sharp, reproachful. Joe looked up and clicked his tongue in annoyance.

"I didn't steal it, Teddy Bear. Well, only from the thief, not an actual owner. I snatched it off F-r-e-d-d-y's shelf as Frowner ran by with me, then passed it to Glue when he grabbed me. I know a man who can sell it for us and give us a good price. And get it to a good home where people will be able to enjoy it like they should," Joe added quickly as he saw Samuel about to object. The twinkle came back to Joe's face, but Samuel didn't care that the mute found his stuffy objections amusing.

"Who owned it before Freddy?" he demanded. An impish smile flitted over Joe's face. He just went back to studying the statue, one finger gently running along the toga's perfect lines. Samuel softened. He could see the quiet admiration and regret hiding behind the mute's mask. The artist in him didn't want to give up this treasure. And probably the man in him too. Samuel slid himself into Joe's shoes, considering the background; grown up a slave unable to call anything his own, tossed in with a rich man, then lost it all at his protector's death, built a life out of his own toil, and then lost it all again in a moment when he ran from the People's Kingdom. And not even twenty yet. And now he held a priceless treasure, something that could set him

up for life.

"What are you purposing?" Samuel asked, suddenly curious what Joe intended. It would be more than fair for the young man to keep a finder's fee. Joe pulled his hand back quickly, as if caught in a vulnerability. He was suddenly all business.

"You stay here, let them think I'm still sleeping. You shouldn't have to actually lie, they'll assume I'm here already. I slip out, meet my man, and mail the funds to you under the name of the IDP leader. I'll use his handwriting, that will make a good clean backer for Knee-High's resurgence."

"Why me?"

"Glue's worn out, Knee-High would object to my using a fence to get money for his war, Beauty and Doctor would yell at me for getting out of bed, and my man won't trust anyone but me. Fences don't give the whole price, of course. But we should get enough for what we need."

"Maybe enough to rebuild a musician's wagon too?" Samuel asked. Joe frowned, his eyes darting away. Samuel had pegged him, again. But he signed without a pause to think, because he had already thought this out.

"No. I don't want another traveling wagon, I want to settle. This is funding to build what I pray will be my own home country too. We only have one shot at this resurgence, and we're going to need every cent to make the effort the best it can be. Deal?"

"All right," Samuel agreed. He bit his tongue as the pillowcase whipped over the statuette again; he wanted to plead for one more moment to admire the beauty. Joe shoved his gloves in one pocket and shrugged on his jacket. A world of memories and some of the old competency filled him as it settled over his shoulders. The warrior showed as he hopped to the window and lowered himself with one hand, his crutch and the statue dangling in the other. The mute dropped out of sight.

Samuel sat back and heaved a little sigh. He prayed he had made the right decision.

Joe watched from the shadows of the alley as the worker rolled the transport mail bin into the grimy building. His crutch tip-tapped on the concrete as he shifted behind the big rusty bin that served as a dumpster, and sank to the ground with a sharp sigh. For a moment he let his head drop back against the wall and just breathed. Everything in him felt weary and aching. But Joe knew his timeline today and he didn't allow himself more than a few seconds. His hand dove into his jacket, relishing the familiar feel, even the smell of years of use. He had never thought to see this old friend again, or gain any of these useful little items hidden in its folds. A thankful smile hovered on his face as he pulled his hologram disc from its pocket and slid the mic into his ear.

Ariel's perfect face flashed to life in the blue lines of the hologram.

"Raven," she stated, her voice guarded. "I didn't expect to hear from you so soon. Honestly, I didn't expect to ever hear from you again, you seemed a little cut up at our last parting."

"How do you know who flashed the signal?" Joe's gloves spoke in their staccato way. He could see her expression freeze, her mind rushing back over the scene she had waltzed into with her boys. Running over the faces she had seen, the options suddenly opening before her. Joe moved the conversation on. He had planted a seed of doubt in her certainty, it was enough for now. "We did cut off one of Wolf's paws that day, most of his agents are no longer a viable asset. Thank you for your assistance."

"Is that sarcasm? It's hard to tell with you, all I can see is this dumb rotating raven, and that computerized voice is just weird. I have to say, Wolf's persona is a lot more flamboyant."

"Different people prefer different styles," Joe signed, quick and irritated. In the shadows by the dumpster he rolled his eyes at himself and gave a little shake. Somehow this lady always managed to derail his control of a conversation and get under his skin. She had a special talent for that. "We are not quite ready to use our leverage."

"Great, you called just to tell me you're letting Wolf win,"

Ariel snapped. Joe's lips pursed, and he worked to keep on topic.

"But I know a way to wound him, and tie a brand to his tail that will burn even after we bring him down."

"Now this interests me," Ariel said, her iron-hard voice as close to a coo as it ever got. "I suppose you aren't going to take the trouble and expense though."

"After we bring him down, why should I care what happens next," Joe signed. He wished his gloves could form it into a question. "Should I send you the information."

"Why not just tell me?"

"Calls have ways of being overheard."

"And you don't like being open long enough to be tracked, all right, all right, send it. But Raven, I want to know before you fade into the darkness again–"

"You will get your treasure. Soon," Joe signed and watched her mouth snap closed and the single nod of her perfect face. *You've already earned it,* he thought silently, but didn't sign. It would be better to keep her on the hook. "Mermaid, the Wolf is not tied as tight as he has been." He saw her stiffen and knew she understood. "And he knows your mercenaries grow tired of the hunt. Watch your back."

Joe shut off the hologram with his toe and swept it up. He tucked it in his pocket with one hand as he slid his crutch under his arm with the other. A sharp pain sliced through the snapped bones in his ankle as he shifted back down the alley, and Joe winced and gave a silent groan. His aches felt more pronounced after the few minutes of rest. But his movements were swift as he wound his mask over his head.

The crutch made no noise on the concrete.

The window above the sorting bin was large and grimy with the dust of years. Joe held his magnet up to the lock and watched as the metal bar slid slowly and smoothly from its place. It thunked into his magnet, he oiled the window's edges, and slid it open an inch. Joe dropped to one knee and put his blowgun to his lips. The metal tube felt cold and light in his fingers, and he silently praised the brilliance of whoever had first

thought of using such a thing as a weapon. It remained one of his most versatile tools. One quick puff, and the pellet smashed onto the cold concrete in the center of the transport mail room.

A cloud of dense orange smoke billowed into the air. Coughs and yells rang as people panicked and rushed for the front door. Joe slid the window open the rest of the way, wiggled half of himself inside, and attached the hoverer discs to the box. He hooked the edge with the top of his crutch and heaved the box so the discs sat under it. The steam pushed off the other packages in the pile, Joe gripped the box and heaved it out the window, puffing and blowing, his face mottled white and red with the effort. It dropped like a stone, then the discs caught again and pushed it a half a foot off the ground. Joe closed the window silently, locked it, clicked his magnet back in place on his jacket sleeve, and clumped away behind the building, pushing the box ahead of him. A whistle slid from him as he stepped into the sunshine and made his way up the street back toward Harry's.

Inside his box rested enough money to fund a resurgence; properly postmarked and addressed, ready for Samuel to wave and declare the whole thing cleanly IDP backed.

And Ariel would take care of that other little matter for him. Revenge could be a useful tool when played right.

"Samuel, there's a box for you!" Peter bellowed from downstairs. Samuel heard Harry and Anna shushing him loudly, and smiled. But his eyes went to the empty bed, and worry crept into him.

A clack came from the window, and Samuel hopped up. Joe's crutch sat on the windowsill and his white hand strained as it pulled. Samuel bounded over and helped heave the mute inside. Joe tumbled through the bay window, bouncing on his good foot and wheezing heavily. He let Samuel help him to the bed. But as the mute sank back with a little gasp, a smile twinkled in his eyes.

"My man paid well," he signed. His hands shook.

7. The Backer

"Oh gosh, this thing is heavy," Peter grunted downstairs.

"Whoa, that is heavy," Nehi agreed. "Samuel!" he yelled up the stairs. Harry and Anna shushed again, loud and annoyed. Joe grinned and made a shooing motion toward the door. Samuel slowly obeyed, but his eyes lingered on the mute. Joe slumped back, going limp against the pillow. A sigh rattled from him and his eyes fluttered closed. Samuel watched Joe's muscles relax as sleep took him. So quickly...

"Samuel!" Nehi called in a half whisper up the stairs, and Samuel deserted the sick room. Nehi's face lit up like an eager child's as he saw his old friend at the top of the stairs. "It's a really heavy box, and it's from the transport lines with no address but Harry's and, 'To the S IDP L,' which we assume means you."

"Harry, don't you think it's a little hazardous to have your IDP position known so clearly anyone can send you boxes like this?" Paul demanded, worry clear on his face. The doctor shrugged, pipe smoke wreathing his head as he leaned in the den's doorway.

"Half my congregation is from drop ins, people who knew what I was and got curious. Besides, how else would weird boxes like this get to you people?" He waved his pipe at the package. "This one could have come from anywhere in the world. The box itself looks as if it could tell us stories."

"I expect it could tell us quite a number of things," Samuel murmured, and let himself be shoved into the kitchen to open his box. Most of the people in the house slipped in after him or crowded around the den door, bored enough to be curious about any strange happening. And a box from the transport line was a strange happening. It sat on the table, tattered and dirty and properly postmarked. Samuel dutifully broke it open.

Bright gold twinkled under the kitchen light. Silence dropped, sudden and complete. Samuel slowly pulled the folded white paper off the top, and eyes widened in the shocked quiet; more gold lay under the paper. Stacks of shiny, newly minted gold, most with the Story Land fern stamped on the front. Anna calculated quickly, taking in the size of the box, the

stacks sitting fifteen by thirty inside... her mouth dropped slowly open and stayed that way.

"It says it's from the IDP leader," Samuel reported, his eyes running over the paper. Joe managed to copy their leader's penmanship very well. He looked up at Daniel and Nehemiah and a smile curved over his face. "He says it's to be used to fund the resurrection of the Sojourners."

Nehi reached out slowly and ran a finger over the shining metal. A laugh spilled from him, tight and excited. His face shone as he spun toward Daniel and Anna, grinning like a fool.

"That's it," he said. "The last piece we were missing, popping up at the door as a miracle dropped by the hand of God. We've got a chance!"

Chapter 8: Rings and Stars

"Iron sharpeneth iron; so a man sharpeneth the countenance of his friend." Proverbs 27:17

Nehemiah gently pushed the door open and stepped inside the sick room. Moonlight played over the wooden floor and the green comforter piled over Joe. His white cast stuck out of the bed and almost gleamed in the light drifting in through the window. Nehi slumped against the wall and sank to a crouch on the floor. Nothing moved in the still room. He let his head drop back and stared at the shadows shifting over the ceiling.

Why had he come here? A part of him recalled the cacophony of snores and crinkling sheets as men moved in their sleep in the upstairs dormitory, and grimaced. Even Paul snored. It made it hard to think. But a part of him...his eyes darted to the bed. Churning inside him was a quiet longing for the way things had been, for Joe's strength to lean on.

Two green eyes glinted in the moonlight as they stared back at him. Wide open, unblinking. Nehi shifted to his feet and stole forward. He could hear the mute's breathing as he drew closer. Tight, controlled, as if he had to think about each one again. The eyes never looked away from Nehi's. Joe's white hands shifted from under the comforter.

"Need out!" he signed. The mute sat up with a jerk and the covers piled beside him. Nehi slid an arm under his friend's shoulders, lifting him easily out of the bed. He felt so light... Nehemiah headed to the window, gripped the sill, hopped over, then dropped. The grass rammed into his feet like concrete. But Nehi's knees bent with it, and he just felt a deep longing for the old times with the wagon. Joe's arm shifted to lean against Nehi's shoulder, using him as a living crutch. The two young men headed toward the bench. Nehi tightened his grip as he clambered over, and took the mute's weight without asking. Joe let himself be mostly carried.

Twelve minutes later they sat on the eight-story office building and watched the waves of the bay sparkle like living

stars in the moonlight. It had been a silent journey. It stayed silent now, as Nehi leaned back on his elbows and sought the sky. A few stars peeked through the clouds shifting endlessly overhead. The moon managed to pierce the wispy trails of clouds at least.

"That gold coming in yesterday was the last link we needed. We're really doing it," Nehemiah said. Joe glanced at him, almost irritated. It melted into amusement in an instant.

"Is that why you snuck in my room tonight? It just hit you?"

"Not everyone is as instantaneously perceptive as you, Raven. Some of us take time to process humongous changes in our lives."

Silence fell around them again. No breeze stirred the air tonight. It hung around them like a physical blanket of humidity.

"You'll do it. And do it well," Joe signed suddenly. Nehi sat up, his expression pleading for an answer.

"Will we win, Joe?"

"Only God knows the future. What I do know is that you're good, and brave, and kind, and whatever comes you'll handle it well. You'll do everything that can be done; and that's all God asks from us."

"At least I have Daniel around to make the big decisions," Nehi murmured and slumped back again to try and pick out stars and lay his worries at their Maker's feet. Joe's face turned toward the bay, blank and quiet. Pleasant stillness fell around Nehi and crept into his soul, stilling the fretting questions over everything the next few weeks might bring. All they could do was their best; God would handle the rest. Peace filled him and even his mind grew still.

After a few quiet minutes Nehi's eye wandered idly to Joe. The mute sat stiffly in the starlight, staring straight ahead at the blackness of the bay. Nehi's mouth opened, wanting to draw him into the pleasant stillness. But words failed as he looked up at the scarred face, set and emotionless, staring at something he couldn't see. His mouth closed again and he tried to guess where to start. *Jesus, I want to help,* he prayed. *Show me how.*

A glint of silver caught the starlight under Joe's shirt, lying

between the buttons. Nehi blinked and focused. The ring. That silver ring with the cross etched in the middle, that Joe had given such painstaking instructions about retrieving from the wagon. Joshua Noble's ring.

"So what's with the ring? And why is it on a chain, why aren't you wearing it?"

Joe blinked, coming back from the darkness with difficulty. He looked at Nehi, leaning back on his elbows, watching him. Nehemiah raised a finger, gesturing to the ring dangling on the IDP chain. Joe looked down and for an instant Nehi saw annoyance shoot over him; the mute hadn't meant it to be visible.

"Is it, maybe, a key to an elaborate play to keep the Gaia Christians from being mowed down? Or an actual key, that you stick in the dragon statue's eye and suddenly the whole battle kingdom region turns green and growing?"

Joe laughed, and his stiffness melted.

"You've been listening to too many of D's stories," he signed, pivoting so Nehi could see his signs better.

"It passes the time." Nehi shrugged. He looked at the mute and waited. Joe's hand rose slowly and pulled the chain from under his shirt. The silver and gold gleamed as his fingers fiddled with the ring. His face went absent again, but this time he didn't retreat into the blankness. Sorrow and shame filled him, a well of mourning and memories etched into his drooped form as he shrank from his tall friend.

"I'm not really a nice person, Knee-High," he signed. "Especially before we met. The people in my life had been... By the time Diamond found me, I could glance at a person and knew their deepest hopes and greatest fears, and just where to push to drive them to the edge of insanity. And I used it to keep people away, and even just because I liked to see it, the power I knew I had over them. I could slip away from anyone I wasn't physically chained to, and did, a lot, just because I knew it drove Diamond wild. By now I've learned how to use the... 'talents' perhaps you could call them, but that doesn't make it much easier to remember what I used to do reflexively. But I–" he broke off, his fists balling. His signs spun off again, his eyes carefully

not meeting his friend's, his movements hurried and tight.

"I had been on a seesaw my whole life, Knee-High, sometimes understanding I was really human and everything I was taught was wrong and searching desperately for what it all meant, other times just an animal trying to survive. Then Diamond showed up and jumped onto the other end. And I went sailing off into a freefall, so scared, so terribly scared, of where I would land." In a spontaneous, quick movement he slid the ring from the chain and pressed it into Nehi's hand. His eyes didn't leave the jewelry as Nehi pivoted into a sitting position, holding it carefully on his open palm.

"This was Diamond's father's. It had been passed to Diamond as an heirloom, the only one besides his faith, the only tangible thing he had from his dad. I stole it. Pretty often, just to watch Diamond ransacking the house, getting more desperate. One time I even planted it where he was framed for a government theft and only just realized what I'd done in time to get him out alive. I did say sorry for that one, and even–"

"Even what?" Nehi prodded quietly, as Joe's fists balled, his head bowed, and his eyes on the silver ring. He could almost feel the shame in the confession from his little friend. He wouldn't let it stay at this point.

"I even handed him a rod. Bared my back. I deserved it. But that was the only time I saw Diamond grow angry. He snapped it in two like it was a matchstick, I never knew he could do that... That was when he pulled the ring off and told me about his dad, and how he had been raised, and so many things I never knew I had missed. At the end of that night he handed it to me. Told me it would be mine when he was old and decrepit and I was the one left to carry on the 'Noble legacy.'" A wet laugh slid

from the mute and he shook his head, his eyes glistening as he stared at the ring, not looking at his friend. "He was such a fool. Always such a trusting, loving, wonderful fool. Even at the end, when I held his broken body, and he couldn't speak for the blood in his lungs, he still moved just to give me that. Such a wonderful, trusting fool." A sniffle came from the mute and his arms stole around his chest.

"But he was right," Nehemiah said. Joe froze. "You've done more than just carry on his legacy, Joe. I've often wondered how you can glance at a person and know exactly how to take over a situation, how you manage stealth moves that excel even those who have trained their whole life for the purpose. You've taken what evil people turned you into, and in the power of God redeemed it. You use what the fears and heartbreaks made in you to keep Christ's own safe, in ways no one else could ever manage. You can do that, because you've chosen to turn evil into talents. You picked the right word, Joe. Have you ever heard the parable of the talents[4], that Jesus told?" Joe shook his head, a small, hesitant movement. Nehi gave him the parable in full, letting his natural dramatics carry it. "And of course you're the one with the hundred talents, Joe. Because of you the IDP has been allowed to live, and multiply and make disciples. If you look at it logically, you probably have thousands not hundreds by now."

"But... I... I've never put that ring on, Knee-High, I can't, I'm not who Diamond was, who he told me I'd become! I'm still covered in blood and fears, you have no idea, and even with you I've let the anger out, I can't–"

Nehi's hand closed over Joe's, cutting off the signs. He slid the ring onto the mute's scarred thumb, sat back, and waited. Joe's hand shook, staring at the silver glinting on his knuckle. Another laugh spilled from him, short and gasping.

"It fits," he signed, the motions tiny.

"Of course it does. Joshua knew you better than you thought. Maybe better than you know yourself. The Master gave the

---

[4] Matthew 25:14-30

talents to the people in that parable. God's been with you Joe, forming you into exactly what His people needed. He didn't cause it, people did that," Nehi paused, his throat tightening on the words as every emotion from the night Joe had said those to him flooded in. He took a deep breath and felt a smile spreading over him, warm and real, tingling from the well of experience the truth blossomed from. "There's a really big difference between causing it to happen and letting it happen. We both know that. But He makes all things work for good in His people, even the worst things. He's worked good in you. He even gave you that name, I'm convinced."

"What name?" Joe asked. He turned his hand slowly, experimentally, watching the moonlight sparkle on the silver.

"The Raven. If more people considered the ravens[5], and what you and Beau have done with your lives through Christ's power and love, it would change the world. You, Joe, are a living testament to God's redemptive love, a shining hope that no situation is too terrible to be reclaimed and remade in the power of Christ. And you've done that. You've chosen to let Him use you."

"Track-Maker said that once…" Joe started to sign, wonder in his eyes. "Maybe I… Knee-High, I… I'm still so weak and lost most days, still so scared I'll even drive you away. I've done things that, had to do things that… I'm not sure you…"

"Oh, I've met your angry fox a couple of times," Nehi shrugged. "It didn't drive me away. Well, only temporarily. I'm not going anywhere, you're stuck with me. Joe, I'll never be you, I can't see what you can. But I think I can see things you can't, because I'm not you. That's one reason God gives us each other and why we need Christian fellowship. We can get so lost in our own heads, only someone on the outside can pull us out again. Stop focusing on the weaknesses and failures and past sins. Joe, I… I understand a little of what you've been through, how an evil master can make you do evil things, and that stains, and clings, and feels like it will never leave. And then without Christ,

---

[5] Luke 12:24

the anger blossoms into a desire for blood and revenge that strangles in the dark and... I get it. Maybe not completely, because I'm not you and Christ has stayed with me always even when I tried to shrug Him off, but... I get it. The stain is real and the scars don't leave. Now listen, and believe. You are a work of Christ Jesus. He lives in you, growing and changing and loving you every day, as you fling yourself into His remaking and loving His people, and it makes you shine brighter than anyone I've ever met. Wear that ring with pride, knowing He is in you."

A breeze blew between them. It caressed the ring, making the silver cold as it twinkled on Joe's hand. He twisted it in the starlight as he watched it shine. The mute's eyes darted to the scars snaking out from under Nehi's light cotton shirt.

"Only because of what you've been through and what I know you understand can I believe what you're telling me tonight," Joe signed. Nehi glanced away, blinking hard. His shoulders hunched, and for a moment the traces of the first days of their constellation parties could be seen in his drawn face. But a smile hovered at the corners of his mouth.

"To me, Joe," he said, his voice soft, "that brings as much comfort and healing as finding out about Atif and his team. Knowing I can help now because of all that went on in the dark changes it somehow, it almost makes the darkness itself..."

Nehi's words drifted off into the still air. Joe nodded. His eyes turned toward the stars as his hands moved in slow, thoughtful signs.

"There are certain lights that nothing but darkness can create."

Chapter 9: Plans

"For thou art my rock and my fortress; therefore for thy name's sake lead me, and guide me." Psalm 31:4

Two days later Joe called a meeting of the Vision Keepers in the back den. The Hillsons spilled in eagerly, even Daniel excited in the hope Joe had something great to tell them. Joe held a paper out to Anna, and she snatched it, reading it out loud for her brothers.

"'I, Harold Pablo, hereby affirm I gave leave (after he drove me crazy whining so much) for Joe to go traipsing with Beau as his steed.'" Her enthusiasm lessened, her words slowing as she read.

"That's so you don't yell at me, Beauty," Joe signed, and Beau said for Daniel's sake. The mute snapped to attention, granting the siblings a bright grin. "Sorry to make this official It's not really worth that. I just couldn't think of another way to get all of us alone in the same room."

"Which means what exactly?" Daniel said.

"All I wanted to tell you was I found a few more of those journal pages–"

"What?"

"Where?"

"Do they have the next page?" the three Hillsons burst out at once. Joe held up his hand with a grin.

"Hold on! Glue and I stashed them somewhere safe–"

"Wait, without letting us see them, or even telling us you had them?" Daniel yelped. Nehemiah and Anna were suddenly and conspicuously quiet as they watched Joe.

"There are still FFs out there," Joe signed, his grin disappearing. "Wolf comes to mind. I think it's very dangerous to have those pages out in the open, even for a brief space of time. If we win this, and Sojourner's Way starts up again, then I'll fetch them and we'll see what we can find. Otherwise, they're better where they are." Daniel started to interrupt furiously, but Anna pinched his arm and he looked at his siblings in

surprise instead.

"Look, if we don't win, what's the use of a false hope?" Joe shrugged. "Dreaming before it can become a reality is hurtful. So, just wanted to let you know, after the war, if we win, we can look at more pages and hopefully figure out what this treasure is finally. That's it, meeting adjourned!" Joe gave a sunny smile, Beau swept him up, and the two hopped out the door, Joe scrambling on his Glue's shoulders as the big man trotted for the garden gate. The three siblings watched them turn out of the yard and trot away, Joe laughing and Beau roaring like an elephant on the rampage. The sound of their passing slowly faded, and the birds fluttered back to the trees.

"What was that all about?" Anna asked, looking at Nehemiah.

"I think he just wanted to rub his control of the situation in our faces," Daniel growled. But he turned to Nehi too.

"I don't know...but it was for something," Nehemiah answered slowly, staring at the back door. He snapped out of his thoughts and smiled at his siblings. "It's one more thing to look forward to once we win! Come on you two, we have a lot to do if we're to leave for our old country and new headquarters tomorrow morning. Ann, we actually get to see our woods again, and Daniel, if we win this you can teach me that trout fishing technique you used to boast about back at that big pond–" Daniel laughed and shoved Nehi towards the door.

"Aren't you counting chickens before we even have the eggs, little brother?" he grinned. "We still have a very large host of mean people to deal with before we can think of peaceful times."

"'The fight draws near!'" Anna quoted an old Sojourner folk song. The second verse broke from her as she swept into the kitchen, her voice strong and lilting, and filling the house.

"There are times in life for peace,
But other times we're called,
To do and dare, till evils cease,
So strike even bloodied and mauled."

Daniel grabbed Anna around the waist, and they whirled

into a dance, her skirts furling in and out like a morning glory on steroids as he spun her through the room. Nehi laughed and went into a rhythm dance as he took up the chorus. The stomping and singing moved with such gusto it shook the doctor's rafters. Heads lifted, and everyone paused what they were doing, listening to the words, filled with sharp meaning as they drew closer to their resurgence.

"To do and dare till Christ's return,
Fight for what you care.
We are called and we must learn,
To do and to dare."

"I thought we agreed to let the bulky luggage come with Harry and Quin in his hoverer?" Daniel complained. Nehi just hefted his package a little higher on his shoulder and stepped up beside his brother. Daniel turned a glare on Joe. The mute shrugged, his expression saying he had no idea what Nehi carried. Beau's huge hand closed over Daniel's shoulder as his other arm wrapped around his master's chest. Peter dropped a hand on Joe, Tanzid unbent enough to grip Peter's shoulder, and the whole party drew a little closer together on the circle of torn up ground outside Harry's house.

Anna stepped up beside Nehi and took his arm in hers. The bag with their lunch felt heavy as it hung from her shoulders, but she hardly noticed it. Her eyes went to the old house, the siding sagging after all the SOLTDs' tugging on it. She might never come back here. If all went well, they were headed... *Home.* A little shiver ran through her and she gripped Nehi's arm tighter. He looked at their group. Everyone nodded, Tanzid's lips a thin line. Nehi hit the button.

The blackness unfolded with its hissing, wild power. It wrapped around them, and Peter felt his breath stolen by the cold and the rushing, screaming power encasing them. The mute sagged under his hand, and he tightened his hold quickly.

Ground slammed into them, and the whole party jerked,

staggering, hands tightening as they tried to keep a hold on each other. Beau held his master carefully, not letting Joe's bad foot close to the ground. The blackness peeled away.

A dense forest stared at the group shivering under a gray sky. They stared at it. This wasn't the tall pines and softwoods of the Sojourner's northern region, fat with wild game and singing with each breeze. This was gnarled, thick, ancient vegetation that crawled with tillandsias and shadows. The party looked over their shoulders, noting the yellow grasslands dotted with ice-covered marshy lakes snaking away behind them. A freezing, humid breeze teased between them and shivers shook the group. Then every eye went to Nehemiah.

Nehi handed his brother the SOLTD. He stepped forward, swinging the package off his shoulder as he moved. The wrapping fell off as he walked, and the others saw a wooden post with a sign attached, the stain new enough it glinted in the gray sunlight. He stopped in front of half a post sticking up from the ground. A broken, slashed piece of wooden plank lay behind it. Understanding began to touch the others' faces as they watched Nehi drive his foot into the broken post, knocking it out of the damp earth. He wrenched it free, knelt, scooped the hole a little deeper, and drove his pole into the ground. Nehemiah's boot piled the dirt back around the hole as he held the post steady and stamped it down. Then he stepped back. When he moved the others could see the sign, the bold metalwork gleaming bright against the lacquered wood.

SOJOURNER'S WAY
"THE LORD HATH MADE BARE HIS HOLY ARM IN THE EYES OF ALL THE NATIONS; AND ALL THE ENDS OF THE EARTH SHALL SEE THE SALVATION OF OUR GOD."
ISAIAH 51:10

Nehi dropped to his knees and his head bowed in front of him, dark curls draping around his face. A smile spread over the mute as he watched. Tanzid and Peter just stood there, stiff and awkward. Anna felt her eyes beginning to sting as she looked at that sign and felt all it meant. All that had happened, the devastation and despair... Could God use even that to show His salvation to the world? The face of the mustached doctor in the cellars flitted through her mind, as she remembered the way he had watched her, learning about her God from how she handled the trials... Could beauty and glory rise even from destruction? Perhaps only from destruction, as the world watched God's people deal with it and saw the only solid hope in existence burning inside them too bright for anything to snuff out.

Sometimes a thing's strength can only be realized after someone's tried to break it.

Anna made herself look away from the sign as she felt her heart swelling inside her at all the questions, and the desperate hope that sign carried. It didn't help. She knew this road. Every emotion of that raw day flooded over her again; running away from their own kingdom, free and alone and broken and wondering what two strangers wanted them for. Her eyes went back to the new sign. No, they hadn't left alone. God traveled every mile with them, and He was here in this new venture too. She would keep leaning on His arm.

Nehemiah stood up and strode back to his group. He stepped between his siblings again, flashed them all a smile, and nodded at the SOLTD.

"Now we're ready," he said. "For whatever comes next."

Daniel hit the button on the SOLTD, and the party disappeared deep into the Sojourner's Kingdom.

The snow piled in deep drifts around the cabin. Every time a SOLTD landed it created a mini blizzard outside. The SOLTDs came and went often during the two months of planning. Daniel and Samuel slipped through the kingdom, setting people up li-

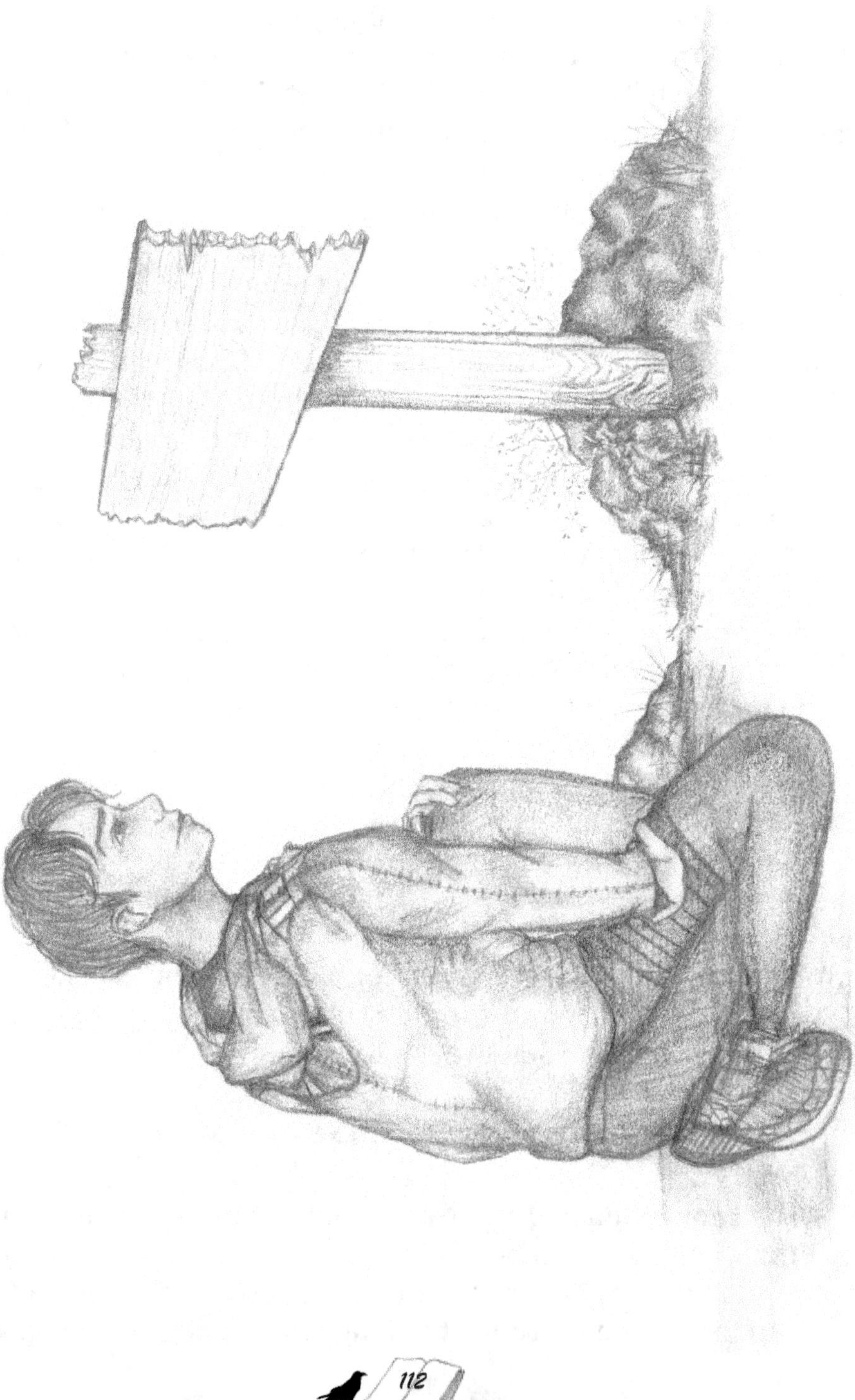

ke game pieces. The trees around the cabin were thick, even in the winter, the pines drooped with the snowfall, and even Joe declared the SOLTDs' light and noise safe enough up here. The invaders didn't care about the upper mountain regions. There wasn't enough capital to be gained by raiding the forests, and they had no interest in traipsing through the winter cold. They were too busy still fleecing the rest of the Sojourner Kingdom.

People came, people went. Soldiers to coordinate, leaders to assuage, people who needed assurance this would work before they considered joining the resurgence. Slowly plans solidified into the names and faces of those who would take on particular pockets of the fight. The days moved in quick succession, and Nehi found it all a blur. Daniel working beside him, Joe slowly up more, Samuel arguing and supporting, Anna carrying light and comfort with her as she worked around them... Faces, places, devastation and hope, it all merged into one picture that seemed to distort the two months into a single surreal moment.

The day before the resurgence finally dawned cold and bright.

It found the same people making the same arguments, and the surreal feeling just grew in Nehi.

"All I'm saying is you're talking about the central part of our plan. The hinge that the rest of this swings on, what makes the whole kingdom's resurgence possible," David Young commented, Samuel's selection from the southern contingent. His hard gaze fastened on Nehemiah. The young man felt like the look seared through him to see every insecurity, failure, and twisted piece. "And you're talking about handing *that* part to the youngest person in the army."

"'Let no man despise thy youth,[6]'" Samuel said. David gave a snort and slumped back in his chair.

"Somehow I knew you were going to quote that one at me," he said.

"You just object to his northern mountain-man tendencies," Andrew, northern contingent leader, put in. His accent rolled

---

[6] 1 Timothy 4:12a

out smooth and thicker than usual, and Nehi did his best to hide a smile; he knew Andrew did it on purpose.

"If you think I would let territorial lines count at a time like this–" David started hotly, but Daniel's voice cut him off, sharp and steely.

"I'm not handing this to Nehi because he's a Hillson," Daniel snapped. "I know that's what you're thinking, and it's what you resent. I'm not giving it to someone who has inferior talents out of sentimentality, or a hoped for 'morale lift' or anything stupid like that. We're not idiots, David. We know how important this is. I also know what I've seen Nehemiah accomplish in the past year, and some of the stunts would knock you off your feet. He's not exactly an untried entity."

"So tell me," growled David, every line of him a sneer that said he didn't believe a word of it. "Tell me what your remarkable younger brother has done that makes him the right choice to lead the first wave."

"Oh, let's see," Daniel drawled, leaning back and letting his hands go behind his head, "He's infiltrated deep into KAM's Institute and taken a prisoner back out with him. He's raided KAM's deportation trucks several times, defying and outsmarting some of the UPC's best in the process. In the People's Kingdom he ran the House gates, taking two blacklisted men with him, and got away with it. He's crossed thousands of miles of wild lands (in a private vehicle, not the armored transports) and not just survived, but outthought and outfought anything that came against him. I've watched him help send the Black Army skittering away from one of their invasions like scared kittens. And that was all before he turned eighteen this year. I could go on, if you want." Daniel leaned forward, his voice snapping with the force of a commander. "In this business, Nehi came to me with a plan that only he can pull off. It's a good plan, and it's tailored perfectly for him and the two agents he's taking in with him. Trust that we know what we're doing, David, and stop acting like a surly five-year-old."

David's eyes flicked to Nehemiah, glaring and angry. Recognition suddenly swept through Nehi as he stared back. That

anger wasn't really directed at him. The meetings this month had stretched on, and on, and even Anna's scones and the scent of her homey baking barely made it endurable. But what Nehi had noticed most in the people who came and went was the same thing he saw now as he stared into David Young's eyes.

Anger.

A deep, broken anger that ran through their very bones and curled in their souls. He recognized it. Nehi knew that feeling too well, Joe had wrestled him out of it in the darkness of the wild lands, and only the Holy Spirit had finally managed to break him free. So much hurt, buried so deep... He wondered who David had lost when the invaders rushed in with their lasers turned on women and children.

"You're awfully quiet suddenly," David snapped.

"It's not my place to answer for myself," Nehi stated, remembering Cuthbert's easy grace as he waited for others to clear him. But Nehi's voice came soft, almost gentle as he stared back at David. The man blinked. His defensive bluster stumbled, cracked by something in the young man's manner.

The door swung open and Anna swept in, a tray in her arms. The scent of fresh bread, sausage, and spices wafted around the meeting room and everyone brightened. Anna sat the tray down and spun to David, her hands going to her hips.

"You're a good man, David Young. Start acting like it," she ordered. "We're set to move tomorrow. We don't have the time for surly five-year-olds, and you know it. Listen to those who have been around these people. You don't know anyone in this room except Andrew, and I remember you were constantly fighting with him even before the disintegration. Don't look so surprised, the dumb waiter in this room connects with the kitchen, we hear everything down there. Here, have a sausage twist and calm down." She pushed a plate into David's hands and swept out of the room. The sounds of her humming drifted from the stairs as she headed back to the kitchen. Everyone stared at the door for a moment.

"Right," Daniel said, reaching for the coffee pot, "I guess that takes care of that. Nehi and his three small teams will go in first

and cut off all communication from the leaders and keep them out of the action. That will create confusion and disarray among the invaders out in the field, and allow the rest of us to sweep in and do our job. Andrew, you and your people wait till you hear from me, we move at the same time. I'll clear the southern half of the kingdom, and it's up to you to take the north. We're going to have a stiff fight on our hands, use the element of surprise for everything it's worth. We need to take them all in one night. If the fight lasts on into the next day, the odds of our winning drop dramatically, and it's even possible the invaders will get outside reinforcements before we can prove our Bible is back. David, you're the last. And no, you're not backup! It's up to you to sweep in and take care of anyone actually causing a problem in the kingdom, you are our failsafe. Without you, we could have any numbers of trouble spots erupt into full scale defeat that overwhelms the rest of us. You're going to need eyes and ears everywhere, and be ready to move in a heartbeat. I gave Nehi two of my best. But all our other top warriors are with you, David."

"Thanks heaps for that compliment," Andrew murmured over his coffee cup. But his eyes twinkled, and he let the briefing move on.

Four rooms away, Joe perched on his bed in the middle of his own meeting. A personal pad sat on the bed in front of him, three different feeds open on the screen. Joe steadily cycled through the feeds, rewinding what his three ravens had seen this past week. He liked to see for himself how the world fared. But while he couldn't be out, he had Beau strap a video monitor to Jewel, Meathead, and Crabby. The trained birds fluttered through the trees, watching the Sojourners and doing raven things. Joe now knew more about the everyday life of a raven than he ever wanted to know.

His finger stopped rewinding Jewel's feed. He stared at the video as it replayed a shaky scene from two days ago. Atif stood

in an old burned out room with his men. And an unknown young soldier. Joe watched their body language, their facial expressions, the words he could read on their lips... A sharp frown cut over the mute and his eyebrows drew together.

Atif was underestimating the Wolf.

Hamfast's fist thundered on the door and Ariel sat back with a petulant huff.

"What?" she demanded. The heavy oak door swung open and the hulking mercenary stepped into the dim lighting of the darkened study. A red-haired, portly man walked in behind him, his small eyes darting around the room. He took in the heavy oak furnishings, the drapes drawn across the windows, the carefully filtered air, the tools and documents on the desk. Several things clicked into place as he began to understand some of the interplay between three of the most powerful people in the underworld; a snarling wolf, a glittering mermaid, and a shadowy raven. This world could be a strange place sometimes. His eyes went to the statuesque woman behind the desk. She stared at him. Her golden hair seemed the brightest thing in this room.

"You look terrible, Freddy," Ariel commented.

"I admit it has been a long few weeks," Frederick Masterton said. He was in no position to take offense at her supercilious attitude, and carefully kept his voice genial. "You are looking well, Miss Athenia." She laughed, a hard bark of a sound in the still room.

"I don't care about civilities, you funny old thing," Ariel said. "You're here because the Wolf is hunting you."

"You have always been well-informed," Freddy said, every inch of him fixed in a differential admiration. She smirked and tossed a hologram disc on her desk. A blue video formed in the air. Freddy found himself staring at Nicky Tarter, trembling as he stood bound to a great black pine. The bubbling of a bog could be heard just under the blubbering of the man. A figure

in a wolf-head's mask stepped into view of the video's feed.

"You earned how much in my service, Nicky?" a distorted voice came from the mask.

"Twenty-three thousand golden marks," Nicky answered. You could hear the despair in his husky whisper. The mask turned slowly, impressively, toward the video feed.

"The gain from working under the Wolf is impressive," the distorted voice spoke up. "Watch now what happens when a man fails the Wolf." The figure turned back to the shaking man bound to the tree. Ariel's trim finger moved and flicked the feed off.

"You know the rest," she said. Her voice came bored, a little contemptuous. Freddy felt bile boiling under his humble attitude. He knew what came next. And it could so easily be him bound to that tree. Ariel leaned back, one perfect arm draping over the back of the chair as she regarded her visitor.

"This one is pretty vicious, even for the Wolf. It's pitiful really, a desperate attempt to grasp at what's slipping through his claws. His business has been wrapped in intimidation from the beginning. Convincing all the people in the underworld that he can see everything and gives generous rewards if you win, but will find you if you fail him. It's worked, he built himself up as such a genius and monster everyone cowered and bowed to his will whenever he bared his teeth. But not anymore, Freddy. He's failed too many times recently. Three heists in a row all gone wrong. Yes, he's found those agents who 'failed him' and made sure the world knows it's 'their fault.' But we all know the Wolf is the one who's failed. He's losing his credibility. All it will take is one more fall, one more heavy blow to his reputation, and no one will ever listen to him again." A smile curved over her pristine face, malicious and delighted. "One more blow... It's coming soon, Freddy. And you hold the key to making sure the Wolf lives for the rest of his life with a brand tied to his tail."

"I will do whatever it takes to make that happen," Freddy snarled, suddenly letting his real self rise to the surface. Ariel laughed and leaned her elbows leisurely on the table, her eyes bright as she watched him.

"I'm told you know of a folder from the Wolf. 'Evidence' he gave you months ago to hold for him. Where is it?" Ariel asked. A smile slowly curved over Freddy's sallow face, shifting his flabby jowls. He reached into his dirty coat and pulled the black folder from an inner pocket. He handed it to the hulking Hamfast hovering near his side.

"It's not in there. But the information to reclaim it from the personage holding the 'evidence' is carefully documented," he stated. "It also contains a gift, from me to you, Miss Athenia."

"Just like that?" Ariel's eyebrows went up. "No demands?" She saw Freddy's eyes dart to the hologram disc before settling on her.

"I would rather see him brought to his knees than anything I can think of demanding," Freddy stated. A grin slowly curved over Ariel's face as she accepted the folder from her mercenary.

"Excellent. I think I could use that kind of attitude, Freddy. Stick around, I'll find you something to do."

For a moment pleasant relief filled Freddy; the mermaid took care of those she accepted as employees, demanding only loyalty back. He could handle that.

But then Freddy's spine prickled. Something invaded his consciousness, tingling with the fear that kept him on the hyper alert since his failure. Ariel's face stiffened as she watched him. Freddy turned toward the hulking Hamfast.

"Do you...smell something?" he asked. Hamfast's eyes flicked to Ariel.

"He lost his sense of smell years ago," she shrugged, "during a confrontation with a group of–"

"Smoke," Freddy broke in. "It's growing stronger."

Ariel came to her feet in one smooth movement. Her arm shot out, pointing Hamfast to the door. He charged it as if it were a monster. They watched his hand grip the gilt knob. They all saw it stick. It stayed unmoving as his muscles bulged and wrenched at it. A thick, angry yell rang from him as he rammed his shoulder into the oak paneling. It didn't move. A wisp of gray smoke crept under the door, twisting with lazy maliciousness.

The blue hologram flicked to life on the desk. A dead wolf head grinned at them as it moved like a puppet.

"That's your collection, Ariel. Ancient documents burn so well," the Wolf said. It came in a distorted snarl, amusement and hatred colliding in it. Ariel's face went white as chalk in her fury. "And now it spreads, racing through your halls." The whisp under the door became a steady flow. They could hear the crackling beyond the door. Somewhere out there a man screamed. "A little gasoline trail makes for an excellent fire, especially in an old house."

A series of low, guttural curses spilled from Ariel as she stood stiff and pale, her eyes burning at the Wolf head. A laugh lilted from the hologram, enjoying every word of her outpour. Freddy leapt forward, swept a shell-shaped paper weight from the desk, and smashed it down on the hologram. The gadget broke into twenty pieces, scattering around the room.

"Get out," he ordered, his voice sharp. His fat hand shot forward as he spoke, gathering the documents on the desk with a reverent touch. Even in that moment he could feel the yellowed paper in their sleeves crinkling under his fingers, and a hint of awe slid into him. Ariel blinked once. Her muscles rippled, losing their stiffness, and she jumped to help Freddy.

"Stop hammering at the door, you idiot!" she shouted at Hamfast. "He'll have that blocked fast." Another scream, higher and more agonized came from beyond the door. Someone hadn't made it out. *Good riddance,* Ariel told herself; it would be whatever agent in her midst Wolf had convinced to work for him. The traitor who had laid that gasoline trail would die, to tie up the loose ends and eliminate all chance of physical proof pointing back to the Wolf.

Smoke streamed under the bottom of the door. Hamfast barreled past the desk, rending coughs breaking from him, his face already splotched with the smoke. He headed toward the large picture windows. Ariel spun on him.

"No, Hammy!" she shouted, her voice mixing with the crackle and roar of the flames. Freddy could feel the heat seeping through the walls as he tucked the last pages into his folder.

What unholy mix of chemicals had the Wolf used to make the fire spread so quickly? "He'll be waiting there." Ariel Athenia snatched up her utility belt, pulled the pin on a grenade, and lobbed it at the far wall.

Freddy heard a bleating shriek come from his lungs as he dropped to the ground, his arms going over his head. A roar shook his insides, jiggling his fat and scorching his skin. Visions of his headquarters collapsing, his agents that no longer existed, shot through him like a red hot poker.

Hamfast's hulking hand closed on the back of his coat. Freddy felt himself jerked to his feet, stumbling backwards. Everywhere around him flames danced and roared. A shower of timbers fell from the ceiling, scattering sparks and flames as they landed.

Then suddenly there was no more floor. Empty, cold air wrapped around Freddy and he tumbled into a free fall. Stars glittered above him.

Flames shot through the hole in the wall, hungry for the oxygen. The stars disappeared as the bright orange fire roared and licked the air.

The ground met his feet with shivering force. Freddy's spine snapped and he collapsed with a gasp, his legs numb. He vaguely wondered how many bones he had just broken. Hamfast heaved him up and Freddy gasped again as pain flared up his shaking legs. The hulking agent looked over his shoulder, staring at something behind them. Freddy turned his head reluctantly, dread screaming inside him.

A figure in a long gray coat stood under the study windows. A netting gun and a tranquilizer rifle rested easily against his leg. A wolf-head mask covered anything human about his features. Freddy could see the fur rippling in the wind from the flames, the orange light playing over him in shifting shadows. A snarl rippled over Hamfast's face and he took a step closer to the figure. Freddy clutched at his arm, leaning back with all his weight, physically holding him from rushing at the figure. His hands were shaking and clammy with the cold sweat soaking him.

A rush of steam cut around the two and Ariel's hoverer spun up next to them.

"Get in," she ordered, her voice deadly cold. Hamfast flung Freddy in and obeyed. But he landed standing in the back, his blazing face turned toward the Wolf. The gray figure raised his rifle in a swift, lazy way, it gave a soft pop, and the giant of a man tumbled backwards into the front seat. Ariel cursed as she fought for control. She shoved a hand into his shoulder and helped Freddy shove his limp form over into the miniscule backseat. He landed with a thud heavy enough it made the hoverer bounce into the ground.

"Is this yours?" Freddy demanded, his voice a squeak. Ariel glanced at him, annoyance sharp. The wind cut between them as she sped up. "The hoverer, is this yours?!"

"What do you think, of course it is!" Sudden understanding flashed over her face, and Freddy saw her fear. "Hold on!"

The hoverer slewed to the left. She aimed deliberately for a half broken bench on the side of the road. The left steam jets hit the bench and it tipped on its side. A sharp gasp came from Freddy as sparks flew into his face from the oval scraping the road. The unconscious Hamfast tumbled out and rolled four yards down the hill. The hoverer came to a screeching stop, butted up against the wooden wall of a house. He could hear the steam jets sputtering as they tried to run bent and jammed. Freddy scrabbled at the road, dragging himself from the hoverer and staggering toward the fallen Hamfast. Voices clamored around him as the town stumbled into the night, fires and hoverer crashes crackling through their town.

Ariel was nowhere to be seen.

A vast heat caught Freddy in the back. The bang rolled over him, as the force knocked him flat on the roadside. Screams and shouts of "Fire!" echoed strangely in his ringing ears as he slowly turned.

The hoverer lay in a twisted heap, the fire from the explosion still roaring around it.

The scent of clean, warm steam overtook the smoke and Freddy staggered up gasping again as another hoverer slewed

to a stop beside him. Ariel hopped from the vehicle, waving a handful of coins at the populace and pointing at the big Hamfast. Freddy didn't wait to be invited. He piled into the passenger seat and sat there blowing and sweating as five people dumped Hamfast into the miniscule back seat. Ariel landed in the driver's seat, and the machine shot off. The wind bubble rose as their speed increased. It cut off the shouts and yells as the town woke to see their wealthiest section steadily being consumed by ravenous flames.

"Stupid, stupid of me to get lost in the anger and fall for that!" Ariel said. Freddy felt his numb fear invaded by shock. Was that her voice shaking? "Of course he let us go, just so we would think we got out before the explosion came. Just like him." A deep breath sucked into her, and the usual stoniness came back over her perfect face. "Most of the boys got out, and he let them leave. The Wolf will use it to confirm he has no quarrel with free agents; just me. But nothing except my manpower can be salvaged from that house!"

Freddy's hand lifted. The black folder he held rustled as he shook, the stack of her ancient documents from the desk sticking partially out the side. A smile spread over her sweaty face. A single nod told him he had done well to keep it through it all. Her hoverer sped up to a smooth two-hundred miles an hour and Freddy could watch her taught muscles start to loosen. She felt the distance was making her safe. Nothing would ever make him feel safe. Her eyes flicked to the still Hamfast in the back. She gave a melodramatic sigh and sank against her seat cushions.

"Silly Hammy. He should know better than to challenge the Wolf when he's the one who's set the scene." Her gaze turned to Freddy, still shaking so his teeth rattled in the quiet, and another smile twisted her perfect lips. "Just wait, Fred. A few more days and it will be our turn to set the scene."

Chapter 10: Stations

"O LORD God of hosts, who is a strong LORD like unto thee? or to thy faithfulness round about thee?" Psalm 89:8

Nehemiah's blood rushed and his head sang with adrenaline as he stepped onto the circle of ripped up dirt and took Daniel's shoulder. He should have slept all day, but everything in him was too keyed up for rest. The time had finally arrived. Allies from Faerie, Geatland, and IDP branches were in place, poised to charge. The Sojourners seething under the conquerors' occupation only waited for a command. In a matter of hours the blow would be struck and all would be won or lost. And now Nehi found himself standing beside his brother, watching his twin's arms snake around herself as she stood on the cabin's wide porch, her smile gone.

The familiar icy, tearing wind closed over him, blackness and swirling power cut off everything else. Quintus had managed to make a workable version smaller, lighter, and more accurate to land than the first Nehi had ridden. He just wished they could be more comfortable too. His head spun and his stomach seemed to drop through the earth's core, catching fire on its way. He ached to leave Anna alone out there at night, and he felt his stomach clench with more than just the ride on the SOLTD. Nehemiah wondered why it felt so different then the times he had gone raiding in KAM. The answer came to him as his feet hit the hard pavement of Tolingbrook, his station for that night, and the SOLTD zipped back into itself with its hissing protest.

"Our world is changing again," he muttered.

"What?" Daniel asked. Nehemiah mumbled an unintelligible answer, not wanting to admit how hard his heart thundered. It was very likely he would die tonight, and whatever the outcome, nothing would be the same. "Yeah, well I can't sit around here listening to you mumble all night."

"Aren't you supposed to be in Crosstown?" Cobeau rumbled in his translating monotone. The two Hillsons jumped, spinning

as their hands dove to their weapons. Joe stood under a lamp-post beside his big friend, his black outfit a strange contrast to the white walking cast on his foot. He laughed at their surprise and leaned comfortably on his big friend.

"You've got to stop popping up like that!" Daniel snapped. "You're going to have my death by heart failure on your hands."

"Sorry," Joe grinned. He indicated the big chimera by his side. "Knee-High has Rock, Frowner has Doctor and P-a-u-l, so D can I leave Glue with you as a sort of body-guard home base?"

"Why?" Daniel asked suspiciously. Joe grinned and dug an elbow into Beau's side.

"I told you he won't buy it," he signed. Nehemiah was sur-prised to see red embarrassment creep over the chimera's hairy face as he translated. "Okay, it's really because Track-Maker's in Crosstown tonight, and Cat got Glue to promise he would look after the warrior." Daniel laughed and nodded.

"Sure, glad to have your skills, just so long as I can get going. Michael's in charge till I get there and he's an awful organizer. I don't even know if my explosives experts have the charges on the barracks set. There's a ton to do and we only have the few hours while we wait for you to do your job, Nehi." Nehemiah found himself pulled close in a crushing bear hug. He squeezed Daniel back, happy warmth colliding with his earlier adrena-line rush and pushing it out. Daniel wasn't much of a hugger. It made it all the more precious when he gave in and chose to show his affection. Daniel shoved him back at arms length, and Nehi thought sure he heard a sniffle from him. "Now enough of the mushy stuff, come on Beau, let's go! See you when this is all over, Nehi. Be careful, okay?"

"You too, Danny. Beau, be safe! Christ go with you in all!" Nehemiah said. Joe hugged his Glue tight, Beau beamed at him, and then the two of them whipped away. Nehemiah took a deep breath to steady himself, and turned to Joe.

"Are you joining my band tonight, Raven? We could cer-tainly use your skill and know-how." Joe pointed at his cast and laughed again, tapping his cane against the ground. "I know you better than that, a simple thing like a broken ankle won't keep

you down."

"I'm staying out of it," Joe signed, more seriously. "I'm better in a lone war, I only get people in trouble in a troop."

"Oh come on, I've seen you work with people. I could really use your help."

"I..." Joe stirred a little uncomfortably, his face troubled. His eyes rose from his feet and met Nehemiah's. "I'm still weak, Knee-High. I'm going to need what strength I can pull together after this is over. Win or lose, I have a job to finish."

"What job?" Nehi demanded.

"Wolf, Knee-High. I can't let him roam, and after this resurgence stops claiming our lives, I need to finish the business. No, don't ask, focus on this fight, brother." A smile cut over him and he shrugged. "Tonight you don't need me. Go cut off the snake's head and win the kingdom back. Make a legend of yourself tonight."

"Most legendary figures are dead, I'd rather not join them just yet," Nehi said, but he only half paid attention to the words. The picture of Anna standing on the mountainside wouldn't leave him alone. His gaze snapped to Joe and he suddenly smiled. "I know where you can do a job, and rest, and be blessed forever for it. Anna's lonely tonight."

"Then I'm gone," Joe signed quickly, pulling out his SOLTD. But he paused with his finger on the button and looked up at Nehi. "You sure you don't mind?"

"I trust you with my sister Joe, and I'd rather she wasn't alone just now. I mean, Wara, Halbred, and Elenore are up there too already, but they're company to be entertained not family like you." Nehi was checking over Hope and missed the sudden flush and elated shine that went over Joe at the words. Nehemiah slid Hope back in her holster and looked up. "And if...if I don't come back, and Daniel doesn't come back, I'd feel a lot better knowing you're there. Not that Anna couldn't handle herself, but I would still feel better." Joe nodded, accepting the duty, his smile gone.

"God be with you, brother," Joe signed, gave him a half silly and half serious salute, pressed his button, and was gone. It was

all done in such quick succession it left Nehemiah a little breathless.

A thin beam of light caught him from the barn door a little to his right. The glowing beam came from the Johnson's old place, where fifty-two men waited for him to explain why they were in a barn tonight. Nehemiah squared his jaw and jogged the last few yards over the soft grass. It felt comfortable and open to stand in the grass. Out here he was alive and free. Inside he became chained as the leader of fifty-two men, and liable to quickly die. Or worse...a lot worse... Abid was still here, still waiting... Darn it, he had sworn to himself he wouldn't think about that! Nehi drew in a deep breath and blew it out again, forcing the thought away, locking it out of his brain. His country needed him. Abid would not get in the way.

Nehemiah slipped inside and found himself immediately flanked by his two lieutenants. Peter and Tanzid stood beside him, their weapons in place, their armor ready, competent and waiting. Nehemiah accepted the comfort of their solid presence, sent a silent prayer flitting heavenward, and let his tension flit away. He didn't have to work this scheme alone. They would do their best together and that's all God asked of them.

Twenty minutes of briefing and everyone had their own part settled. Nehemiah gave them a little speech, feeling like a leader should at a time like this. Then he shook hands with the Squad leaders, and stepped out into the night with his small team.

Just him, Tanzid, Peter, and the open sky now. And they had to clear the way for the fifty men coming behind them.

The old boards creaked under Anna's feet as she shifted her weight and rubbed her arms. The cold seeped into her out here. Her eyes stayed fixed on the bare circle of dirt where the SOLTDs had been coming and going for the past weeks. Her brothers' SOLTD had disappeared what felt like an age ago, but she stayed on the porch, her mind numb and tired. So tired.

There was only waiting to do now, for hours and hours. The past years had been so busy she had had very little time to reflect on anything, and no time for simple life. Anna suddenly realized she had been a nomad for over two years and, oh, how much she longed for a real life again. At least Nehi had been with her through all the roaming.

But now she stood alone.

Numbly Anna thought she should go inside and do the dishes. But she stayed in the cold on the old porch, the pines rustling and creaking around her in the mountain breeze, staring at the circle of dirt.

What would she do if they lost? If Nehemiah never came back? Oh, she would be fine materially. But who would she laugh with? Who would she tease? Who would she cry with when the old sorrow came again and Mom and Dad's faces wouldn't leave her mind? To face the years alone, continually on the run, striving to survive and be a pillar of hope and light for those who came into her life...the vision of life after tonight ended in ruin paraded through her, and Anna's breath choked. The wind seemed to howl a dismal tune instead of the cheery mountain breeze, and even God was silent in that moment. It felt as if only Anna, shivering and sniffling, stood on the porch and a voice whispered in her ear that it would always be so.

A blanket of her uncle's fell over her shoulders, flapping around so it enclosed her in its comfort. Anna drew it around her like the old friend it was and looked behind her. She saw Joe's sharp features as he looked at her in concern. He gave her half a smile, plopped on an old rocking chair, stretched his walking cast out painfully in front of him, and tilted his head on the side, inviting confidence.

"Hello, Joe," she said, her voice soft and warm. The furrows on her face evened out as she looked at him. She pulled the blanket closer and sank on the ground across from his chair. "I don't know, I...I'm scared for Nehemiah and Daniel. And tired. And depressed. And I don't want to wait. Maybe I should have found something to do during this time. To wait and wait, alone and wondering..."

"At least not alone," Joe signed. "I met Knee-High on his way to his station, and we thought I might settle here for the few hours of waiting. I'm not needed right now. You have the ending card, I don't blame you for being nervous. I'll stick, if you want me. Jesus has the troops, Beauty. Remember, whatever happens Jesus is in charge. Keep the vision; we will always be His." A joyful, catching smile broke over his face and Anna suddenly found she could smile back.

"Neither height nor depth, that's right," Anna said quietly.

"Nor governments, or soldiers, or death, or loss, or pink hairdos can take us from His strong hands," Joe signed.

"Pink hairdos?" Anna asked, trying to decide if she had seen that right.

"You never know, the color pink can be pretty powerful sometimes," Joe shrugged, a telltale twinkle showing in his eyes, and Anna laughed.

"I have a confession to make, Joe," she said, a little of her usual winning cheerfulness coming back. "Until you said 'the troops' I had forgotten all about the rest of our men, Beau and Wiglaf and Atif and Tanzid and Peter... On top of being depressed and tired, I'm a terrible friend too." Joe gave a little grin and changed the subject.

"I noticed the dishes were still dirty on my way through the house looking for you." He didn't tell her he had analyzed the dirty dishes and realized these weren't the I'm-so-relaxed-I-don't-care dirty dishes. This time it was a sure sign of Anna being very depressed and worn down somewhere, and how utterly heartbreaking that had been for him. "I'll wash, you dry and put away?" Anna nodded and stood up, the blanket swirling around her and accenting her perfect form. The mountain breeze stirred her black hair as she turned her profile to him, looking back at the SOLTD landing pad, the moonlight setting it all in silver; Joe could almost believe the tales of goddesses of the woods.

"I'm glad you came, Joe. It's nicer with you," she said, and moved inside. Joe was behind her getting his cane situated. She missed the color that flew into his face, the look of elation and hope at her words. He replaced it with his normal cheerful, even look in an instant. Joe swung and thumped quickly through the house, moving fast enough he bypassed Anna on his way. He already stood at the sink when she stepped into the old fashioned kitchen. He began to whistle Anna's favorite hymn as the dishes clinked, and she smiled. Cleaning helped. Joe near helped more. When he reached the chorus, he looked pointedly at her (his hands busy with the dishes) and she began to sing along. At first it was only because Joe had asked, and there was no heart to it. But as she continued to sing, the words came alive to her again, and the depression disappeared. She could lift her head and face whatever may come in the next few hours. God would be by her side, He made all things well for His people.

And somehow she knew Joe wouldn't be far off, no matter what happened. And if the little mute stayed near, life would manage to be good no matter what circumstances broke in. She dried the last dish, wiped her hands on the dish towel, and spun on the mute ordering him off to the living room to rest his ankle.

Chapter 11: Kingdom's Hope

"And ye shall tread down the wicked: for they shall be ashes under the soles of your feet in the day that I shall do this, saith the LORD of hosts." Malachi 4:3

His black hair whipped and flailed in Nehemiah's face as the grappling line zipped toward the roof of the Judge's House. The crisp night air, the adrenaline and fear, for a moment it was overshadowed by a scene playing in his memory; he and Peter, in a dead-end alleyway, a toaster facing them, and Joe dropping into their midst like a black falling star. The relief and joy of that moment made Nehemiah smile as he scrambled up the last few feet over the decorative molding. He heaved himself onto the flat roof, rolling to break the sound of his landing. Tanzid loomed in the dark next to him, and the blob that was Peter dropped over the molding, landing silently on his toes.

"Glad I don't have a hole in my arm this time," Peter murmured to Nehemiah. Apparently he wasn't the only one thinking about that night.

"Tanzid, take the south side, Pete take the north," Nehemiah ordered. His two cohorts slipped into the darkness to make sure they hadn't been noticed, as Nehi checked the gadget Joe had handed him again. According to the mute, it "fuzzed their progress" on the security monitors, so they could move as practically invisible. Nehemiah thanked God for the weird talents of his little friend as he moved swiftly over the roof, raising dust and listening to the silence tingling around him. It only took a minute to find the hatch. Nehi knelt in the dust beside it and slowly loosened the old hinges. He found himself thanking heaven again for a curious childhood and an equally curious sister to egg him on. He knew every inch of this house. The hatch was old and disused, and it stuck. Nehi pulled a switchblade from his pocket. The click of it opening rang in his ears, and moonlight gleamed on the silver blade. He ran it around the edges of the hatch, slipped it under the door, and jacked it up.

The hatch lifted with a slight crack, dust cascading off it. He waved to his two men and the three dropped through the opening.

A cloud of dust spurted up as their boots landed in the dank darkness. Tanzid pulled the hatch closed above them as Nehi switched on his pen light. The little beam lit up floating dust specks, and dirty wooden walls of an old, narrow passageway, winding down into the house. Nehemiah moved with the steady step of a man who knew his way and had a good light. Down two dusty unused tunnels, through an air duct, down a rickety stair, through a dust-filled narrow hallway, onto a bleak metal staircase. Dust rose around them in clouds. It flew into their noses and eyes until it seemed to be an integral part of them. The place smelled musty and disused. Nehemiah finally stopped outside a plain wood door.

"Plant the first one, Pete," he muttered in his friend's ear, and swiveled the light. It fell on Peter's calloused hands as he swiftly pulled tubing, a timer, and a vial of green sludge from his vest. Two minutes later he stepped back and nodded at Nehemiah.

Nehi oiled the hinges on the door as he shook the dust off himself. They didn't want a trail drifting behind them. No noise came from the other side. He waited for thirty slow seconds, and still only heard silence beyond the door. Nehi opened it swiftly and slid through.

"Nice, the security level already," Tanzid murmured as he stepped into the white tiled hallway. The tasteful hanging lights above them seemed glaring after the dim tunnels.

"How did we get here?" Peter whispered. "I thought it was supposed to be well guarded."

"They don't know this way in," Nehemiah answered, and pointed. The door melded with the white-washed wall, leaving only the tiniest hairline crack to be seen. "Ever wonder how the IDP got its genius for disguising their tunnels?"

Tanzid glanced up and down the hall and turned left. This was his expertise, he had been here as an agent and knew what the invaders had done with the place. Three steps and the team

scattered, darting out of sight as the sharp thump of booted feet came from around the corner. A group of five security officers swung into the hall, marching in tight formation. Their boots thumped over the tile till they spun around the next corner. Nehemiah let go of two of the swinging lights, dropped off the ceiling, and looked for his men. He saw Tanzid peel himself out from behind a janitor's cart, but he couldn't see Peter. A door opened on his left, and Nehemiah swung around, Hope jerking up. Peter's blond head and grinning face poked out, and Nehi's taut muscles relaxed again. A yellow Story Land uniform covered the lanky Peter, and he made a sweeping motion over the canvas material.

"What do you think?" he asked.

"You look like a banana," Nehemiah smiled. "But the idea is great." Tanzid's hand shoved into his back and Nehi stumbled into the room with Peter as footsteps began to come towards them again. It was a plain gray locker room, but looked wonderful to the three men. It didn't take long for Nehemiah and Tanzid to find uniforms bulky enough to cover their utility vests, and the three stepped out into the bright light again. They marched down the hallways as if they belonged there, and no one gave the three men a second glance. After walking in what felt like circles for ten minutes, Tanzid found what he was looking for. He stopped at a door marked Controls, painted an official red instead of the ordinary white of the other doors. He twisted the knob and swaggered in with all the stiff arrogance of an officer. Panels and screens covered the walls, while three soldiers lounged in black chairs. They started and jerked up, cards from the deck they had been flicking at the light fixture scattering over the floor. One swiped a hand over the nearest instrument panel and monitor, knocking the doughnut crumbs to the ground.

"Hello," Tanzid said. He leveled his Brunhiem and motioned their hands up. Six arms rose, as the men gaped, staring into the red circle of the laser's barrel. Peter and Nehi moved behind them. Two sharp cracks, like melons being split with a rubber mallet, filled the little room. Pete spun and landed his cosh on

the third guard's head, and he sank boneless onto his companions. Nehi glanced up as he unwound the rope coiled around his waist, and his eye caught a movement on one of the security cameras. His first squad neared their target, ready to hold the gate and let the other teams in to clear out the invaders.

"Pete, Squad One is on the way, be quick," he snapped. Peter shoved Tanzid towards the myriad of buttons, switches, and microphones. The agent handed him a microphone, flipped two switches and pointed at his companion. Peter slouched and his tone changed to a nasal voice not at all like his own, but very much like the commander of the People's Kingdom contingent. "This is General Colchi. I am in the Controls Room and want fifteen of you up here. Now. There's been a breach in our security level, someone is here that's not supposed to be." Nehemiah glanced up as he finished with the last soldier and smiled as he watched most of the guards at the West Gate peel off at a trot towards the House. He held two fingers up to Tanzid. The agent flipped more switches, and pointed at Peter again. Pete's spine straightened with a jerk and he did a bit of a swagger.

"East Gateman, I'm calling whoever is in charge of this gate!" Peter barked, his KAM accent strong, the tone every inch General Ronoch's. An answering crackle came over the radio. Peter's legs went rigid, his head snapped up, and an invisible pointer twiddled through his fingers. "I want your best men up here in the Controls Room immediately, there has been a breach of security. Repeat, there has been a breach of security. Hurry it up, man, send at least twenty and tell them not to dilly-dally in conversation along the way." He looked at Tanzid, and the agent flipped more switches.

"Okay, we're offline," Tanzid said. "What next?"

"Tanzid, start up the jammer Quintus made us. Peter, set the second vial, then help me smash everything." Nehemiah rammed his laser butt into the security camera hanging in the corner. It jerked off its mounting, sparking and turning lazily on one frayed cord. Tinkling glass, heavy cracks, the sound of destruction followed him as he moved systematically around the room. Soon there were no more working security cameras,

communication channels, alarm systems, or even walky talkies in the Judge's House.

"Nice of them to put it all in one room for us," Peter grunted as he finished with the last camera.

"When we have you set up here as Judge," Tanzid commented to Nehi as he ran the last check to be certain the jammer was working, "I suggest better security measures."

"Me?" Nehemiah said, his eyebrows shooting up. "I'm not sure I want that,"

"You should have thought of that before you made that speech about justice instead of bloody revenge tonight in the barn," Tanzid said.

"Me? Judge? No, I don't want me as Judge! I'll help you set up Daniel, he's the one you want," Nehemiah said as he smashed the last switch.

"I want a Judge that could think of the people who murdered his parents and handed him to a torturer, and then order his men not to get cruel with the leaders so justice could have them later," Tanzid replied steadily.

"No kidding!" Peter half smiled. His stomach still churned enough it was a little difficult to smile with this conversation. He had known the disintegration had been hard on his friend, but he hadn't known how hard until tonight. "When word of that gets out, Nehi, I expect you'll be stuck with it."

"No, Daniel's got it, thankfully, and I have absolutely no intention of being in the running."

"I bet *his* speech went something like, 'Remember what they've done, and go at it!'" Peter commented.

"Are you sure all the channels are jammed?" Nehemiah asked Tanzid, firmly changing the subject. The agent noticed he didn't deny Peter's statement.

"You can't get anything through here except by word of mouth now," Tanzid smiled. Nehemiah grinned back and motioned them toward the door. It was a rare treat to see Tanzid smile. The three stepped into the hallway and moved to where the white wall turned a crisp corner a few feet away. Tanzid crouched around the corner watching for their men to come to

the Control Room. Nehemiah slipped his goggles on, slid the safety off Hope, and stood looking over Tanzid's shoulder. Peter fingered a knock-out grenade where he stood behind the other two, watching their back.

"Here they come," Tanzid reported, feeling the floor vibrate with the marching feet. Nehi watched as the fifteen soldiers from the West gate trotted into the white hallway and headed toward the Control Room. A tall man with thick curling black locks moved in the lead. He pushed at the half open door and gingerly stepped inside, his voice ringing as he called for General Colchi. The man stopped dead, his eyes going wide as he took in the wreckage. Tanzid and Nehemiah stepped out be-hind the soldiers, lasers leveled.

"Inside," Nehemiah ordered. The soldiers spun toward them, shock and anger playing over their faces. "Inside," Nehi repeated, his voice low and dangerous. They didn't move. One grizzled fellow fingered his rifle. Nehi's finger tightened on Hope's trigger, dropping a young soldier who looked healthy enough to take a creased head and still be fine tomorrow. The man folded on himself without a sound, steam lifting in a stink-ing tendril from his head. "Pick him up and get inside," he growled. The soldiers swallowed, swept him up, and obeyed. A smoking knock-out grenade flew into the room after them, and Tanzid snapped the door closed.

"Good timing, Pete," the agent said.

"Get over here," Peter hissed back, "the next group is almost in place." Nehemiah and Tanzid darted around the corner to start again. Twenty seconds later they had the eighteen men from the East Gate firmly locked in the Controls Room with their fellow gatemen. But this time Nehemiah stopped Peter be-fore he threw another knock-out grenade. They wanted the noise now. Nehemiah listened to the pounding and cursing as he marched across the yellow and blue floor tiles, leading the way through the halls.

"Dear, dear, I'm glad Lizzy can't hear that language," Peter commented. The noise behind them became a series of loud bangs as the door was attacked from the inside. The little group

started jogging.

"Running away from the noise is going to be noticed," Tanzid murmured, as doors began to open and heads poked out. A curious mutter rose around them as the noise penetrated through the floor level.

"Just keep up," Nehemiah answered and started to run. The halls began to fill as alarm spread through soldiers and security officers. The patterns on the little diamond shaped tiles were lost to sight as pounding feet raced for the Control Room. Nehemiah pushed through the crowd, breaking quickly into an unpopulated hallway. As Peter spun around the corner and raced after the broad shoulders of his friend, he noted the pretty tiles suddenly became bare concrete, and the nice hanging lights changed to intermediate neon bulbs that left large patches dim. Tanzid slid easily past the people, his feet landing just behind Peter's, his trained eyes noting a film of dust here that hadn't been in the other hallways, and that it was a short run till it took a strategic sharp turn.

A shout sounded behind them. They had finally been spotted. Nehemiah ran harder.

Nehi's hand caught the corner and swung around the bend. There it was; a crack in the wall, hardly perceptible under the thin layer of dust, outlining a hole about three feet by two. He threw himself on the hidden catch under the baseboard and the small doorway popped open. Nehemiah dove inside and felt his two cohorts scrambling in after him. The door clicked into place just before feet pounded around the corner. Confused shouts from outside their hiding place filled the close air and pushed past them farther down the hall. Perfect. They hadn't spotted the dust trail, and now the crowd had traipsed through it, obliterating his small band's footprints.

The dark closed in. Deep, close dark. Sweat pooled on Nehemiah's forehead and started to congeal on his backbone. The four walls of the passageway seemed to push into his body. He had been a lot smaller the last time he and Anna ran through this place. His hand darted to his pocket, before he remembered he left his pen light in his other pants, back in that gray

locker room.

"Light," he murmured. The knowledge his old master was only a couple of stories below him and coming closer rose with the bile in his stomach, singing in his ears and sending his heart skipping beats. That fear had pulsed under the surface, every moment of tonight, and now he couldn't keep it from breaking through into panic. "Light?" he hissed, a desperate pleading, his fingernails biting into the palms of his hands. A thin beam of light snapped on, and Nehemiah dragged in a breath again.

"Are you sure it's a good idea?" Tanzid murmured as the noise of their pursuers moved just outside their little door.

"No, but if you want me to be functional leave it on," Nehi muttered back, his voice shaking hard.

"Hold it so he can get to his vest," Peter whispered. "Tanzid I need your vial, and Nehi point that thing this way." Nehemiah found a pen light pressed into his trembling hand and turned the thin beam toward Peter. His friend's yellow jacket was off and he dug into the utility vest, pulling out clear plastic tubes, another vile filled with green sludge, and a third timer. The noise grew louder in the hall outside. It came and went, as their hunters raced up and down the bare hall looking for their invisible quarry.

"Hurry Pete," Nehemiah muttered, swiping the cold sweat off his forehead and glancing at his watch. Boy, he hated tight spaces. A grunt was his only answer. Nehemiah and Tanzid watched in silence as Peter set the third vial of gas to spill out into the security level.

"Done," Peter said after another minute. Nehemiah shuffled off, leading the way down the wooden passageway. The sides pressed close against them, making the air hot and stuffy. The lowering ceiling forced every move into a stooping shuffle. Nehemiah was very glad of that pen light. Eight minutes of scuttling along, gathering dust and splinters, and the passageway dead-ended at a wooden wall. Nehemiah dropped to his knees, pressed his ear to the floor, and fingered the catch. A minute passed in silence. The air grew closer and the passageway seemed smaller. Sweat trickled down Peter's back. He told

himself it was just from the hot passageway and ignored it. Another minute ticked slowly past. It was the silence that was so bad.

"Can you hear them?" Peter murmured to Nehemiah, as the young man knelt, unnaturally still.

"Yes," he murmured. "A lot of people have passed, most of the security officers should be up on that level now. And here come the two we're waiting for."

"Who?" Tanzid asked. The words dragged through his dry throat and he found himself swallowing. He must be out of practice at this kind of work.

"Al Abid and a man named Ban from the Battle Kingdom," Nehemiah whispered. "They're the two strong enough to really make trouble for us tonight if they aren't contained."

"How can you be sure it's them?" Peter hissed, trying to shift into a more comfortable position. His spine ached.

"I would know those footsteps anywhere," Nehi murmured, his voice barely audible. A shaky, wet breath rattled into the darkness as Nehemiah forced his lungs to expand. When he spoke again it came a little stronger. "Ready?" Two lasers started up their soft whine behind Nehemiah, their red glow adding to the pen light. They were ready. And that fact made this night bearable. He heard the door to the security level open below him and two steady sets of footsteps begin to walk up the metal stairs. His body was soaked with sweat, and the shakes wouldn't stop. But he successfully kept from whimpering at that sound combined with the close festering dark, and took a firmer grip on the tube of door sealant in his hand. He closed his eyes, breathed out one more scattered prayer, switched the pen light off, and pressed the catch.

The floor fell away beneath him, and Nehi landed feet first on thick red carpet. The yellow light reflected off the crenellated white walls, and it felt like it seared through his eyes. Tanzid and Peter landed next to him on the thick crimson carpet, and Nehemiah felt the comfort of their protection as he shot forward. He leapt toward the door to the security level, fingers curling around the metal edge, his eyes down; he didn't want to

see Abid, ever, ever again. He heaved and it slammed shut with a bang that echoed around him.

Nehi's hand shot up, running the tube of sealant along the crack. A furious yell sounded from the other side and Nehemiah worked faster, his heartbeat hiccupping as it raced. The thick line of yellow from his tube expanded on contact with the iron door, sizzling, and melting the metals together. And no manner of hammering could open it, despite what the two people on the other side of the door thought. Peter watched the last crack sizzle and melt. He activated the trigger to release the vials they had left behind. The furious shouts intensified, panicked, suddenly changed to coughing, and then silence.

Nehemiah slumped face first against the cool iron. His knees shook. All of him felt weak and shaky. He hadn't realized how strung up he had been over being so close to this man and this place again. Simmons' soundproofed room stood just at the top of those stairs. He could feel it through the metal, the old hurts pulsing under his scars. The thought of his master dragging him up those metal stairs, to that horrible–

"Well, there went that level. They're all out cold, and will stay that way," Tanzid interrupted Nehi's thoughts. Nehemiah glanced at him, his lowered eyes lifting to his friend's face. Tanzid watched him, waiting to see the effect, and Nehi knew the comment had come just to break up the horrors rushing through him. A smile spread over Nehi as a thank you, and he found he felt that too, deep inside him.

"And most of the security in the house ought to be up there after all the commotion we caused," Nehemiah answered, capping his tube of sealant.

"We make a pretty good team," Peter commented with a smile, dropping a hand on Nehi's shoulder. "We stopped all communications."

"Cleared the gates," Tanzid added.

"And the house of most of its security," Peter finished. "We should stick together when you become Judge, Nehi."

"I like that idea. You'll need bodyguards," Tanzid nodded.

"I'm not going to be Judge! But there's a room at the top of

the stairs I'll let you destroy for me after we win."

"I have training as an explosive engineer," Tanzid nodded.

"That can be your first official Judge command," Peter commented.

"Stop it!" Nehemiah grinned.

"What? Now's the time to speak of happy things, the House is clear for us," Peter said.

"Not quite, Pete, not quite," Nehemiah answered, sliding Hope into his hand and smiling at the two men beside him. They had seen his weaknesses tonight; they knew he was broken inside, and still didn't mind working with him. Nehemiah would probably never admit even to himself how grateful he was for that. "Come on. Let's go make sure this war is won."

He spun and trotted up the main corridor, Hope ready, listening to the sounds of people rushing toward this level, scared at the chaos and alarms that had suddenly and eerily stopped. He spun into a small room jutting off the main corridor, threw open a door, and stood to the side as Hope swept the area. A simple stairwell yawned at him, and a dusty wooden stair spiraled down into the lower levels of the house.

"Servant's stairway?" Peter asked. Nehemiah nodded and headed down, the stairs creaking at his weight.

"I thought you lived here too, Pete," Tanzid commented, bringing up the rear.

"Yeah, but I didn't know this was here," Pete grinned. "I guess that's why we have a Hillson with us."

"Quiet," Nehi muttered over his shoulder. He stopped on a stairwell with two plain white doors and pressed his ear against one. He stood still for twenty seconds, every muscle rigid as he listened. Only silence drifted from the other side. He spun on his heel and fired a quick blast into the second door's lock. A deep male voice gave a shocked expletive from behind it. Nehi kicked it open and stepped aside. Cuthbert, huge, gleaming, and menacing in his red metal plates, stepped through. His long lance dragged half out the door, blocking the way for the five other mail clad Knights of Faerie waiting to crowd inside.

"Thy directions art exemplary, Sir Hillson," Cuthbert murmured in a booming whisper. "No untoward difficulties annoyed our passage. Until thou nearly melted my hand. Art thine enemies near?"

"Glory awaits," a knight murmured, his voice rolling through the dark.

Nehemiah gestured at the second door set in this little stairwell. A wolfish smile curved over Cuthbert's face, twisting his blond beard. He gripped his lance and tapped it on the door handle. A burst of blue electricity lit up the little area, and a hole shivered in the door. The clank of metal filled the room as the knight's helmet deployed, plates sliding over each other to cover his face, leaving only slits for his eyes and mouth. A roar burst from him and he smashed into the weakened door, splintering it and barreling through. Five clanking knights rushed behind him, shouting war cries, lances, maces, and swords sparkling in the light streaming through the smashed door.

Nehemiah stood on the stairs with Peter and Tanzid, watching the flood run by. Screams, crunches, battle cries, power bursts, anger and agony and terror and lust of war, it all drifted through the broken door. The noise moved away, steadily deeper into the building, leaving only a quiet whimpering and a few groans behind.

"I don't think the enemy expected that," Tanzid commented. Peter laughed, primed his laser, and turned back up the stairs.

"Somehow I don't think that bunch needs our help. Let's see what's happening up here, shall we?"

Chapter 12: The Return

"Let the high praises of God be in their mouth, and a twoedged sword in their hand." Psalm 149:6

Darkness clung to the People's Kingdom outworks, grown up among the Sojourner wreckage. The soldiers were barracked between a series of control buildings scattered throughout Crosstown and the surrounding agricultural area.

Most of the land under their control lay in blackened heaps. But they kept some farms tilled by the Sojourners, and they yielded enough to send some back to the motherland. The farms watched over by the KAM soldiers yielded more, as they allowed the slaves to work the land as they had for generations; the People's Kingdom could not be shaken from doing things as their homeland did them.

Tonight the forced labor worked slowly under the moonlight. Their tools barely touched the earth, and their gaze kept darting over their shoulders. Watching each other. Eyeing the soldiers prowling among them. Staring at the shadows.

The shadows thickened. They began to turn to shapes and spilled over the barren earth, edging toward the buildings. Some raced hunched toward the soldiers in their blue and green. The night suddenly filled with dark-clothed enemies, vengeance smoldering in their eyes. The soldiers spun with a shout, red alerts lighting on their belts like evil fireflies as their hands dove for their weapons.

Hoes, sticks, even bare hands and dirt clods suddenly turned on them with a ferocious hatred. As Daniel's shadowy force reached the fields, most of the soldiers lay unmoving in their own blood, or writhing under the blows of those they had ruled for two and a half years.

But their alarms made it through. Yellow lights lit barracks across the southern region, as alarms caterwauled through the countryside. Everywhere officers slammed their hands onto their holograms and radios to report a mutinous situation. Terrifying silence greeted each attempt to reach their leaders.

They tried new channels. Different methods. Attempted to reach aides, and even secretaries, as they searched desperately for what had happened. The silence remained. And while they stayed in their control room, trying method after method to break the silence, chaos bubbled through their troops.

Conflicting stories and orders ran like wildfire as the soldiers rolled out of bed and frantically grabbed for uniforms and weapons. The alarms blared over it all. Soldiers spilled from their barracks into the darkness of a country that wasn't their own. Laser fire lit up in their midst. A constant stream of bursts, with no way to tell where the shooters lay, no chance to fire back with any certainty of hitting their mark. Soldiers fought each other in a panic to get back into their brick barracks, the screams of their wounded surrounding them.

The first company piled inside and slammed the bars over the door.

They never heard the crackle of the fuses light.

The first fireball lit the southern region. Bricks cascaded into the air and came down again in sizzling molten masses. The second explosion followed five seconds later. Four more went up in quick succession before the invaders realized their mistake and stopped piling back into their barracks.

Soldiers from KAM, the People's Kingdom, and Kallipolis charged into the darkness, daring the white bursts to bring them all down before they found the shooters. KAM came the fastest, the best prepared, the most dangerous. Screams filled the silence and the night lit with laser fire like small imploding stars.

The fight for the south raged ragged over the scorched earth.

But in the north, the blackness waited. It listened to the silence from their leaders and calculated without panic. And it moved like one dark entity, never shaken as the enemy rose from the night. Andrew staggered as he stumbled into an abandoned stone building in the center of Selah, main city in the northern section. Story Land, Gaia, and four minor kingdoms ranged over this territory, steadily picking away at the precious

gems, metalwork, and factory output splayed over the hilly ground. But the Kingdom of the Prophet's Peace, based here in Selah, held the real power. They knew how to quell a new land and bend it without breaking it, drawing the useful commodities out like a steady stream of honey dripped into a jar. The others were willing to let their expertise lead the way.

Tonight Andrew cursed the unwarlike tendencies of Story Land and Gaia that had let the Prophet's Peace take over. He could watch his men on his radar slowly being picked off and whittled down. The Black Army didn't panic. It took more than sudden silence from their leaders and a few buildings blown to bits to break their soldiers and make them run. Andrew looked up at the moon and his lips pursed. They had waited as long as they could. He gave a mental sigh and hit the button connecting him to David Young.

"It's a man to man fight here with no real advantages. We could really use your people, David," he told his button. Andrew snapped it off, prayed it had reached their backup, nodded at his lieutenant, and darted back out into the fight.

Bursts of laser fire lit the air around him. His lieutenant hit the ground, ominously silent. A scream ripped from Andrew as he rushed the church-turned-mosque in front of him, where the heaviest fire came in this street. His back slammed into the stones, and he could feel the heat seeping through the walls from the constant stream of lasers. Did they have the women and children inside?! The thought haunted Andrew, they had scattered the most vulnerable slaves throughout the city when the fight first started; flinging grenades at random could mean hundreds of his own dead.

Sojourners rushed from around corners and out of buildings, following his lead. The Black Army met them at every turn. Laser fire and screams flowed through Selah, and Andrew prayed the name could once again be true for his people as he raged against the black tide.

Balls of sucking wind and pure power spasmed through the dark. The white lines cutting over the SOLTDs created a surreal cadence to the scene. The noise cut through everything.

Andrew felt as if someone prodded his brain with invisible fingers. He hadn't realized how many of those things the strange old inventor had managed to conjure up for the resurgence. The blackness peeled back and Faerie red and gold gleamed amongst the mismatched bands of the Sojourner soldiers. Pent up lust for war and pain at two and a half years of heartbreak and abuse burst onto the invaders. The Black Army wavered, some contingents literally pulled apart by terrifying black balls dropping new soldiers into their midst.

A massive ball landed pulsing just outside of town. It peeled back, mushrooming up and into itself, tearing up grass and hills around it. It left battle-grimed southerners massed on the hills. Their own region lay in their hands. Hard faces and dripping weapons spoke of their fury waiting to burst into the enemy in this new sector. The southerners broke into a run, shouts ripping from them as the years rolled through their souls and poured out through the weapons in their hands.

The tide rolled through Selah with a horrendous noise of bloodshed and terror. Andrew squinted at a figure on the torn up hill, and his goggles zoomed in obediently.

Daniel Hillson, blood-grimed and greatcoat ripped in tattered shreds, stood on the torn hill outside of town. His mouth moved in shouted orders, his black curls whipping in the breeze of coming SOLTDs, his face fierce and hard. He looked like a general ready to do anything necessary to win.

The thick form of David Young rounded the bend at a run. A squad of southerners rushed around him, screaming battle cries and bloodlust. They poured into the mosque and Andrew could hear the tide turning against the Black Army. David's jog turned to a stroll, and Andrew straightened with and effort as he came nearer.

"You did need the help," David commented.

"Black has never been our color in the north," Andrew admitted, his voice a little shaky.

"We favor green really down south," David admitted. For a moment Andrew saw a wince go over his friend's face as he looked over Andrew's shoulder into what had once been a

peaceful church. David's eyes flicked back to Andrew's. "KAM kept a meticulous record of all the Sojourners 'pressed' into work." Hope and dread flared through Andrew and he felt his face flush with it. Sarah, was she... David nodded, his face softening. "She's alive, Drew. She's still alive. And we know where she is. We know where everyone is."

"Then, Little Blue Turtle saw the whale!" Anna wiggled her hand through the old trough, moving the twig that was Little Blue Turtle toward the floating pinecone. A wisp of steam lifted from the trough as the battery heated water met the winter air. Elenore leaned closer, her eyes wide and flicking back and forth between the twig and Joe's signs, as he lounged on the porch out of the snow and translated Anna's words. Halbred's hand went over his mouth, a little gasp sliding from him. "It was huge! The biggest thing Little Blue Turtle had ever seen." Anna wiggled the stick around the pinecone, wracking her brain for somewhere to take the story. Little Blue Turtle had been everywhere by now, in an effort to keep the two children from weeping in a corner, or ripping apart the house in exuberant childhood. They didn't have much use for anything between the two extremes.

Anna recalled Wiglaf's murmured apology and his rueful glance over the pretty interior of the cabin before he slipped out to man his station and left his adopted children with her. His reaction made sense now that she knew them better. She felt honored he had picked her to keep these two spitfires, it meant he thought her capable of great strategy as well as childcare. They didn't sleep much either. Wara, the children's chimera nursemaid, still lay snoring in the upstairs bed, and the children had been up for hours already. At least it eliminated the chance of dwelling on the waiting; trying to handle these two broken wild-things made the time speed by. Wiglaf had his hands full.

But stories caught their attention. A little smile played over

Joe's face as he began to sign, and Anna spoke his words for Halbred, relieved to not have to think for a little bit.

"The whale spouted, water blowing out the top of its head," Joe signed and Anna said, "and Little Blue Turtle was caught in it! Up he flew, up, up, into the clear blue sky, and light filled all the world. Beauty, freshness, so much light, it was everywhere. The water tumbled down as the whale stopped blowing, and Little Blue tumbled with it, back into the waters of his homeland. But he knew, as he flapped and swished, that he would never forget that. There was a place above him where light and safety and beauty dwelt, and waited for him. One day, he would go there. And the fear of the sharks wouldn't be able to follow him into the light."

Anna met Joe's eyes as he signed. The little smile stayed on his face, but it wasn't amusement. It was Joe who managed to drag the children from the corners, made them look up and hope. He was so good at this. Joe's foot suddenly slammed into the trough, spraying them with the warm, rust-laden water. The children pulled back, laughing and spluttering. "Then a dolphin splashed into him, and Little Blue spun with the laughing fish!" Anna found herself laughing too, as Joe made the water slough everywhere, and the conversations between the turtle and dolphin grew sillier and sillier. The game turned into mud pies after a moment, and she found herself laughing harder as she shook her head over the mess. The fun Joe had with it took Anna by surprise. The hidden child in him, that had never had the chance to be a child, seemed to wake up and leap with the chore of keeping these two entertained and cared for.

A soft beeping suddenly started in Joe's pocket.

The mute jerked up, each line on his face hardening as his hand shot into his pocket. Every eye riveted on him, the imaginary turtle forgotten. Elenore's gaze went wide, her lip trembling as she pulled back, automatically getting away from anyone's reach. Anna drew her close, wrapping her arms around the little girl; Elenore needed to learn to seek out human sympathy when scared, not pull away. And Anna didn't care about the mud steadily dripping on her from the girl's hands. Joe

drew out the middle section of his SOLTD. A red light blinked on the programmer's box, and the beeping went in time with it. Anna laid a hand on Halbred's shaking arm.

"What's that mean?" she said quietly, her voice trembling despite herself.

"It means it's over…" Joe signed back, staring at the light as if his life depended on not missing a beep.

"Which is it, success or devastation?" Anna asked, her voice almost squeaking. The beeping stopped, and the light started flashing green. Joe lit up. Excited joy radiated from him. He threw the SOLTD section into the air with a silent whoop, and caught Anna's hand. He spun her in a tight circle, caught the SOLTD as it returned to earth, somehow attaching the two ends to it at the same instant, and started flipping and walking on his hands around the porch, whistling a delightedly happy tune.

"We did it?" Anna asked breathlessly. Joe flipped beside her, bouncing on his one good leg.

"Yes! Yes, yes, yes, yes, God gave us victory, Beauty, and we live again!" he grabbed Halbred's shaking hands. "We did it! The war is over, we won!" Joe signed with the boy's fingers. The mute's palms shoved into Anna's shoulders and pushed her toward the door. She understood and took off in a run, flying up the porch steps, into the bright mustiness of the old cabin, and on up the creaking old staircase toward the meeting room. Her breath seemed to fly from her and her ears hummed.

Success! Sojourners Kingdom back as a light on the earth, Jesus had granted them another chance. Her home! Anna gasped in joy so hard it hurt and ran faster. She had a home on earth again, and they could settle down, Nehemiah, Daniel, Joe and Beau. A place to call her very own, while she helped her brothers put the kingdom back on its feet! And Joe, what would a settled home mean for him?

The cold metal of the handle bit into her hand and Anna fumbled at the catch to the door. She paused and stood still for three seconds, forcing her breathing even. She shut the elation out, for now, and pushed open the door.

The book lay on the table. So large, so magnificent. Anna slid

on a pair of white gloves and stepped gingerly toward it, feeling clumsy and awkward as her fingers slid under the tooled leather and gathered the book into her arms. She forced herself to stop shaking as she settled it in its protective box, grabbed the velvet bag, and slid the ancient book inside. She held their life right here.

This book meant resurrection.

It took an instant to toss the gloves in, draw the bag closed, and swing it over her shoulder. She felt it settle at her hip as she spun toward the door and flew back down the stairs toward the outside. As she darted onto the porch, the rustling pine needles seemed more vibrant, the dawn air more alive, the sunshine a visible song. Joe's arm suddenly held a wet rag in front of her. Anna rocked to a stop to keep from barreling over the mute. She took it with a breathless, half sobbing laugh and wiped the mud from her boots and the larger spots off her dress. As she looked up she found a package held toward her. She took it from Joe's hands and quickly ripped off the paper, trying not to show her impatience with all this preparation.

A jacket fell into shape in her hands as the paper came off. A hundred concerts in a hundred different towns flashed through her, and memories of long boring days of travel, laughter and adventures. Years of memories with Joe and Beau and Nehi. It was the same make as the concert coat Joe had given her that first time the twins joined him in a show. But this coat was white as salt.

"When you wear it remember you're helping preserve the world for our Savior," Joe signed. Joe held his SOLTD up in front of her and the cold metal stung as she wrapped her fingers around it.

"Won't you come with me?" Anna asked, her voice trembling with the high emotions rolling through her. Joe shook his head and tapped his cane on the porch.

"I would slow you down. This is your job, Beauty. Take it home."

Anna spun off the porch onto the circle of torn up ground, her dark eyes bright. Joe plopped on the old porch and the

children huddled into him. His face was flushed, his eyes bright, and a half-smile twisted over his scarred face as he watched her. He gave her his half-silly, half-real salute. Anna smiled, and hit the button.

Cold energy swirled around her, sucking her dress and hair, and seeming to suck even her life out with it. The hissing wind screamed in her head, shooting through her nervous system and quivering in her bones. Her brain ached and spun as if it was being stirred with a metal spoon, and her stomach flew off somewhere without her. Hard dirt slammed into her boots, whiplash snapped up her spine, and the hissing wind wailed away back into itself.

Anna knelt on one knee, panting and clutching the velvet bag with one hand, a strafing laser pistol in her other. She was in the courtyard of the Judge's House. The ancient oak, fire blackened but alive, stood two yards to her right. The courtyard stared back at her empty. Anna shoved herself up and ran for the humped domes behind the great house. Her memory filled the empty landscape with people, populating it with the ghosts of that night; the conquered people bunched by the door, soldiers in the moonlight shouting and menacing, and the four months of her life sucked into the dark of these buildings. Anna's stomach tied in knots as she pushed open the door, gripped the metal railing, and raced down the stairs. But her arm stayed wrapped around the velvet bag and her precious package.

"And the LORD, he it is that doth go before thee; he will be with thee, he will not fail thee, neither forsake thee: fear not, neither be dismayed[7]."

The words flew through her and she clutched the book closer. The God who spoke those words moved with her now. He was the reality. These hollow buildings only held shadows.

The cellars were empty, as she knew they would be. All activity had been moved to the new buildings, a quarter mile behind these storerooms. This place stood deserted, and rank

---

[7] Deuteronomy 31:8

with the smells of what no one had bothered to clean up. Anna shut it all out and ran. Her feet knew these halls. Her mind did too. Old memories of her child-self gathering things with her mother filled her, and her eyes stung. The hall changed to concrete, and newer memories of sobbing brothers and sisters and numb horror took over. Anna's cheeks were wet as she spun into the last hall, pushed the ugly metal door open with a grunt, and slammed her hand down on the elevator's button. But her mouth was a tight line of determination and her head held high.

The chains creaked and groaned as the elevator dropped toward her. Anna took the moment to shrug into the coat. As her fingers flew down the buttons, Joe's sharp face displaced the dark memories. Her eyes were bright and her spine straight as the elevator shook to a stop. Metal shrieked against metal and the door pulled open. Anna stepped gingerly into the cage, her knuckles white as she gripped her strafer. The chains groaned, gave another metallic shriek, and the elevator began to jerk up. It swayed and hummed, and Anna prayed it wouldn't break now. But the freight cage kept lifting, steadily rising from underground. Another groan, a sharp jerk, and Anna moved beside the door, her laser pistol ready as it began to squeak open. Anna shifted her grip on the stock and prayed again it wouldn't be needed.

The door creaked and groaned open. A bare, dusty entryway greeted her. Ominous sick brown patches stained the concrete floor, and only dim, dirty light managed to drift in. But it was sunlight, and Anna breathed easier as she stepped out of the elevator. The door's metal handle stuck, stiff with disuse. Her boot rammed into it, her foot stinging with the force of the kick, and she tried it again. The knob turned, still stiff, but she could hear the latch drawing back. She flung herself against the rusty knob, wrenching at it. A loud click rang through the stained entryway, and the heavy door jerked open. Dust motes and the stale darkness of a hall greeted her, and Anna coughed and slid through. She strained her ears as she began to run, listening to the sounds that drifted through the walls.

Shouts and whining laser blasts echoed over her head. The

fight went on up there, probably in isolated pockets, the last enemies resisting. That meant she still had time. Anna bent into her run, flying up the dusty hallway. The old doctor Tara had told her about this place, a connecting door with the kitchens in the main house, because someone had thought it was a good idea. But the elevator moved too slow and awkward, and no one ever used it. Another plain metal door filled the end of the tunnel, and Anna's hand flew to the knob. Her wrist wrenched as the knob stuck. This one was locked.

She snapped her goggles over her eyes and the world took on a weird blue tint. Anna murmured a quick prayer, begging that she wasn't going to kill anyone on the other side, or alert an enemy, and stuck her pistol barrel against the lock. Light filled the little area, as steam and heat rushed out at her. The metal melted, dripping away. Anna let go of the trigger, pulled her hand away from the heat, and blew on her fingers. The door swung open.

Pots and pans sat neglected on the stovetops. Something had gone rancid in the commercial sized mixer, and Anna's nose wrinkled as she stepped out onto the tiled floor, her smoking pistol held ready. An empty room stared back at her, just like she had hoped. A kitchen is the first place forgotten when a fight starts, and the first place remembered when peace comes and bellies get hungry. She still had time. Anna's boots rang as she pounded over the tile, jerked open the door to the third servant's entrance, and raced up the spiraling stairs.

Shouts drifted through the walls as she raced past doorways. Battle cries, victory whoops, screams of the wounded. It melded into a din that made her hairs stand up and her skin prickle. But there were no more lasers that she could detect. The house was theirs. Even the pockets of rebellion were squashed. Anna spun up the stairway, praising God for an intricate knowledge of the house, and how hard it was to find this little stairwell. It might as well have been a secret passageway for all the traffic it got. One story, two, three, four, five. Anna's hand tightened on the metal railing and her boots jerked to a stop. Her skirts flared out and then swirled back around her as

she stood holding her breath, staring at the door, listening.

No sound came from the other side. She gently reached out and touched the plain metal knob. Her hand tightened, twisted, and shoved in one swift motion, and Anna stepped through into the Judge's House.

Graffiti scrawled over the scratched walls. The gilt paneling had been scraped clean exposing bare wood, scratched and scored mercilessly. The intricate white moldings were blackened with dirt and tabaco residue. The beautiful paintings hung ripped and mutilated. Tabaco stains and garbage reeked up from the hallway's carpeting. Anna's eyes found the picture of her parents almost against her will. A crude saying scrawled over the canvas, a gaping tear cut through the two elegant figures, and her father's face had been childishly doodled with devil horns and fangs. Heat raced through her, and her throat tightened, choking her. But she moved steadily toward her goal. Anna ran over the ruined carpet and into the domed Room of the Book.

The mosaics were still here. Someone had used the room to house a campfire, and the white marble was scarred and the ceiling blackened. But it had been too much trouble to break down the pieces, and the dome still sparkled with the beautiful biblical scenes of Moses the lawgiver, Paul the Letter-Writer, Daniel the Prophet, so many faces used by God to write his words. Anna gripped the pedestal (shoved over in the corner and used as a bench for too many unwashed bodies) and levered it upright. She panted and blew as it settled with a clack on the marble. But she could hear other sounds too. Marching feet, and someone complaining loudly, fear in the voice.

They were coming.

Anna whipped the white gloves on, slid the velvet bag off the box, drew out the Bible, slapped the bag on the pedestal, and gently, carefully laid the great book on the black velvet. Her hand ran through her hair as she slid the pistol in her belt with the other and straightened her skirt. She spun and faced the door, ready for her job.

The doorway began to fill with people. Men and women

filed in, some whom she recognized, some she only knew by name. Most were disheveled and looked terrified. All of them gaped at her.

A tall young woman, her dark beauty perfect, calm and courageous and graceful. The white coat and gloves shone in the dawn's sunlight spraying in from the hallway, pristine and almost angelic. Each person stilled, silent, just staring at the apparition. Nehi smiled as he stood behind the grouped leaders; they thought a goddess had just dropped in their midst, and it wiped every other thought from their mind. Joe had been right, Anna was the perfect one for this job. Just the sight of her imposing, serene beauty quelled their fight and made them want to listen. And it felt impossible to think of her telling a lie. Anna pointed at the great book on the pedestal.

"Our base has returned." Her voice rolled through the room, striking the round walls and coming back at them in an echo. Anna slid a gloved hand under the book, lifted it and gently drew it open. Paper crackled, and a murmur of incredulity and awe ran through the gathered leaders. Anna paced past them, carefully turning to new passages to prove it was a full book and not simply a few pages. "We have our foundation, our book has returned. Sojourner's Way takes its place among the kingdoms of the world again. You have no right to be here."

Nehemiah swung beside the pedestal as Anna laid the Bible back on the black velvet. He stood tall, as imposing as his sister with Hope hanging from his hand and the grime of war covering him.

"You will be returned to your countries," he stated. Shoulders and faces sagged in sudden relief. "Inform your kingdoms what you have seen here. We have risen again."

12. The Return
Psalm 149:6

Pg. 249

Chapter 13: The Raven and the Wolf

"Behold, I send you forth as sheep in the midst of wolves: be ye therefore wise as serpents, and harmless as doves."

Matthew 10:6

Hours, what felt like days later, the resurgence was officially finished. Anna walked beside Nehi, dully listening as the talk flew between he and Peter and Tanzid. The leaders had been transported back to their countries to report the Bible returned and the Sojourners alive again. Their enemies had been subdued and placed in holding cells. Those that were still alive, at least. A few still ran through the countryside of course, but squads swept the kingdom, steadily picking up the stragglers.

Anna had spent the last six hours mostly helping with the wounded. She had forgotten how advanced the hospitals were here. The invaders had kept them up, and skin grafts, infusions, tissue repair, even limb replacement in some cases, sent soldiers who had been carried in half dead walking back out only hours later.

But some of that time she spent wandering the ruined halls of her home. Her elation at winning this war felt like a distant memory already. Only bare, unfixable ruins were left here. So much ruin, so much destruction and death. Anna's footsteps slowed as she neared the doorway to the great hall. The path was so easy to walk in one sense, her feet knew the way without thinking about it, she had run it every day to fetch her father home and walk hand in hand with him to their little happy set of rooms. But then it had all died. The last time she had walked this hall, Nehi had been a battered husk of a human...

Anna lifted her tired head and her red eyes landed on Joe waiting by the great doors. He leaned on his cane, laughing with Nehi as her twin trotted past into the room. Joe didn't follow and the door swung shut. He turned and caught Anna's gaze. The twinkle left his face. He understood.

"You'll be all right in here. Trust me." Joe winked encouragingly as he signed it. Anna felt her twisted soul straighten out

again. Trust Joe? With all her heart. Life didn't have to be as it used to be, as long as Joe and Nehi were around it would be what she wanted. "It won't be like the last two times you were in this room, Beauty. I don't promise comfort or even peace... but it will be all right in the end." Anna wondered vaguely why he looked at his toes that way, but her mind had already wandered off. Anna stared at the two big doors leading into the great hall. Happy shouts filtered through the heavy wood. She recognized the voices of her friends.

"You ready?" Joe signed. Anna smiled at him. He really was a very understanding little person. She nodded, and Joe heaved the door open. Bright noon light flung into her face, calling her to look up again, and she stepped through with a smile hovering on her lips. Joe's cane tapped away from her as he shuffled off to congratulate Beau on still being alive.

"Don't use that ankle too much," she called after him reflexively, her nurse's side coming to the top.

Nehi spun away from the great table at the sound of her voice, a grin on his tired face. Anna walked toward him. But she couldn't help a small shudder as she crossed in front of the old meeting table, the night of the Disintegration playing through her. Nehemiah felt it and sobered.

"I know, it's pretty awful memories now," he said quietly. "But we're going to make new memories here, Anna. We're going to use this hall for judgment again, and justice, and mercy, and set the light on the hill, and re-salt the earth, and– And isn't God good!" Anna smiled and nodded, unable to reply any other way; her heart felt enlarged and like it was trying to crawl out her throat and choke her. This happy, strong, wise Nehemiah was so different than the cowed, frightened, beaten one she had seen last in that hall. For Anna, so many answered prayers and whispered hopes played over Nehemiah as she watched him standing in the sunshine, laying out plans for the future. God's healing and goodness on display in a living vessel.

The gigantic oak table and its intricately carved chairs had already been cleaned and reset; pockmarks and scratches still showed, but a little stain would help. Someone had scoured the

floors, and pulled rugs in to cover the grisly stains. Two of the enormous bay windows stood open and a fresh breeze rolled through the hall, bringing sunlight and the scent of good dirt. Anna drew in a deep breath and let herself remember the way the earth is renewed in a rain, how the forest is reborn after a fire. Their kingdom would grow again. What couldn't be washed away could be painted and remade. Quiet happiness and hope filled her as she sat down at the table next to Daniel, with Nehemiah on her other side, and her brothers began to explain the events of the night. Anna listened and gasped at all the right spots, as she watched people bustle in and out of the door, and they waited for the selected few to arrive for the post-battle conference about the future.

Samuel settled across from the Hillsons, his wise old face so happy it made Anna want to laugh and cheer and cry all at once. Boy, she could use a nap. The remaining chairs began to fill, noisily and happily as Peter and the four leaders from the So-journer's IDP found their places; the voices of the people. Quintus, Cuthbert, Tanzid, Paul, and Harry tumbled into their chairs, still raucously giddy; the voices of the outside world. The group at the table spoke at a deafening level, and Nehemiah chuckled, wondering how they thought they'd get any business done at that roaring volume. He noticed Samuel wasn't joining in. He seemed to be looking for someone.

Nehi scanned the faces around him for the missing person. Wiglaf and Atif weren't there, but Samuel had been there when they had asked to be excused from the meeting on some business of their own. Joe. Of course, where was Joe? He ought to be here.

The hinges squealed as the twenty-foot-tall door pushed open. John Mickelson's laser shot up and aimed at the crack. The eleven other men in his squad spun into a tight formation around the pillar with the book, lasers swinging up as their nerves tightened.

A small white-blond head peeked around the door, and a bushy black haired one towered over it in a perfect imitation.

Shoulders slumped and rifle muzzles dropped as the soldiers recognized the Ravens. Mickelson's aim didn't shift. A red circle played over Joe's face as the mute gave a smile and slid tentatively into the room.

"I'm leaving the house today," Joe signed. The chimera's translating rumble echoed in the vaulted room, bouncing back at Mickelson. "Just to another part of town but... Can I look at it one more time before I go?" Longing scored the mute as he glanced up from lowered lids, not quite daring to meet the squad leader's eyes. John Mickelson wavered. He knew Nehemiah held these two in high regard and trusted them with the kingdom...

"Sure," he said, and felt the word burn in him. He was entrusted with this precious book that had just brought life back to their kingdom. And here he was letting someone come in to page through it! But as the mute's face lit up with eagerness and he crossed over and gently started shifting through the ancient pages, Mickelson found himself relaxing. It felt right, somehow, and no worries plagued him as the seconds ticked slowly into minutes and the mute kept paging through the crinkling pages, devouring the words. The squad steadily dropped back to the boredom of a long watch.

The snap of the cover closing echoed around the room. John Mickelson looked over, still with a sense of peace inside him. He saw the mute give a sigh of pleasure, letting one velvet gloved hand run over the ancient leather cover. Joe's eyes rose and met Mickelson's. A sunny smile cut over his face.

"Thank you," Joe signed. Mickelson nodded as the chimera's rumble wrapped the words around the squad. Beau swept his master onto his shoulder and the Ravens trotted out of the room and closed the door gently behind them. Mickelson relaxed enough to turn the safety on his laser. The barrel's glowing red circle dimmed and then slowly died.

The door opened creakily and Nehi turned toward it. Joe's small form and Cobeau's huge one slid in and headed for the table, Joe's cane clacking on the floor. The Ravens moved behind the Hillsons, joking and jostling each other happily. Beau jostled Joe a little too hard and he crashed into Anna's chair and fell across Daniel's lap, hard enough to knock the chair over. The mute sprang up laughing, bouncing on his good foot, and jerking Daniel's chair back in place as Cobeau apologized loudly and tried to help. Joe grabbed his huge friend by the coat collar, plunked him down in a seat between Daniel and Paul, and slid around the table. He dropped in a spot next to Samuel and gave a grinning wink at the silver-haired gent. He laid a black notebook on the table and slid it across to Nehemiah.

"What's this?" Nehemiah asked as he picked it up.

"A souvenir I've gathered. Remember? The promised fruit of victory," Joe signed and Nehemiah looked at him sharply. Something lurked behind the sudden appearance of this precious notebook.

"Before this goes any farther, I would like to state that I don't know Joe's language and have no idea what's going on," Daniel drawled. It came almost indulgent, amusement running under the words. Joe gave his translation whistle, signed what he had said earlier with Beau rumbling it this time, then gave Nehemiah a 'where were we' look.

"I don't suppose you would tell us why you chose to bring it now?" Nehemiah asked.

"We were busy before," Joe signed airily and Beau rumbled. "Besides, I thought it would be best to wait till we were able to do something about it."

"About what?" Anna asked, leaning over Nehemiah's shoulder as he opened the notebook.

"Here we go, more of the journal from the last world!" Nehemiah murmured, his eyes shining.

"I added the ones we've collected to this batch, and it makes it almost complete," Joe signed. Nehemiah began to read. Anna and Daniel looked over his shoulder and read along. Soon their abnormal silence made people notice. The council grew quieter

as they began to watch the group at the head of the table.

"Lou sounds cute," Anna commented, and Nehemiah and Joe grinned at her.

"There Nehi, it's the page that cut off so abruptly," Daniel cut in, his voice fast, excited, as he read the excerpt. "'This really is a treasure, this–'" Nehemiah turned the page slowly, biting his tongue in his effort to keep from moving too fast. The yellowed paper crinkled and shook as he shifted it under its protective plastic. Anna's finger shot out, pointing at the top of the next page.

"I know that word! 'AmazonKindle,' I know that word!" she yelped.

"That's what this treasure's called. Anna, how can you know that and never have told me?" Daniel snapped. Anna ignored it, she was fumbling with her leather drawing notebook. The corner caught on the seam of her pocket and she had to shove it back in and start over. Silence tingled in the room as everyone stared.

"It's my notebook, the white pad I use to draw on, the one Mom gave me, it has that same word printed on it! Hold on, I've almost got it–" Anna pulled the notebook from her pocket and Nehemiah moved eagerly to look at it. Joe's hand landed on top of Anna's pressing the notebook down on the table. The scarred hand left almost immediately as he began to sign swiftly.

"Wait, Beauty, I don't think this is the place for it." The mute glanced over his shoulder, as if he suspected some evil being hovered there. "Too exposed, too easy for someone to walk out with it."

"I've been carrying it in my pocket for years, Joe–" Anna started, a little smile quirked over her face. Joe didn't smile back as he interrupted.

"That was before anyone realized what it was," he signed.

"We still don't know what it is!" Nehi said.

"Valuable," Samuel struck in, the word heavy with meaning. He nodded at the mute. "I think he's right. Whatever this is, it destroyed our country once. Let's get this thing to a secure location, then talk about what to do next."

"Oh come on, it's just us here," Daniel scoffed. But Nehi's eyes went to the open windows, and the great hall doors without locks. He and Daniel were the only ones still armed in this room, even Tanzid had let his blaster rest against the wall four yards behind him for the conference.

"Well, Dan, they have a point," he murmured. Anna stared at the notebook with startled eyes, as if it might transform into a viper.

"You're right, Joe," she said. "Let's take it to the Hall of the Book and put it into Mickelson's keeping before we do anything else."

"With the order not to let *anyone* touch it," Samuel said.

"I'll send Tanzid with a second squad of men to stay with it," Nehi, nodded, shifting his chair back to take point for his sister.

An iron strong hand clamped onto the back of his neck, slamming him down into the chair. A small, cold round hole pressed against the back of his head. Instinct kicked in and Nehi twisted, one leg shooting back toward where the knee of his attacker should be. His foot met empty air. The hand closed harder and the gun barrel dug into his scalp, forcing his head uncomfortably forward. Hope's weight lifted from his thigh and he heard her clatter to the ground, bouncing out of reach under the table.

"I'll take that, Ann," Daniel ordered. Nehemiah's head buzzed, his breath strangled, as he tried to recognize his brother's voice. It carried no trace of the cynical Hillson. This voice was icy, dangerous, and hard. "Unless of course you want your twin to meet an untimely demise where he's already spent so many unhappy hours." Nehemiah could see Anna staring past him at Daniel, face graying, mouth open, eyes wide and fixed. Silence tingled as everyone sat frozen, gaping at Daniel. That hand squeezed, its force bruising. It hurt. It was almost worse because of its natural, living heat. A cold metal clamp would have been better than that warm, live hand that dug into his flesh and breathed icy treachery into his heart.

"Oh come on, I don't have all day, especially since I had to do this in front of a crowd," Daniel prodded. The gun dug harder

into Nehemiah's scalp and he hoped he didn't grimace. Everyone sat frozen.

Everyone except Joe.

The mute slid slowly and smoothly onto the table. He took the notebook from Anna's limp hands and held it out toward Daniel, every action deliberate and open. Daniel jerked his chin, motioning for the notebook to be slid towards him.

"Let go of Knee-High first," Joe signed and Cobeau rumbled automatically. The chimera's muscles bulged as he gripped the arms of his chair, glaring at Daniel's head.

"Do you really think I'm dumb enough for that one?" Daniel scoffed.

"I promise you will have the notebook, and can step back to a good vantage point," Joe signed.

"Like I should believe you, the Raven who's been such a pest?" Daniel said.

"I haven't lied to you yet and I'm not starting it now," Joe signed and Beau's rumble filled the quiet. "You've lied to me ever since I met you. I'm not trusting a steady liar. You want the book, you step away." Joe pulled the notebook back sharply, showing he meant what he said. Daniel studied him for a moment. The hand let go, and he took a step toward the windows, covering the table with his pistol. Nehemiah slumped forward, sucking in a breath; his mind felt broken and numb, and the thing he registered clearest at that moment was the relief of having that hand gone. Joe sat the notebook on the ground, slid it over to Daniel with his foot, then sat back up again on the table. The mute stared at him.

"What, Raven?" Daniel demanded irritably, his fingers fumbling around the notebook and shifting it into his greatcoat pocket. Joe opened the fingers on his right hand and put them to his face, then drew them outward, closing them to form a sharp snout. Daniel had finally earned a sign from Joe. Seeing it broke the twins.

"Wolf. That's you, and soon to be a very disappointed person. That notebook doesn't mean anything to you."

"You don't know everything, beasty," Daniel said with a cold

smile. He pulled a SOLTD from his belt where it had been hidden by his long leather coat, and backed toward an open window. His fingers flew over the programming tablet, the ghostly green glow of the screen lighting his face as he punched in his destination. His pistol never wavered from the table. "I'm about to start up my business again. You won't be here to see it I'm afraid, the Raven has pestered the Wolf long enough. You're coming along and going to be very useful, for a little while, before I kill you." A different screen lit his face, blue mottling the green, as he hit the control panel for a bone plant. Nothing happened. His eyes narrowed and he hit it again. Joe's shoulders lifted in a little shrug, his face hard. A low chuckle, menace and disappointment mixed in it, came from Daniel. He echoed the mute's shrug. "So you cut your own chain before I had the chance. I didn't know someone could survive frying a slave plant. Oh well, I'll just kill you now instead."

"Daniel, what are you doing?" Nehemiah burst out, his voice thick and strangled. A part of him even at the moment knew it was an idiotic statement. But most of him simply couldn't comprehend what he watched. "You can't murder someone just because you don't trust them! God's word says–"

"God? You still think I believe in that superstitious deity?" A short laugh rang from Daniel. "Come on Nehi, grow up. There is no God, there is no point, we're only a bunch of circuits wired together with life for a little while. I decided a long time ago that I was going to get what I wanted while my circuits still worked." A frown twitched over him as his eyes flitted to the twins, and for an instant pain crinkled in lines around his eyes. "If you decided to grow up, you could come and join me. We could do big things together, Nehi you've got nerve and Anna you make a mean dish of tiramisu. I make a mean pile of money with what I do." The sneer came back, stiffening his features as if they were bronzed. "But no, you're both too sunk in your superstitions. I gave up on you a long time ago. You even picked a GI beast and chimera as your closest friends. That's ridiculous, they shouldn't even be alive." Daniel glanced down at his SOLTD and moved his finger towards the launch button. He looked up and the gun barrel leveled at Joe's head. A snarl flickered on Cobeau's face, his knuckles whitening. But Daniel paused before the chimera could jump for the gun. He looked at the mute, curiosity playing over him. "You don't seem worried, beasty. Or surprised for that matter. Don't tell me you were expecting this." Joe nodded, a grim smile shifting his face. "You really mean you knew *I* was this Wolf in the flock you've been looking for? For how long?"

"About a year now," Joe signed with half a shrug. Every head swiveled to stare at the mute, even forgetting the gun.

"A year," Daniel said incredulously. "Yet you kept traveling with me, and never said a word." A laugh barked from him, then cut off. "Yeah, wrong choice of words for you. But I admit I'm even impressed by your acting abilities, you really had me believing you didn't know who I was."

"A little inflating of an ego can go a long way in some people," Joe signed. "I think it limited your movements pretty well to have you travel with us, you had to keep your identity quiet and play the good-guy IDP persona. Look, I suggest you move on your way, Wolf. Someone is going to get curious about the lack of noise in here soon. Oh, and don't fire that pistol. I have a tracker on me for your SOLTD, it's activated now but I promise if you leave without bloodshed I won't use it."

"Yeah?" Daniel asked suspiciously.

"Promise," Joe signed and Cobeau rumbled, the chimera's tension lessening visibly. Daniel studied the cool green eyes for a moment in silence. Joe crossed his heart and held up his right hand. Daniel Hillson nodded and leaned out the window. A sharp hissing shot through the hall, table, chairs, and people jerked toward the swirling black bubble, and then he was gone; along with the window and a portion of one wall.

The room erupted. Everyone spoke at once, most of them clamoring for Joe to use his tracker and catch him. Anna and Nehemiah sat still and silent, faces gray, staring glassy eyed at the wreckage of the wall. Joe didn't look at the twins, and he drew the rest of the table's gazes as he flipped the tracker out of his pocket and erased it without looking at it.

"What?" Harry roared, leaping to his feet, drowning out the others. "Joe, there is such a thing as taking a promise too far! You just said he's the dirty murderer that's been taking your brothers and turning them in to be tormented and killed, didn't you?"

"He is," Joe signed, his manner quiet, and Beau rumbled. The chimera's mind drifted off to other matters now that the threat to Joe was gone. Peace rested on his big face, and his eyes were distant as he automatically translated.

"And you just let him go, to do it again? Joe, I know you don't think much of revenge, but justice comes into it too." Harry's voice trembled. He had dealt with the fallout from the Wolf's snatching up Christians in Story Land. It wasn't something you just forgot.

"Vengeance is the Lord's[8], Doctor, you know that," Joe signed and Beau still rumbled. "But you're right, and I didn't let him go. That SOLTD is jammed on one co-ordinance. Wolf's down in the courtyard where Track-Maker and Frowner were waiting with a strong welcoming committee. He's being led to a cell." Harry sat down abruptly, staring at Joe as if seeing him for the first time.

"So why did you wait a full year to catch this bloody traitor if you knew who he was all that time?" Tanzid asked, his tone carefully neutral. Joe looked down at the table, and if possible his face went blanker than before.

"I needed force behind me. Enough strength to stop Wolf for good and keep him from destroying us."

"From what?" several voices snapped.

"Wolf has been the mastermind and organizer of a group that's been stealing books and then blackmailing the countries they stole them from to get money. It's a lucrative business, I doubt you would believe their net profits if I quoted them to you. That kind of business gets kingdoms riled at you. He needed a scapegoat for his retirement, he didn't want to be chased the rest of his life, where's the enjoyment in that? So he

---

[8] Psalm 94:1

picked the IDP."

"What?" every voice cried, even Nehemiah and Anna shocked out of their previous shock.

"Perfect, really. Everyone hates and suspects us already. Let a word drop to the UPC or some other big group that it's their old enemy the members of the Way stealing books, and Wolf could relax and watch the fun of the hunt for the rest of his days. He's had the 'proof' of it set and ready to release for a year now, with orders to do it if he wasn't heard from for several months. I couldn't get my hands on his 'evidence.' But I could get to him. So I kept him alive and as much out of trouble as I could manage. The IDP couldn't survive the shock wave of the entire world inflamed against us for book thefts and disintegration as well as our usual truth, and I wasn't about to let it happen while I lived."

"You had to be sure you had him fast before you confronted him," Samuel said, watching his little friend with fascination. Joe nodded.

"Among other things," he signed quietly, so quietly even Beau didn't notice as his thoughts wandered off to hissers and ladies.

"But what about Nehi, just now?" Peter burst out. "You deliberately provoked Daniel into that, he could have shot anytime he wanted!"

"I switched guns on Wolf when Glue knocked me into him a few minutes ago," Joe signed. "The one he has is no good, it couldn't fire even if it had bullets in it."

"All right, well what about that notebook," Quintus objected. "He still has that."

"Yes, and I'm sorry for it," Joe signed.

"Sorry for it?" Quintus interjected. "Joe, that is a very precious thing he's carrying, whatever it is. He's liable to destroy it just out of spite."

"It is precious," Joe signed. "But not the way you think. It doesn't have the treasure in it."

"But I–" Anna started her voice shaky and thick, but Joe held up a hand. He reached into his jacket and drew out a thin, white

piece of hard plastic. He handed it to Anna without meeting her eyes.

"Sorry I swiped it," he signed. "I couldn't think of any other way to keep it safe."

"When did you switch them out?" Samuel asked. He leaned over and wonderingly traced the word 'Kindle' on the back of the white piece of plastic. Anna gripped it without seeing it, her hand shaking.

"One day in Doctor's house when Beauty booby-trapped her notebook with sneezing powder. The prank helped, I almost convinced myself it was just a prank I pulled back." Joe slid into his chair, his face blank and his green eyes not meeting those around him. Silence tingled as the room focused on Joe.

"Well I'll be a jiggered turnip," Andrew said suddenly. "I was told you were bright, Joe, but I never thought you were this elaborately brilliant!" He started to chuckle, and soon the rest of the table caught the relieved humor. Talk began to fly at a faster rate than it had before the confrontation started. Quintus took the Kindle with Anna's distracted permission and began to carefully probe it. Everyone except those at the top of the table watched with fascination.

The top of the table stayed uncharacteristically silent. Joe fidgeted and stared at his hands as the twins sat silent and stunned. Samuel was about to say something to try and help move the situation along the right direction, when Joe suddenly looked at Nehemiah, determination almost shooting from him. He leaned over the table to catch his friend's attention, giving Beau his little whistle to stop translation.

"Knee-High, I know this is a bad time for this, especially coming from me right now. But the longer we leave Wolf down there the closer he gets to making his escape, and people will get hurt. Knee-High, when you're offered the position of Judge by the people, will you accept it?"

"What?" Nehemiah asked, his voice soft and husky.

"I know this isn't what you want to hear right now, and I know I should wait. But it's not over," Joe signed. "There's more to this story, more that Wolf holds that we need, and I have to

know the answer to that question. Will you accept the Judgeship and govern the political part of this nation?"

"Joe, I... Disintegration came during my father's service; I know it had nothing to do with him, but it still did. And now my older brother... Joe, are you sure?" It came out desperate and sharp, a cry more than a question. Anna reached out and gripped his hand, her lips tight and eyes unfocused.

"I'm sure," Joe signed simply, every emotion tucked away behind a serious blankness. "D-a-n-i-e-l is the Wolf. I know this is a lot to take in, and I should give you time. But we don't have time, Knee-High. You don't know him like I do, we can't leave him down there. I need to bring him an offer he might consider before he kills more people and we lose our only chance at getting the coordinates to something truly wonderful, and I need the backing of the Judge to do that. Knee-High, will you accept when you're offered the position?"

"Me as Judge? I don't know if I want that," Nehemiah said, voice husky and slow. He ran a hand over his face, as his other tightened spasmodically over Anna's. They looked so young, Samuel thought, so drawn and lost. So broken.

"Believe me, I know this kind of thing," Joe signed. "You will be offered the position soon. Knee-High, whether you want it or not you need to take it, at least temporarily. What about all your hopes and dreams about putting this table back to its proper use?" Joe waited for a moment, studying his friend. When no response came he signed again, apologetically. "I need an answer, Knee-High." Nehemiah stirred and looked at Samuel. The old tutor smiled as best as he could into those questioning, hurting eyes and nodded. Nehemiah gave a little sigh and sat up.

"Yes," he said. "I guess I would accept if I'm offered the position of Judge. At least for a little while."

"Okay," Joe signed with a nod and took a deep breath. "Here comes the really hard part. Knee-High, I need you to come and talk with Wolf with me now."

"What?" Samuel, Anna, and Nehemiah all snapped together. The rest of the table stopped talking and looked at them.

"That's going a little far, don't you think, Joe?" Samuel said sharply.

"Now?" Nehemiah stuttered. "You do realize I had no idea, don't you? I mean, I had no idea! I should have...now?"

"If we don't do it now," Joe signed, all emotion but a serious earnestness carefully tucked away out of sight, "we're putting all the brave lives down in that courtyard and converted cellar of a prison in danger, and we'll miss our only chance at–" Joe stopped and pursed his lips together. "I can't sign about that here. Not yet. Please, Knee-High. Trust me blindly one more time. I need you. And so does this country that's just trying to come back to life, and the whole world when it comes down to it. I'll leave you alone after this, honest. If you come with me now, I promise I'll step away and let you and Beauty go your own direction. You won't even see me unless you let me know you really want me, I promise that to you. But I need you now. Please?" Silence rested in the room as everyone looked from Joe to Nehemiah and back again, wondering what was happening.

"All right," Nehemiah said finally. He got heavily to his feet with Anna beside him. Joe hopped up, slid Hope back to his friend, and moved toward the door, Beau lumbering behind. Several stood up to follow but Samuel waved them back down. He watched the group go out the door on whatever business Joe had going, then turned to those gathered around the table.

"All right men. While the Ravens and their cohorts are tending to the Wolf, let's start on the business of reconstructing this country." He put his fingers together, sat them on the table, and looked around him. "David, do you have any suggestions for what needs done in the next few days?"

Chapter 14: Traitors in the Dark

"For the LORD knoweth the way of the righteous: but the way of the ungodly shall perish." Psalm 1:6

Joe led the way behind the house and along the well-known path toward the old cellars. The buildings spilled over each other in concrete domes, ugly and stark, additions made by the invaders. Anna's hand gripped Nehemiah's harder as they came closer to it, and her steps slowed. He threw an arm around her shoulders and they walked on in silence. The little group drew to a stop at the entrance, and Wiglaf pulled the iron door open for them.

"All is well, Ravenswing Ashe-Maker," he reported. Four pairs of eyes looked at him. The Geatish hero bit his tongue and wished he could bite it off. "I mean, he is secured below. Atif watches with a strong contingent of young warriors."

"'Contingent?' How many did Frowner choose?" Joe signed, suddenly wary. The warrior raised one eyebrow.

"I know not all the names. He selected each especially and made certain of their mettle."

"That doesn't make much difference if Wolf got to one first..." Joe's signs trailed away, apprehension tightening his face. He moved through the door, and the darkness engulfed him. The sound of his cane tapping on the metal stairs descended deeper and deeper. Anna stood rooted, her knees locked. Her clammy hand let go of Nehi and she stepped back jerkily.

"I think I'll wait out here," she said quietly. Nehemiah just nodded and followed Joe and Wiglaf. Nehi held onto the metal rail as he walked down the cellar stairs. It felt cold. His skin prickled against the rough metal, and his eyes flashed with white dots after coming out of the sunlight. The sensations claimed his focus. A numb film covered his brain. He dully knew he should be thinking of what to do with his brother. If Joe was right and he was elected Judge, it would be his duty to judge Daniel. But could Joe really be right about *this*? Nehemiah

shivered, and wondered why all of him suddenly felt cold. He decided it must be being underground and let his mind go numb again.

Joe waited for him at the bottom. Wiglaf stationed himself in front of the stairs, his sword hanging at his side and his laser ready in his arms. The two young men began to pace down the dark, concrete hallway. Soldiers stood posted every four yards, all of them staring straight ahead and ignoring Joe and Nehi.

"Why so many guards?" Nehemiah asked, his voice low.

"There shouldn't be!" Joe snapped, his hands chopping the air, his lips a tight line of frustration. Nehi watched as the emotion faded into his blank mask. "I told Frowner to use just his team, but he thought I underestimated Wolf. I didn't, Knee-High, Frowner did. If any one of these men has fallen under his spell, we're in trouble. He's a very dangerous man. Brilliant, a genius in his chosen field." Nehemiah thought of his chosen field and his mind jolted, some of it coming back into focus. The pain flared into anger.

"If you say he's so dangerous, why have you let him loose for a year?" he growled.

"We've done our best not to let him loose, Glue and I," Joe signed evenly. But even in his anger Nehemiah noticed the mute's mask was firmly in place. "Ever since he started recovering enough to do damage again we've had someone latched onto him all the time. Why do you think Glue's been sleeping so much these past months? He had night detail most of the time, since Glue can see better in the dark. Wolf is good and he managed to get away from us occasionally. Those mornings he 'slept in' and missed breakfast, for instance. It took me too long to catch on to that simple trick. But for the most part, between us all, we held him in check."

"That's what you've meant this whole time." Nehi rocked to a stop, blinking. "When you've said Anna and I were helping, even without knowing it. We were the ones tying the Wolf down. It was the way we latched onto him as the long-lost brother, keeping him close..." He swayed, his knees locked and his head swimming. "Joe, why didn't you tell me?" It burst from

him in a vibrant, bitter growl. He might have imagined it, but it looked like the small form hunched forward as if a great weight fell on it and it hurt. Nothing showed on his face though as the mute spun and faced Nehi.

"You can't act, Knee-High," Joe signed. "Wolf would have known you knew right away and it would have gotten all of us slaughtered. Look, I'll answer every question you ask me in a few hours, but right now we have to finish this business." He pointed a few more yards down the hall at a heavy iron door, and stumped off toward it. Atif stood across from the iron, his matching Healy's glowing and ready, a young soldier standing stiff and silent beside him.

"Every question?" Nehemiah asked as he automatically followed. The humming buzz of anger in his mind quieted. If Joe really meant that, he was opening a door that had been firmly closed inside the mute since they had met, and finally beckoning Nehemiah in. The mute nodded and stopped in front of the grim young warrior.

"It has been quiet," Atif reported. "Too quiet." Joe didn't respond. He studied the sandy-haired soldier beside Atif from under half-lidded eyes. Nehi noted the mute's tense shoulders, the way he moved like a warrior carefully keeping his weight centered ready to leap in any direction. Nehi felt his own muscles tightening in response to the tension hanging in the air. His eyes went to the iron door. His brother was the one bringing that tension. Surely it couldn't be warranted. Someone must have made a mistake! Nehi stepped forward and dropped a hand on Joe's shoulder, the words on the tip of his tongue, ready to wrestle the mute's reasons from him and argue for Daniel's sake.

White hot heat blasted into him.

The darkness closed over her twin, and Anna couldn't see him anymore. She stood staring, her fists clenched and face stricken. A huge hand dropped on Anna's shoulder and she

drew in a shaky breath, her lungs expanding again. Beau pulled her gently toward the large oak tree where they could see the entrance, one of the few trees that had survived the occupation. He sat down under it and patted the ground as he looked up at her. Anna dropped obediently beside him. The frozen mud felt hard and terribly cold.

"Nice tree," he rumbled. "Reminds me of the one Joe painted in the wagon. With the ravens. Remember?" Anna nodded absently, her eyes searching the doorway and seeing much more than the iron and wood. She suddenly spun on the chimera.

"Beau, how does Joe know Daniel is this Wolf he's been chasing?" Anguish rode her words, a desperate need for Joe to be wrong.

"Watched him hunt," Beau rumbled, and a growl underlaid the words. "Not nice."

"Yes, but...'

"Trust Joe, Miss Beauty. He is doing good, protecting God's people. Serves well."

"I know he does, but–"

"Miss Beauty, God is still in charge. He can change even a Wolf's heart." Anna looked up and focused slowly on the chimera's simple, hairy face.

"That's true, isn't it Beau?" she whispered.

"Of course it's true. Remember it only takes one touch of God to change a heart. No matter how dark. We all have dark hearts, Miss Beauty, until God sends His light."

"That's right. I had forgotten for a moment," Anna murmured.

"Dark when we forget Him. Darker than dark. He's the only light. Pray for Wolf, Miss Beauty, that's the best thing for you and him. Jesus listens. Always." Anna nodded slowly.

"The more I'm around you, Beau, the more I see why Joe calls you his Glue. You never forget God, do you?"

"He never forgets me, Miss Beauty," Beau answered, a delighted smile shifting the lines of his face and making his beard bristle. Anna couldn't smile back. Sorrow ate away at her soul like a roaring fire, and denial fed it hot fuel. A sniffle broke from

her and she leaned into the solid bulk of her big friend.

"Pray with me now, please Beau?" she asked softly. "I'm not sure...I don't think I have the words." Cobeau nodded. His simple, truth-wrung sentences rumbled deep into the earth around them, wrapping even around the oak's roots. Anna curled against his side, crying softly, sentences breaking from her sometimes, heartbroken and pleading, flung to the throne of the only One who remained steady no matter what shifted and died around her. The seconds ticked gently on under the tree's sheltering old branches.

But the quiet didn't last.

The blast shot the metal door from its bolts and it slammed into Nehi. He collided with Joe and Atif, and the three of them hit the wall, pressed against it by the heavy iron door. Fire burst around the metal, licking the walls and heating the door. Then the noise hit. The bang slammed through Nehemiah's insides and he felt as if it punched through his ears and crushed his head. Nehi saw the fire hit the young soldier. It consumed him, too fast for the man to even scream.

The flames fell away as fast as they came. The red hot door crushed Nehemiah, and he felt Joe and Atif squirming beside him, trying to push it off. His limbs hung stunned, burnt and useless, his head singing so hard he knew he wasn't fully there.

A hand reached around the door. Even in that moment, Nehemiah recognized the olive skin, the strong thin fingers that wrapped around the SOLTD hanging half off Atif's belt. The hand snapped the belt and disappeared with the SOLTD. Nehi's neck burned with a different kind of heat as he felt the warmth of those fingers holding him helpless in his chair again. A gasp ripped through his lungs, and with it came a desperate need to move. To be free of this pressing weight. To be free enough to defend himself.

Nehi flung his weight against the door. His strength added to Joe and Atif's and the door tipped, then hit the ground. Ash

and smoke furled away from it in a cloud. It must have made a fearsome clang, but Nehi heard nothing except the ringing in his ears as he gasped and leaned hard against the wall. Atif staggered up the hall, his greatcoat smoking, his hands and face burnt, smoke trailing from the right side of his hair. He stumbled to one knee, and Nehi could see his breath shudder through him.

Joe's hand landed on Nehemiah's shoulder. The mute tugged, his fingers biting and strong, his green eyes burning. The mute shot down the hall, his cane gone, the bumpy leather on his left arm trailing a thin line of smoke, his cast half blasted away. He dragged Nehi along with him. Nehemiah staggered several yards behind, obeying the pull. Joe shuddered as his left ankle buckled, and his hand tightened on his friend's shoulder like a vice. It lifted Nehi out of his shock. He shifted forward, slid an arm under the mute's shoulders, and started to move without being pulled; Joe's urgency burned off the mute into Nehi, and he raced through the hallways.

The two young men dodged past soldiers shouting and pounding down the hall toward the explosion, ducked those trying to block their way, leapt over those still on the ground with their ringing heads in their hands. In half a minute they raced up the stairs and burst into the crisp air of the courtyard. Anna and Beau raced toward them.

Joe's face seared into Anna; pale, thin lines sharp and stiff, eyes wide and burning, alarm radiating off his taut muscles. In that instant she felt the danger Daniel posed to all Joe held sacred. And she believed it. The truth shuddered through her as if someone poured molten metal into her veins.

Her own brother was the wolf in the flock. Heat flushed her as she shook, and a dry sob ripped from her throat.

Nehi swayed beside the mute, blinking in the bright sunlight. His head still swam and as he stood still he felt his limbs tingling with the physical shock of that explosion. But something was wrong with the sunshine, something dimmed it somewhere... Nehi blinked toward the odd darkness and found himself staring up at the bronze dome, the crowning

monument on the Judge's House; under that dome mosaics spoke of the lawgivers, and the kingdom's precious book rested on a marble pillar. He vaguely registered Joe signing words Nehi didn't recognize at the chimera and pulling a little box from his coat pocket. But most of Nehi stayed focused on the dome.

A jagged hole stared at the sky, sharp edges bent inward, as if someone had punched through the bronze metal. Shifting darkness played from it, punctuated with sharp white lights, lightning bolts or laser fire. Or both. Nehi stared at it, unblinking, slowly grasping what he saw. A SOLTD pulsed inside the room. It must have been programed to enter from the outside. A daring, dangerous maneuver... But why was it still running? Tanzid's voice rang in Nehi's memory, *"Weapons. Messy, bad ones you can't guard against because they just pop up, tearing everything around them apart."* His stomach tightened and he felt his breath snatched from him as he stared. For an instant the darkness of the SOLTD disappeared. Then a dense blackness shot off, something so fast Nehi registered it like the white dots that cut into his vision when he went inside from a bright day.

The sun dimmed and freezing power cut into Nehi as Joe's SOLTD flashed into life. His joints screamed and Anna clutched at his arm. Another started in front of the twins, manipulating gravity and dragging their bodies toward it, the freezing wind tearing at them.

Both SOLTDs zipped off, and Nehi sagged, gasping for breath, his skin tingling with the cold on his burns. The Ravens were gone. Around them soldiers poured out of the cellars, rushing toward the Judge's House. He began to hear the voices through the ringing in his ears and the dead numbness in his mind. Yelling. Shouted orders. Up in that domed room a dying wail drifted gently into silence. He had heard too many of those last night during the fighting. Nehi gripped his stomach feeling like he was about to be sick and his knees wobbled. A part of him realized it had only been a minute since the explosion, a certain amount of physical shock was normal. But he knew that

was only a small part of it.

The Ravens were gone. Chasing Daniel. The two Ravens went separate places, obviously, since they took two SOLTDs, but... Joe was off somewhere in the world hunting Daniel, ready to engage in a final standoff with his great enemy. Where did that leave Nehi? Surely the enemy couldn't be among those three, his closest brothers! A wail like the one that had echoed from the Judge's House shuddered through Nehemiah's insides. It drowned out the thoughts and he let the numbness take him again. Nehi focused on the sensations around him.

Anna's grip on his arm hurt. The courtyard began to clear as everyone poured into the House toward the scene of the destruction. Sunshine and distant shouts swirled around him. Nehemiah leaned down and picked up a little black box lying against the toe of his boot. He and anna stared at it.

"Joe's tracker," Anna breathed. Nehi nodded, looking at the numbers saved on the little device. Anna's face was the color of ash, but her lips tightened. "I'll find Tanzid and the others and send you backup. You go after him, now."

Anna's fingers left his arm and she started to run, a white streak dashing across the courtyard toward the house. Nehi stared at the numbers. Go after him...did she mean as support, or a hunter? And which *him*? Nehemiah's eyes closed and a sharp breath dragged into his lungs. He didn't know. He didn't know anything right now, all of reality felt in flux, a strange place with no solidity under his feet. He let the numbness slide over him again and pounded toward the hall where his SOLTD waited. He didn't know where he was going, or what he would do. But Anna was right.

Somewhere out there death stalked as a Raven and a Wolf hunted each other.

He had to find them, now.

Anna's soul screamed at her as she bolted toward the House, the faces of her brothers and the Ravens swimming in

front of her. But she channeled the desperation and horror tearing her apart inside, letting it flow into energy that shot her forward. She had to find out what had happened to their book, regroup their people, and send Nehi help in whatever situation he ended up in out there. Should she have sent him on his own? For an instant horrible doubt raged in her, with visions of her twin lying bloodied and dead somewhere. But she shut it out and ran. Too late now.

Anna spun through the servant's door and darted up the winding, dusty stairs. She could hear people shouting confused orders and questions on the other side of the wall as she moved steadily upward. But no one remembered this shortcut, and she knew she ran ahead of the crowd.

Anna darted up the last stairway and spun onto the top floor. At the end of the hall, the huge doors to the room of the book were flung open. One hung crooked, the hinge twisted and broken. Anna's breath came in sharp little spurts as she darted past the open door.

A pool of light spilled through the rent hole in the roof. Broken tiling from the mosaic and pieces of wood and metal from the ceiling littered the floor. Torn, white pieces of paper fluttered around her feet.

Pieces of men littered the room too.

John Mickelson leaned against the wall, his clothes ripped and bloodied, his Brunhiem rifle bent at a ninety-degree angle. Anna's eyes darted past him, registering the eight other men staggering back to their feet. And the one writhing near the center of the room. A young man with jet black hair, like Nehemiah's, and half his leg gone. Anna's steps never slowed. She darted into the room, snatched a rifle from a soldier swaying on the broken tiling his eyes glassy with shock, and kept going to the black-haired one. The rifle snapped up to her shoulder, and horrified shouts rang around her. She vaguely noted Mickelson straightening with a jerk and fumbling for his broken laser as he stared at her with panic on his face, and three of the soldiers darting forward to tackle her. Then she pulled the trigger.

The white blast hit the soldier directly on his severed knee. His scream rang through the vaulted room, and the shouts rose in volume around her. But Mickelson's yell drowned out the others.

"Back, don't touch her!" he roared. The three soldiers staggered back a step, slipping on the slick ground as they obeyed. "She cauterized it." Eyes turned toward their mate, shaking on the ground. The stump of his leg flecked with ash and stank like burnt meat. But the blood flow had stopped. For a few moments at least. Help should come before it started seeping past the burnt flesh. Anna flung the rifle to the nearest soldier and tore the white jacket from her dress. She knelt beside the black-haired one, carefully tucking the coat around him and giving him a smile.

"You did well," she told him, and ran a hand over his forehead to get the sweaty hair out of his eyes. She could feel his clammy skin and the shock shaking him violently. He was far from out of danger. "Let Jesus hold you. Lie still and pray, soldier, then you can go home for leave."

The crowds from the house finally began to trickle through the door. A medic trotted over and knelt on his other side. Anna swept to her feet, dismissing him to better prepared hands, and let her focus turn to the rest of the room.

Her eyes went to the papers fluttering around her feet. Starkly white until they found the sticky crimson of the floor. She picked out marble pebbles that used to be a pillar and shreds of ancient leather. Her gaze shot up and focused on John Mickelson. Samuel stood by his side, and she noticed his arm under the commander's shoulder, giving him support as Harry ripped the fabric from Mickelson's right arm and began to wrap the shredded skin with bandages. Mickelson met her eyes as the bandages quickly turned from white to bright red.

"Your brother," he said, his voice tight and confused. "A SOLTD landed in the center of the room and just kept running. It tore apart my men, and..." He swallowed hard and Anna could see his jaw tremble before he went on. "The book. He kept it running, the black ball just kept pulling and ripping...nothing

we fired did any good, and the longer it ran the more it ripped... He turned it off for an instant to reprogram it, and that's when I knew it was Daniel, but he had a Kerr on, and we couldn't... The book is gone. Sucked into that black ball." It came out in a rush, despair shaking it. Anna's eyes went to the paper shreds again.

Blank papers.

"Don't loose hope, Mickelson," she ordered. Her voice cut through the sobs and horrified murmurs in the room. "Learn from the Raven. Even the blackness can be turned into a weapon that fights for you."

"Who?" Mickelson murmured, his face pale as the second wad of bandages steadily turned bright red.

"You don't fight alone," Anna just answered him. She swept toward the door. "Where's Tanzid and Peter?" she demanded of the crowd in the doorway.

"They can't do anything to fix this," David Young muttered, despair slurring his words as he stared at the wreckage with terrified awe. Anna felt her hand tingle in the desire to slap him. Every muscle in her was tight, her heart pounding and her head singing with her pulse.

"I don't want them to fix this! Joe and Nehi followed the enemy responsible, and they're out there alone," she snapped.

"How do you know that?" David blinked at her.

"She's right," Atif broke in from the back of the crowd. Every eye turned to see the grim young warrior leaning heavily on the big Otar, half his face and both hands blistered, his greatcoat shredded.

"What happened?" David snapped.

"One of the soldiers I conscripted turned. The Wolf must have charmed him first. He slid in place when I ordered a search of the prisoner, and heaven help me I let him do it instead of doing it myself."

"Where is this traitor?" Mickelson thundered.

"Dead. He stood beside me when the Wolf blasted his way out, and the fire incinerated him." *That was purposeful*, Anna's brain supplied, and she felt her heart hiccupping inside her at

the picture of the real Daniel rearranging inside her. *He ordered him beside Atif, because he didn't want a living witness able to explain his real work here.* Atif's eyes flicked to her. "As I made it out of the cellars I saw Joe watch the SOLTD flash away, and then he and the chimera zipped off. Nehemiah is also missing. We don't know where any of them went."

"They're out there somewhere, fighting a desperate, dangerous enemy determined to get revenge," Anna said, and spun on the rest of those in the doorway. "I have the coordinates we need to go after them. Stop standing there staring and gear up!"

Chapter 15: Ruins and Shadows

"Rejoice not against me, O mine enemy: when I fall, I shall arise; when I sit in darkness, the LORD shall be a light unto me." Micha 7:8

The ancient trees stood gnarled and bent, huge monuments to time. Tillandsias hung in their twisted branches like colored paper lanterns at a party. The tall meadow grasses rustled in the breeze and it sounded as if they laughed and chattered at the solemn old trees standing sentinel around them.

The huge building resting in the midst of the grasses and trees seemed utterly out of place. A crumbling giant, it loomed over the far side of the meadow, a stark outsider with its unnatural concrete. Windows broken, doors hanging off their hinges, a hole torn in the metal roof. A lost artifact of a past era, neglected and forgotten.

Until today.

A black ball of terrifying power flashed into life in the meadow. It whined and pulsed, and the laughing grass tore up from their roots and swirled into a tornado around it. The blackness mushroomed up and sucked into the two balls on the edge of the wand. A black glove dropped the copper wand as the blackness still hissed into it. The SOLTD bounced into the soft earth of the meadow, and the Raven darted away, ducking underneath the grass till the light turned green around him.

All the secrets, all the years of lonely work, all the dreams gently laid aside to die, it all brought him to this. Adrenaline danced through Joe's veins as the grass whipped the black leather of his mask. He could feel the strength he had so carefully hoarded already seeping away, and his ankle ached beneath the jury-rigged brace tied on with strips of leather.

The Wolf waited for him at that ruined building.

And the Raven ran half plucked, a grounded, pitiful thing limping to his last fight.

He wouldn't need that SOLTD to take him back.

184

The light changed from green to bright white as he neared the building and the grass grew shorter and sparser. Joe paused where the grass barely covered him, staring into the muddy wasteland surrounding the ancient concrete building. His ankle pulsed and his eyes tightened with the pain as he studied the area, finding the strategic positions, memorizing the layout, and searching for the perfect entry point. Part of him stayed focused on the work. But he let a part of him, the Joe deep inside the Raven, free for just a moment; he lifted into a prayer, soft and sad and ready.

Jesus, I'm here. You've kept me alive for this purpose, to stand between the enemy of your people and preserve this one light for a dark world. Oh Jesus, I need help. I don't expect to come out of it alive. I'm not asking for that kind of miracle, I'm content with where You've led me. I'm not needed after this, I know. But Oh Jesus, please let me protect them. Don't let the Wolf destroy those boxes, and don't let him leave to finish slaughtering your people. I'm here. Use me to protect Your own, one last time.

The Raven focused on a gray square cut into the wall, four feet off the ground, the remains of a corrugated door hanging off it in rusted shreds. His entry point.

A black figure darted through the mud wastes, his boots hardly touching the ground. The tail of his mask sailed behind him in epic swirls at his speed, as the Raven flew toward one last fight.

The dust of centuries soared up around the black boot and danced into the sunbeams slanting through the huge broken doorway. The light shifted, plunging the dust motes into darkness, as the Wolf blocked the light.

Daniel watched the lighting change in this ruined building, eyed the one rusted hinge holding up the fifteen-foot door, and listened for any sound of approach from outside. There wouldn't be. He alone knew of this place. There had been one other, but she was a trusting fool and it had been ridiculously

simple to snap her neck. But it still paid to be cautious.

A trail of boot prints imprinted in the dust behind him as he walked past the broken windows letting the slanting sunbeams into the dark ruin. On his other side machines stood silent and lost. Let them stay lost. It wasn't good for business for these ancients to be discovered. A few more days, and he would have Ariel in his claws, and then all of these antiques could twist and melt.

For now he just had to remove the boxes. One flame should do it in this dry air. A slanting sunbeam cut through the last broken window in the line. A little smile flitted over the Wolf's scarred face as the beam played over the crates. Eighteen of them, simple wooden squares stacked neatly against the crumbling concrete wall. Revenge was so easy in this book base age. It was time to keep it easy. The light shining on the crates flickered and died as the Wolf stepped in front of the last window. He pulled a spring gun from his fur-covered greatcoat and leisurely slipped four firebombs into the clear barrel. A whistled "To Do and Dare" slid from him into the gray dustiness of the ruin. It bounced off the walls to echo back at him, and Anna's voice sang in his mind. He saw her dancing in his arms, Nehi laughing and singing along behind them. His smile died.

A scowl cut over Daniel's face as he snapped the gun to his shoulder and fired. The firebomb sailed in a perfect arch for the eighteen crates with their precious contents.

Two copper ovals clanged into the ground and rolled against the corners of the crates. The shimmering red of a Kerr shield sprung into the dim dustiness of the ruin. The firebomb hit the hexagonal shapes and deflected out. The Wolf leapt backward in a roll, curses growling from him. Flames blossomed into the air above the last window in the ruin and bloomed like a deadly orange rose. It consumed the dust, feeding off the detritus of centuries.

The Wolf gained his feet with the easy grace of a predator. He spun and focused on the shadow cast by a six foot monster of metal and plexiglass and rollers. His greatcoat flared in the heat of the flames as the fire played over his face with an orange

glow and reflected in his burning eyes.

Joe shuddered in the shadow of the machine, his body tingling as if those eyes pricked him with a hundred burning needles. The Raven held perfectly still, knowing his blocker ran strong and no scanners gave away his presence, the Wolf couldn't know he knelt here. But everything in Joe screamed at him to run. Green eyes stared into dark burning brown ones, filled with the fury and hatred only a human predator could obtain. Joe's lungs constricted as he shook in the shadows, just waiting for those clawed gloves to wrap around his throat. His eyes darted to the Kerr shield and the crates it protected. *"Lo, I am with you always...[9]"* The words slid through Joe like a cooling stream. His trembling muscles slowly relaxed.

The flames died. Dim dustiness crept back over the building.

The Wolf was gone.

The Raven blinked, his eyes darting everywhere, fear rushing through him. The enemy had disappeared. Gone to ground behind any of these hundreds of machines in this acre-wide ruin. The Raven slid a hologram disc into the corner near a broken side door. He pulled his black gloves over his leather ones as he slipped through the shadows, moving in a smooth, swift shuffle.

"I hear you..."

The walls caught Daniel's voice and sent it bouncing in echoes. It curled around Joe, and his aching muscles shuddered again. The Wolf hunted in the dark, with the crippled Raven as his prey. Joe let his eyes dart to the crates as he crept forward another foot. *"...we are more than conquerors through him that loved us[10]."* The truth cut through the panic, Joe sucked in a breath, and focused on the task of surviving a few more minutes.

"So you decided to come play again, Raven?" the Wolf called into the shadows. Dark, teasing amusement rode the words, and Joe's lips pursed tighter. "You really shouldn't have. You

---

[9] Matthew 28:20
[10] Romans 8:37

know revenge isn't just a pleasant pastime for me, it's part of my business."

"You have to keep up your reputation or no one would fear you enough to obey," the Raven agreed. The automated tones drifting from the hologram's speaker somehow fit in the midst of the ancient machines and concrete. Five yards away from the voice, Joe crept forward another foot, searching the shadows and watching the light patterns, every sense tingling, desperate to find his enemy. Running a blocker meant none of his own scanners worked either.

"I can't have the world thinking the Wolf has turned into a meek pussycat," Daniel agreed. The voice bounced and deflected off the concrete walls, and Joe couldn't pinpoint the speaker's position. "And you, Raven, oh you deserve a special kind of revenge. I admit I underestimated you, I never thought a GI beast could setup a con game intricate enough to last three years, and play even me. Are those journal pages even real?"

"They are real." The Raven slid under a long metal table loaded with stacks of huge white papers covered in gray dust. His eyes focused on the shadows between two machines eight yards ahead of him. Something moved there. "'Con' is too strong a word. I did not set it up, just left it for you to find. I hoped to identify the Wolf of the underworld. But you were too fast for me." Yes, something shifted in the shadows, a deeper patch of blackness. The Raven gripped his dart gun. He would have one shot, one opportunity to end this here. Joe shifted silently to the edge of his shadow, his eyes never leaving the dark blotch eight yards ahead of him. Was that the enemy? He needed to see it move again. "I never would have left it if I guessed you would start picking up Christians for information, and even kill your own country."

"Both were logical," Daniel answered, factual, steady, no regret riding even the undertones. "I couldn't snatch the most useful people for information, the Sojourners were too strong inside their own country. But Dad worked with the IDP enough someone there ought to have known something." *Move, darn it!* "And everyone gets tired of waiting eventually. I still say Mom

and Dad knew about that journal and never told me."

The black patch shifted a centimeter. The Raven jerked up on one knee. The pop of the little dart gun was swallowed by the dark. A sharp "ping" echoed back to Joe as his dart hit metal and sailed harmlessly off into the shadows. Joe spun, horror washing through him.

Gray fur filled his vision.

A glove slashed his hand, the black claws slicing through skin and muscle. A silent yell slid from the Raven as he dove to the right, his dart gun clattering to the ground. Fingers gripped his hair, the claws ripping through his mask and raking his scalp. A sharp kick sent his legs out from him, and Joe jerked back, flailing helplessly. Warm blood oozed down his head. An electric wrist cuff slid around his arms and a gasp broke from Joe. Daniel's laughter drowned it out, echoing off the walls.

Nehi's SOLTD peeled away, and he stared up at a giant of a gnarled tree. It towered hundreds of feet over his head, enormous tillandsias hanging in its branches like colorful balls a child had thrown and lost.

Everything good eventually gets lost. Nehi's eye twitched. He spun quickly to take stock of the area, forcing himself to focus on the task. Find Daniel and Joe. That's all he knew to do right now.

But once found, what next? Whose side was he on?

The questions screamed in him, and Nehi gasped into his military mask as his hands shook. Could Daniel really be...

Nehi focused on the area. A grassy meadow spread out in front of him, waving gently in the breeze, so peaceful... His eyes went to the patch of frozen mud he stood on, and the ripped up dying grass lying in a circle around it. *Destruction always comes. And we bring it.* He gave a violent shake and forced his back straight as he studied the area again. A few pieces of black and gray rocks lay under the grass, and he kicked one, turning it over. That looked like... He hit scan on his mask. It focused on

the rocks and flashed a probable date of origin as three hundred years ago. He was looking at the ancient remains of a road from the past world.

Nehi didn't feel the wonder. Not today. He hit the next button on the mask. Joe's tracker pulsed about an acre ahead, past the gnarled old tree towering in front of him. Nehi jogged forward. More black and gray rocks lay on his path every few feet. He moved out into a large meadow of the peaceful, long grass and his mouth dropped open. A huge building rose into the blue sky, blocking out the horizon. Its ancient cement crumbled, and the windows were black holes like hundreds of empty eye sockets in some vast creature.

His mask flashed a double warning and zoomed in on the corners facing him.

Two white packs of high explosives adhered to those corners. Four wires ran from them to an activation mechanism resting inside a gaping black rectangle of a doorway. Nehi blinked at it, trying to grasp what he was seeing. That was enough explosives to take out at least half that giant ruin, and probably most of this meadow too. Not to mention any living thing nearby. Nehi acknowledged the warnings and his mask went back to tracking.

Joe's tracker pulsed just on the other side of that wall.

Urgency slammed into Nehi like a physical blow. He stumbled into a run, pounding through the grass toward the ruin.

His mask suddenly shorted out, blocked by something running inside that huge building. Nehi swept it off, flung it into the grass, and put all his heart into his run.

"Two can lay out a decoy, Raven," the Wolf barked, amusement dancing on the words as he stared at the mute writhing in his claws.

Joe's left hand shot out. A ring of extra black leather stayed stuck to the cuff, a trap for the gadget. He palm struck the Wolf's chest. Three electric nodes flared into life. They caught the

Wolf's own electricity and blue lightning shot over his form, and on into Joe. But the Raven was prepared for it. Joe's good leg shot out as the nodes pulsed, smashing into Daniel's knee-cap with a snap kick. The Wolf hit the concrete ground, a furious roar breaking from him. Joe jerked free and rolled off into the shadows, his heart hiccupping with the electrical charge. He scrambled over the ground, dodging between two square metal machines. He slid down the aisle, immediately picked out the deepest shadows at the side of the ruin, and rolled into it. The Raven slid to a stop, panting hard, perched on his fingers and good foot, ready to spring. His green eyes raked the warehouse.

Gray dust floated gently in the air, catching the sickly beams of sunlight sliding through the broken windows. A hole in the ancient roof cast brighter beams farther toward the center. There was no sign of Daniel. Only the dust swirled and moved. The Raven's gaze fastened on the hole in the roof as he panted and tried desperately to gather his strength.

A blast of white laser fire hit the wall behind him, melting the concrete and killing his shadows.

The Raven kicked up into a cartwheel and turned it into a double flip that took him sharply deeper into the ruin and kept his weight on his hands.

"I hear you," the Wolf sang again. The words echoed around Joe as he moved, and his lined face tightened. His mind danced through options, sorting, rejecting, furiously searching for any way to cheat death a few minutes longer. Green eyes, crinkled with weary pain, darted to the crates behind the shimmering red wall. *The race is not to the swift...*[11] He pulled his movements back, deliberately slowing.

A white blast of light hit the wall a half a foot in front of his head; exactly where he would have been at his normal speed. The Raven rolled into the darkness of an eight-foot machine with paddles and metal blades. He sprang up and flew through the shadows. Joe could feel Daniel's footsteps pounding on the concrete. Rushing toward him.

---

[11] Ecclesiastes 9:11

"You can't hide from me, beasty!" The Wolf's voice swirled with the dust rising into the ruin in a steady cloud. Joe struggled to breathe as he zig-zagged, moving steadily closer to the middle of the building.

A gray figure spun into the beam of light streaming through the hole in the roof; his coat flared around his legs, the wolf's-head hood pulled over his hair so that only a little smile could be seen playing over his scarred face. A small copper pen glinted in his hands. Joe's lips pursed as he recognized his own Dark Ray. When he switched guns on Daniel in the hall, it seemed the Wolf had also been busy. The Raven never stopped moving, his green eyes shining as he calculated. He darted straight for the Wolf. His old-fashioned projectile pistol barked twice in quick succession, the noise echoing like thunder off the walls. One bounced harmlessly off the body armor on the Wolf's chest, the other hit directly in his forehead and seemed absorbed by the lead-lined gray fur.

A cone of pure black shot from the ray. It cut over Joe, his body bent nearly double as he dashed forward. He felt the sting of the cold, and his joints popped as the PUDRE effect tugged in opposite directions. But behind him, where the main force hit, he heard metal and wood rip apart as it was sucked into the blackness. For an instant he remembered the drip of a little cave and an inner voice quietly telling him to leave Dark Ray on high... Then the yellow sunbeam touched Joe's mask, and the next three seconds went by in a blur of movement.

The Wolf's claw slashed out at his head. The Raven grabbed the forearm as it swept toward him and used it like a gymnast's bar. He spun under it and shot up, legs held close together, spine straightening as he moved perpendicular to the cement floor. One hand shot out, and a black line sailed toward the hole in the roof. Out of the corner of his eye, he saw gray fur swiping at him. Joe's other hand pushed off his enemy and lifted, and for a fraction of a second he hovered in midair, suspended by nothing but his own momentum. One bloodied finger hit the button on his belt to retract his rope. The other hand shot out and a little blade sprung into his palm. The blade met gray glove as

the claws swiped at his face. A howl came from the Wolf, and Joe fumbled for Dark Ray as it tumbled from Daniel's numb fingers.

The Wolf's head smashed into Joe's. Everything went black. His muscles went limp, and utter terror flooded him as he could not call them back. A sharp metallic tinkle reached his ears as the PURDRE bounced onto the cement ground and rolled away. The Wolf's claws touched his face. Before they could bite, his rope retracted, and dry air whipped around Joe as he jerked toward the ceiling. Sharp claws ripped across his forehead and a silent cry of pain came from him.

Daniel's face contorted in a scowl, his scarred half mottled red and white in his fury. His hand darted for his SOLTD, ready to rip the Raven to pieces. His fingers fumbled in an empty sling. Daniel's gaze shot up. A copper SOLTD glinted in Joe's bloodied glove.

Sharp, furious, hate-filled curses rang around the Raven as he flew toward the sunshine.

Chapter 16: The Cache

"For where your treasure is, there will your heart be also."

Matthew 6:21

Nehemiah pulled on the last wire with infinite care, his tongue sticking from between his teeth. It slowly slid out of the white explosives with a soft slucking sound. A short beep came from the activator box. Nehi sagged in relief, his legs weak as he stepped back from the horrifying white paste. A groan broke from him as he lifted the box and heaved it away. It rolled into the meadow and disappeared, swallowed by the four-foot grass. At least that whiteness couldn't be exploded by the touch of a button now.

Exhaustion pulled at Nehemiah's limbs. How long had he been up? Twenty-four hours? Probably longer. He steadied himself, and focused on the black door yawning in front of him. Nehi suddenly found he had Hope in his hands. He stared down at her, the Compton's weight pulling at him. Joe and Daniel laughing around the campfire on one of their hundreds of days of travel slid through his mind and his hand shook. Nehi slid the laser back in her holster strapped to his thigh and stepped through the door.

Dim light fell over him and swirling dust flew into his face. Nehi held back a cough and stepped to the side, out of the light spilling through the doorway. His hip bumped a stack of wooden crates, covered in gray dust. They stood in a line eighteen long, stretching across the wall. He didn't try to guess what might be in them. He didn't have the energy.

Sharp curses bounced off the walls and drifted to him in whispers of sound. But even in whispers, he could hear the deep hatred that filled the words. Nehi recognized his brother's voice. The years swirled up into the young man's mind, that voice intertwined with so much living, so much... The curses rose louder, deep and malicious, spewing into a promise that rang through the ruin.

"I'll tear everything you've worked for apart, Raven! You've seen me do it before, it only takes a moment to destroy

everything you've spent years sweating to protect." The voice mixed with the memories swirling in Nehi, but it twisted them into nightmares burning inside him. How long had Daniel been living a double life? "I'll send the 'proof' the IDP are book thieves, and it will be believed. Add one quick note to the UPC that the Sojourner's don't really have their book, a nudge to KAM about the mines the invaders missed in the mountains, a few incentives thrown out in the underworld. Maybe even a loan of a few SOLTDs. The ones who die first in this hunt will be the lucky ones." How long had Daniel been this...monster? A sob broke from Nehi and he stood rigid and sick, staring into the dim ruin trying to tell where the voice came from. "I'll start here, Raven, I know why you came. You'll watch it sucked to nothing before I tear into you!"

A black cone closed over the crates farthest from Nehi. A gasp broke from him as freezing blackness hit him in the side. It tugged him violently to the right. He fell between the crates and the wall, fighting a scream as his joints popped and every sinew seemed torn apart. Wood ripped from the boxes and concrete jerked from the wall and crumbled into dust.

The ray shifted, and the debris thudded back under gravity's pull. A chunk of concrete settled with a sharp thud, pinning Nehi's leg against a box. The roof above him ripped apart and concrete rocks and metal shingles cascaded onto Nehemiah. A six-foot metal shingle shaved off the top of his hair as it slammed on the boxes and cut into the wall, shutting out his light. Debris rattled on top it with sharp thuds and pings, and Nehi ducked away from the dents poking into his skull, choking, half blinded by dust, whimpering as the dark closed him in a tight prison. The box beside Nehi's head cracked open under the strain, and its contents poured out, burying him deeper. Panic flooded him. He fought wildly to pull his arms free, hyperventilating in the dark. A sharp corner cut into his cheek, and Nehi gasped and shoved it away.

His fingers brushed paper.

Everything around him dropped suddenly into a surreal unreality. His entire focus went to the thing under his fingers. A book. He could feel it, nothing else had those papery corners and delicious shape. One sick shaft of light cut through the corner of his prison, and through the swirling dust and pressing weight, Nehi saw a rectangular, priceless, miraculous book. Two words stared at him, embossed on the simple black cover.

Holy Bible.

His stinging eyes sought through the dark as his fingers grubbed among the weights pressing into him. Ten, twenty, maybe fifty of them spilling from this crate! These weren't like the ancient filigreed leather one kept by his country. These were old, yes, but pristine, simple, almost in perfect condition. Nehi gasped again, dimly wondering if he was in a strange dream, a part of the detached numbness that claimed him when his life fell in pieces. The Bible under his hands fell open and the dirty beam played over the page. The phrases punched into his sick heart.

"For God, who commanded the light to shine out of darkness, hath shined in our hearts, to give the light of the knowledge of the glory of God... We are troubled on every side, yet not distressed; we are perplexed, but not in despair; ... For our light affliction, which is but for a moment, worketh for us a far more exceeding and eternal weight of glory...[12]."

Nehemiah's raging soul settled into a smooth sea as the truth of the words sunk into him. The numbness from denial sped away, as his heart remembered it was bound with iron bands of eternity that would not let it burst. Everything else could shift and turn into destruction and monsters. But God never changed; and his Father still held him fast.

As suddenly as it had come, the peace shifted into a steady flow of purpose. His hands shot up and shoved against the metal shingle. Daniel was trying to destroy these Bibles, this precious treasure holding the light of God's knowledge. Nehi would not let that happen. The weight of the concrete pressed into him, and he couldn't feel his leg. But the thought of Joe filled him, out there in trouble alone, giving everything in him to protect this miracle. Nehi knew where he belonged. Between Daniel and the Raven; between his brother and this priceless

---

[12] 2 Corinthians 4:6-18

treasure. In a sudden burst of strength, Nehi tugged his legs free and struggled to his knees in the silt and rocks and books. He shoved his shoulders under the shingle, drew in a sharp breath, blew out a prayer, and shoved. He felt his burnt skin tearing and his muscles shaking. His eyes closed and he pushed harder.

The world came back to Joe in a series of white dots and fuzzy sensations. Dry wind tore into him and he could hear the "zip" of his rope retracting. He forced himself to move, and one hand reached clumsily for the rope. The Raven landed on his fingers and one good foot. The clang of the SOLTD against the metal sheeting on this flat roof rang like a bell.

"I'll tear everything you've worked for apart, Raven," the Wolf roared from below him. *You have to get out first,* Joe thought, shaking with exhaustion. He stumbled to his feet as the Wolf kept yammering, hauled up the SOLTD, and heaved it like a discus. It spun beautifully in the sunlight, landed in the four-foot meadow grass, and disappeared. Joe staggered, breathing in wheezing gasps. His ears suddenly pricked and he paid attention to Daniel's words again. "I'll start here, Raven, I know why you came. You'll watch it sucked to nothing before I tear into you!"

Horror spread through Joe in a spiderweb of tingling urgency. He leapt to the hole and peered in. A cone of light-eating darkness swept over the crates. A silent scream ripped from Joe as if the pain of the breaking wood cut into his own flesh and blood. But his hands already moved. Drawing the enemy's fire. That's all he could count on, the Wolf was too good to let a bullet end his career. But he could pull the Wolf's teeth from the books to sink into the crippled raven.

His hands shot up with his projectile pistol. He poised over the hole, the toes of his good foot gripping the edge. The Wolf saw his enemy's movement. Daniel swiveled out of the light. The black cone shot up toward the roof, eating a jagged line in

the ceiling before it cut off. The crack of Joe's pistol broke through the still air, the echo thundering off the walls. The gray coat swirled up over Daniel's head and the magnetic plates inside caught the bullet and bound it to the lead-lined fabric. The Wolf whipped toward Joe as his coat swirled back in place, his body rigid, his face flaming.

The sun struck the metal sheeting and reflected up at the bloodied Raven as he swayed, exhausted, and grim. But he would not just stand here and take it. In a blur of movement, he snatched his new collapsible hoverboard, unfolded it, slid his good foot into the slot, and hit the power. The steam pushed off the roof and he shot forward. The Raven leaned into the movement, trying to balance as the board wobbled on the corrugated metal sheets.

Cold stung him. A cone of blackness cut through the hole and devoured the light. Concrete and metal crumpled, folding in on itself. The roar of the roof tearing apart covered everything. Joe's board wobbled, his foundation falling away behind him as the roof folded on itself and disappeared down into the ruin. The board hesitated, spitting and sputtering as the back jets found nothing to push against but air. Joe dropped to a crouch and gripped the front with his hands, willing it forward. The front jets caught and the board leapt off.

The destruction followed him. Metal roofing sheets ripped and twisted behind him, shrieking in their agony. The thunder of falling debris echoed up from the ruin below. A thick, jagged line cut through the roof, metal and concrete bubbling like a monstrous soup, chasing a small hunched figure in black.

The roof bubbled in front of his board. Joe slewed to the side as a hole melted in his path. A firebomb sailed through the hole.

"Let's see you fly, Raven!" Daniel roared.

Joe's left arm shot out in a desperate side strike. The bumpy tail lizard skin hit the firebomb. It shot back three feet, and burst into a fiery flower. Heat slammed into Joe like a giant's fist. His body lifted into the air and spun, the steam from his board creating a white cloud around him. The flames cut through his clothes, shredding and melting, and scorched his skin. Hot metal roof tiles slammed into him, and in a dim haze,

Joe felt himself slipping into a dark hole.

Oh help! Joe found the prayer rushing from him as concrete dust filled his nose and eyes, and he spun into a free fall. The Wolf waited for him thirty feet below. Joe twisted and spread his gliding wings. He could hear the wind whistling through the flapping tatters of their shreds. But there was just enough material left to catch his fall and send it into a steep glide deeper into the building. Joe kicked his board around and hit the steam on high. The jets pushed off the ground, slowing his landing a fraction.

Concrete flooring cracked under his board and Joe felt as if every bone in his body cracked with it. He thudded into a roll, dragging his burnt skin over the concrete. A metal machine met his back with a sharp clang. Joe's spine shuddered, then his body turned slowly, and he crashed face first on the ground.

The Raven lay in a heap of black leather and concrete dust, ash flaking off his burnt clothes, every muscle and bone shrieking at him. His mind sparked. But the thought of the Wolf out there kept him conscious. The Wolf and those precious, precious boxes. Joe gasped and sobbed, and tried to drag himself up. But nothing in him felt capable of movement.

In the shadows to his right he heard the Wolf hunting.

Just a shuffle of movement. So small a sound amid the debris still settling from the jagged line torn in the roof.

Move! the voice inside Joe yelled at him. He shifted his elbows under him and levered his body up. *You're in the open. Move, now!* His fingers found the top of the machine as his right foot planted on the ground and pushed. A silent scream ripped from him as Joe dragged himself upright, leaning heavily against the machine. His vision sparked, but the voice inside drove him on. In the open he was nothing but target practice.

The Raven staggered into the shadows.

"I hear you..." the Wolf sang after him. Joe dragged a breath through the dust and the sharp stabs of pain from his ribs, and lunged for another machine. His foot dragged across the ground with a sharp scrape, and he couldn't keep the gasp back as his burnt hands caught the edge of something surrounded by plexiglass. He couldn't move in silence, not like this, not with

one good leg. No, even that leg only half worked. The muscles felt torn apart. Joe's shaking hand slid into his shredded jacket. He pulled out a second pair of black gloves. Two bloody handprints shone on the metal as he hopped awkwardly into the deeper darkness on the other side of this monster of metal and plastic.

The Wolf's chuckle followed him. Playing with his prey.

A shudder ran through Joe, shaking his thin shoulders. But he pushed his hands into the gloves.

"You think you have everything going your way," the staccato voice of the Raven cut through the ruined building. A smile twisted over Daniel's face. He took two steps closer, his laser swinging in his hand.

"Oh, but I do, Beasty. You don't know everything."

Joe dragged himself to the edge of the ruin, into the deepest shadows. Behind him, the Wolf's footsteps rang against the concrete.

"I know I have been busy these past months while in bed." The footsteps paused. Joe drew in a breath and hopped farther away as his gloves moved in the dark. "I found your bank accounts, Wolf. Glue has been running errands for me."

"You little–" A sharp blast of laser fire cut off the furious growl. It met concrete wall, melting it into a liquid trail that bubbled toward the ground. But it lit the shadows for a fraction of a second. The tail of a black mask was just caught in the glow before it whisked away. The rifle shifted. The Raven pushed himself forward, dredging up the last drops from an inner well of strength. A second blast lit the shadows. A pinprick of pure sunshine flowed through the hole as the glow died. The Raven was nowhere in sight.

"You've just wanted the money all along," the Wolf growled, furious, iced with a hatred so deep it changed the tenor of his voice, deepening it and killing every hint of the bantering, cynical Daniel.

"You know me better than that, Wolf," the automated voice said from the corner of the warehouse. Half an acre away Joe dragged himself another foot forward. Even the salt from his own sweat hurt as it soaked into his burns and cuts. His gadgets

were dented, melted, and cracked. His body felt shredded. His last strength flitted off like the dying whisper of an old friend. He sank gently to his knees in the black shadow of a looming machine, blinking up at the huge white papers stacked neatly on the rollers. His hands still moved. Distracting, buying time for just a few seconds more. "Knowing me, what do you think I did with your money?" He watched the Wolf step into the beam of sunlight, four feet away from him, the dust cloud furling away with his movement. The gray fur on the coat stirred in a tiny breeze, and another shudder racked the Raven.

"You gave it back to the countries I took it from," the Wolf growled, his voice still deep with the hatred. "Anonymously, with some superstitious note attached. In your opinion its tainted with blood and tears, and you wouldn't sully your clean hands with that." The sarcastic irony of the words dripped like liquid fire through Joe's veins. The Wolf focused on the papers, gleaming white in the darkness. Joe watched as his enemy's eyes dropped to the black shadow underneath them. The Raven felt those dark eyes burning into his skin. Everything in him begged to run. To leap off and scramble away. But he couldn't. Joe held perfectly still, not breathing. Not blinking. Staring back into those dark, burning eyes. He saw death stalking in their depths.

The Wolf's black boots thudded against the concrete as he stepped closer. Joe's eyes dropped to the rifle. A prayer for it to fire, to end it quickly, slid from the Raven before he could stop it. There were only the two of them in this dim ruin. The Raven and the Wolf, and the hunt was over. His eyes closed slowly. The sharp thumps of the Wolf's steps jarred through Joe as he knelt in the shadows and waited. The steps stopped, two feet from him. Silence tingled in the dark.

"You wish I would fire," the Wolf whispered into Joe's ear. The mute pulled back, his lips opening in a silent cry, crushing himself against the metal machine. "End it quickly. But now that I have you, why should I?" A gray glove closed over his throat and squeezed. The Wolf drew him out of the shadows. "You've been such a pest, Raven. Since you were what? Thirteen? You've earned more than just a laser blast to the chest."

Joe found the Wolf's thumb and pulled; but he had no more strength than a child. His feet dangled as his hands pulled uselessly at the gray fingers clamped over his trachea. Memories began to slice through his marrow. Held helpless. Too young and small and weak to fight back. Joe writhed in the Wolf's claws, his vision starring and seeing scenes he could never forget. But newer scenes invaded too. Held by gentle hands, with a silver cross sparkling on a ring. Verses spouted from two friends laughing in the sunlight. A voice drifting from a bloodied crack in a dry desert oval... He wasn't alone. Never alone. Jesus held him, and he had a *home*. Joe's vision slowly blacked. But held helpless, death curling around him, a voice that wasn't really his cried out stronger than he had ever known it. Peace, freedom, love, it sang louder than any fear. A sharp longing to live a little longer, bring more people to know this voice, beat inside him. But his arm dropped to his side and he couldn't call it back. Death wrapped a little tighter around the Raven.

Heat cut through the gray glove and into the skin beneath. A sharp intake of breath came from the Wolf, and Joe gagged as the hand jerked, shaking the mute. The fingers shifted, and a wet cough rent from the Raven as he sucked in a breath. Two pairs of eyes shifted, picking out a third form through the cement dust and ash swirling around them like a gray snowstorm.

Nehi stepped into a shaft of light spinning from the torn ceiling. Black curls plastered against his head with sweat and dust, face drawn and caked with gray mud, pants ripped showing a bloody leg; but his shoulders were squared, his stance ready, everything about him set with a determination the Wolf and Raven both recognized. He would protect what needed it. Hope's copper glinted in the shaft of sunlight, her muzzle leveled at the Wolf's hand.

"Put him down gently, Dan." Nehemiah's voice didn't ring. It drifted out soft and sad, twisting with the gray dust in a dance of mourning. "Or the next shot will sever your hand from your body."

The Wolf didn't move, his face inscrutable as he stared at Nehi. The harsh rattle of the Raven fighting in a breath cut between them. Daniel's expression changed, rippling with

202

sadness, and even a little horror. His voice trembled, dripping with shocked hurt and sorrow.

"So you still choose a sneak thief and liar over your own brother?"

"Coming from you, right now, that's incredible irony. Put him down," Nehi ordered, his voice hardening. Daniel stared at him, hurt betrayal pouring from the injured older brother. But his fingers slid, rearranging their hold. Ready to crush Joe's trachea. The mute felt the movement; the Wolf, so sure he had the situation under control, so sure he had the whole world under control.

Nehi fired.

A yelp rent from Daniel. He pulled back, cradling his smoking wrist to his chest. Joe crumpled like a limp doll on the concrete. Nehemiah leapt forward, Hope swinging like a club at Daniel's head. The Wolf swept out of the way, all trace of the hurt brother gone, the flame back in his eyes. His hand slashed out, and Nehi ducked left, carefully keeping his weight centered. Knuckles glanced off his temple, and he saw stars in the dim swirling dust. He shot in, trying to get under Daniel's guard. His brother's fist slammed into his stomach. Pain flared through Nehi and his body folded on itself. But his leg shot out, hooked around Daniel's knee, and jerked back.

Daniel hit the ground with a thud that shook the floor under Nehi's feet. But the Wolf rolled up in an instant. He darted at Nehi. Nehemiah fell back a step and pulled Hope up. Daniel moved faster than Nehi ever knew he could, and batted the Compton away. A jab slammed into his kidney, and he folded over, pain flaying his insides. Nehi caught a flash of gray gloves headed for his belly, black claws glinting in the few stray pieces of light that pierced through the dust and ash.

A sharp cry rang from Daniel and he stumbled to one knee. Joe's dirk stuck out of his leg like a perverse syringe. The Wolf staggered back, cursing under his breath, one hand going to the blade in his leg. The other slid under his coat. Joe's eyes widened, and a spasm went through him as he tried to jump for his enemy.

"You two meddlers, watch it all twists and flame!" Daniel

cried in a furious growl. His thumb hit a button. Nothing happened. Nehi straightened with an effort.

"I disconnected it," he said in a strained grunt. "There is no box."

Heat flushed Daniel's face, murderous anger swelling the veins on his neck. A sharp, short whistle came from Joe and Nehi's gaze shot to him. Two fingers ran along the concrete: "Move!" Nehemiah lunged forward, dodging under the Wolf's swipe as he roared, black claws aimed at his brother's back. Nehi swept up the tattered bundle of his friend and sprinted behind the nearest machine, a looming box with rollers and screens and a hole gaping inside it ready to suck something in. He knelt on the ground, shifted Joe to one shoulder, and carefully leaned around the edge of his cover.

Daniel was gone. Melted into the shadows.

Gray dust and ash swirled everywhere. An eight-foot piece of concrete broke from the crack in the ceiling, tumbled to the ground, and exploded with a deafening bang. More concrete dust mushroomed out into the air, swirling and covering everything. Nehi held back a cough as he tried to breathe.

"Where is he, curse him," he growled. A click came from Joe and he looked at his torn little friend.

"Let me go," Joe signed, each movement a jerky, tortuous thing.

"I'm not leaving you with him on the loose!" Nehemiah hissed. Everything in him felt strung to the breaking point. He felt like that block of concrete, lost in a free fall and then exploded into a million tiny shreds. "I should have stayed to take him down!"

"Can't win in hand to hand," Joe signed. "Take the shot if you have it, don't underestimate him. Now turn off blocker. Warn them. You have to keep her safe."

"I can't just leave you here," Nehi blurted. "With him on the loose, you could be–"

"I'm protected." A smile tweaked the corners of Joe's blistered face, and for an instant the green eyes gained their

twinkle as they glanced back at the boxes. "'*Nor height, nor depth*[13],' remember?" His eyes darted around the machine, and one finger gestured out. *Go.* Nehi obeyed, his muscles aching and seeming like someone else's arms. He propped Joe gently against the machine, trying to ignore the gasp from the little mute, and stole into the aisle between the two machines.

A gray blizzard swirled around him, swallowing the broken Raven and enclosing him in his own private nightmare.

Nehi stole forward in a crouch, moving the direction Joe had pointed. He couldn't hear anything but the building wailing as the destruction settled; rocks and metal sheets falling with great clanging booms, slipping from their piles of rubble to smash into more rubble. Ancient artifacts of a past civilization rose around him in the gloom. Sweat soaked him, trickling into his eyes in muddy gray streams. Nehi slid under a metal table stacked with huge papers, and peered out into an aisle between the looming machines. He could see his entry point, the side door next to the splintered boxes. The precious books spilled onto the floor.

"Look up," a speaker in the corner spouted Joe's words. Nehi's attention snapped to the ceiling. A small circle sailed in a gentle arch toward the crates. Hope leapt up, and an invisible gamma ray hit it.

Firey orange blossomed inside the ruin, spraying out and lighting everything for an instant. Nehi started back as the firelight revealed a tall figure in the corner in gray fur, a wolf's snarling head where the face should be. The empty eye sockets stared straight at Nehi.

"And I thought a quick little push of a button would take care of everything here," Daniel's voice echoed off the walls. The firebomb played out above them, leaving more ash and smoke swirling. Daniel flicked the hood off his head and stepped through the door into the bright sunlight. He stood still, studying the grass. Looking for his activator box? "You've turned into one of the Raven's little pets, Nehi, running his errands, dancing to his music...I should have taken care of you

---

[13] Romans 8:39

months ago."

"You've tried." Nehi stepped into the aisle, Hope held in front of him. Daniel turned and brown eyes stared into brown eyes as gray dust and ash swirled between the brothers. Nehi kept Hope aimed at Daniel's heart. Daniel's hands hung empty at his side, but that meant nothing; Nehi knew now how fast he could move. "You ruined our country. Your agents murdered our parents. You sent... It was you that sent me into Abid's hands!" The Compton wavered and shook, and anguish scored Nehi's face. A breath sucked into him, wet and harsh. "Why? You've always known the truth, how could you... Why?"

"Why reject your 'Truth'? Mainly because I don't like what He says about how I have to live. *'Do unto others as you would have them do to you[14],' 'Thou shalt not steal[15],' 'Thou shalt not covet[16],' 'The love of money is the root of all evil[17],' 'Thou shalt not commit adultery[18].'* All those lovely things Mother and Father made sure we all learned. Not for me, Nehi. I grew out of those fast." He turned, his movements almost lazy, staring back out at the grass. Nehi noticed the bloodied bandage tied around his brother's leg. Fear shot through Nehemiah, flashing with the memory of those black claws headed straight for his belly; Daniel would kill him.

Nehi flung himself to the side as he squeezed two shots from Hope. A white light shot the shadows to pieces beside him, and his leg went limp. He caught a glimpse of Daniel, dark eyes peering over his shoulder, the hidden muzzle of his laser melding with the gray fur of his coat. Hope's shots seared into the back of the coat at the shoulder. But they didn't leave a mark on the skins under the fur. Nehi slammed into the ground behind a cover of a metal machine of rollers and plexiglass.

Daniel had tried to kill him.

It screamed through him, louder than any yet, and Nehi couldn't shut it out. A sob broke from him as he sat up and

---

[14] Matthew 7:12
[15] Exodus 20:15
[16] Exodus 20:17
[17] 1 Titus 6:10
[18] Exodus 20:14

reached for the wound starting to pulse in his thigh. That shot had been meant for his stomach. And he hadn't even touched Dan yet. *"Take the shot if you have it."* He had tried. Nehi glanced back at the door, his mind still swirling as his heart hiccuped inside him.

The door yawned empty. Great. Where was he now? And why had he come here anyway, he already knew the box was deactivated. Joe's other words shot through Nehi. *"Take out the blocker. Warn them."* His body went cold.

Daniel had come for those explosives. Enough to blow up the whole meadow. *"You have to keep her safe."*

Anna. She was on her way with backup, she would never stay behind with all three of them here. Any second now, she would touch down in that meadow and a fiery annihilation waited for her.

Nehemiah's hand shot to his Grady as he broke from his cover. Pain burned up his leg and he staggered, nearly toppling to the ground. His mind raced down a list of people with bone plants while he spun in a circle and looked everywhere for the blocker. This was Joe, the Raven in the shadows, it could be anywhere!

"Here," an automated voice swirled from the shadows by the door. Nehi spun before the sound ended and pressed Hope's trigger. A sharp fizz and a short flash of circuits shorting out cut through the corner. Nehi's thumb smashed down his Grady's communication button and he chose the two he knew would be coming for him.

"There's a bomb, Pete, Tanzid, I need you to answer!" he shouted. His hand went to his leg, pressing against the wound to try and stabilize it. A crackle came from the other end of his Grady. They heard him. He didn't wait for any kind of greeting. "Explosives, when you land, the Wolf is waiting, don't–"

A vast boom cut out every word. The ground under him shook and more rubble tumbled from the jagged hole in the ceiling. A scream rushed from Nehi's gut toward his throat as he stumbled out the door, watching the yellow fireball eating the grass, seeing the carnage in his mind's eye, his sister and friends–

16. The Cache
Matthew 6:21

"Got it," Peter's steady voice cut over the Grady. "Tanzid came prepared, as always. Your warning came just in time to pull out the shield. But it still damaged the equipment, we're falling back into the giant trees to recheck before we come for you."

"Right," Nehi answered, shut the communication down, and slumped against the door frame. He didn't trust himself to say anything else. He ripped a strip from his already torn pants and tied a quick, dirty bandage over the wound starting to ooze blood through the ash. He tested his leg with a grunt. He could still move. But where to?

The sun sprayed through the windows in tainted gray shafts, filled with so many dust motes they seemed to be tiny monsters eating the light. Nehi grimaced and slid back through the door into the darkness. He couldn't stay out here in the open. Nehi limped toward the towering machines. His eyes kept going to the ceiling, watching for more firebombs headed toward the crates. Or explosives equipped with wings. Or... A deep sigh rattled from Nehi. He had no idea what to expect from the brother he had known for his whole eighteen years.

"All right, Nehi." Daniel's drawl echoed into the ruin. His old caustic note rode it. But knowing the real man behind the tone turned it into a monstrosity and sent a shudder through Nehi. He turned in a slow circle, trying to pinpoint the origin of the voice. *Where was he, curse him?* "I'll let you have a choice." The voice bounced from wall to wall, surrounding him. "Your life; a desperate run for the books; or the little Raven with the clipped wings. If you choose the first, you'll almost certainly get to keep it. Either of the other two? Eh, we'll see how fast you can run on that leg." Nehi turned in a circle again, searching through the dust and ash swirling in the ruin, a cold sweat steadily soaking him. He saw Joe, thirty yards away, drag himself into the aisle and prop himself against a metal square that looked like it might once have been turquoise. "Want to guess my meaning, Nehi? Tell you what, I'll give you a clue." Nehemiah limped into the aisle and started toward Joe, his muscles rigid, Hope held in both hands ready to snap up. *Where was he, curse him?!* "What's white, and sticky, and you thought there were only two?"

Horror clamped down on Nehi's throat till he gagged. That's why Daniel had walked out the door. Why he couldn't find him now. This whole building was about to go up in a fiery explosion. He broke into a mad run, racing for Joe as the Raven reached for the machine above him, slowly dragging himself to his feet. The Wolf's voice swirled around them in a ghostly echo, malicious amusement twisting every word.

"Five... four..."

Nehi's leg gave out and he fell against a machine, ancient plexiglass shield biting into his hands. Twenty yards in front of him Joe's green eyes flicked to the huge, broken front door, staring at something through his dirty blond hair hanging in sweaty strands. A smile shifted the Raven's bloody lip. Nehi pushed off the machine and ran again.

"...three... two..."

Joe's eyes darted to Nehi. He caught his friend's gaze as Nehi staggered into the light spinning through the huge open doorway. The mute's fingers closed into fists with the thumbs up. He scraped his right thumb away from his left fist in a quick movement: "Dodge."

Nehemiah didn't think, he just trusted.

He flung himself to the side, letting his shoulder slam into the ground. Something whistled past him, swirling the dust and ash into crazed tornados. Nehi followed it with his eyes. He was just in time to see Daniel framed in a small doorway on the other side of the building. A tiny pop echoed off the walls, and Daniel's legs folded. Thick netting slammed into the Wolf. The weights wrapped around him with a sickening thump that echoed through the ruin. He crashed to the ground in a tangle of wires. A huge form stepped up next to him. Nehemiah pushed back to his feet in a daze, staring at the scene framed in the little doorway, the huge trees in the background like the scenery of a play.

Cobeau towered over Daniel, a tiny spring gun in his massive hand. Daniel lay limp on the mud just outside the little door, his muscles jelly. Nehi could just see a small black box tumble out of the Wolf's hand. The light shifted behind Nehi, and he turned to look at the main doorway.

Soldiers stepped into it, shifting the beams of light cutting into the swirling dust. The red and black body armor of the Tao shone in the sunbeams. A tall man marched past the soldiers, an empty netting gun resting on his impossibly muscular arm, his armor pure red, an officer's pigtail hanging from his conical helmet. He strode past Nehi without giving him a glance as the chimera trotted over to scoop up the little mute.

"How…" Nehi heard himself slurring.

"Classic misdirection," the mute signed, an exhausted smile on his face. "I've been buying time until the real force got here. With his ego, Wolf forgot what he considered an insignificant force. Thanks, Glue." The Tao soldiers fanned out, perfectly focused on their orders. The officer stepped beside the still form in the muddied gray coat, lying wrapped in the silvery net. Beau's big hand landed on Nehemiah's shoulder and pulled gently. Nehi's joints obeyed stiffly, automatically. The shadows engulfed him again as the officer stirred Daniel's shoulder with one boot.

"Daniel Hillson, you are charged with breaking arrest and causing the death of two Tao warriors in your attempt," the officer's voice rolled out, deep and almost bored. "You are hereby sentenced to twenty-five years of solitary in cell block fifteen." Beau's hand tugged. Nehi turned, focused with difficulty on the pile of tattered leathers and blood in the chimera's arms, and followed the Ravens through the shadows toward the boxes. The deep voice rolled on behind him, and he heard the scrape of the nets as they dragged across concrete. Nehi kept walking. A soft whistle came, and Nehi looked at the huddled form of the mute.

"I'm sorry I had to do it this way," he signed, the movements stiff and small. "So sorry. Stay for me. Finish the last thing here."

"What is this place?" Nehi asked, his voice gritty and monotone. Tired, so tired.

"It's where they made books," Joe signed. Nehi stopped again, swaying on his feet. He blinked around him at the huge machines.

Made…books?

Could you do that?

Could *they* do that?

A twinkle teased at the edges of the pain in Joe's green eyes. He nodded once, and for what felt like the hundredth time that day, Nehi's brain sang and numbed with the possibilities. Beau stopped in the corner across from the books, straddling the melted remains of a blocker and hologram speaker. Nehi stood still, blinking at the books spilling onto the concrete. A corner of his brain noticed the Sojourner backup (Pete, Tanzid, and Anna at the front of the group) jogging in a tight formation through the grass. They paused, and black and red uniforms stepped up to meet them. They seemed to be having a conversation. He thought he could see something gray hanging between two of the black and red soldiers. His eyes closed for one long moment and he swayed. When he opened them again he saw Joe's hands moving, signing at the chimera.

"You still have it?"

Beau pulled a white protective box from his coat then shoved it back in. Nehi blinked wondering why they had the case for the Bible while the book rested under guard back in the – Oh.

"When did you steal it?" he asked. Even his voice was tired, husky and slow. Joe's eyes darted to him. Reluctant? Apologetic?

"I didn't know Wolf would try to destroy it. I hoped he wouldn't get the chance. But–"

"–it pays to be cautious, yes, I know," Nehi finished the sentence. How had he never suspected any of this?

The sharp whine and stinging cold of a SOLTD closed over him and his eyes flew to the door again. Black energy mushroomed into a copper wand just outside the door, and a familiar form stood on the muddy ground outside. Her blue-green suit sparkled in the afternoon light, and her lips were just as ruby red and ruthless as Nehi remembered. A click came from the mute and Nehi looked at him.

"She found Wolf's 'proof' and destroyed it for us, and then exposed him to the rest of the world as the real book thief. The IDP is safely out of the Wolf's jaws. She deserves it. Up to you, Judge."

The mermaid stepped through the door and stopped, staring at the books. She moved slowly to the next crate and slid the lid off. It toppled to the ground with a clatter, and another cloud of dust swirled up around her. Red-backed books lay stacked neatly in that crate. Her lips twitched, and for a moment Nehi thought he saw her eyes glisten in the light trying to cut through the dust and ash. He stepped into the sunbeam. The mermaid's eyes flicked to him.

"Choose what you want," Nehi heard himself saying. It didn't sound like him. He didn't feel like him. "You deserve it. Even if you did come late to the fight today." A smile quirked over her face.

"Some of us know it's better to avoid certain fights," she answered, her hard voice perfect and beautiful. *She's afraid of him, even now,* Nehi's brain supplied. Tired, so tired. "So..." She let the word hang, but her gaze went hungrily to the ancient machines standing like soldiers in the gloom.

"We keep the setup," he said. Authority rang in his voice, surprising him more than anyone. A pretty pout cut over her face. "This is on our land, property of the Sojourners, and we have sole command over what's made here. But you may have a say, later, after we work out the details and get it running. Right now you can choose your own treasure." He gestured at the eighteen crates, and slowly the awe slid through him, pulsing gently against the numbness. A little smile crept over his mud-streaked face as he looked at the miracle, the incredible, priceless treasure lying in this ancient ruin swirling with dust and ash. "There's enough for all of us."

Chapter 17: Repairs

"...A time to kill, and a time to heal; a time to break down,

and a time to build up; ..." Ecclesiastes 3:3

The monitor strapped on Joe's wrist gave a rhythmic beep for each heartbeat. Soft and steady and annoying, it filled the little room. Baby blue paint covered the walls, and pretty white moldings gave the hospital room a cheerful air. But nothing felt cheerful tonight. Nehi perched on his chair, his leg strapped in the tissue repair tube, his body high on pain killers, and his mind just tired. So tired. A soft whistle melded with the beep, and Nehi looked listlessly at the bed. It dwarfed the mute as he curled on the white sheet. Beau had programed Nehi's SOLTD and drawn them all back to Tolingbrook five hours ago, where Harry had promptly taken over and whisked them all here.

Now Harry was off somewhere, snatching a nap or arguing with the hospital doctor about something. Beau perched on the ground beside his master's bed, one huge hand engulfing the mute's knee, his rhythmic snores nearly drowning out the annoying beeps. Joe's skin looked weirdly mottled, the twenty-three skin grafts pink against his natural coloring. The facial ones overlayed most of his earlier scarring, and Nehi idly wondered if it would wipe them out as it continued to heal, or just become a new layer rippled over the old scars.

"I didn't expect to come back. Thank you," Joe signed. His green eyes focused on the sheets, not meeting his friend's eyes. Nehi couldn't think of an answer. Joe's pink hands moved again before Nehi could get his sluggish mind to come up with something. "I'm so sorry I had to do it this way, Knee-High. I'm sorry I had to tag your brother, I know how much it hurts when someone you trusted turns out evil. It's the last thing I could have wished for you in this life." A sigh spilled from the mute, and he began to sign swiftly, not meeting Nehi's gaze.

"I knew it was someone from the Judge's family. At first I thought you and Beauty must be in on it, especially when I saw

she had the treasure—"

"You've known from that first night!" Nehemiah's voice choked, trying to comprehend it all.

"Why do you think it was so hard to believe your simple stories, that you could be as good and innocent as you seemed? I assumed you knew more than you said, and was listening for anything to help in my work. You did give me a clue, I didn't know F-r-e-d-d-y had been there at the very beginning of the disintegration until you two mentioned it. Trusting you wasn't easy, Knee-High. But then you two went after me in the Institute, and I let myself believe you. Which meant D was Wolf. I... I helped Mermaid set up a death trap for him in the Tao. I wasn't out there to rescue him, Knee-High. I was there to make sure he died. But then, while I waited, I overheard his conversation with F-r-e-d and found out about the IDP frame he had setup. I knew I couldn't recover that information, and I couldn't cope with the aftermath if Wolf died and F obeyed and released that on the world. So I rescued him from my own plan." Joe looked up, meeting his friend's reddened eyes. Something in the determined set to the mute's mouth told Nehi it took a lot of courage for Joe to go into this.

"On the way back to KAM after Glue pulled me out of Evil's plan to catch the Black Raider I did nothing but mental summersaults for three days and two nights. I tried and tried to come up with another way to tie down Wolf. I kept coming back to the same conclusion. It would take you and Beauty, wonderful latch-ons that you are, to hamper his movements and keep him in a place Glue and I could watch. Offer him hints and clues of that treasure to keep him watering for it, put you in his path combined with the threat of the Mermaid's assassins still after him, and he would stick. That treasure had become the one thing in his life he couldn't obtain, the only thing he couldn't control and twist to his own ways. It obsessed him. He couldn't risk giving himself away, not until he had everything he wanted. But I thought you two were safe. I thought the real man behind the mask..."

"Actually cared about Anna and me. That's why you

apologized when you came for me in the People's Kingdom," Nehi said. "You thought Daniel still had a smattering of love, that Anna and I at least were safe with him." Joe's eyes held Nehi's as he signed.

"I was wrong. Watching him today, the man behind the others still does care, Knee-High. He could have killed you ten times over today. I know he still almost did, but... But there is still something there."

"Why just me?" Nehi asked, his voice small and choked. "He turned me in to the FFs, twice, why just..."

"Because..." Joe's quick signs stilled, his eyes moving to the sheets as he paused, new pink skin drawn into lines on his forehead. "I thought Wolf was just holding Beauty in reserve, in case he didn't learn anything from you. But watching today, I think that's the excuse he used to satisfy the Wolf and a part of him still felt...what? I don't know, Knee-High." The signs came small, a whisper of movement. His hands moved faster as he rushed it on. "That day in Geatland when he saw your scars and found out about you and Evil, Wolf's anger was real, I could tell. At first I assumed it was what it looked like, anger over the pain you had gone through. Then when he turned you in, I thought I had misread it, and instead it was anger at slighted pride, that Evil hadn't told him everything, that they almost had you then and Evil blew it... Now I think probably a combination of the two went through him, as the Wolf and the man behind Wolf collided. Either way, I shouldn't have left you and Beauty with him in the People's Kingdom. And I couldn't tell you any of it. If he found out you knew who he really was, you would be dead, the IDP would be destroyed, Glue and I would be dead, the printing press would explode, and Wolf would win. So I said nothing. And worked beside you, never telling you what you were working on. I'm sorry."

"Joe, you kept all this a secret for so long. You let him free for so long. But you kept telling us how dangerous this Wolf is, how even talking about him could somehow bring his fangs around our necks! I don't understand, I..."

"Wolf has always had two obsessions. Himself, and gain.

Pride is one of his main features. I had to keep him believing I didn't know his identity, or he would have wrung the Raven's neck immediately. I kept inflating his ego. As often as I could, and as much as I could without exaggerating so much it became obvious. It worked, he believed he was smarter than any of us, that he had us all on the hook. He was confident enough of it he took that bomb off me at Doctor's, curious to see if he could gain access to the 'other Joe' you and Beauty told him about, maybe finally learn where Mermaid was, and if I had more journal pages. A lot of what I told you wasn't exaggeration though. He had lots of contacts, and all of them were scared of him for good reason. Just this month he murdered four people who failed him."

Nehi sat slumped and drawn. His reddened, listless eyes slowly closed as he leaned his head back against the wall. A grimace cut over Joe. His mouth formed a whistle, ready to ask for attention again. But his hands balled into fists and the mute's lips closed to a thin slit.

A sharp knock rang on the door. It opened before the sound died, and Harry and the hospital doctor in charge of their cases swept in. Both doctors looked hot in the face, and Nehi idly knew there had been heavy arguments going on in the halls. It should have been funny. Why didn't it feel funny? A nurse stepped up beside Nehi, gave him a little smile, and began to unstrap the tube around his leg. The doctor shoved a clipboard at him.

"You're dismissed. I have enough people who need that tube for life-altering wounds, be thankful you're a hero of the hour and got it first," he snapped.

"Thank you?" Nehi murmured. The doctor spun and pointed at Joe.

"You are staying overnight, I don't care what your private physician says. I'm not releasing you till I see your vitals in the morning." He spun on Harry. "So there!" The doctor stomped out of the room, the nurse sidled out after him, and Nehi blinked at the light blue door as it closed softly behind her.

"Did he actually just say, 'So there'?" Nehi asked.

"Yes, the stubborn numbskull," Harry snorted. "But I will admit he cares about his patients. A little too much, sorry Joe, I tried to get you out tonight since I know how much you hate places like this. You're well enough to leave now, especially with the fancy fluids they filled you with and that new ankle brace. But you'll have to promise to stay in bed for a few days even after you get out of here. Right now, I delivered your white box to Mickelson and Atif, and whatever was in it they looked ready to hug you and strangle you, in that order. I'll stick and keep an eye on things, don't worry. Nehemiah, Peter's party just got back five minutes ago and Anna is asking for you."

"What..." Nehemiah let his voice drift off. Did he really want to know where they escorted those Tao soldiers, what happened to Daniel? He squeezed his eyes shut and rubbed his forehead. So very tired.

"Get some sleep soon," Harry told him, his voice soft.

"Yeah," Nehi murmured, stood up, and walked out to find his sister.

Nehemiah found her standing by the great oak tree in the courtyard, staring up at the old branches. Her hair flew in unruly tangles around her head, her face ashy and...old. She glanced at him as he walked up, her eyes puffy and red.

"Do you remember when Dad made us a fort in this tree?" she asked. Nehi stopped beside her and looked up at the old fire-blackened branches.

"We spent whole days up there," he said. "Until I pushed you out."

A laugh, short and wet but real, broke from Anna.

"Mom shrieked so loud, and I had to spend the rest of the day in bed even though I didn't even have a headache. It was... I never realized how precious those days would feel."

"I was mad at you for not doing things my way," Nehi said, his voice husky as he stared up at the branches. "I didn't mean to do any real damage, but, Anna... There's some murderer in

me too."

"There is in all of us. It doesn't excuse Daniel actually committing murder. But we all have dark hearts until God sends His light."

"Yes. God still claims us, and changes us," Nehi whispered. His lungs expanded in a long sigh, and his spine straightened. "He can do it again with Dan." Anna's arm slid around his and she leaned into her twin.

"God can still claim him and change him. Just like He has for us." The breeze caught it and teased the words around the twins like a gentle spell. A nightingale landed in the tree branches and her song trilled into the night. They listened in silence, as the stars began to shine with the cold brilliance of a winter night. "We left him in the Tao. I upheld their prior claim to him. They have Daniel on jail-breaking, with guards killed in the attempt. He currently has twenty-five years, with no chance of talking to the guards or other inmates to try and trick his way out."

"Oh, he'll try."

"But he won't be able to. It's not a nice place. But it's not cruel, and it is extremely secure. Tanzid told me no one has successfully escaped alive."

"Daniel wouldn't have that first time without Joe's help." Nehi took a deep breath and launched into what Joe had told him in the cellars and hospital, what he had seen of the real Daniel in the ruins. Anna took over explaining more details of their escorting the Wolf to his new quarters. She had been able to say goodbye. Daniel hadn't answered.

Their words flowed on, and they settled under the sheltering old oak, watching the stars through the branches. Their heartache and sorrow poured out in a steady stream, about Daniel and his treachery, the suddenly recovered country, devastation and recovery, and the hundreds of other things on their hearts. The stars moved in their ancient paths, and Nehemiah and Anna gradually grew still. They sat in silence, exhausted and curiously empty. As if the tears and sorrow had worn through their souls and left only a shell. But it was an

iron-strong shell; the adamant Truth that would never leave them, and that held them together even through this. This life was just a blink in reality. Yes, the pain was real and scarring and deep. But it shaped them, somehow, for what God needed them to do, and all scars would be healed in the end. Their job was to serve while still here, to do their best with what came and went in their lives. Silence hung in the cold air around them. But it wrapped gently around the twins, a blanket of familiarity after the air cleared.

"He is all right, you're sure?" Anna suddenly asked. Nehemiah smiled and nodded.

"Joe's new burns and wounds are all taken care of, and Harry seemed to think he could have walked out tonight. Well, maybe been carried out by Beau. Harry ordered Joe to stay in bed for a while after the fight in that ruin." Nehi sat up, excitement filling his pale face. "Anna, you should have seen all those books! So many of them lined up in the crates, and I don't even know what they all were! A whole box of bibles, think of it, a whole box. And if we can get those machines working again, we can print off more. The world wouldn't let us invent a way, but if we already have it, we can let them complain while we hand them fresh copies of their own works. It will make all the difference. And we can print off Bibles."

"Pastors able to study the scripture for themselves," Anna said, her voice awed at the possibilities, "maybe even one for every Sojourner. Think of it! Able to go to God's word anytime we wanted, to know more than just what Mom and Dad made us learn growing up, to read *all* of it... It's..."

"It's a miracle," Nehi nodded, a smile on his tired face. "And I still don't know what the other books are in there, when the Mermaid opened the second crate, they were different. A whole new book!"

"I bet Joe knows. Are you sure he said he would answer every question?"

"Yes. Joe seemed a little surprised too, but he said it, and we can make him stick to it."

"I already know some of it. He sent Dan and I to take the

note to the UPC when you were caught for more than just delivery service. It got the Wolf out of the country. Suddenly Daniel couldn't just waltz in and pick up the *Manifesto*, he was miles away dealing with a whole different job. And that situation in Story Land the first time we went felt like an elaborate play because it was. Joe set it up, placed us in just the spot to be taken for Rachel and the Trio, probably even sent that necklace to her in the first place. All so Daniel would find those journal pages on his own, and be caught deeper into that treasure obsession."

"It helped spook the Trio and send them skittering out of the country too, and kept the Wolf tied to us and our business instead of doing his own nasty things in Story Land."

"The main purpose, though, was so Dan knew the Raven planted the pages with the Trio."

"True. That was one major thing keeping Joe alive for a year while he traveled with his worst enemy in his own camp, the assumption he knew where the Mermaid was, and where to find more of those pages. They did hold the key in the end, somehow Daniel must have known that. And of course Joe did know where to find more. I bet he had them in the wagon the whole time."

"He waved the idea of getting at them under Daniel's nose just before leaving Harry's, to offer one good reason for the Wolf to actually be on our side in this resurgence."

"'If we win...' Joe repeated it several times in that strange little meeting he called," Nehi nodded. His head fell back against the tree with a dull thunk, his reddened eyes staring up at the sky without seeing it. "And we kept wondering why Dan and Joe couldn't get along!"

"Looking back it does make us seem little fools, doesn't it?" Anna murmured.

"Well, we really couldn't have guessed our own brother..." Nehi heaved a long sigh and silence fell around them. The nightingale sang again, high and clear, her song trilling into the night.

"Do you know what, Anna?" Nehemiah said softly. "I think Daniel is more honest with himself than most of the other lost ones we've met in our travels."

"What do you mean?" asked Anna.

"In Gaia the Recyclers say they kill the Christians because they're holding the race back from a collective consciousness, and that makes it a good thing."

"I think I see what you mean," Anna interrupted. "In Natropia, it's nature being higher than people, and that obviously made it right to reject God and hurt people. And in KAM..." Anna stopped and shivered again, not really out of the growing cold.

"In the Kingdom of Autonomous Man," Nehemiah took up, "and the People's Kingdom too, they can declare incompletes and chimeras animals, and kill and enslave them as much as they like; because science said so."

"And steal from their people because it's 'best' for the most people."

"And Story Land even declares truth void because they say it's the 'right' way to think. But Daniel admitted the real truth to himself. He said he rejected God and what He says because he wanted his own way, the evil and not the good."

"Yes," Anna said softly. "It all stems from that, a love of self and sin more than God and His laws. All the evil we've seen–"

"It all comes back to that, no matter what name they give it and what reason they have for declaring their evil good. It all just comes from a desire to be gods–"

"Just like Adam and Eve at the very beginning. Daniel is more honest with himself. At least he admits it was because he didn't like God's commands and wanted to do it his own way. There's some hope in that. The first step toward God calling a person is to make him see his ways are not God's ways." Anna stopped and shivered again. Nehemiah sighed and stood up.

"It's getting colder out here. Come on, let's go in and face everyone."

"We might as well get it over with tonight," Anna said, taking his offered hand and pulling herself to her feet. "Then we can start tomorrow with a clear mind, nothing bad staring us in the face. A fresh start."

"I wonder if that's part of the reason Joe chose now to bring all this out? A fresh start, knowing everything bad in the past?

And he made sure we have all the building blocks to a new future. Anna, this is going to be a good year, I can feel it in my bones."

"I agree, and I don't have to feel it in my bones," Anna smiled. "Sounds decidedly uncomfortable."

"If someone has a bone to pick, let them do it tonight," Nehi commented, a smile creeping over him.

"Well, tibia honest, I hope they don't," Anna answered him, one finger digging into his ribs as they made their way through the deserted courtyard.

"Come on, pick it up, I'm bone tired."

Anna answered it quickly, and by the time they moved inside humor hung on the twins despite their reddened eyes and weary hearts. As Nehi followed the soldier delegated to guide him to a bedroom, the weariness of the past hours crawled into him. He gave the man a little wave to say thanks, stepped inside the room, and fell onto the bed without even taking off his filth-crusted boots. He gave one yawn, and a single thought flitted through his mind as sleep shut him down.

Tomorrow would start yet another new life.

Chapter 18: The Beginning

"I will seek that which was lost, and bring again that which was driven away, and will bind up that which was broken, and will strengthen that which was sick..." Ezekiel 34:16a

Ninety-three, ninety-four, ninety-five..." The coins clinked and Gregory Talbot shook his head, staring into his cash pocket. His eyes lifted to the small-framed mute, pulling the tarp back over the instruments lining the side of the street. The setting sun glinted off his cropped blond hair, making it look almost white; it was very hard to guess his age. "You are a wonder, Master Joe! I don't even have a roof over my store yet, and my first shipment of instruments is sold twice over." Joe gave a shrug, jammed the spike through the last tarp corner and strolled toward Mr. Talbot. The brace on his ankle didn't seem to hinder his movements. The old man held out a handful of coins. Joe stared at the dulled metals. He frowned, and didn't move to take them.

"I have enough to fulfill the orders, and eat for this next week," Mr. Talbot said, amusement and thankfulness mingling in his tone. He slid a plastic change bag out of his pocket, dumped the coins in, and held it out again. "Take it, this is your cut." Joe hesitated for another moment. Then he took it and nodded his thanks. Not quite meeting Mr. Talbot's eye, the music store owner noticed. The mute never did. But that was none of his business. Mr. Talbot swung into the street, his cane tapping merrily on the ancient cobbles as it helped his twisted leg along. Joe walked the opposite direction, tucking the bag of money out of sight. This was a lot for playing music for an afternoon. It sure beat loitering, wondering what to do with himself. Or lying on Samuel's couch, hurting every time he tried to move, like the first days of these two weeks. At least Harry had kept him company some of the second day, that had helped, a lot. His playing had drawn a lot of customers (most of them churches trying to reestablish their musical section). And

223

during a time when the kingdom was just trying to get its feet under itself, that was pretty good, Joe admitted even to himself. But he still felt guilty taking a quarter of the cut.

He walked over the cobbles, his feet wanting to turn it to a trot, automatically shifting into the shadows of the buildings. He had a pocketful of money. His head lifted a little higher and a spring came to his tired steps. It was a strange, freeing thing to have a wad of cash that was all his and not needed for weapons or a desperate ransom or something. That meant he could do... What? His stomach growled. Maybe try a restaurant. Joe paused, staring across the busy street, as people scurried to finish the day's work before the last of the sun failed. A large window shed warm yellow light into the street, and illumined people settled at white covered tables, enjoying peace and stability. He had never been in a restaurant. Well, except chained in the back kitchen, but that didn't count.

Joe stood still in a pool of dark shadow cast from a derelict building. The shadows dropped into heavier blackness. People went in, people came out. Joe didn't move. He wasn't invisible, Joe was all too conscious of his bright hair and the green three-quarter-sleeve jacket he had bought second hand. People could see him; he felt vulnerable, and horribly self-conscious. But he still didn't move. After fifteen minutes, a spasm of determination went over his face and he stepped into the street. Joe crossed legally at the crosswalk (the new hologram lines glaring in the evening sun), spun onto the sidewalk and began to stride toward the restaurant as if it were a monster he would slay. In a way, it was. Fourteen days had come and gone since he had started to be "normal." It took all his courage to pretend he wasn't terrified every time a stranger looked his way. To seem to be easy and cool when inside he was forcing himself not to duck into alleyways and slink over roofs. Being "normal" was not normal. But normal people ate out when they had the spare funds, Joe knew it from watching the world. So he would do it.

His steps slowed as the warm yellow light drew close. The toe of his soft boot showed in the bright glow and panic

snapped over Joe's face. An instant, and the mute had ducked into the quickest way to disappear, his boots slipping and squelching on soft mud. The scent of garbage filled his head as he gulped in panicked gasps, cursing himself soundly, burning with shame, his teeth biting down on his lower lip that *would* tremble, just to make everything worse.

Something clanged into metal, reverberating around the alleyway. Joe spun toward the sound, his back slamming into the brick wall. A man started away from him, almost cowering as he jerked aside from the dumpster standing outside the restaurant's kitchen. The man stared at Joe, his thin chest heaving, eyes defiant and ashamed. Joe stared back, steely blankness covering his laboring heart and his furious annoyance at being found in an alley. Again.

"I didn't think anyone would care," the stranger said, his voice surly, defensive. "All we need is enough to get us by till next week, when the loan comes through. I can order the material and tools for my cobblery trade then. It isn't much to ask for trash no one else needs, my little girl–"

The man's voice strangled as a bagful of coins shoved into his hands. He stared at the bag weighing down his palm, the coins dull with much handling. He blinked stupidly, trying to decide if it was real. His head snapped up, stammering out something about an IOU.

The alley stared back at him empty. As he turned in a tight circle and found no one, James Curn found himself slowly growing still inside. The emotions of finding his family again, suddenly being free, destitute, lost in a sea of others wallowing in the same trials, it had all translated into a deep struggle with anger and doubt aimed at the God who hadn't answered prayers.

And now here he stood, free, with a bag of coins that would pay for the first two weeks of an apartment, clothes, food, even probably a little chocolate for his wife. Heaven knew she needed it after... James slowly lifted his eyes to the sky, his cheeks wet. His anger drained with the tears dripping down his face.

"Well God... A scarred white-headed angel boy wasn't what I expected. But I should know by now You don't come to us with the expected. And the scars... You bear them too, Lord Jesus. I forgot. Thank you." The words drained just like the anger. James Curn tucked the coins into his pocket and trudged out of the alley, empty and still inside. But peace sang in his emptiness like he hadn't known it in two long, long years.

Joe kicked off the roof support, slid down the tiles, and felt the comforting jar of the rain gutter slamming into the boot of his good foot. The cast no longer enclosed his ankle, but his foot still twinged and ached under the brace. He made a move to flip off over the edge to the next roof, but paused. Joe swayed as he braced against the gutter, his eyes slits against the pain, the weakness that just kept returning. He turned and labored back up the ridge to crouch behind the soot-blackened chimney. He stayed there for a five minutes, panting, his eyes closed. It wasn't like he had anyone around who needed him, no one to spend a wad of cash on. Besides he had a yogurt in the fridge back at Samuel's. Joe's eyes flew open and his mouth twitched into a frown. He kicked off the chimney, slid down the roof, dropped into an alley, and walked into the street. He held his head high as he flagged down a transport.

Ten minutes later he climbed up the metal stairs to Wiglaf's apartment, leaning heavily on the railing. His breathing wheezed out of him and his feet dragged as he made it to the door, his eyes crinkled in weariness. But a smile touched the mute at the rushing, thumping, merry shrieks of two children who objected to the fact it was bedtime. Joe stopped outside the door, calculating as he listened to Wiglaf trying to bring order. If Wara were here, she would wrap an arm around each and hold them till they went to sleep. If she wasn't here, she was with Beau. And that meant, Beau was somewhere else, out with Wara. Joe let a sigh slide from him. He turned and climbed down the stairs without knocking.

Fifteen minutes, three blocks, and one transport line later, Joe banged on the red door of the cottage resting beside the Judge's House. He forced himself not to turn around and study

the windows glowing in the great white mansion. He didn't know which one was hers anyway. *You could find out,* a voice inside him whispered, *just a little climbing.* Joe's lips pursed and he shook his head sharply. *Or slip in and look at the records. In and out in five minutes,* the same voice whispered, a little nagging fiend. *That's not me anymore! Remember, I retired, I'm NORMAL.* Joe told himself desperately. His shoulders slumped as he realized what a lie that was. Laughter and conversation drifted through the heavy wood, warm yellow light seeping under the crack onto Joe's boots. Eight men, Joe's brain automatically supplied, giving him their estimated ages, weights, and assessing their probable fighting strengths. The frown twitched over his face as he knocked again.

The door jerked open. A middle-aged portly man with a drink in one hand and a smile on his face stood framed in the light, half turned back toward his companions, half toward the interruption at the door. Joe was suddenly all carefree smiles as he handed over a note. The man took it with a little surprise and played trombone with his arm for a minute to get the focus.

"Oh, Harry!" he burst out, his voice jovial and loud as he looked back at Joe. "Sorry, he's out right now, doing something with the Judge again."

"Probably prescribing nerve tonics," one man called, and a roar of hilarity greeted it. The drinks had been flowing a little too long, Joe guessed in amusement.

"Anything I can do for you?" the portly one at the door asked. "Is it that ankle? Harry let you up last week, but make sure you rest it, that foot still has healing to do." Joe shrugged, gave a little salute to the man as a goodbye and thank you, and walked away. He wanted to make it a cheerful trot, but his body didn't agree. His slow steps turned toward the transport lines. Another four jerky stops, and he stepped out and started walking again. His walk slowed till it turned to a shuffle, his head down as he labored. Away from the streetlights, onto smaller lanes, keeping his distance from people. Ten minutes later he stopped and gripped a gate. He made to hop over it automatically, stopped, and stood blinking as he swayed on the

sidewalk, his eyes slits against the weary pain.

The catch clicked as the gate swung open. Joe trudged over cracked garden flagstones onto a sagging porch. The house was a simple square, the yard a neglected garden, the blue paint fading from the door. The mute studied the door closely as he strolled up, then his eye ran along the worn old porch boards to see if anything had fallen off. Joe pulled a key from his pocket, scanned it on the lock, slid inside, pushed the two deadbolts home automatically, shoved the light switch down, and spun, his eyes searching the polished wood floor in front of the door, looking for something that wasn't there.

He moved to the mantlepiece above the tiny, soot-blackened fireplace. His hand ran along the cold stone top. Nothing but dust flew from his fingertips as his trembling hand slid off the other end. Blankness covered the mute as he walked into the tiny kitchen. He headed for the small refrigerator humming in the corner, pulled open the door, grabbed a glass cup of yogurt, closed the fridge, and took a red pen from where it perched over a magnetic calendar. Fourteen days had been bracketed in red. Thirteen had large red x's slashed messily through them. The last had a crooked line of text scrawled over it.

The last day I can hope they'll send for me.

Joe uncapped the pen, slashed an x through the day, stuck the pen neatly back over the calendar, pulled a spoon from the drawer, and turned to the tiny table. He slid into the circular booth built into the bay window of the breakfast nook, pulled the cover off his yogurt, stuck his spoon in, and sat staring at it.

The refrigerator hummed. A board on the porch creaked as it settled back in place. Above the kitchen sink, a clock ticked rhythmically. It ticked, tocked, and ticked relentlessly. Joe sat still, staring at his dinner. The clock ticked on. It filled his mind, echoing in the emptiness. Screaming it was empty.

Joe bit his lip, pushed the yogurt back, slid to his feet and walked into the living room, switching off the light as he moved. The old green couch squealed at him as he flung himself on it

and drew the blue knitted throw over himself. Joe lay for a moment, staring up at the ceiling.

Silence roared around him.

A muscle twitched along his jaw.

He turned on his side, his feet tucking up as he curled into a ball. The throw drew up farther, till it draped over even his head.

Soft, wild, sobbing breaths filled the silence of the little house.

The smell of new paint tickled Nehi's nostrils as he strode down the hallway. The ends of his dressing gown tie trailed after him, and a part of his brain wondered if he looked as tattered as this old hall, with filthy wallpaper stripped for new paint to go on. Twelve days? Had it only been twelve days since he had stood on the temporary bandstand and listened in terrified awe as Samuel pronounced him Judge, or had he miscounted somewhere in there? It seemed like two lifetimes ago, and he regretted sleeping through the last of his life without being tied down as Judge; the last two days he could claim as a free man.

Most of his brain stayed occupied by the voice of the short, pedantic man almost trotting beside him. Oliver Tolley had stood up among the wreckage as the only man who knew the state of the kingdom's coffers, all the nuances of policy, and even the intricacies of a tax form. He slid naturally into position as Nehi's aide. His thin voice sounded even thinner this morning as he stared at the paperwork in his hands and read for Nehi.

"...when the party of the second part defaults on a vow in this treaty, the party of the first part has the right, nay, the duty, to call the party of the second part out upon their deeds of misfaith–"

"We're not going to war with the Battle Kingdom, that's what they want," Nehi growled, interrupting the little man's

reading. Anna rolled her eyes and gave a little sigh of relief when the reading stopped. She found it hard enough to stay awake and take notes like she was supposed to as Nehi's secretary. Oliver shoved his cracked glasses up on his nose and glanced behind him for the hundredth time. Tanzid moved a few paces behind them, as always. The bodyguard's gold flecked eyes stared back into Oliver's watery brown ones. The little man's Adam's apple bobbed and he looked at his papers, shuffling through them hastily. The papers rattled like a disturbed snake, and Anna glanced over at the aide. His hands shook almost uncontrollably.

"There is a clause in the ancient treaty, Sir, stating that if the Battle Kingdom defaults on their vows, we have the right to charge them for it."

"We're not going to war with them, even though they deserve to be called out for this!"

"No, Sir, I mean charge them the monetary value laid out by our ancestors," Oliver corrected. Nehi paused. The little group stopped in the hallway, standing on the rough wooden boards laid over the new carpets so the painters could do their work. Oliver swayed for a moment, before his backbone went rigid.

"You mean according to the treaty, if they invade us, we can demand money off them?" Nehi asked.

"'For injuries and oath-breaking,' yes, Sir," Oliver nodded, reading off the papers. He looked up, his thin shoulders rising in a shrug as he blinked owlishly at the Hillsons. "But how we would make them pay it when their soldiers are already crossing our borders–"

"Oliver, get me KAM's president," Nehi interrupted, in the sharp crack he used when he was scheming. "KAM is always looking for money. We'll agree to split the fee if they back us up. With KAM behind us, the Battle Kingdom will have to retreat, they don't have enough men to stand up to both of us."

"That might work," Oliver muttered, respect dawning on his face as he eyed the handsome young Judge. His finger pushed his glasses up again. It took two tries, he was shaking so hard. "It will take a few minutes to rouse him, the President never

likes to be woken up, Sir."

"Oliver?" Anna interrupted, as the thin little aide started to hurry off. He paused and looked back at the group. "I don't mean to pry, but have you slept at all this week?" Color flew into the man's sunken cheeks and he muttered something inaudible. It sounded like an apology. Nehi looked at him as a man, not a dictionary, for the first time in days. Oliver Tolley was stick thin, his skin almost translucent, his eyes bloodshot behind his cracked glasses. A deep bruise was still trying to fade off his cheekbone.

"I'll make the call, get something from the kitchens and go to sleep," Anna ordered.

"Don't get up for the meeting tomorrow. I mean today." Nehi pinched the bridge of his nose, his bleary eyes closing as he wondered how long it would take the sun to rise, and which day it actually was. They all seemed to run together. "Sleep till you're called." Oliver's mouth opened, his eyes blinking as his face fell, looking like a man just told he was useless. Nehi's tense shoulders slumped, and the worry lines faded into a soft, tired smile as he dropped a hand on Oliver's boney shoulder. "Rest up. I need you with a sharp mind, and would rather not have to make Tanzid carry you on a litter. If I find something I have to have you answer immediately, I'll send Peter to chase you back to work." Nehi gave the man a friendly push down the hall and started marching. Anna watched as his shoulders tightened and his face stiffened for the fight ahead.

"He was kept here," she said, trotting beside her brother. He glanced at her, blinking as his mind came back to the hallway and away from the call he had to make and the army he had to drive off. "Chained in a closet-sized room on the top floor. The invaders found Oliver's extensive knowledge almost as useful as you do."

"How did you find out?" Nehi asked, his voice quiet and strained. So many lives wrecked, so many stories of horrors, of his people treated like animals.

"I asked him, obviously," Anna grinned at him, and Nehi's tight face eased a little with a smile. She called herself his

secretary, and did an excellent job with the notes and paper-work and getting him to appointments on time. But Anna knew she was really his stress relief, the ribbon of solid family love reminding him of why he stuck at it, holding him together as he rushed around like a mad thing, trying to keep the newly re-born kingdom from being smashed to bits. She gave a pert or-der to go by the kitchens on the way to the conference room and bring her a sandwich too, and peeled off to get the presi-dent out of bed.

It took a full hour and all the wheedling and bossiness she had in her to get the president to answer the call. But Anna did it. She slumped back against the conference room wall, blowing a loose hair out of her eyes and watching Nehi talking rapidly to the holographic lines of the KAM president's head. She could watch the president's expression change from irritation to hes-itating interest. Nehi would make this scheme work, just like he had the others these interminable two weeks. Anna's eyes strayed to the wall of windows.

A beam of sunlight lanced over the horizon, stretching out over the town, calling the kingdom to rise and serve and be for another day. The buildings stretched off into the distance, melding with the western forest until the town disappeared, lost amidst the trees. The day's bustle began out there. She could see movement, as the rubble and ashes were cleared, new buildings sprung up like mushrooms in the night, and the people rebuilt their lives. There had been enough money left over from the revolution's fund to loan out to qualifying busi-nesses to let them rebuild. Anna idly wondered again how the IDP leader had acquired so much, and from there her tired mind traveled a worn path. Who was the IDP leader anyway? Was he safe, no one had heard from him. Joe probably knew who he was, and would help if he was needed.

Joe. Where was he? Why hadn't he shown up? The mute's knowledge and skills would have been really useful in some of the crises Nehi had to deal with. Why hadn't he come back?

The thoughts had run through Anna so often she could al-most feel the groove left in her brain. She let a sigh slip from

her, and automatically looked toward the door as the hinges creaked. Samuel walked in, moving slowly as if his bones ached, his silver hair tousled and unwashed. It had been a really long two weeks. Fifteen days, with the rising of that sun. Anna's mouth tightened into a line, and she shot forward, intercepting her old friend as he headed for the conference table.

"Samuel, does Joe have a place to stay? I haven't seen him here. Beau didn't say anything about it when he showed up with Wara to tell us about their engagement. But he mentioned you." It was a demand more than a question. Samuel paused, his blue eyes meeting hers, his mouth turned down in a frown. Anna suddenly felt on the defensive, had no idea why, and resented it. "I know Joe's grown very fond of you with all the private conferences you two have had, and I'm glad he trusts you enough to let you work out his accommodations. But he might have at least told us he needed a room!" She felt her face flushing and clamped her mouth down on the annoyance that would climb to a lecture in a moment if she let it. For once they were on their territory, the twin's country. Why hadn't he come to them? Why hadn't he come for her? Samuel's jawbone shifted, and his eyes softened.

"Joe has been staying at my little place. I think. I've hardly been in it enough to tell," Samuel said. He smothered a yawn. "Last night what sleep I had I got on a bench in the foyer."

"You haven't been checking on him?" Anna asked, her annoyance flying off with all the quickness of a woman realizing a loved one needed something. What if he was too hurt from the fight with Daniel to come? The name of her brother scalded through her brain. Anna winced, her arms snaking around her as the horrible, familiar cold hollowness closed in again. "You haven't been checking on him?" she asked again.

"I've hardly had the time, have I?" Samuel demanded, irritation in his exhausted voice. He waved a hand at the gaggle of people gathering around the hologram and a 3D map of the kingdom's Eastern border. "What's all this? Another crisis already this morning?"

"No, it started long before morning," Anna murmured

absently. Her eyes went to the door. The rest of her followed the look, and Anna slipped quietly out of the conference room and headed for the nearest exit at a trot. Only Samuel noticed. His reddened eyes crinkled in a smile, and a little of his usual cheery bounce came back in his step as he moved toward the table. It was about time she went looking for him!

Anna's knuckles stung as she rapped at Wiglaf's door, out of breath after her run from Samuel's little house. Joe hadn't been there. Her knock reverberated through the little apartment, but an exuberant, boyish yell eclipsed it. A smile crept over Anna as she heard the thunder of small feet tripping over themselves rushing to answer the bell. Wiglaf bellowed for them to wait an instant, and Anna grinned; whoever spoke of the 'pitter-patter' of children had never actually been around many children. Wiglaf's voice carried strong exasperation, and Anna did her best to swallow her amusement. Poor man. Choosing to love could be hard when it came to everyday living.

The words sunk into her heart and on into her chest, twisting there. Joe's face revolved in her mind, expressions playing over him in a swift stream; fear, anger, infuriating blankness, impish spite, weary sorrow...but the happy smile he wore most around her shone strongest. Anna sucked in a breath and her shoulders squared again. It was worth it. Loving someone who needs it is a tangible way to show the world God. It creates a picture of how Jesus loves, projecting the vision of ultimate hope like a beam of brilliant light pointed straight to heaven.

The door jerked open, and a smile sprung to Anna's face. Wiglaf stood with an apron wrapped around his waist, a pan in one hand, and his two children just behind him waiting for an opening to push forward. Anna waved at Elenore and gave Halbred a cheery hello. Then she turned back to Wiglaf.

"I'm sorry to interrupt your day, I was just wondering if you've seen Beau. I'm looking for Joe and can't find him. I assumed Beau would know where he is, and since Wara is usually

here–"

"They're at the blacksmith's!" the boy broke in. "Beau's working, and Wara likes to be with him." There was a sulky note to his tone as he spoke of his huge nursemaid, and defensiveness rose in Anna; of course she wanted to be near her man. But she squelched it quickly and just offered her thanks. Wiglaf nodded, caught Elenore by the back of the dress as she made a move to rush out, closed the door, and Anna heard the deadbolt slide home. She knew it wasn't meant for her, and grinned as she turned and trotted down the apartment stairs. She offered a quick prayer for patience for Wiglaf today, and made a mental note to offer to take the children for him tomorrow and give him a break.

The heavy scent of acrid smoke told her she was getting close before she actually found the shop. The Sojourners prized a job well done, and a skilled blacksmith could make things personal, and things that lasted for generations. A line already stretched out front as Anna approached, and the heavy rhythmic ping of metal on anvils mixed with the smoky air. It spoke of industry and things getting back to normal.

But as Anna drew closer, she only saw the building that used to house the stables. The horses had been slaughtered by the invaders. Every one. She prayed a breeding pair might be possible to acquire sometime, as the picture of her sweet mare returned to her. Such beauty and grace, mixed with power and superb control... Even the smell of her riding days came back to Anna's memory as she walked that path.

Ash and acrid smoke invaded her nostrils and she coughed. It turned to a sniffle, then her shoulders squared again and she broke into a trot.

Anna skirted the line and turned into the dark, muddy alley leading to the back of the building. Sunlight beckoned her on, and she trotted through the squelching mud to burst out in a small complex of open stalls, each with a burly man busy near a smoking fire. Every head lifted, and every eyebrow rose. A whistle slid from one man, but Anna chose to pretend she didn't hear it. A roar of welcome came from her left, great arms closed

18. The Beginning
Ezekiel 34:16a

around her and lifted her into the air, and Anna pounded on Cobeau's shoulder to tell him she couldn't breathe. He plunked her on the ground and she staggered back a step, one hand snaking around her ribs as she laughed and gasped.

"Can I help you?" a business-like bark flew at her. Anna spun and found it matched the man well. He was tall, well built, sweaty, and frowning at her. To him she was a distraction to his employees. Anna gave him her best disarming smile.

"I'm looking for someone. May I borrow Mr. Cobeau? I'll pay for his time," she said.

"Joe?" Beau asked, his smile so wide his beard bristled around it.

"Yes, do you know where he is?" Anna asked quickly, her eagerness betraying itself. Beau's face fell. He shook his head, and Anna noticed a huge hand slide into his. She offered Wara a little smile, though her stomach suddenly tightened. If Beau didn't know...had Joe been alone? For two whole weeks?

"She's mine next month," Beau rumbled, motioning to Wara. His voice cracked. "Joe says I have to switch masters. Won't let me stick as close." Anna quickly laid a hand on his arm, interrupting before he could say it.

"Don't apologize! He's right," she told him. A breath, huge and noisy, sucked into Beau's lungs. He nodded and his hand tightened around Wara's.

"Joe said he wanted freedom and green," Wara rumbled. Anna looked at her, and one huge eyelid slid down and up again in a slow, conspiratorial wink. "Try gardens."

"Gardens, right," Anna nodded, refusing to let herself blush. She gave a quick thank you and ran off, through the alley and back to the streets. Freedom and green. Somewhere without crowds. No, without people, strangers would make him nervous if he was alone, and nervousness didn't fit with freedom. Anna's feet turned to well known paths. She had ridden through the city beside Nehi on his triumphal parade (Nehi's smile had been sickly, but he made it through town without vomiting or screaming, "I don't want the job!"). Now she mentally ticked off the areas that might pass for gardens as she

trotted along. The streets teemed with builders and people dragging away refuse, families and friends suddenly reunited falling into each other's arms, people begging jobs and breakfast. A city slowly reclaiming life from what the invaders had left behind.

She would try the old public gardens attached to the Judge's House, rippling away on the east side. They used to stretch for fifty acres, filled with roses, intricate mazes, a children's castle, so many beauties. The invaders set a burning brand to it, of course, until everything green had been consumed.

But that was two and a half years ago. Now, as Anna trotted into the shambles, she saw green shoots peeking out of the small snow drifts and cold mud. Her path took her over a hill and she swung to a sudden stop. A patch of pansies came in view in a host of colors, delicate blooms turned to the sun. An old, weather-beaten man and a young woman, a few years younger than Anna, knelt working among the blooms. They looked up at her as she stood transfixed by the sudden beauty. The man tipped his battered felt hat to Anna and a smile crossed the young woman's face. Vibrant violet eyes stared into Anna's wide, wet ones.

"Things grow back, miss," the violet-eyed girl said. "Men can try to kill the earth. But it heals itself after they're long dead. No one is here today because there's not much to enjoy. Come back in three months, then you'll see." Anna only nodded. It was all she could do; words had deserted her. She turned and wandered back toward the streets. Her boots landed on hard pavement again and Anna's chin shot up. She had a mission to finish, no time for getting sentimental over flowers. Her eyes closed and she concentrated, trying to think with the humming, busy town rushing around her. A scene that had flashed by in that triumphal hoverer ride, one of hundreds of the horrible scenes of destruction, came again to her.

The parade began at the open-air theater, where the Judges were officially sworn in, plays and concerts had gone on year round, and beautiful church services resounded every Sunday. Nicknamed the Pit, it was an oval dug into the ground, with

perfect acoustics playing through the bowl. Fire did little to damage the place. So the invaders had turned it into their dump heap. For the first year refuse from the kitchens had been flung into the Pit, until the stench made it too close to town to be desirable, and they had hunted out another dump.

There had been green there, Anna realized.

She darted into the street to catch a transport. Green, and no people wanted near it. The bodies had been dumped there too, "refuse" of the invaders. Oh, they had been buried a few months later by their conscripted countrymen, to keep disease down. But to those who had lived it, that did little to change the horror. A three storied giant of metal shot down the street, and Anna chased it. The cars were filthy and run down, and the lines dangerously unkept. But it still ran. The towering hunk of metal crawled to a stop and Anna leapt through the door, shoving a coin into the driver's hand. He gaped at the shining gold.

"Just wait, you'll see more of them," Anna told him. "The Judge has started the smelter again."

"Yes, but what's he found for metal?" the man asked.

"The invaders in the house were allowed to take their lives back home with them. But nothing else," Anna grinned at him. "Want to guess what they were hoarding in the cellars and closets? The official announcement comes out later today. For now, give me my change, I'll give you a tip, and then get me to the theater."

"The theater? You mean the Pit?" the man gaped again. A woman shouted at him to start moving and stop flirting with pretty passengers, and he grumbled loudly as he turned back to his work. Anna took her change, handed a heavy tip to the man, and slid to the back of the transport to stand by the back door. The lumbering purring thing felt like it crawled today, and she bounced with impatience. Four stops, eight people on, ten people off, and the machine crawled to a halt again. The metal plates began to slide on top one another, opening the doorway. Metal clanked against metal with a sharp clang and the whirr of a sick machine, and the two middle plates ground together, clacking rhythmically as one tried to get over the

other. Anna grunted in annoyance, hunched over and slid under what opening had been made. She was in no mood to wait while the driver fiddled with the mechanics.

A vast dome sunk into the ground in front of her feet. An acre from end to end, and three hundred stairs to the bottom. Broken white marble lay scattered around the mouth, the steps cracked, chipped, and irregular as they wound down into the Pit. She saw barely a trace of the carved marble seating, or the carefully designed bandstand and orchestra pit. A remnant of the refuse smell lingered in the air. But most of the scent wafting around her was just dirt. Dirt and living green. With the drainage clogged, rainwater had collected in the Pit. Water, sunshine, and thirty months of revolving days had done what no human had dared to come near to do. The refuse had rotted, decomposed, and become a rich layer of black dirt. Grass, shrubs, vegetables, flowers, even fruit trees had begun to take root here, popping up even in the winter as the sun poured its bright light into the Pit.

Anna stared at a wild sunken garden, surrounded by the ruins of past lives. It was beautiful.

The bustle of the city didn't touch this place. No one rushed past, no builders argued over what to do next, no transports rattled and coughed through it, no reuniting friends wept and laughed. But it wasn't silence. The breeze stirred, and with the perfect acoustics of the Pit, Anna could hear the rustling of the few leaves from where she stood. And she could hear the recorder's song.

Soft, low, not meant for a crowd, the notes didn't dance. They lingered on the air, fell with a gentle touch, and died on the rich black ground. The tune didn't wail, and it didn't sing, it only mourned. No black despair hung in the notes. But no hope sang through it either. It was a song to something that had died, never to be seen again. A song of soul-rending letting go. Anna's eyes filled and her throat grew hot. Her feet flashed in the sunlight, scattering small puddles of rainwater as she rushed down the cracked stairs. The song crescendoed, then died into a whisper. Her feet hit the soft earth at the bottom of the Pit, and Anna

trotted into the chaos of new shoots and plants and half-melted snow. No, it wasn't quite chaos. Someone had cleared a path, pushing away the snow and ripping up the grass to allow the earth to see the sun. It wound through the few shrubs toward a single pine sapling set off the main bandstand. A small tree, but it couldn't have grown in two years. Someone had brought it here. Anna's flurry faded as she neared the tree. Her steps slowed, then came to a crawl as she turned the last gentle curve.

A new Joe slumped under the pine's green boughs. Instead of his habitual black he wore a green three-quarter sleeve jacket over a blue cotton shirt, and his blond mop of hair had been cut and tamed. It seemed unnatural to see that hair gleaming short and clean. His face pressed into his knees. Not violently, but just lay there, like his flaccid hands on the ground beside him. As if he had no heart left to move. He had just stopped. Like a clockwork figure, worn down.

"You didn't come."

Joe spun to his feet at Anna's words, a white, scared face turning to her as he stood rigid, poised to run.

"You didn't come," Anna said again. Even she felt surprised by the hurt carried in the words.

"I promised not to," Joe signed. Anna blinked at him.

"Oh."

The two stood and stared at each other for a long moment. The green needles of the pine whispered in the breeze.

"I forgot." Anna's whisper drifted out quieter than the breeze. She blinked again, but this time it was because the tears would come. Her words spurted from her, filling the quiet of the garden. "Oh Joe, I'm so sorry, we forgot! There was so much happening, so much breaking, I didn't think you meant it, neither of us did. That promise didn't come across as a promise, it was just words in a mix of acid burning a hole in me, I didn't think you meant you would actually stay away! I've been waiting for you to show up again like you always do, to come find us. To come find me. So much has changed, so much is changing, the city trying to come alive again, our world falling apart and coming back in new colors, and you weren't there!"

The sobs came, sloppy and wet. The memories crawled through her, standing here amidst the place she had spent so many happy hours with family and friends. Now all of it lay in ruins. But beautiful ruins, growing into something new and wonderful.

Cold, clammy hands closed over her wrists, gently drawing her hands from her face. Anna gulped in air and looked up through burning eyes. Just at that moment her main thought was the realization her face was blotchy, covered in salty tears and snot, her hair a wreck. Joe stared at her, his face working with concern. But a spark showed there, a vibrancy that he had been missing a moment ago. That his song had been missing. Hope. A cautious, wild hope, desperately searching her for something. His hands let go and formed words. The shadows of the waving branches of the tree mottled him, light dancing on and off his white skin and green jacket.

"You came looking for me," he signed.

"Of course I did," Anna sniffed, running a sleeve over her nose. "I've been waiting for you for two weeks, wondering how you were every day."

"Waiting for me! But, but, wouldn't I have just made it worse?" His eyes still searched her face, that taut wildness strong in him. "I'm the one that kept Wolf's secret, remember? The one who sprung it on you, spilled the acid out." Anna shook her head, a little smile creeping over her face.

"No, Joe. You're the one who protected us before we knew we needed it. Who gave us our kingdom back and a new life after Daniel ripped the other to bits. Made it worse?" She sucked in a breath, shaky with the sobs of a moment ago. "I want you near, Joe. I need you near."

He drew back, astonishment, wonder, a hint of fear playing over him. But the wild, joyful hope was so strong it seemed to pulse off his tight muscles. She wanted him. They wanted him, even after the secrets were out, she was here, he hadn't been dumped! He laughed, a short, overwhelmed movement, and turned a radiant face to her, questioning, begging to hear it once more.

"We never would have left you on your own, even for a day, if we had realized! We need you with us so badly right now." His radiant grin grew even wider, sending his twinkle dancing into his eyes. Anna's sweet smile crept back on her face, still wet with the tears. No, it wasn't her normal smile, it was warmer, different...all for him. The hope turned to wild happiness, a silent laugh breaking from him as he fell back another step, and she could see the understanding run through him in a shudder.

"You..." he started to sign, shook himself into some sort of coherent thought and started again. "You came for me. Thank you. For finding me. I needed to know, to hear that you two hadn't dumped me."

"I want you near, Joe," Anna said, her voice soft, that peculiar smile strong. Joe's eyes met hers with a laughing smile that beautified even the scars; he understood. But then he took another step back and looked away. In an instant it all tucked inside of him.

"I don't want there to be more secrets, no more hidden meanings," he signed. She saw him steel himself, then he looked up, his smile gone. "Beauty, look. You don't deserve someone like me, a GI that has nothing to give you but his love and himself. I've already given you that. But I was never going to let you know about it, for good reasons. You don't want me, really you don't. I'm more evil than I've ever let you know, I have blood on my hands, Beauty. And broken too, a lot more than I've let on. Just look at me, I've got the frame of a twelve-year-old and I don't know anything about regular life. The thought of having to live one scares me to death, and being scared depresses me so much sometimes I deliberately go hide in a corner for hours and hope no one notices. It took me three days just to work up the courage to get a haircut! I'm more of a shattered soul than you know. And look at you! Perfect, gentle, godly, strong, wise, joyful, brave, and more beautiful than a host of stars and oceans. I don't have anything to offer you. Beauty, I don't have *anything* to give. I don't have a job, I don't have a house, I don't have a family. I don't even have a last name to give you!"

"I like Ravenswing, the way Wiglaf uses it," Anna said. Joe gaped stupidly at her. She shrugged. "I'm not discounting your words. I know you're broken. I am too." One hand went to her hip as the usual pert Anna came back. "Honestly, I've known you for two years, through some pretty hairy circumstances, and haven't run away yet. Aren't you satisfied by now that I want to be with you?"

"Beauty, you deserve so much better than I can give you. I can't ask you to share my life. I don't even have a life to give you! My old one ended when I turned Wolf over to Knee-High and I..." Joe's eyes shut, his face scored with shame, sorrow, and a deep-seated fear. "I haven't had the courage to start another one yet. I've tried, these past weeks. But I...alone, I...was crippled, inside and out. I'm more broken than you know. I'll probably never really feel well again, not like I used to. I'm weak, and dirty, and..." He looked up at her, suddenly more weary than anything, and shrugged. "You want someone better than me."

"Did it ever occur to your brilliant mind that I might not want 'better,' Joe? I want you. And why are you trying to convince me to leave?" Anna asked, cocking her head in annoyance. "I'm not sure I feel flattered." His mouth fell open as he gaped at her again. Her toe started to tap the black earth. "First I had to be the one to come out here and find you, and now you're trying to convince me to leave. If I didn't know you better, I would say you didn't want me." Anna took a step forward, her head high, inquiring and challenging. "Joe, I'm going to ask this once, and you've promised you wouldn't lie. No dodging with clever mental twists to the words, you know what I'm asking. Do you love me?"

A smile broke over the mute's face, beaming, tender, and hesitant all at the same moment. It was a smile Anna had thought she had seen from the corner of her eye sometimes when she turned suddenly and caught his gaze. But she had never seen it in the open. Joe nodded, his eyes dropping and face flushed. His hands started to move, fumbled over the signs, then started again in a blur.

"Don't ask the next question, please." He was looking at anything but her. "Because I love you I'm not going to ask–"

A thick body collided with Joe, long arms wrapping around him and squeezing, lifting the mute off the ground. Sudden terror snapped on Joe's face. Then realization caught up, and Joe pounded a fist irritably into Nehi's shoulder, shoving himself out of his friend's grip.

"You're an idiot, Joe," Nehi barked, giving the mute a shove in the chest. It sent Joe staggering three steps, and they both noticed he favored his right ankle heavily. "When Anna slipped off today I figured she was coming to find you–"

"But you had to follow my earing trackers and check," Anna interposed, irritation in her voice. Nehemiah didn't seem to hear.

"–and I'm glad she did, we've missed you. A lot. Why have you kept away so long? I needed you!"

"You too?" Joe signed, frustration strong on his expressive face. "I promised to stay away!"

"You..." Realization dawned on Nehi. A groan slid from him, as his whole form wilted. One hand went over his face. "I forgot. It's not an excuse, just a truth." He pulled his hand back and his face was strained; even Anna was surprised at how far the stress lines furrowed into his face. "Look, I'm sorry, Joe. It was...I let myself get lost in the whole Daniel thing, and...well, I guess I got lost in it, I didn't really get a choice, and then the judgeship–" The mute's arms suddenly shot around him, squeezing in a bear hug that cut off his words. A grin covered Joe as he pulled away.

"You're the idiot, Knee-High, I'm not mad at you, stop apologizing. It's been hard, I know. Thanks for coming for me. It means the world."

"Two weeks!" Nehi burst out. "I let you think we weren't around for two weeks. I'm sorry, Joe." His hand clamped onto Joe's bony shoulder. "You know I didn't mean it, right? We may not be geniuses, Anna and I, but we recognize a friend when we see one. You're a brother to me, Joe, under Jesus and, well..." He glanced at Anna and ran on with a different thought. "I never

would have dumped you. I never will." The hand on Joe's shoulder shoved again, Nehi's turn to be irritated. "Don't let us desert you like that again, we were waiting for you to suddenly materialize, like you always have before!"

"Ok, ok," Joe chuckled, his feet shuffling as if he could dance on the air. But under the joy, Anna could still see the nervousness. And he wouldn't look at her. "What are you doing here now, did they kick you out of office already?"

"Unfortunately no, I'm still stuck with it," Nehi said, and shrugged. "Anna finally got tired of waiting for me, and slid off to find you on her own, and I got lonely for you both." Joe and Anna looked at him. Nehemiah threw up his hands in defeat. "All right, so I was worried about her traipsing around town on her own, there's still a lot of unsavory people left-over from the overthrow. But she found you, so it all worked. You look different. I almost don't recognize you without the crazy mop." Nehi said, studying Joe. Anna rolled her eyes at him. "It's a good different, honest," he fumbled. Something hovered in the air, he sensed it, but couldn't quite pinpoint it. "You sure you don't want to punch me, you know, to get it out of your system?" Joe laughed, his feet still shuffling on the soft earth, too happy to stand still. Though his eyes refused to settle on any object for more than a few seconds, and he wouldn't look at Anna.

"I wasn't mad at you, honest, Beauty already told me you forgot, and I get it." The mute's grin turned to a wry half smile, and a hint of a blush showed under his scars. "You just showed up suddenly is all." Nehi's eyebrows rose and he glanced from one to the other.

"Did I miss the proposal? Oh shoot, I probably barged in on it," he said, in boyish bluntness. "Joe, you can have my sister, if she wants you. There, I didn't even make you ask. When's the date?" Joe's lips parted as he gaped at him.

"If you do that much more this afternoon, your face is going to freeze like that," Anna commented icily. Joe's eyes darted to her for a moment, but went back to Nehemiah, his jaw setting and eyes snapping.

"Some brother you are!" he signed, his hands chopping the

air. "I'm trying to talk some sense into her and here you come barging in with that." Nehi's eyebrows rose. A little smile twitched over his face and his eyes darted to the silver ring sparkling on the mute's thumb. Joe's fingers ran over it subconsciously, confusion suddenly his main emotion.

"Have you forgotten already?" Nehemiah commented, his voice soft. "If more people considered the Ravens, if more were like you, Joe, living out God's diamond love every day, well... My job would be done for me." Joe just stared at him, suddenly still. "I'm not just happy Anna's chosen my best friend. I'm thankful God's blessed her with a man that He can take delight in." Joe blinked at him, his hands closing into a fist on the silver ring.

"Very pretty, Nehi," Anna broke the silence. "Now, go help clear more of the path for a minute, will you?" His good-natured laugh echoed around the Pit as he turned and strolled off into the plants shooting into the sun. Anna waited till she couldn't hear his movements anymore, then spun to the mute. "Well, Joe, you heard him. There's nothing standing in the way, except you."

"Technically, there's two bushes and a pine," Nehi's voice drifted to them, and Anna spun to face it, an acidic reply on her lips.

A shaking hand took hers. She could feel the cold sweat on his palm, and he shook so hard his hand spasmed. Anna turned slowly back, a new wonderful sensation running through her at that hand in hers. Joe knelt on one knee in front of her. His other hand closed over hers, encasing it between his. Two green eyes lifted to hers, bright pools begging her to understand, terrified of what he was asking. He looked about to faint. Anna dropped to her knees, joining him where he was, in the mottled shadow and light. She let her forehead tip gently to rest against his.

"I will always be yours, dear," she whispered. She felt the sobbing intake of breath run through him, the smile that took over his whole form, lifting his slumped shoulders and filling every inch of him with energy and delight.

"Always," Joe signed, his face radiant. "On beyond death, and into new life. I am yours." The pine whispered above them, as if

it laughed in the joy of the lovers nestled under its young branches.

"Sheesh. I'm going to have to endure a lot of this, aren't I?" Nehi muttered from somewhere on their left. Joe spun to his feet and heaved a dirt clod at him.

The acoustics drifting out of the Pit are exemplary. Even Joe's laughter could be heard, in sharp happy breaths, intermingling with the twin's guffaws and busy chatter. From the shrieks and yells it sounded like a mock battle went on down there. Tanzid looked over at Peter.

"We're going to be here a while, aren't we?" he asked. Peter shrugged philosophically and glanced up at the relentless sun.

"That's what we get for signing up as bodyguards."

The noise of clinking glasses and plates moved through the huge ballroom. It mingled with polite conversation, light laughter, the hum of hundreds of humanity all pretending to have fun and being sickly polite. Nehi wondered if he would ever get used to these "parties" as his job went on. The great hall danced with firelight and twinkling chandeliers, the lights glittering off the crystal glassware and the ladies' jewelry. He absently thought it would be ripe pickings for a good thief, and smiled to himself.

"That's better," Lady Margaret purred, and Nehi turned to look at the Gaia dignitary. He expected the high stiff collar on his white jacket to chafe, but it didn't. These tailored items fit too well, more comfortably than his old worn traveling jacket, and Nehi felt surprised, pleased, and a little uneasy about it. The comfort whispered to him that he fit the job, and would grow just as comfortable in it as the clothes that went along with his new occupation. But he never forgot the bright red

Celtic cross splashed across the right side and shoulder of his jacket. He was here for a reason and would account for every word to his Boss when the time came.

"What's better?" Nehi asked, not bothering to correct his grammar or compliment Lady Margaret on something. Maybe the gauzy white dress that shimmered and flowed every time she moved, Nehi thought idly. No, he didn't want to be like these dignitaries, and wasn't going to try; fake, pretty lies flowing in compliments they didn't mean, saying all the "right" things.

"I was beginning to think we bored you," she said. The smile on her face seemed more genuine than most he had seen tonight. "I am aware you would be better pleased with a younger crowd, one more suitable to your tastes."

"His tastes," President Beatle of KAM grinned, a scoff just beneath the words. He had been drinking a little too much, Nehi had noticed. The real man was coming out stronger than most of the dignitaries, though it still lay buried under the polite veneer. "I hear they run along channels more than just younger than us, Margaret. Are you really going to allow that gorgeous beauty of a sister to marry a GI?" Every eye in the little group around Nehi turned to the stunning young lady playing hostess a few yards off.

"I hear he's only an assistant at a music shop," another member of the party murmured.

"I admit, I saw him yesterday and was shocked," Mrs. Beatle commented. "He's...not at all handsome."

President Beatle leaned a little closer, and Nehi smelled the spinach dip on his breath. "I wouldn't bring this up, except in your youth you might need the counsel. Have you considered what an advantage that sister could be, if the marriage was to a more suitable personage?"

"Your definition of 'suitable' and mine don't tally," Nehi shrugged. "I couldn't be happier with Anna's choice. Joe is the best friend I've ever had, and as a bonus, he's an incredible asset to the kingdom." The words were carefully chosen, Margaret noticed with approval. "Choice," "friend," "asset," it smashed

the hovering theory that Anna had been coerced in some way by an ugly GI beast, without coming right out and yelling at them all for a pack of gossiping meddlers. This Judge may be young, but he was no fool. He would do well.

"Asset?" President Beatle asked, his eyebrows rising.

"Even ignoring his genius with music and an artist's brush, he has genuine brilliance in government policies." (Nehi was aware he meant "he's a great spy," and for an instant a twinge touched his conscience. But the same voice whispered there was a big difference between dirty liar and diplomatic.) "But even putting that aside, Joe is a good man, and serves my Savior well. He and Anna are well suited to making a strong family. And it's strong, godly families that are the backbone of our kingdom." The people around him blinked, trying to decide where to take his sudden turn of conversation, awkward to almost all their philosophies. Nehi noticed Margaret's lips twitched as she held back a laugh at their reaction, and he liked her better for it. He caught a crystal glass of sparkling water as a waiter swept past him and lifted it to his lips. It was hot in this crowded room, and he found himself praying they would all go to bed soon and leave him alone. But he was surviving, and even shaking up their ridiculous philosophies. Maybe he could actually do this job.

"I've heard down my grapevine of news," Jarrod Polock changed the subject, Kingdom of the Wise ambassador, "that you have a surprise in store for us."

A smile cut across Nehi's face. Lady Margaret noticed every woman who saw it sagged, and even her aide nearly swooned at the young Judge. But for her, his handsomeness was marred by the look not enhanced; it was too daring of a smile. Something lurked behind it she didn't think she or her country would like. Nehi sat his empty glass on a tray as another waiter swept by, silently wondering how much Joe had learned about the printing process and how long it would take Quintus to get them running, and aching to be out there joining them. He chose his words and answered the question.

"Give me two weeks. Then I think we'll be ready to tell you

about it."

Atif swept the crowded great hall again, but his contact still registered nothing out of sort. Even Gor had come unarmed. Of course the Battle Kingdom leader was a weapon by himself, but Tanzid kept an eye on him, never more than a few yards from the big man. The hum of humanity buzzed around Atif. His head filled with it, ears ringing and chest tight. His head began to throb. Atif spun, shoving out the side door on his left. Bracing, spring air washed over him, the artificial glittering lights replaced by cool darkness. The door swung closed behind him, latching home with a sharp click. Humanities' hum became eclipsed by the breeze in the ancient oak and a lone cricket, chirruping mournfully. He gave a sigh and took another step onto the pretty little porch.

A low whistle drifted from the darkness on his left. Atif spun, one hand slipping automatically to his Healy. Two wicker chairs and a little glass-covered tabletop rested on the corner of the porch. Joe splayed in one of the chairs, a bowl of grapes perched on his belly as one leg dangled over the arm of the chair. The mute's fingers slid into the pocket of his tailored gray jacket and came out with a pair of black gloves. As Joe slipped them on, Atif silently theorized on the likelihood of the mute's fiancé lecturing him about wasted finery and desertion of duty. He hadn't seen Joe in the hall at all tonight.

"Too filled in there," Joe's gloves said, in their computerized voice.

"Too many normal people," Atif agreed. His mouth snapped closed, pressing into a tight line, aware he had given himself away. He turned toward the door, stiff, pretending to concentrate on his duty again.

"We have blood on our hands, you and me." The words sounded awkward and strange coming in the stilted voice of the gloves. Atif came to a gentle stop, rocking back on his heels. He looked to the left. Joe's green eyes glittered in the shadows of the porch.

"Hard for people like us to be with so many who. Who do not know what it is like." The computerized voice stated it, no emotion behind the words. But the mute's face was lined, his eyes haunted with the same things that crawled behind Atif's dark gaze. Joe waved a hand at the seat beside him as he pivoted to a regular sitting position. The glove spouted random gibberish but both men ignored it.

"I am a part of the security team. I need to return to watch," Atif stated. He laid his hand on the doorknob and twisted it.

"Knee-High forgave you."

Atif froze, every muscle tensing.

"God forgave you." The computerized voice seemed to pulse in his mind, and Atif turned slowly, reluctantly. Joe's eyes bored into him, a world of experience and dark knowledge behind the mute's scarred face.

"Have you any right not to forgive yourself?"

The color drained from Atif's face. He stood rigid, staring at Joe; but the mute could see the absence in the other man's eyes, and knew Atif wasn't actually looking at him. Joe waited, signing nothing. The minutes ticked slowly by on the little porch. Second by second, Atif's rigidity melted till he stood hunched and trembling, his head bowed too low for Joe to see any expression on his face. The muffled hum of voices and clinking dishes seeped through the wall. The cricket chirped monotonously, never changing his dismal tune. Joe held out the bowl.

"Grape." The gloves stated it, but Joe's expression made it a question. Atif shifted forward jerkily, as if he had to unglue his feet from the porch, and dropped into the seat beside Joe. The mute held the bowl out again.

The two men sat in silence, the contents of the bowl slowly disappearing. Twenty minutes shifted along the annals of time. The cricket finally finished its song, and the night grew quieter around them. Somewhere inside a glass broke with a bright tinkle of sound.

"I'm not actually needed in there," Atif said. His voice came comfortably quiet. The usual snappishness was missing, Joe noted, and he smiled. His words had settled deep. Good.

"Tanzid, Peter, and you have the new Judge well protected."

"I am just a musician now," Joe signed. Atif gave him a look. Joe grinned at him and shrugged. "Truth. I do not want to be that man anymore. I have retired."

"From what, exactly?" Atif asked bluntly. A twinkle sprung into Joe's face, and a half smile twisted his lips as he studied the man beside him.

"Glad you asked, Frowner. A job you would be good at, where you are needed."

"The IDP leader hasn't been heard from for months," Atif stated. Someone else might have thought it was a change of topic. "I wrung a fact from Harry that fascinates me, do you know the IDP leader sometimes uses trained birds to send his messages back and forth?" Joe's teeth flashed in a grin. He settled back in the wicker chair and started to sign. Atif's eyes glittered in the moonlight as he listened. A smile slowly spread over his stiff features. It changed the dark eyes, warming them and forcing away the sorrow that always lurked there. He began to nod slowly.

This was something he could do for his King.

A rectangle of light swung out and illumined the old oak tree as the door shoved open. Joe watched the changing light with abstracted interest as the door swung back again and snapped closed. Chiffon and silk rustled, one pearl clacked against another, and the smell of lavender wafted gently over Joe. Warmth and love, comfort and safety, closed over him with the sensations. Anna dropped into the empty chair beside him. She blew a strand of hair out of her face and flopped back, blinking at nothing. Her hand swept up Joe's, almost an automatic response after four months being engaged. He slid his fingers in between hers and gently drew her arm close, cradling it in his.

"I don't think I like playing hostess for Nehi," she said. Joe smiled at her, that warm smile that was all for her. The flame of love for his Beauty flared higher. Anna hadn't said, "Why have

you been out here alone all night?" He had a remarkable woman.

"We'll have to find him a wife, so you can duck out," Joe signed. "Things are breaking up in there?"

"Yes," Anna said, letting go of Joe's arm to pull off her silver high-heels. Her toes wiggled in the moonlight. "The dress I like, but the shoes need improvement."

"You looked like a shooting star tonight," Joe smiled, allowing himself to stare at the beautiful creature beside him.

"You mean darting everywhere with my feet on fire?" Anna asked with a quirk to her lips. Joe rolled his eyes and she mended her ways.

"I think you look good in gray," she said, and mentally reminded herself to work on the compliments. "I would even say dashing." Joe grinned at her, a twinkle in his eyes telling her he was considering a snappy reply. Anna had dragged him to the tailors, and it had taken all of her skill at wheedling. Once there, desperation had made her brilliant and she pointed out how useful the pockets might be when he could order anything from a skilled needle. It worked, he had stood still and stopped whining as they measured him. Joe swallowed whatever remark had come to mind and just took her hand in his, looking out at the moonlight. The lone cricket started up its chirp again. Joe started to count, his fingers moving against Anna's palm.

"Five, four, three, two, one…" His head tipped, waiting, a little smile on his face.

The door swung open, light spilling over the oak and then swung closed. Nehi stomped out, leaned against the porch's support post and dropped to sit on the ground with a little groan. Anna laughed. He looked up at her curiously, then decided not to bother asking, and let his aching head drop back against the pillar again. Joe sat still, his eyes shining and dancing in the moonlight as they flitted back and forth between the two. *Family*. He felt almost dizzy as the word shivered through him again. He had a real, honest to goodness family now. Who loved him no matter what, and were stuck with him. Joe sucked in a deep breath, cradling Anna's arm a little closer, and wishing

the next two months of waiting could just disappear, so he could call her...he swallowed, looking at her with those dancing eyes. *Wife.*

"I hope we don't have to do those often," Nehemiah groaned.

"'Semi-annual gatherings are the expected duty of the Judge,'" Anna said, mimicking Oliver's pedantic manner. "Next time you're hiring a majordomo or something, and I'm staying home."

"What, you would desert me to those peacocks and pretenders?" Nehi asked, and faked a pout. "You get a fella and suddenly I'm deserted, I knew that's the way it would be." Anna threw one of her shoes at his head, and he laughed, doing him a world of good. "So you didn't enjoy all the ogling men and the sickeningly sweet ladies talking politics all night?"

"Oh my word, I nearly fell asleep on so many conversations!" Anna cried, her head drooping and one hand massaging the tight muscles in her neck. "Politics are so boring!"

"Boring?" Joe's face twisted. "Boy, you've got the wrong impression. Politics are ideas, worldviews put into action." He laughed, no humor in the movement, his eyes narrowing as the scenes played in his mind. "If you knew how many times Glue and I have almost died from someone's politics, you wouldn't call them boring." His attention snapped to Nehi and a grin split his face. "Did they completely drain you?"

"That depends on why you're asking..." Nehi drawled, sitting a little straighter.

"I was thinking of visiting Q tonight," Joe signed, "and seeing if he's managed to get the k-i-n-d-l-e working." Joe paused and gave his sign for the device, then went on. "I want to see what's on there."

"What is it?" the twins burst out at once. Joe's eyebrows rose.

"You don't know yet?" he asked, then held up a hand to say wait, his other slipping under his gray jacket. Joe pulled out Anna's drawing notebook, glanced at her with an apology on his face for keeping it this long, and flipped to a page. Nehi swiveled to his knees, and he and Anna bent over the sketchbook,

staring at the picture the mute held out.

A huge room viewed from above, with other rooms branching off from it and shelves all around it. The shelves reached high up to the ceiling and lined the floor, with just enough space to walk comfortably between them. Every shelf was lined with books. Books were everywhere, people browsing among the shelves or holding whole stacks of books. The lighting looked quiet and peaceful. Every face looked like the light, quiet and peaceful and happy. It was so realistic and yet so optimistically perfect it could only have come from Joe's soul onto the page.

"You mean..." Nehemiah said then stopped, unable to get the words out.

"I've been carrying that around in my little notebook, drawing on it?" Anna gasped, her eyes so wide they gleamed. They both looked up at Joe and began to fire off questions; what books were there, were there really this many, could they get them off and print them, did he really think they could make a room like this in reality – Joe held up a hand, laughing.

"I don't know," he signed. "I don't know those answers. But that is what the Kindle is supposed to have on it."

"Golly gee," Nehi breathed.

"Can there really be that many books in the world?" Anna asked, her voice low with wonder.

"I counted twenty-five different titles in the printing room," Joe signed, grinning at Nehi. The Judge grimaced and threw Anna's shoe at the mute. He hadn't had a moment free to go back to the miraculous concrete building with all the books. Joe had. It was a sore point for Nehi. Joe snatched the shoe out of the air with a laugh, and tossed it back to Anna. "The Kindle is supposed to have much more than that. If we can find a way to access it, who knows what wonders we might find!"

"That's a lot of words," Anna said, her eyes still glued on the picture. Joe handed her the notebook, hopped to his feet and started strolling over the moonlit grounds toward the north side of the house, where Quintus had stationed himself. Anna and Nehi ran to catch up, Anna's shoes dangling from her hand, her skirts twinkling in the moonlight as they swirled around

her.

"That many books," Nehi murmured, excitement playing over him. "What could we learn from so many different authors!"

"It's a lot of knowledge," Joe nodded, and looked at Nehi, suddenly serious. "And knowledge is power, Judge. You could use this as a tool to hold over the rest of the world. The only kingdom able to print books." But Nehemiah shook his head.

"No, that's not what this gift is for. The world is such a dark place, Joe. This is like...it's like a light maker. We have the chance to print off more than just knowledge, we can print Bibles. And once we have enough, we can start sending them out into the world, like shafts of sunshine. God's own words, ready to say it again: 'Let there be light.'" Nehi's voice rang, clear, reverberating around the three as they walked, his eyes focused on something none of them could see in its entirety; the future, drifting off before them. Joe nodded slowly as he watched his friend.

"The truth does act like a spotlight," he signed, but his mind wasn't really on words. It was on two pools of clear blue, as he looked into Joshua Noble's eyes, and the young man saw through every lie, straight into a torn child, and pulled a cowering soul into the light of burning love. "It can reach where nothing else can, and show up every dirty secret. The truth, if couched in love, can burn away the dark. But it sometimes takes a fight."

"Oh, it will be a fight," Anna said, tossing her hair as the fancy plated braid tumbled off into a jumble of black curls. "But we have God on our side, and the Raven too." Her arm slid through Joe's, and she leaned into him, feeling his heartbeat rhythmically speeding up as a smile spread over him again. "I don't fear anything. Whatever comes next."

"One thing is certain," Joe signed. A shiver of cold, pure joy washed through him as he walked between the twins and his eye went to the lion constellation revolving in its steady dance above them. An adventurous smile twisted his lips and crinkled his green eyes. "Books will change the world."

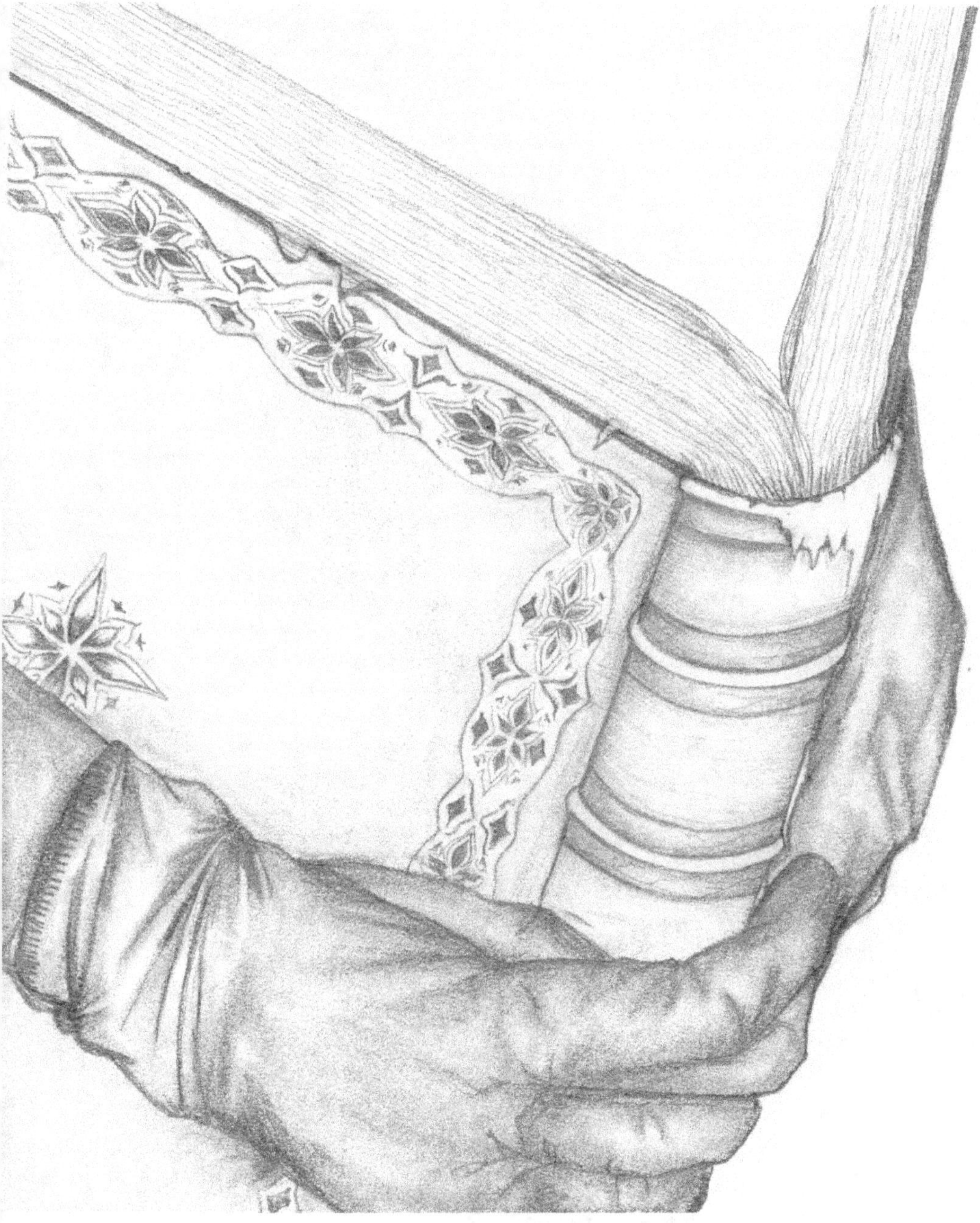

Epilogue

I like the black one," Joe signed. Anna's nose wrinkled, and he signed again quickly. "Or not."

"You are allowed to have opinions."

"So say the wives. We husbands know better."

"Different opinions are important. But the wife's opinion usually wins," Anna stated with a teasing smile. "Now stop joking, this is an important decision, it's going to be a big part of our lives for years." She lost the smile and concentrated on the choices. Four couches sat lined up under a bargainer's awning, as the rain trickled from a gray sky. Joe and Anna didn't mind the rain. They were on their honeymoon. Nothing short of a tsunami could have interrupted their happiness. Anna's hand lifted and she pointed at the last in the line, a blue and white checkered couch, ordinary gingham fabric looking dull and uninteresting in the dim light. Joe's eyebrow rose. He quickly morphed into a smile and nodded, but Anna made a face at him.

"You don't have to pretend to try and please me, silly. But I do think it will look very nice in the farmhouse." She leaned closer, speaking into his ear. A wonderful tingle ran through the mute at having her so near. "It's the least expensive," Anna whispered. A smile twitched over Joe. "If we get that one, we can have enough left to ship it back home and don't have to have someone come out here and pick it up, with all the visiting that goes along with it." Joe's finger shot out and pointed at the blue and white gingham.

"That one," he signed. Anna laughed, and started to stroll around the store, leaving her husband to pay.

Nehemiah slumped behind his desk, staring blearily at the paper in front of him. It would be really nice to get a normal night's sleep. He had held this job for a year and a half now, and it hadn't improved much. He stood up with a little groan and moved toward the espresso maker in the corner. Oh well, there

were a few perks. Like making enough money for good coffee and being able to buy the farmhouse for Anna and Joe. By now he felt pretty fond of his apartment behind the sprawling farmhouse too. He leaned against the wall, a little smile on his face as he listened to the coffee hissing into his cup, and tried to come up with another scheme to make Joe stop insisting on paying out his half of the mortgage.

"Whoa, stop and be recognized, Joe!" Peter's voice drifted from the door, and Nehemiah laughed into his cup at the ridiculous statement. But his bodyguards had been pretty high-strung after the last assassination attempt, poor guys, and he wouldn't have let Pete see his amusement for the world.

"Identification, we have to–" Tanzid barked. It broke off into a yell, as something heavy thumped into the floor. Peter shouted, the door clicked open, and Joe darted through. Nehi just caught a glimpse of Tanzid hopping on one foot holding his other, and Peter lunging at the mute, then the door slammed. The deadbolt clicked in place and Joe spun on his heel. Terror almost beamed from him. Nehemiah straightened with a jerk, coffee sloshing out the top of the white porcelain espresso cup, all humor squelched.

"What's wrong, Anna, she's been snatched, there's–" Nehi gasped, but then Joe was in front of him, slamming a palm into his chest to make him shut up.

"She's pregnant!"

Nehemiah blinked. His pattering heartbeat slowed down, then sped up in a different direction.

"I'm an uncle!" Nehi yelped, throwing his arms up in delight. Coffee splashed up the wall to the ceiling. Joe's foot started to smash down on top his friend's, but he spun out of it, and took a step back. He stumbled, and Nehemiah automatically noticed the way he avoided his bad ankle. Joe must have run the whole way, it showed in his slowed reflexes; that wasn't going to go over well with Anna when he got home. The mute stood as tense as a bow string, his breathing hard. "Joe, you had me terrified! What's the matter?"

"Matter?!" The sign slashed out as he stared his incredulity.

"Oh come on, did you never consider this might happen?" Nehi chuckled. Joe folded into the leather chair in front of Nehi's desk, his hand going to his hair.

"Knee-High, I..." Two desperate green eyes looked up into Nehemiah's and the mute's hands locked together, dropping to his lap. Nehemiah turned back to the espresso maker, letting Joe gather himself. He glanced up at the wall and grimaced. Mrs. Appletree, his exacting secretary, wasn't going to be happy about that. *"A diplomat's office must be orderly and pristine, reflecting the country's purity,"* she had said when she swept in and decorated the place. Well, his would reflect coffee too. Nehemiah turned back with two little cups, sat one in front of his friend and dropped into his chair.

"Ok, what's the problem?"

"What's the problem! I don't know how to be a father! I can't, I'm terrible with people, I can't just accept people like you and Beauty–"

"Even you don't mistrust babies," Nehi murmured over his cup.

"I couldn't discipline it, I'd never be able to raise my hand. I never had a dad, Knee-High! I've never even known a good dad, not really! Ok, maybe Rock, but... What do I do? I don't know the first thing about fatherhood, and what if... What if it's a GI because of me!" It came out a wail, then his hands darted over his face and he curled in the chair.

"Did you happen to mention any of this to Anna?" Nehi asked, his voice neutral. Joe's hands came away and he gave Nehi a 'What kind of fool do you take me for?' look.

"I told her I was excited, which was sure true, waited till her back was turned trying to decide if she wanted to move the couch for the hundredth time, and jumped out the window to run to you. Knee-High, what do I do?" *Poor Ann,* Nehemiah silently thought, but managed to hold his grin back at the mental image of the lecture Joe was in for when he got back.

"Ok, well first off a baby isn't an 'it,' refer to the tyke as 'he' until further notice. Next, it's not a big deal if the little one is a GI." The mute's hands jerked up but Nehemiah went on, rolling

over the stumbled signs. "You're not in KAM anymore, it's ok, Joe. Get the world's thinking out of your head. God's the one Who fashions and makes just as He wants." Porcelain tinked against the wooden desk and Nehemiah made a mental note to defy Mrs. Appletree and get a cup that didn't "tink" at the first opportunity. "Look, Joe, you like kids. You play with Martha all the time and are great with Wiglaf's children when they come visiting during the interkingdom gatherings."

"They aren't mine! I'm not the one they're looking up to! I'm not the one responsible for being the figurehead, the main teacher, I..." A sigh welled from the mute and he slumped, his head dropping on the back of the chair as he blinked at the ceiling.

"I had a great dad," Nehemiah said. "Let me tell you the one secret I know about how it works." Joe's head lifted, staring at him, devouring the advice. Nehemiah leaned over the desk, tapping his finger on the wood to accent each word of the sentence. "A good man makes a good father. That's all it takes. Although we both know 'all it takes' isn't the right phrase for that, it's not easy to be good. But a man who's doing his best to follow Jesus falls naturally into place as a great dad. Just be you, Joe. Be you following Christ, and you have nothing to worry over. You'll do great."

"You're kidding," Joe signed, his face wrinkling as if a nasty smell rolled through. "That's all you've got? Be me?" Nehemiah laughed and pushed his finger against the button unlocking the door. It clicked and Peter and Tanzid shoved in, glowering at Joe. Tanzid limped heavily.

"Go home," Nehemiah chuckled. "Be happy, and don't just pretend to be." Joe rose smoothly to his feet glaring at Nehi.

"When you come to me for help in a crisis, just wait," the mute signed, "I'll tell you to, 'Be you and go be happy.'" Nehemiah laughed again as Joe hopped out the third story window to avoid Mrs. Appletree's glare.

Joe swung the bedroom door slowly closed, his gaze lingering on Anna's black curls splayed over the pillow. She was sleeping easily. His eyes darted to the bundle in his arms. The baby squirmed, but didn't make an outcry. He padded down the stairs into the bright living room, moving around Nehi where he lay passed out on the recliner. Harry and the midwife had left hours ago, everyone had eaten, and gotten the chance to coo and ogle the newcomer. Now came the time to sleep and regroup. The bundle squirmed again and Joe held him close, clicking gently, comfortingly. His eyes darted down and he rocked to a stop.

Blue eyes stared up into his. Tiny, blurry pinpricks of light. The baby opened his mouth and gave a sort of bleat. Joe bounced him gently, so gently, in his arms. One hand escaped from the swaddle, and Joe automatically reached for it. Tiny fingers curled around his skinny thumb, brushing over the silver ring.

So small. So alive.

A smile spread over the mute. It kept spreading, into his bones, through his blood, till he tingled with the warmth and his heart felt as if it might burst. Joe brought the tiny hand to his lips, kissing it softly. Another "awck" sound came from the baby, and Joe laughed. He dropped to the couch, laid the baby on his lap and looked at him.

"Just you and me now, son," he signed. His lip tucked between his teeth and his eyes shone. *Son.* A sharp intake of breath, and Joe started to sign again, just to the child on his lap.

"It's ok. Nobody will hurt you. I'll protect you, always." Blue eyes blinked into his, then slowly closed, and the baby slept. So beautiful. So small. So helpless. Joe drooped, till his forehead touched the tiny, pink, wrinkled, fuzzy head of his son. His signs moved through the bright morning sunlight, elegantly, softly, silent in the still house.

"I will always love you."

"How do you know he's safe?" Peter demanded. The words snapped, an edge to them that cut through the humid air. Anna glanced up, her hand going out automatically to catch little Michael as he did his best to squirm away from the changing pad, giggling maniacally.

"Catherine, give that back to your brother!" she called over her shoulder, and Catherine reluctantly handed the toy back to the sobbing Paul. "I don't know, Peter, but I'm not worried about him. Nehi isn't a wilting flower, even if you and Tanzid treat him like it."

"He's been gone for three days," Tanzid growled. Rain pounded on the windows of the sprawling farmhouse, and Anna silently hated it as she wrestled the diaper on Michael and caught him just as he barreled headfirst off the checkered couch. If only she could send the children outside to run!

"It's also been flooding for three days," Anna said, snatching back Timothy's hand as the toddler reached for the electrical socket with a spoon handle. "Many people were displaced and had to hole up wherever they could when the floods started. Even your trackers short out in heavy rain."

"Why couldn't he just let us use a bone plant?" Tanzid growled. His knuckles were white as his hands squeezed into fists, and Anna didn't bother to reply. They all knew Nehi had declared he didn't like implants, didn't trust them, and refused every model. This was the first time Nehemiah had gone missing in the eight years of his judgeship, and Anna didn't blame his bodyguards for their panic. She just wished they would find someone else to bother about it. Paul's mighty bellow cut through the air, and Anna spun, glaring at Catherine. The little girl handed the toy back meekly and slunk off to pout in a corner. Her twin, Hannah, bounced over with her usual cheerful grin to cheer her up, and Anna quietly prayed Catherine wouldn't pull her red curls out.

A whining, high-pitched hum cut through the air, sizzling and pulsing in their minds. A brilliant white light showed for an instant on the enclosed SOLTD landing pad. A cry of delight went up from seven little people, even Michael understanding

what the noise meant. Peter heaved a sigh, Anna saw Tanzid's face brighten, and she suddenly understood why they were here. She couldn't help a smile, though she kept it turned toward her children. A small figure opened the SOLTD door and made a dash for the farmhouse, a worn gray jacket pulled over his head. Anna flung the side door open and Joe spun in, splashing water off and grinning as he shook himself like a dog. Six little people barreled into him, Michael crawling in a blur and giggling, trying to join the rest. Joe fell back against the wall, laughing, patting heads, and kissing cheeks. He swept Timothy into one arm and Michael in another, making a face at the two youngest and getting a giggle out of all seven. Anna leaned forward and he planted a kiss soundly on his wife, coming away beaming and rosy with his run; and with the delight of being in the midst of his family again.

"How did the commission go, dear?" Anna asked, throwing a towel she had kept warming by the fire over Joe's wet head. He plunked the babies down, settled cross-legged on the ground and signed as children clambered all over him, vying to see who could stay on his lap the longest without getting knocked off.

"Gaia now has their own Ravenswing mural splayed over the central square's wall," Joe signed. "They paid well. Very well. You know, Beauty, I think we can start choosing our commissions at this point, with your marvelous salesmanship and managing, we're rolling in the stuff."

"It's your skill dear," Anna smiled. Joe lifted one shoulder in a shrug.

"Split the difference, you're managing the business end of my skill. Hopefully Gaia thinks it's worth it. The work will do. I would have liked another day to make it perfect, but then I would have missed you for another day, and it wasn't worth that." He winked, grinning at his wife, and was rewarded by a flirtatious half smile thrown back at him as she headed toward the kitchen.

"Nehi's gone missing," Peter said. Joe's expression stiffened and he looked his question. "Three days ago, he went for a walk

in the gardens and dropped from sight."

"'Went for a walk,' is a little bit of an understatement," Tanzid growled, "he stormed out of his office declaring he hated the smell of the coffee maker and had a headache."

"It's been a while since he's had a vacation," Joe signed. *And since I had the chance to have a constellation party with him*, the mute mentally added, berating himself. Usually he made the time at least twice a month, slipping out to Nehi's little apartment in the back yard and rattling rocks on his window to get his friend up. There was an ancient tower on the farmhouse property where they liked to go and spend a few hours under the stars. Lately life had been too busy.

"He's disappeared!" Peter almost wailed.

Joshua barreled into Joe like a speeding train, taking him shoulder to shoulder, and the mute went tumbling backward in a tangle of little arms and legs. Michael tumbled from his lap and started screaming in frustration, as Catherine stamped her foot, signing it wasn't fair. Catherine and Hannah had only been theirs for two years, and the first three years in the work stations would never really be eradicated from the little girls' souls. Fit throwing was one of Catherine's ways of dealing with it, and Joe could see the tremors starting that he knew would lead to her pounding on the floor in a minute. He rolled out from under his roughhousing boys and caught her up, wrapping his arms around the little girl and holding her tight as he kissed her cheek. For a moment she fought back. Then every muscle relaxed and her arms slid around her daddy's neck, her pretty head dropping onto his shoulder. Tanzid's lips pressed tight, and Joe could tell he and Peter were having a hard time not yelling at all the children interrupting.

Anna swept back into the room, holding a tray with the scent of fresh-baked ginger gooiness wafting off it in waves. She plunked it on the coffee table, held out one hand to stop the rush, and began handing out cookies and sippy cups of milk. A minute later, the children were happily plunked in their play room, munching and riveted by the new toys their father had brought from his trip. A sigh of relief slid from Anna as she

settled onto the checkered gingham couch and slid closer to her husband.

"Now, tell me again," Joe signed at the two bodyguards. "He dropped out of sight three days ago?"

"It also started flooding three days ago," Anna murmured, and Joe's eyes flicked to her.

"Nothing's online, not a single one of our trackers," Peter took up. "And we can't get anything launched for an aerial search with all this weather."

"I took a party out yesterday," Tanzid reported, "and combed as much as we could in kayaks. But I almost lost two men when their boat swamped, and there's no way to track a person through all this flooding. There's no sign of him."

"Map?" Joe signed. Tanzid flipped a Grady 2.4 out of its clip on his belt and held it up. A topical map sprung into the air, twisting gently to allow the company to see it from all angles. Tanzid slid it onto the nicked, scratched coffee table and the four leaned in to study the botanical gardens attached to the Judge's House. Joe pointed.

"That? It's the old gardener's house," Peter said. "A man named Kenneth O'Toole and his granddaughter Violet. We tried to get a message through, but he's an old timer who doesn't have any of the modern communication devices."

"Because those are working so well for us now," Anna said, and Joe grinned at her. He hopped up, grabbed his sopping gray jacket again, took a breath, and plunged out into the pouring rain. They watched him dash for the little apartment in the back of the farmhouse, where Nehemiah officially lived. Though in his rare off-duty hours he was usually found in the midst of Joe and Anna's large family, enjoying the semi-controlled chaos. Joe disappeared inside the apartment, and the others waited. Peter sat cross-legged on the ground and reached for a cookie. Tanzid started pacing. Anna leaned back and picked up her latest book, ready to use any moment of peace. The door swung open and Joe spun in again, shaking more water off. A little packet dangled from his hand. He gave another shake, draped his jacket over the fireplace shield, pulled out a dagger, and

moved toward the wall. A sharp thunk sounded in the room as the dagger dug deep into the painted wood.

"Really dear, I had to tell Joshua not to do that yesterday, how am I to explain your doing it now?" Anna commented mildly. Joe just kept digging a hole in the wall, carefully chipping away till an electrical cord could be seen. He detached it with a rubber glove, slid a gadget from the packet onto the cord, and began to program something. A second gadget tumbled from the packet, and Tanzid swept it off the floor. It had a long cord attached to what looked like a pump handle with a plunger on one end poised over a metal circle.

"This thing is illegal," Tanzid muttered. "It makes it too easy to tap into people's houses." Joe winked at him, swept up the gadget's cord, jammed it into the other gadget, and began to tap on the handle. A rhythmic beeping filled the little room.

"That's Mickelson's code," Peter said. He swept a pencil and paper from his pocket and began to jot down the message.

Nehi it's Joe. Answer please.

The mute tapped it out twice, then paused, waiting. He reached for the tray and happily devoured cookies, chatting with Anna about the Gaia job and what he had missed of the children's antics as he ate. After two minutes he reached for the machine and tapped out the same message again. Then he went back to the cookies.

"Is this all you plan on doing?" Tanzid barked.

The machine began to vibrate. A series of beeps came through the chord in the wall, and Peter wrote furiously.

Back again? Bet Anna's glad.

Joe smiled and reached for the handle.

P and T freaking out. You safe?

"We weren't freaking out," Peter defended, his mouth full of ginger cookie.

"Yes we were," Tanzid shrugged. The conversation tapped on between Joe and Nehi and the others watched Peter's pencil fly with the dialogue.

I was. Now I've dug a hole in wall. Host may not be happy.

Sorry. Picked up some news for you while I was out. Anna

270

grimaced and the two bodyguards exchanged a look. When the mute went news gathering even Tanzid and Peter weren't allowed in on his debriefings with the Judge. But everyone close to Nehi suspected the mute's "contact trips" had a lot to do with the uncanny way the young Judge was able to keep the country running safe and smooth.

Thanks for reminding me. Not thinking about work.

Enjoying vacation?

Met a girl. Every eye in the living room widened. For eight years the whole world had been watching the handsome young judge, the most eligible bachelor alive, but Nehi had shown no interest in even looking. *Knows every hymn. Wields a mean rake. Violet eyes. I'm going to marry her. She doesn't know it yet. Met you once.*

I remember her. Joe tapped, his mind flitting back to that dark run, pushing an unconscious traitor and a scared young girl along a scorched, barren ground. *Congrats, brother. Come home when you can. Kids miss you.*

Right. Better patch up wall before host sees.

Joe tossed the gadget to Tanzid and reached for the cookies again. Anna pointed at the gaping hole in her wall, her chin lifting at the bodyguards.

"I expect you two to fix that. There are tools in the closet kitchen."

The two agents glanced at each other, then moved toward the kitchen, heads down, feet shuffling, looking like two scolded schoolboys. Anna leaned toward Joe.

"You went spying again. I know you're capable, and it's been two years since the weakness plagued you, and even your migraines have almost disappeared," Anna said. Her mouth twitched into a frown. "But I still worry when you do that. How long were you out?"

"Nine days. It only took four to paint the mural," Joe signed, meeting her gaze. "It was spur of the moment, Beauty, and once on the site it wasn't safe to contact anyone. I wasn't keeping it from you on purpose. Frowner is still out there and he needed me for something. He's doing good work."

"Is there any news of…" Anna's hands rubbed together, an old, hollow sorrow deep in her eyes. Joe's lips pursed and his eyes darted away, and she knew the answer. No news of Daniel that she wanted to hear; prayed to hear every single day. The noise of the two bodyguards thumping back interrupted, and Anna sat up quickly. "Peter, tell Lizzy to bring the little ones to visit soon, before the children go crazy from all this rain."

A piercing scream split through the room, followed by a babble of voices calling out, "I didn't do it!" Anna grimaced. Joe laughed, hopped up, and trotted for the play room.

Joe's whistle danced around the kitchen, and Anna let it sing alone for a verse, feeling the beauty swell her heart with love and joy. She joined in as she moved to the drying rack. All the children had come home this weekend, and with the fifteen grandchildren along too, it made for a lot of dishes to clean and put away. They had made it a full family gathering the last day, with Wara and Beau and their son and daughter, and Nehi's four grown children, and it had been a noisy, wonderful time. Anna joined in the song, and the two sung through the kitchen work, dancing around each other as they cleaned and put things away. Bright sunshine spilled through the big picture windows and splayed over the husband and wife. Joe's bald spot gleamed in the sunlight, and the gray hairs scattered among Anna's curls seemed to glow. The back door shoved open and Joe spun to look through the barn-like kitchen doors. He laughed and crooked a finger under his nose.

"I can grow it long now that your Joshua's taken over the judgeship," Nehi grinned at him, self-consciously running a hand over his salt and pepper mustache.

"I like it," Violet smiled, giving her husband a quick peck on the cheek.

"I'm glad *you* do," Anna said, making it clear the new bush didn't have a sister's approval as she bustled in from the kitchen. She absentmindedly wiped her soapy hands on hips

that were no longer thin and shapely, then quickly wrapped Violet in a hug. The two ladies moved into the kitchen to finish up the work, chattering about the spring gardens and grandchildren.

"Sorry we missed the gathering," Nehi commented, dropping onto the worn old checkered couch in the living room. He let out a sigh, relishing in the well-known comfort. "And that's not all we missed apparently. I get back and immediately get bombarded with news of an assassination attempt."

"A new guard stepped in and foiled it," Joe nodded. "I heard the guard is going to pull through, but nothing else."

"Yes, a Charlie Green Jr., I was told. I recommended him for promotion, of course. What's the look for?"

"I think I met his parents once," Joe signed slowly, a queer little smile on his face, his eyes focused on something in the past. "Long ago... funny how God works through time." He snapped back into the present, smiling at his brother. "How was the trip? A worthy celebration of twenty years married?" Joe signed. Nehi reached into his coat pocket and handed a paper to Joe.

"This made it about perfect," he said. Joe flipped it open. He dropped suddenly onto the ottoman, his eyes riveted on the paper. A smile stood on Nehi's face as he watched. "It's true. All the work stations are closed, not one is left. You and Anna started it, back when you first got married and began your campaign to rescue the GIs and chimeras. Now there just aren't enough available to feed the work station fires anymore. I don't think the People's Kingdom is going to make it much longer."

"They refused the Bible," Joe signed, his eyes still on the paper. Those green eyes were absent, seeing more than just the words. For a moment, as he sat there thinking of the past, Nehemiah could see the old Joe; the fright, defensiveness, the inward scars almost as visible as the ones marring his skin. He hadn't seen that Joe in years. Nehi let him just sit for a moment before he answered.

"That's true, and I'm sure it's one reason the kingdom's failing. All the other kingdoms at least took a complimentary copy.

Though no one really paid attention."

"Some did," Joe signed with a shrug. "The smaller ones. Of course I haven't been out in... golly, it must be six years since I checked on the state of the world."

"It's getting brighter, Joe," Nehi murmured. "The dark is still there, but...it's not what it was. Gor is long since dead and I've heard rumors about the arena changing to only voluntary fights. The Story Land IDP is blossoming like a field of wildflowers, individuals there are responding to the Bible's truths. Our missionary foundation is sending out Bible wielding light-makers every single day, and it's showing. Slowly. But it's showing. I think Joshua is going to have an easier job of it than we did."

"You've made our place secure in the world," Joe signed. A musical tinkling ran through the bright farmhouse, the first few notes of Joe's world-wide hit, "Holding Together." Joe hopped up and headed for the door. Anna called that Lizzy's pie plate was on the entry table if it was her, and Joe whistled back to say he heard as he pushed down the latch and pulled the door open. A warm summer breeze laden with the scent of the apple orchard blew in. Anna's old white horse Honeysuckle nickered and Pressley, the giant pig who shared the pasture, whistled back.

The breeze skirted past a tattered old man shifting from foot to foot on the mat.

"Hello Joe." His voice was hoarse, anxiety and embarrassment playing through it. Joe hardly recognized it as the cool, cynical voice of Daniel. But he knew the face, wasted and faded as it was. Joe stood with the doorlatch in his hand, just staring. Daniel's dark eyes suddenly looked like a hunted deer and his voice cracked as he spoke again.

"I know I should have left you alone, you don't need me back in your lives, any of you. But I just had to come by and say that...I'm sorry. I'm dying, see, the doctors don't give me much longer and I couldn't go without telling you and Anna and Nehemiah...especially Nehi. I'm not expecting forgiveness or anything, I just thought–"

"Joe, who is it?" Anna's cheerful voice called from the

kitchen. Panic twitched over Daniel's wasted face. He spun to go, hunched and trembling. Joe's hand shot out, wrapped around his arm, and drew him inside. He plunked Daniel down in the entryway wing-backed chair, whistling for Anna. Joe's hand rose and patted Daniel's shoulder.

"I'm glad you came, Wolf," he signed. "And we all forgave you a long time ago." Daniel's tired, frightened eyes suddenly grew wet. The soft sound of his weeping filled the room.

"You were right," Daniel croaked. "All of you, you had the truth all along. Eternity is the only thing that matters in the end."

"And God shall wipe away all tears from their eyes; and there shall be no more death, neither sorrow, nor crying, neither shall there be any more pain: for the former things are passed away.[19]"

---

[19] Revelations 21:4

Appendices

March 234: Born in KAM, marked as GI, "adopted" by the Incomplete Keepers of the People's Kingdom.
April 238: Successfully ran from the IK Station.
August 238: Picked up by Geego Thomle's slaver caravan.
January 239: Sold to Bart Meilson as a pet for his ninth birthday present.
February 240: Acquired by the Advancers of KAM for testing.
March 241: Bought by Jarl Furt, the Music Maker, traveling musician and cat burglar.
April 243: Upon the death of Furt, able to slip off into the streets of Hurn in the Kingdom of the Wise.
June 244: Captured by Gretta Netters, Purveyor of Inferior Peoples.
September 244: Sold to Valus, pawn shop owner in Kallipolis, for odd-jobbing, renting out, and venting anger.

He shifted, trying again to get the open cuts on his back to stop pressing against the shelf. His chains clanked and he felt his Owner's eyes turn to him. He froze, barely breathing. His green eyes dull, his matted hair clumped over his face. A part of him wished he could just stop breathing completely. Just end the pain. Nothing but more of it would ever come to him. His lips twitched as he realized that was his hope now.

And it wouldn't take long to realize it.

Another rental from the mad scientist across the street. Or the smuggler using him as a living jug to transport his drugs. Or just a few more weeks with this Owner and his anger fits. A few months, and the bugs would eat him down to the bone, and he wouldn't have to worry about it anymore.

He laid his head on his bruised, boney arm, resting on the bottom of a metal shelf near the back of the pawn shop. Black mold crawled over the shelf above him, alive with insects. He just lay, almost in a stupor. Not even bothering to remember his name. He was done trying. It didn't matter. No one used it but himself. No one ever would.

The bell above the door tinkled faintly as someone entered. He didn't look up to see who. Owner moved on the stool behind the counter, and he noticed that. A part of him stayed always aware of the threat in the room, always watching for the next blow. Footsteps shifted through the

aisles. Heavy, even, rarely stopping to look at anything. A man, he recognized listlessly as he stared across the aisle at the shelf containing old paint cans.

A pair of leather dress shoes stepped in front of the cans. Pleated pants creased as the customer knelt. Green eyes suddenly stared into two large, blue ones. A young man, in a full blue suit complete with vest, obviously not from Kallipolis. His face was round and open, his ears large and sticking off his head like discs. The rental lay frozen, staring like a rabbit caught in a field. An incomplete never met a normal person's eyes. He lay still, muscles taut, waiting for the storm to burst.

A tear slid down the young man's cheek. The customer's hand stretched out toward him.

He pulled back, curling into himself, the chains clanking and biting harder as he moved. His green eyes closed, too tired to watch as the storm came.

Shoes squeaked, then the heavy footsteps paced quickly toward Owner's counter.

"I want that boy," a voice spoke, in a quick, determined voice. "How much?"

"What boy?" Owner asked, confusion in his voice. A chuckle, thick and spiteful, filled the store. "You mean the little beasty? He's an hourly rental, the rates are clearly marked–"

"No, he's coming home with me. Today, now." The voice came quicker, agitated, and even a little angry. "Just tell me the price and get those chains off him." Silence filled the room, and dragged into a slow thirty seconds, as Owner thought it over. The rental tried not to care. Tried to ignore the whole situation, maybe just to sleep; though he knew the tearing pain in his back made that impossible. But still... what if Owner said yes? What if he got out of this place still breathing? Would that be a good thing? Or would a relatively quick death be better here?

"Four-hundred hannins," Owner grunted. The rental sagged. He hadn't realized how much he cared until that price made it impossible.

Coins clinked in the silence of the store. The rental's eyes

fluttered open. He focused on the customer standing in front of the counter and felt his mind slowly numbing in disbelief. Gold coins clinked steadily onto the dirty metal. Owner's eyes kept growing wider and wider in his fat face. The rental lay still, staring at the growing pile. His eyes flew to the face of the big-eared customer. Why would he pay that much? What did he want him for? The rental's empty, bruised stomach tightened.

"Get those chains off him, now." It was an order as the customer continued to count, but the voice shook with emotion. What emotion, the rental wondered wildly. Excitement for what was coming? Sorrow over the mistreatment of a beast? Disbelief he had just paid that much? Keys clinked from behind the counter and the rental dropped his gaze to the cold metal shelf. He could feel his Owner's footsteps coming toward him. Hot, fat hands gripped his torn wrist and a key slid in the lock.

The chains came off, one by one. Ringing as they fell into the metal shelf. Owner gripped him by the back of the neck, dragging the rental toward the door. He didn't try to get his feet under him. He knew they would just be kicked away even if he managed to stand with that hammy hand pulling him.

A sleek hoverer stood just outside the pawn shop's door. A two-seater, red leather seats, copper shiny and elegant in the morning light. Owner hefted and dropped the rental into the passenger side. His hand pressed against the back of the rental's skinny neck, shoving him against the dashboard as he drew his bloodied wrists together and pushed them onto the door handle. Two leather ties quickly tightened around his wrists and the hand let go.

"I don't know why he wants you so bad," Owner whispered into his ear, as the rental shrank back, unable to get away from that hot breath, that hated face. The words came slow and amused, as if he tasted each one and liked it before he spoke. "But he has a thick ring with a cross on one finger. These Christians, I've heard they offer what they call 'living sacrifices' to their God. Enjoy." One fat hand slapped the copper band running around the top of the hoverer, and Owner strode for the shop again. The bell above the door tinkled,

and the rental heard a quick exchange, agreeing the money was complete, the customer's voice eager to be gone. No. Not the customer. The new owner. His head began to swim as his heart palpitated. He pulled against the ties binding him to the hoverer, desperate for a chance to slip away. He gained nothing but more ripped skin.

The hoverer shook as the young man hopped into the driver's side and pushed the primer down. His other hand pumped the wind bubble as the vehicle began to rise smoothly, shutting off the sounds of the city. The sounds of the Pawn Man chuckling over his new fee. The stench of the shop. Except the stench the rental carried with him.

The hoverer whooshed off, smoothly and quickly, turning the world into a blur. Turning everything except this new unknown presence beside him into an unreachable unreality.

"Can you understand me?" the young man asked. Even through the ringing in the rental's ears, he knew the tone was gentle. Soft. "I mean, can you hear when I speak to you?" The rental made a quick choice. Try servile obedience first. If that didn't work, he could always play stupid idiot later. His head bobbed. "Ok, that's a start! Here, I have a paper around here somewhere..." The hoverer shook as the young man began to look around his seat. He turned, facing the miniscule trunk, and the vehicle wove back and forth in a bouncy irregular pattern. The rental sat blinking, suddenly sure he wouldn't have to worry about anything else after this ride, except what he would look like as a steamed corpse. "Aha, I knew I had it!" The big eared one spun around, and the ride evened out. He held a bright silver pen and a notebook with pristine white paper. "Can you write?" He bobbed his head. "It's ok, you don't have to be afraid." Ha! This character must be the stupid idiot, to think he could believe that. "Take these and–"

The words stopped and the hoverer hiccupped, darting to the left. The steam cut off so suddenly the vehicle bounced into the ground and slid for twenty feet. He tensed, his fingers stiffening as his arms automatically tried to lift to protect himself in the crash. The hoverer slid to a slow stop.

Silence buzzed around his head.

"I didn't tell him to do that." The words were staccato and wet, clearly upset. "I'm sorry, so sorry, let me get my pen-knife." His gaze shifted from staring at the thick forest around them and wondering how close to the wild lands that ride had taken them, to darting down to a knife blade hovering over the leather ties. His hands were discolored and he could feel the blood dripping from his wrists. But he still didn't like the idea of that blade coming closer.

"It's so tight!" This new owner sounded like he might cry. Or throw up. Maybe both. He didn't dare look at him to make a better guess. "I'll be as quick as possible, ok? Just hold still." The blade slid between the ties and he tried not to scream as the sickness from the pain rolled through him. But this new one was quick, and a moment later he lay panting in his seat with nothing holding him there.

It had been four months in the pawn shop, and two with the slaver before that. It felt strange, wonderfully strange, to have nothing clamping him down. Not even a bone chip marking out an invisible radius. Weirdly, weirdly strange.

"Please, can you tell me your name?" the new one asked. A sniffle came from him, and green eyes shot up to his face despite himself, confusion mounting. He didn't know what to make of this new owner. No one asked his name. No one assumed he had one. No one cared. The paper and pen pushed across the dashboard toward him, gentle, inviting. He hadn't held a pen in two years. He blinked, slowly reaching for the silver metal. Remembering the feel as it slid into his boney fingers. Remembering himself as he scrawled the three letters over the page.

Joe

The new owner nodded, tears clear in his eyes as he tried to smile. Another sniffle slid from him.

"Thank you. It's a strong name, Joe, I like it."

Joe's tired, tired mind fuzzed, his vision shaking as the words slid into his consciousness. This man had just called him by name. He stirred, forcing his mind back into focus, looking out at the trees moving outside the hoverer's bubble.

Nothing held him down. Joe's eyes went to the new owner, assessing him as the man dug into his trunk. The owner kept talking, in a distressed sort of way. He seemed unsuspecting, completely oblivious to any thought of danger. The rental eyed the prominent Adam's apple bobbing on the man's throat, considering how much force he would need to kick it in and slip out. Or maybe wait till this new owner finished scrabbling and gasping from a collapsed windpipe. He could dump the body and figure out how to drive off in this sleek new machine, start a new life with it. Joe knew he was weak, desperately weak... But that sort of blow, if he did it quick, he could still manage. To be completely free again...

A bag of prepacked energy bars landed on the seat between them. Two water bottles thumped into the floor and rolled against Joe's feet. The new one spun to him, wrapping soft washcloths around the mute's bleeding wrists. Joe pulled away from his grip automatically, pressing himself against the door. But he fingered the material, wrapping it a little tighter around his wounds. It was so soft. He had never felt anything so soft.

"It's ok," the new one said again, his voice gentle and quiet, that distress still lacing it. "You don't have to be scared, it's ok." The hoverer hissed steam again and spun out into the road. The trees turned to a blur, and Joe slumped back against the leather seat. He had missed his opportunity.

"I'm not your owner. I didn't buy you." Green eyes shot up again, confusion, even anger moving over the wasted, sharp face. "I bought your freedom. Just like a Friend bought mine, a long time ago." A heavy metal ring dropped into Joe's hand, and he spun it automatically, staring at the golden cross etched beautifully into the silver. "It's going to be all right, Joe, trust me. I'll introduce you to Him."

February 245: *Freedom purchased and home established by Joshua Noble.*

March 4ᵗʰ, 246: *Renewed by Christ, resolves to serve his new Master by being the IDP's troubleshooter.*

October 246: *Rescues the chimera Cobeau in the People's Kingdom.*

July 247: *Runs across the FFs for the first time.*
November 248: *Joshua Noble betrayed and slaughtered in the arena of the Battle Kingdom.*
December 250: *Met Nehemiah and Anna Hillson.*

The Wolf

240 (15): *Uncle dies of drowning, begins to question God, which leads to questioning his way of life.*
243 (18): *Uses the persona of a Wolf for the first time in the Underground Market while gathering supplies, contacts, money, and a reputation.*
244 (19): *Steals his first book while on a diplomatic mission for his father.*
245 (20): *Meets Freddy and his FFs.*
February 247 (22): *His alternate career in full swing, stolen the Kingdom of the Wise book, and Gaia, attained excellent fees for the books return. The Wolf is enjoying the "high life" he lives.*
July 247: *The Black Raider first appears to annoy the Wolf.*

July 247: The Raven first learns of the FFs and begins to probe more about

them.

November 248 (23): *Convinced he is in complete control of his world, fully swallowed by his Wolf career, only home for visits before he creates an excuse to scoot off again. Parents put it down to restless feet of a young man who enjoys traveling and spreading his wings; the Wolf always completes Daniel's Sojourner missions with perfection.*
March 249 (24): *Set in his attempt to steal the KAM book by unknown agents. Violently angry, the first of the recordings of the Wolf hunting travels through the underworld. Marks a turning point, no return for Daniel from the murder and thefts.*

March 249: Barely manages to save the KAM book with the help of two

UPC agents, nearly gets his head chopped off in the process.

August 249: *Succeeds in KAM heist, and takes Kallipolis book the same month. Back on top, pleased with his life choices.*
January 250 (25): *Slips the Sojourner book in his coat on his rounds. Takes it out of the country when he leaves as Daniel Hillson*

to "hunt for the thief."

March 250: Knows the Judge family is involved in the Sojourner book theft. Leaves the journal pages where he knows the Wolf can find them, misses seeing Daniel Hillson pick them up.

April 250: Finds the first of the journal pages, and hears of the treasure his family is supposed to have.

September 250: "Leaks" the news of the Sojourner's book to the world, sends the FFs in to try and snag the other Hillsons, convinced the rest of his family is hiding things from him.

September 250: Disintegration comes on the Sojourner Kingdom. Titus Hillson and his wife murdered, Anna and Nehemiah enslaved. Raven too far to do any good for the Sojourners. Hunts down Daniel.

October 250: Meets Joe and Beau, traveling musicians, and they latch onto him. Ditches Ariel.

December 250: Knows the Hillsons involved with the Wolf, desperate to find the Bible. Gets Daniel caught in the Tao to keep him in one place and out of trouble, heads for the Sojourner wreckage to learn what he can.

December 250: Caught in the Tao, interned for an indefinite time. Begins to cultivate contacts within the prison, working his way steadily out.

January 251: Anna and Nehemiah rescued by the Ravens. Joe sees Anna has the treasure.

July 251: Manages the theft and ransom of the Tao book while comfortably interned (by now living in luxury even though still technically in jail). Ego rises a little higher, considers himself capable of anything.

September 251 (26): Escape setup offered, he takes it. Hover crash that leaves him in a coma. Raven pulls him out and stashes him in his cabin.

November 251: Wakes for the first time. Grooming the old grumpy couple to use in his business.

December 251: Contacts Freddy, begins running his business again.

January 252: Up and about, plotting the Geat and Prophet's Peace heists with the FFs. Secretly already planning heist for the Story

Land book.

February 252: *One of Ariel's assassins find him, and he barely manages to kill the killer first. Realizes he's going to have to drop out of sight until he can deal with the mermaid.*

March 252 (27): *The twins find him at the cabin, he pretends he has just started moving in the last few months. Thoughts of the "treasure" mentioned by the journal pages reenters his calculations.*

March 252: Manages to set the Wolf in the Goat and Prophet's Peace heists with the twins' help. Carefully leads Daniel to stay latched to the twins, and sets him up to find the next journal pages.

May 252: *Meets with the Trio, frustrates the Raven's attempt to regain the Bible, misses out on the Story Land book. Interest in both the Raven's knowledge and the treasure rises a little higher. Begins to probe the Raven as Daniel Hillson.*

August 252: *Heads in for the People's Kingdom book. Again set by the Raven at the last minute. His reputation in the underworld beginning to teeter. Obsessed with the treasure, as the one thing in his life he can't seem to control and obtain.*

August 252: Retires officially from the Black Raider. Begins the process of retiring as IDP leader.

September 252: Sets out to recover the Bible. Manages to regain the book, but only by being caught.

September 252: *Uses FFs to capture the Raven, and murders the Ill Trio as agents who failed the Wolf twice, makes sure their end recorded and sent out to the underworld. Loses the FFs as a viable option for agents.*

October 252: *Aware the Raven is crippled, acts on his hunch that the Raven slipped away in Walden for a purpose; finds Ariel's hideaway. She barely gets out alive.*

October 252: Raven realizes he's letting Wolf loose too long as his wings stay tattered. Has to rely on others' help, brings in Atif.

November 252: *Helping the Sojourners rise again as Daniel Hillson, tied down by Nehi's plans, Atif's requests for help, etc. He enjoys helping, as he knows in a year or two the Wolf can enjoy the fruits of his labor in a fat book ransom from the Sojourners. Contentedly*

planning thefts of the Story Land and Prophet's Peace books, slotted for spring of the next year.

November 252: Still mostly tied to bed, but scheming and working through others. Helps the process of resurrecting the Sojourners and planning the Wolf's eventual downfall after the resurgence.

January 253:

Sojourners surge up under their oppressors, regain their kingdom.

The Raven drives the Wolf into the open. Catches him in a carefully laid net.

The Wolf surges up in revenge for his ignominious defeat, destroys the Sojourner book and heads to the printing press to be certain the extra copies are also destroyed; thus, in the thinking of the Book Base Age, annihilating Christianity. But miscalculates by discounting Beau as an animal incapable of any real thought. Ends by being retaken by the Tao.

The Raven retires in the Sojourner Kingdom, hands over his IDP duties to Atif, and marries his sweetheart.

Chimeras

The pain seared through him, eclipsing every thought. A small hand shoved something into his mouth, something thick, that muffled the noises coming from his throat. Darkness closed over Cobeau's head. But it wasn't unconsciousness; they had taken even that from him with their drugs. Something pushed against his back. It pushed him up and the thing moved. Steam hit his dragging arms.

The pain shrieked and he echoed it.

Small hands gripped his. He felt his hands pulled up till their edges touched, then brought back down to his sides in a sharp movement. The word seeped into him and he understood the order.

Quiet!

Cobeau lay still, the blackness shifting high above him with a familiar, dark tinkling sound. Black pines, with their hard needles. His hands flopped over his chest and he felt skinny arms around his legs, heard someone blowing hard with the effort of holding him. He moved, hovering under the dark. Something else... he heard howls, shrieks. Something he should know... For an instant the faces of Calla and Ydara resurfaced. It came as a lightning bolt, cutting through even the pain. It took the last strength Cobeau had left, and blankness claimed him. No more thoughts disturbed his silence. He lay flaccid and stared at the shifting blackness above him without seeing it.

His arms slid slowly off his chest and thumped into the forest floor. An annoyed gasp came from the small form panting with the effort of moving the chimera through these woods. He pursed his lips and forced himself into a run trying to get a better grip on the heavy legs. The image of a hairy, happy, rabbit-like oval pulsed in his mind as he pushed the straining hoverboard forward. If he could just reach that gigantic animal and get this hulking chimera on her, they could make it out before the CKs noticed him missing.

Other images cut through his mind and the thin lips pressed so tight they couldn't be seen. The CKs were busy right now with their other captives. They wouldn't turn back to look for this one until the others were dead. The mute found himself praying the end came quickly for the two he hadn't been able to rescue.

A black pine shifted above them and for an instant the moon broke through and shone on the small form struggling to push the huge one through the forest. It glinted off two glittering streams of tears on a sharp, scarred face that should have been young.

~~~

Bright sunlight cut through his eyelids. Slowly he opened them. The yellow sun shone on him. No dark trees in the way. No dark faces or black boxes. The chimera stared, unblinking. The One moved that great yellow ball. He took away the dark.

Fur. He lay on fur. And it felt warm and rippling and alive. It moved. The chimera tried to shift his head to see more.

Pain sliced through him and for an instant the sun cut off into dark splotches.

A whistle slid through his mind and the chimera blinked his vision back into focus. A sharp, small face stared at him. The fur under him had stopped moving now. A water skin pressed against his lips and the chimera drank, emptying the skin. As it came away he saw the face again. Smiling. Such a strange, unfamiliar thing. A smile.

"Hello," the boy waved. "Don't try to move, you are hurt very badly. Do you understand me?" The chimera stared at him. The thin hands came into view again and shifted slowly in the sunlight. "No move."

The chimera understood and obeyed. He always obeyed.

Sleep crawled over him and he let the scene fade.

His eyes opened slowly. Now the light crackled and shifted. Darkness clung to the edges, trying to take his feet. A little gurgle of terror came from him and he tried to pull away from the dark, to get into that light. He managed to turn on his side in the power of his fear. He felt the fur fall away, and he tipped.

Two small hands rammed into his chest, heaving him back again. Sharp gasping and panting came, and he flopped onto his back again. The soft fur rippled under him. The crackling light shifted, closing all around him. Shutting the dark into a circle somewhere outside. The chimera blinked as the small, sharp face appeared again. A lit torch in his hand crackled and shifted, casting the light. He made that light. He kept the dark off. Again came the water, a little food. That light held steady as the fur shifted and

the something he lay on trilled to the night. Strength slowly started to flow back through his limbs. The small sharp one watched as the chimera flexed his hands and rolled his shoulders. Slowly the small hands lifted and moved in the torch light.

"Do you remember?" the boy asked. The chimera blinked at him blankly. Joe couldn't decide whether to be relieved or sick. He recognized the blankness on the face of the man in front of him. No memories rested behind it. It was all wiped clean by the trauma. Right now, Joe would choose to be thankful he didn't have to deal with the added pain of a chimera grieving his packmember's loss. "You wore a tag. C-o-b-e-a-u?" The chimera's shoulder lifted in a shrug. His expression held nothing, no sign to say he cared.

"Quiet?" the chimera rumbled, his voice still so hoarse it came barely audible. Joe shook his head.

"No more quiet, it's ok."

"Master?" the chimera rumbled. Joe shook his head sharply, a frown cutting over him.

"No. Friend." For a moment green eyes stared back into blank brown ones. The mute made the choice to risk offering more. Joe's thin hand slid under his shirt and pulled out a metal cross on a chain. "The One who made the light sent me." Interest sparked in the brown eyes.

"You know Him?" the chimera rumbled, his voice hoarse. The mute nodded. He slid the chain from his neck and let the cross fall into the huge open hand. The hairy fingers closed over it, gently, as if he held a precious treasure that might be crushed. This he remembered. Most chimeras innately recognized the Someone above everything else, but there were some who wanted more and some who didn't care. This one wanted more. The deep brown eyes stared, begging for more, for even just a name, a tiny fact about the Creator he felt but had never been allowed to know. Joe took a deep breath and committed himself.

"Lie still, we have a long way to go. It's going to be all right. I'll introduce you to Him."

Lasers and Gadgets

In the early days of research, the main problems with using lasers as a weapon were the source of energy and the heat emitted by the process. It takes so much power to create a weaponized laser, the apparatus used to excite the atoms was too heavy for even a tank to carry, and handheld weapons were out of the question. Also, most of a laser's energy burns off as heat, before the laser light becomes strong enough to be useful. One more problem with the practicality of lasers was atmospheric interference. A high concentration of dust or water in the air might tamper with a laser's accuracy, bending the beam, or causing it to reflect off the atmospheric conditions.

The first two problems were finally solved by the Pylum battery. A man named Ralph Pylum, in the year 20 of the Book Base Age, discovered a battery powered by heat. It is the perfect solution for a laser weapon energy source. The Pylum battery requires an initial charge, which it uses to start the lasing process in a weapon. The laser passes through its chosen medium and begins to bounce between a complicated series of mirrors, increasing the atoms' excitement and thus the power of the la-ser. This is called priming. Some take more time than others to reach a weaponized level of energy, it depends on many factors, including the size of the battery and the medium chosen. But as it primes, the laser is giving off wave after wave of heat. The Pylum battery absorbs it and uses the energy. This creates a weapon which basically powers itself. If allowed to sit unused for some time the battery loses its charge and needs a "jump start" of external heat to start the lasing process. But if kept in proper order, a Pylum battery laser will provide its own energy indefinitely.

Atmospheric conditions are still an issue with some lasers, throwing off the accuracy. The lens of a laser (what the beam is finally sent through, after the energy has climbed to useful levels) as well as the lasing medium affect the accuracy. It is possible for the beams to be reflected back, or even scattered. This kind of reflection would be too weak to cause much damage, unless they landed in a person's fragile eyes. Because of this danger lasers are never to be fired without safety-dyed goggles.

Brunhiem

The laser of choice for the Sojourner Guards, the Brunhiem is a compact liquid fiber laser. The lasing medium is optical fibers, coiled to pack more power into a weapon that is smaller, lighter, and more easily maneuverable than most of its contemporaries. The Brunhiem employs three separate packets of carefully coiled optical fibers. The packets each have access to the Pylum battery, a relatively small affair for a laser. Because of the smaller size, the Pylum does not consume all the heat created by the lasing process, and so is surround-ed by a liquid coolant, running through tubes wrapped around the battery. The separate beams from the three packets combine in the reflective chamber as the weapon primes.

Priming: 3 seconds
Health Length Without Charging: 2 weeks
Weight: 9.27 pounds
Accuracy: Excellent

Compton

A revolutionary weapon, the Compton laser is the first to uti-lize dark energy and matter as an energy source. Two balls of care-fully fashioned Z shielding are bound next to each other in a copper fitting. Inside one is a ball of dark matter, inside the other dark energy; they are small enough as to be almost trace amounts. But when activated, a "window" is cracked between the two. Dark matter and dark energy excite each other when combined, and create what science currently sees as an inexhaustible source of energy. The gun then utilizes Compton scattering between the two balls to harvest gamma rays. The rays are fired through a crystal lens fashioned after the Krackmens' excellent design. Gamma rays are invisible to the human eye, and so most Compton guns are sold with specially dyed goggles to allow the shooter to see where his rays land. Currently thought inexhaustible, nearly unbreakable, and as small as a Ruby laser (though considerably heavier), a Compton is viewed as the best weapons breakthrough since the Pylum battery.

Priming: 0 seconds
Health Length Without Charging: Unknown
Weight: 9.4 pounds
Accuracy: Very Exceptional

Healy

Termed by some a variation of a Brunhiem, the Healy laser is a liquid fiber laser, with the battery wrapped in liquid coolant, as the heat from the lasing process is not fully consumed by the Pylum. It contains four chambers of optical fibers. With the smaller size, and the four chambers placed directly against the Pylum battery, the priming time is excessively short, and the energy impressive especially with being emitted almost immediately.

Priming: 1.5 seconds
Health Length Without Charging: 2 weeks
Weight: 9.47 pounds
Accuracy: Excellent

Krackmen

The Krackmen is a prepossessing weapon with its intricately crafted red carbon stock. It is a dye laser utilizing rhodamine, and the accuracy is legendary, though the priming time is a serious drawback to the weapon.

Priming: 7 seconds
Health Length Without Charging: 1 week
Weight: 15.9 pounds
Accuracy: Exceptional

Ruby

A mass market weapon, the Ruby is a solid-state laser found in most kingdoms during the Book Base Age. It employs a synthetic ruby rod as a medium and is prized for its small size. Because of the single-handed size, the battery is necessarily smaller, making the power less effective. It creates a lethal laser shot, but only at a range of up to six feet. A popular choice for personal

defense, but not optimal as an army weapon.

    Priming: 4 seconds
    Health Length Without Charging: 5 days
    Weight: 6.3 pounds
    Accuracy: Average

Strafer

Setup very like a Ruby laser, this is a close range weapon used for personal defense. It is small enough even for concealment upon a person, a rare thing with a weaponized laser. The strafer varies from the Ruby in the makeup of its lenses. The strafer has a combination of five lenses, carefully overlaid with one an-other, capable of being aligned into one stronger beam, or shift-ed to create up to eight different beams. In a close quarters fight it can be used to take down multiple enemies, making it ideal for self defense.

    Priming: 4 seconds
    Health Length Without Charging: 5 days
    Weight: 6.5 pounds
    Accuracy: Average

Toaster

A large optic laser employing several stages of photon conversions for optimum interaction with the target. The Toaster starts in the first chamber as infrared beams, travels through special optics to become green light, then converts to ultraviolet in a third chamber. By the time it releases from the third chamber, the Toaster beam is one of the more powerful laser weapons employed. The three different phases of the photons how-ever make it too large for a handheld weapon, and most used in the field are from KAM's design of a truck-mounted version.

    Priming: 15 seconds
    Health Length Without Charging: 10 days
    Weight: 208.6 pounds
    Accuracy: Tolerable
    Strength: Decimating

PUDRE Dark Ray

The Pulsating Ultrasonic Dark Ray Emitter, or PUDRE, came on the market ten years after the invention of the first Compton laser pistol. Observing the interaction between the dark matter and dark energy, the inventor of the PUDRE foresaw a different use than the laser; through careful experimentation he discovered how to form a localized, directed black hole effect. The ray beams a concentrated black hole, sucking anything it hits into the devastating dark force. It is capable of twisting steel and titanium, breaking diamond glass, generally wrecking anything it hits. The distance and concentration of the beam can be adjust-ed, its range being between six yards to twelve yards.

Speed of Light Transportation Device - SOLTD

A foray into new technology during the mid-200s of the Book Age, the SOLTD utilizes dark matter and dark energy to form what the inventor, Quintus Leeman, terms a space-warp bubble. Originally he was searching for a method of time travel, and speculated on the possibility of creating a time-warp bubble by the use of the black hole. Through careful experimentation he discovered there is a calm at the center of the massive force caused by mixing dark matter and energy, and it is possible to be enclosed safely in the midst of the swirling mass of a black hole by intentionally causing it. The bioelectricity of living beings is "felt out" by the black hole as it forms, and it molds itself around it. The SOLTD makes it possible to move large amounts of living things at the speed of light, if there is no break in the chain of bioelectricity within the center of the hole.

The inventor admits it was an accident that set him in history as the first SOLTD traveler. During an experiment his assistant en-tered, opening the specially-reinforced door. The black hole currently formed in his lab sensed a small source of other dark matter and energy and the inventor found himself dis-placed, suddenly in the Kingdom of the Wise quite literally crashing in on the inventor of the PUDRE, as Hyram Grange completed his work on that gadget. Leeman did not travel through time as he had origi-nally hoped, instead he found he had moved kingdoms with

almost no time involved. He was quick to see the possibilities of the SOLTD as a transportation device.

The method of programming the direction of travel took him two years to perfect, and to this day only those specially li-censed to build the SOLTDs are allowed to know the intricacies of the method involved. We do know it employs small bits of dark mat-ter and dark energy, attracted to particular places through the pe-culiarities of the earth's magnetism. The smaller pieces are care-fully introduced to the larger pieces contained in each individual SOLTD's Z shielding balls. Through this they come to "know" each other, thus eliminating the possibility of multiple SOLTDs detect-ing the same pieces of matter and energy and intersecting.

The SOLTD changed the course of the Book Age, allowing those kingdoms and peoples who first attained proficiency in the gadget to gain a solid foothold over those slower to acknowledge the incredible usefulness of being able to "zap" people anywhere on the planet. To this day it marks a turning point in the technol-ogies of mankind.

Kingdom's Worldviews

Story Land

Book Base

Ducky's Big Pond, Vlanderbelt, Vera, Ducky's Big Pond. Illustrated by Laura Moler, Penguin Random House, 3466.

Government Structure

"I will go for a walk today. Perhaps I will find something to do." (Pg. 1)

Let me tell you a story. There once was a man named Jarrod Talum. As he traveled along the coastline, he came to realize that people understood things differently according to their own experiences and interpretation of the world. And why not? Why should there be one thing that's true for everyone, instead of each individual having their own truths? The more he spoke to people, the more he realized that none of them really understood what he meant. This confirmed his theory that truth could only be grasped by the individual, and that it changes from person to person.

It was about this time *Ducky's Big Pond* came into Talum's hands. He flipped through the book and enjoyed the bright illustrations. Gradually he came to see the small duck's journey to find something to do as an allegorical expression of life. We are all, according to Talum, on a journey to find something to do. And the answer comes differently for each of us. Each individual sees life through their own lens. Sharing viewpoints, or "truth" as most of the world call it, is practically impossible. Even the duck in the book came under Talum's own interpretation. When the duck said, "Quack, quack," to the cat did he mean, "Chase me," or "Please look at the blue sky." The cat heard, "Chase me," but Talum heard, "Look at the blue sky." Both were true according to the different individuals who heard it.

Talum settled along the coast. Gradually others settled around him, those who either agreed with his assumption that truth changes according to each person's perception, and those who

simply preferred the tropical flowers and unrestrictive kingdom.

It didn't form into an actual kingdom until a woman named Beria approached Talum with a desperate plea for help to recover her three-year-old son from her husband-turned-nasty. Talum turned to his best friend, a man named Greg. History has lost his last name, it seems everyone knew him as Greg. They also knew him for being just and brave. He listened to Beria, immediately declared that interpretation went only so far as the single individual, when it invaded other individual's lives to their hurt, intervention became necessary. He formed a posse and restored Beria's son to his mother in less than an hour.

For most, that day marks the formal creation of Story Land. Of course there are some who interpret it as other days, that is in the nature of the kingdom. But for most, Story Land formed the day the one law came into being: If one individual's interpretation causes harm to another individual, there is just cause to intervene. Of course there are thousands of interpretations of that one law, but in the history of the kingdom we find people who are willing to draw a line and step in: those are the people keeping the kingdom functioning as a kingdom. Because of their work, social interactions are possible within Story Land. They gradually became known as the Social Workers, and they have a strict hierarchy and long work hours.

Those who term themselves in charge of Story Land, the government, change frequently. When anyone can extrapolate their own meaning from the kingdom's book, anyone can claim their own form of leadership. Usually the overthrows come by employing mercenaries from outside and the seedier elements within the kingdom. (A kingdom with only one law naturally caters to those who prefer not to follow laws.) But after the dust clears and a new form of governing comes into play, the SW is still there, and still keeps the kingdom's general structure.

Incompletes and Chimeras

"'What's your name?' Ducky asked the frog. But the frog just stared." (Pg. 20)

Once there was a governor named Janet Grange. She admired KAM very much, and declared incompletes and chimeras not

wholly human, and therefore not entitled to full rights. But one day she was overthrown by the Neil Family. The Neils, like the other governors of Story Land, took this portion of the book, and the strong leaning toward individualism throughout the kingdom, and choose to see incompletes and chimeras as the same as anyone else.

Art and Music

"When the leaf fell from the tree, it danced. Ducky watched as it swirled and spun. 'It needs music to dance to,' thought Ducky. She began to sing." (Pg. 11)

Let me tell you about Ben Carson. Here is a man who loves music. Ben Carson lived in Story Land in the year 100 of the Book Base Age. It seemed a very significant number to him, and somehow needed marked and celebrated. His interpretation for marking the 100th year turned into the Seal Annual Music Festival, so named after his favorite animal (at that time abundant in great herds on the beaches of Story Land). Let me tell you of another individual, Ben's wife Henrietta Carson. Thanks to Henrietta's exceptional organizational and promotional skills, the SAMF quickly became a worldwide sensation. Any band stamped with the label, "SAMF Champion," can be assured of their future popularity.

Naturally, as the home of the SAMF, musicians and artists abound within the kingdom. Most of them also appreciate the "anything goes" attitude of Story Land, and settle happily within the borders.

Science and Advancements

"Ducky waddled on, leaving the frog, and the cat, and the leaf. The pond seemed to stretch out forever in front of her. 'Maybe it does go on forever! How do I find out?' she wondered." (Pg. 21)

Violeta Yin loved science. She grew up longing for nothing so much as to be a scientist and help the people around her by finding new things. Story Land welcomed her ambitions, and others like her, and she enjoyed a long career in the Neil Science Hall.

Some of her interpretation of the world, however, other kingdoms find it hard to agree with. Violeta loved the color violet. She loved it so much, she placed violet dye in her permanent contacts, and thereafter declared the world could only be observed in shades of purple. Another time, she published a widely read paper stating popcorn balls were overgrown atoms humans felt compelled to create, because of outside influence from the stars.

There are many similar storylines of scientists within Story Land. If a scientist has a desire for worldwide recognition, emigration to KAM or the Sojourners is the most often sought course.

Army

"The dog ran at Ducky, and his teeth looked very sharp. Ducky fluttered her wings and landed gently in the pond. The dog slid to a stop at the edge and stared at her. 'There you war hound,' Ducky quacked as she paddled, 'you will not eat me today.'" (Pg. 13)

Once a Story Land governor named Wilt Umtern chose to see the world in red. The export fees had been high that season, the coffers of the kingdom full. He used it to outfit a great army, and marched off to war. They overthrew two kingdoms before Umtern met his death at the hands of a Battle Kingdom spear, and the army dispersed with their kits.

During his lifetime Wilt Umtern expressed a great loneliness, because no one in the past or present of his kingdom seemed to adhere to his truth. It is a kindness he did not know the future. The coming governors, like those in the past, looked at the dog section of the book, and their own personal stories, and decided being the attacker is not wisdom.

There was another man named Vergal the Vicious, Wazir of the Prophet's Peace, who saw overrunning new kingdoms as his main truth. The year 92 of the BB Age saw his black army ranged against the Story Land border. The citizens decided they did not like the idea of Vergal the Vicious, and raided a local munitions plant. Vergal the Vicious was forced into retreat with only a quarter of his army left alive.

Social Structure

"And so Ducky arrived back at her nest. She fluffed the downy

feathers and settled in for a rest, suddenly very tired. 'I suppose "having an adventure" was what I did to-day,' she said to herself. 'But I am glad I'm home.'" (Pg. 22)

There are some interpretations which state Talum lived on the verge of insanity, and just happened on good friends and good luck. Other interpretations place him as one of the smartest leaders in history, who used a philosophy to his advantage. Whichever story you choose, Story Land sits on the best coastland for trading known to the Book Base Age. The import and export fees are usually kept low, which facilitates a great deal of movement back and forth. The busy port creates revenue for the kingdom, and lots of jobs. The high turn-around of governments combined with the heavy emphasis on individual stories fosters factories with almost no government regulations, and medium to low tax rates.

Like Frank and Myra Yeals, makers of personalized bone plants, most of the people of story land enjoy prosperity. This allows them leisure to enjoy each other, and find time to foster the things they love. Architects find a great deal of work around the country, as the citizens enjoy expressing their personal stories through their building styles.

It would take much too long to tell all the stories of the living styles, work ethics, school tactics, and religious preferences of Story Land. Just so long as no serious harm comes to someone against their will, anything is allowed. Some things are quite unpopular, such as holding to a truth that tells others their stories are untrue, or believing there is only actually one truth which ought to be applied to everyone. Usually any who do hold to viewpoints of that nature (completely at odds with the basic Story Land premise) merely face extreme peer pressure and dislike from their fellow citizens. But there are times the dislike becomes hatred. The lack of laws and government oversight tends to foster a criminal element in Story Land, which are always for hire: those holding fast to the belief there is only one real truth sometimes find their neighbors' hatred flare into violent action against them.

But on the whole, the social structure of Story Land can be summed up in the words, "eclectic and individualistic."

Sojourner's Kingdom

Book Base
The Holy Bible: Authorized King James Version. Blue Heron Book-craft, Family Edition, 3011.

Government Structure
"Now therefore, our God, we thank thee, and praise thy glorious name. But who am I, and what is my people, that we should be able to offer so willingly after this sort? for all things come of thee, and of thine own have we given thee. For we are strangers before thee, and sojourners, as were all our fathers: our days on the earth are as a shadow, and there is none abiding. O LORD our God, all this store that we have prepared to build thee an house for thine holy name cometh of thine hand, and is all thine own." (1 Chronicles 29:13-16)

The citizens of the Sojourner's Kingdom term their government an elected Judgeship under a theocracy. A careful reading of their book base made the Sojourners distrustful of kings, and they had lost the idea of presidents in the past. The name "Judge" is taken from the sections of the Bible wherein God speaks through prophets and judges to His people, exhorting them to stay truthful to Him and so be safe and prosperous. The Judge of the Sojourners never presumes to speak with the very voice of God, but is expected to act according to the words of God given in the Bible.

The Judge is elected by the general citizenry, and he must know his scripture if he expects to be selected. When first organized into a kingdom in the year 2 of the newly declared Book Base Age, a Reverend John Hillson was unanimously elected by the citizens as the first Judge. Any citizen of the country can be elected Judge by law, but it became traditional to have a member of the Hillson family elected. In the history of the kingdom, only one other line has been elected, and they were cousins to the Hillsons. The Judge is the undisputed ruler over the smaller bodies of state government, such as local court judges, the army, and the penal system. It is the state's duty to deal with the malefactors, outside diplomacy, and protect the kingdom.

It must be noted, the state is seen as only one part of what

keeps the kingdom running.

Picture three circles, state, church, and family. Each are their own separate entities, but they join in the center. This is a simplistic explanation of how Sojourner's Way functions. Only one circle is state government. The other two are independent of the state, but it is understood that the kingdom lives and breathes in that small triangular shaped section where all three circles join.

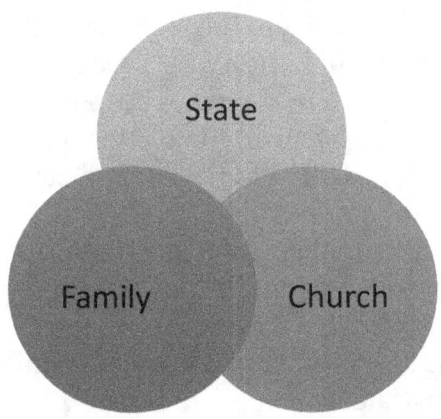

"The church" encompasses all denominations, it speaks of the universal church as represented by the individual congregations scattered throughout the kingdom.

"Let us hold fast the profession of our faith without wavering; (for he is faithful that promised;) and let us consider one another to provoke unto love and to good works: not forsaking the assembling of ourselves together, as the manner of some is; but exhorting one another: and so much the more, as ye see the day approaching." (Hebrews 10:23-25)

This circle inspires a firm sense of local community, as the separate churches serve their cities and neighborhoods. The churches are in charge of charity, seeing to the needs of the poor, the orphan, the widow, and of course shepherding the kingdom's citizens in religious matters. Involved in that shepherding is the church's opinion on a candidate for state office, especially on if the person in question is truly a Christian. The church has no say as

to who is appointed in the state, but they have a traditional role in offering advice to their congregations. They also have a very definite role in the formation of laws.

When a need for a new or amended law is found, a Law Court is formed, consisting of fourteen elected members of the church and fourteen elected members of the local court system, presided over by the Judge. The vote must be unanimous for a law to be passed or amended, and the Judge has the right to refer the law to the general public after the decision has been passed. If over half the citizens vote for a second debate, a Law Court of thirty pastors and thirty local judges will be called, and the process gone through again, with an eighty percent majority needed to pass the new law or amendment. The ruling of the second Law Court is undebatable.

Families are the single small entities that make up the entirety of the kingdom. The point is obvious, but unlike some of the other kingdoms, the Sojourners not only recognize the fact, they encourage it by acknowledging strong Christian families are the backbone of their subsistence.

"Lo, children are an heritage of the LORD: and the fruit of the womb is his reward. As arrows are in the hand of a mighty man; so are children of the youth. Happy is the man that hath his quiver full of them: they shall not be ashamed, but they shall speak with the enemies in the gate." (Psalm 127:3-5)

"And these words, which I command thee this day, shall be in thine heart: and thou shalt teach them diligently unto thy children, and shalt talk of them when thou sittest in thine house, and when thou walkest by the way, and when thou liest down, and when thou risest up." (Deuteronomy 6:6-7)

Families, by working their own individual jobs, are in charge of the economy of the kingdom. By seeing to their own children, they are in charge of the education of the next generation. And by voting, families choose the leaders in the state.

The state has no right to interfere in either church or family, unless an individual in those entities comes under the heading of malefactor.

Incompletes and Chimeras

"There is neither Jew nor Greek, there is neither bond nor

free, there is neither male nor female; for ye are all one in
Christ Jesus." (Galatians 3:28)

"Thou shalt not curse the deaf, nor put a stumblingblock be-
fore the blind, but shalt fear thy God: I am the LORD." (Levit-
icus 19:14)

"If a brother or sister be naked, and destitute of daily food,
and one of you say unto them, Depart in peace, be ye warmed
and filled; notwithstanding ye give them not those things
which are needful to the body; what doth it profit? Even so
faith, if it hath not works, is dead, being alone." (James 2:15-
17)

Most Sojourners would not understand if asked what they thought of incompletes. Inside the Sojourner's Kingdom there are no incompletes, only humans. There are numerous passages in the Bible where we find the blind, halt, deaf, etc. as objects of compassion, specially pulled from the crowd to be healed by Jesus and His followers. Mercy and practical help are also stressed in the Sojourner's book. If someone needs assistance, the Sojourners are one of the most likely places to obtain it.

Chimeras are undeniably different, but still considered fully human amongst the Sojourners. They are generally looked on with indulgence and can easily become objects of charity from the church or individuals as the chimeras attempt to make a living for themselves. Some live on stipends from local churches and do small, menial tasks among the congregation. Sometimes, a job is created in a company especially for a chimera's unique job skill or lack of intellect, solely to ensure the chimera sufficient funds to live on. A chimera is never turned away at the border or discouraged from creating a family and living as normally as possible.

Art and Music

"Sing unto him a new song; play skillfully with a loud noise."
(Psalm 33:3)

"And thou shalt make holy garments for Aaron thy brother
for glory and for beauty." (Exodus 28:2)

Music is a commanded way to praise God, it is prevalent throughout the country. Most music created is sacred, but there

are many instances of music used only as personal expression.

Art in Sojourner's Way notes how the Bible is poetic, paints many word pictures, and begins with a creative God making things of beauty. Art is encouraged, prized, and there is a plethora of styles and mediums employed in its making. The majority of the artistic works are realistic and hopeful; they depict what they see, because God made the seen and the unseen and pronounced them good.

Science and Advancements

Jesus was a healer when here on earth, Solomon a naturalist.

Within Sojourner's Way the freedom to pursue one's interests combines with little government control and a robust economy. Added to that are the Bible's obvious commands to help our fellow men when we can, Jesus' many acts of healing the sick, and instances of various naturalists recording their observations.

Combine those facts, and you have the perfect position for the sciences to thrive. The study of science, and the uses derived from its advancements, are prevalent throughout the kingdom. The rest of the world is reluctant to acknowledge the Sojourners proficiency at new medical and scientific breakthroughs, but often find themselves using their methods. Ingenuity runs rampant within the kingdom.

Army

"Happy is he that hath the God of Jacob for his help, whose hope is in the LORD his God: Which made heaven, and earth, the sea, and all that therein is: which keepeth truth for ever: Which executeth judgment for the oppressed: which giveth food to the hungry. The LORD looseth the prisoners: The LORD openeth the eyes of the blind: the LORD raiseth them that are bowed down: the LORD loveth the righteous: The LORD preserveth the strangers; he relieveth the fatherless and widow: but the way of the wicked he turneth upside down." (Psalm 146:5-9)

We see God's people making war throughout the Bible. But it isn't wantonly, there's always a reason behind it. Usually it's defense, sometimes it's a direct command from God in a select

circumstance. In the New Testament, Jesus puts forth the command to "turn the other cheek," (Matt. 5:39) and "he who lives by the sword shall die by it." (Matt. 26:52) Sojourners are a strong people, with no love of war but the willingness and ability to defeat anyone coming against them, and a desire to protect those who cannot protect themselves.

A standing army is necessary, both to patrol the borders to keep the wild beasts at bay and to stave off attacks from the rest of the world. In the history of the Sojourners, almost all the kingdoms have attacked at one time or another. The Sojourners are adept at warfare, their soldiers are some of the best trained and best outfitted in the world. Both sexes are taught defense, but only the men make a career of it in the nation's army, as this is the principle laid out in their book.

After the first hundred years of the Book Base Age, Sojourner's Way found itself with peace on its borders and a large number of trained soldiers with nothing to do but patrol. Jeremiah Hillson, the Judge at that period in the kingdom's history, allowed soldiers to place their names in the newly formed International Site of Warriors, making it possible to hire themselves out as mercenaries. The Sojourners were in high demand from small countries without the standing armies to contend with threats. Jeremiah quickly found a few rules had to be put in place (such as, a force of more than twenty men needs the Judge's approval, and a rotation system to ensure enough men on hand for the Sojourner's use). If the cause is a just one, the Sojourners tend to hire themselves at "discount prices" to those who cannot afford their services. It is a politic move, for any kingdom favorably minded toward the Sojourners, and not swallowed by larger enemies, means a little more safety for Sojourner's Way.

Social Structure
"And that ye study to be quiet, and to do your own business, and to work with your own hands, as we commanded you; that ye may walk honestly toward them that are without, and that ye may have lack of nothing." (1 Thessalonians 4:22-12)

"But if any provide not for his own, and specially for those of his own house, he had denied the faith, and is worse than an infidel." (1 Timothy 5:8)

Industry is a national pastime. Private property is a strongly-felt right in the kingdom, as God is the One Who gives and takes away; not other people. The taxes are kept only high enough to keep the kingdom safe (i.e., keep the judicial system, army, and Judgeship in good order). Any interest is allowed to be pursued, so long as it is not directly against the laws of the kingdom (based on commandments laid out in their book). With the freedom to hone any skill, the philosophical and social urge toward hard work, and the safety to enjoy peace, the economy within the Sojourner's Kingdom booms.

"So God created man in his own image, in the image of God created he him; male and female created he them." (Genesis 1:27)

"There is neither Jew nor Greek, there is neither bond nor free, there is neither male nor female: for ye are all one in Christ Jesus." (Galatians 3:28)

"Now therefore ye are no more strangers and foreigners, but fellowcitizens with the saints, and of the household of God..." (Ephesians 2:19)

No man or woman is above another in humanity or purpose. All are all born of the same line, created in God's image. If someone is a Christian, they are even part of the same family and will share the same home for all of eternity. God gives and takes away life, in His own wisdom. Therefore, every life is to be protected and cared for, as the soul is also nurtured.

"Wives, submit yourselves unto your own husbands, as unto the Lord. For the husband is the head of the wife, even as Christ is the head of the church: and he is the saviour of the body. Therefore as the church is subject unto Christ, so let the wives be to their own husbands in every thing. Husbands, love your wives, even as Christ also loved the church, and gave himself for it... So ought men to love their wives as their own bodies. He that loveth his wife loveth himself... Children, obey your parents in the Lord: for this is right... And, ye fathers, provoke not your children to wrath: but bring them up in the nurture and admonition of the Lord." (Ephesians 5:22-

25, 28, 6:1,4)

Women inside the Sojourner Kingdom are not meant to be public leaders. They are to give way in those spheres to their menfolk. You will note, however, that their book says "submit to your <u>own</u> husbands." Women are not called to obey all men, only those God has directly placed in their lives as headship figures. Also note the text immediately after speaks of husbands loving their wives as much as Christ loved the church. A careful reading of their book produces men who respect, protect, and genuinely love the women under their care, which allows a woman to respect, and even enjoy, their man's headship. Recall there is a strong sense of community flowing outward from the church's work. If man in a family is failing in his job as protector and Christ-like leadership (especially if a woman's situation becomes dangerous) there are those around the family who will notice and step in to help. When operating correctly and following the Sojourner's book, a family becomes both a steadfast rock against anything the world can throw at it, and a haven of rest to all those inside it.

> *"The aged women likewise, that they be in behaviour as becometh holiness, not false accusers, not given to much wine, teachers of good things; that they may teach the young women to be sober, to love their husbands, to love their children, to be discreet, chaste, keepers at home, good, obedient to their own husbands, that the word of God be not blasphemed." (Titus 2:3-5)*

Women are generally expected to work in the family sphere. But unlike some other kingdoms in the Book Base Age, they are respected and even in many cases revered. The women hold a high standard for the men, and it is much of what keeps the kingdom stable; deadbeats and jerks aren't likely to catch their sweethearts.

One summation of everything said above can be found in Colossians:

> *"Lie not one to another, seeing that ye have put off the old man with his deeds; and have put on the new man, which is renewed in knowledge after the image of him that created him: where there is neither Greek nor Jew, circumcision nor uncircumcision, Barbarian, Scythian, bond nor free: but*

Christ is all, and in all. Put on therefore, as the elect of God, holy and beloved, bowels of mercies, kindness, humbleness of mind, meekness, longsuffering; forbearing one another, and forgiving one another, if any man have a quarrel against any: even as Christ forgave you, so also do ye. And above all these things put on charity, which is the bond of perfectness. And let the peace of God rule in your hearts, to the which also ye are called in one body; and be ye thankful. Let the word of Christ dwell in you richly in all wisdom; teaching and admonishing one another in psalms and hymns and spiritual songs, singing with grace in your hearts to the Lord. And whatsoever ye do in word or deed, do all in the name of the Lord Jesus, giving thanks to God and the Father by him." (Colossians 3:9-17)

All Christians are one in Christ, Who is all in all. And all in Christ are to act like Him, the One who gave His life for the outcasts and sinners. Christians are to be kind to strangers, fierce against evil, watch out for one another, and do their work without causing trouble.

Strangers, those who are not Christians, are welcome within the borders of the kingdom. Their book base has a great deal to say on how a stranger ought to be treated, and it usually comes with the reminder that God's people too were strangers and sojourners in a foreign land (Exodus 22:21, Leviticus 19:34, etc.). Anyone can come into the border professing whatever religion they espouse. But if the stranger deliberately breaks laws in professing their religion, they will find the full weight of the government on their heads, just as any citizen would. Part of a Judge's job is to know the basic tenants of the other kingdoms of the world. This aids them in foreign policy, but it is also very useful in knowing which strangers entering their border ought to be surreptitiously checked on during their stay, in order to best protect their citizens. To become a citizen with voting rights, however, a person must profess the basic tenants of Christianity and be a member in good standing of a local church within the kingdom.

"Behold, I send you forth as sheep in the midst of wolves: be ye therefore wise as serpents, and harmless as doves." (Matthew 10:16)

The Sojourners strive to be open and kind, but not stupid.

Recipes

Pumpkin Spice Latte

1 tbs butter
1/4 cup pumpkin puree
1/4 cup brown sugar (or to taste)
1 tsp pumpkin pie spice
3/4 cup heavy cream *or* 1 cup half n' half
2 cups espresso *or* your favorite coffee

Melt butter in a skillet. Place pumpkin, brown sugar, and spice in skillet on medium heat, and stir until combined and sugar is dissolved. Add cream and heat to boiling, stirring often. Add coffee. Enjoy with a good book and a good friend.

Alternative: In place of the pumpkin, sugar, and spice, use a 1/3 cup of Libby's Pumpkin Pie mix instead.
Serves 2.

Sausage Twist

2 cans croissant rolls
½ pound sausage
8 oz cream cheese
3 tbs butter
½ cup cheddar cheese

Flavor Profile 1:
2 garlic cloves
2 tbs. Parsley
1 tbs rosemary
½ cup parmesan cheese

Flavor Profile 2:
½ cup diced green chilis (or salsa) + 2 tbs
½ cup Monterrey jack cheese

Preheat oven to 350.

Brown and drain the sausage. Warm the cream cheese in a bowl big enough to mix all the ingredients. Add the sausage and cheddar to the cream cheese. Melt butter and choose your flavor profile. For 1, add parsley, rosemary, and parmesan to the cream cheese mix, and crush the garlic into the butter. For 2, add the half cup green chilis and Monterrey to the cream cheese mix, and the extra 2 tbs green chilis to the butter.

Grease a cookie sheet and lay out one can of the croissant roll dough on the sheet. Roll or press it thin, then spread the cream cheese mix on the dough, trying to get the filling all the way to the edge. Press or roll the second can of dough flat, and lay it over the top of the spread out cream cheese. Brush the top of the dough with the flavored melted butter.

Take a sharp knife and slice the dough into one-inch-width branches down each side of the rectangle of dough, taking care to leave about an inch and a half in the middle untouched. You should end up with a trunk of untouched dough, and lots of little branches on each side. Take each of those branches and give it three or four twists. Brush with another layer of butter, and place in the oven. Bake for twenty to twenty-five minutes until golden brown. Brush with the rest of the butter and serve hot.

NOTE: if you like a thicker filling layer, double the filling. You may have some leftover that doesn't fit on the dough, but hey, it's yummy for a dip, or just to munch.

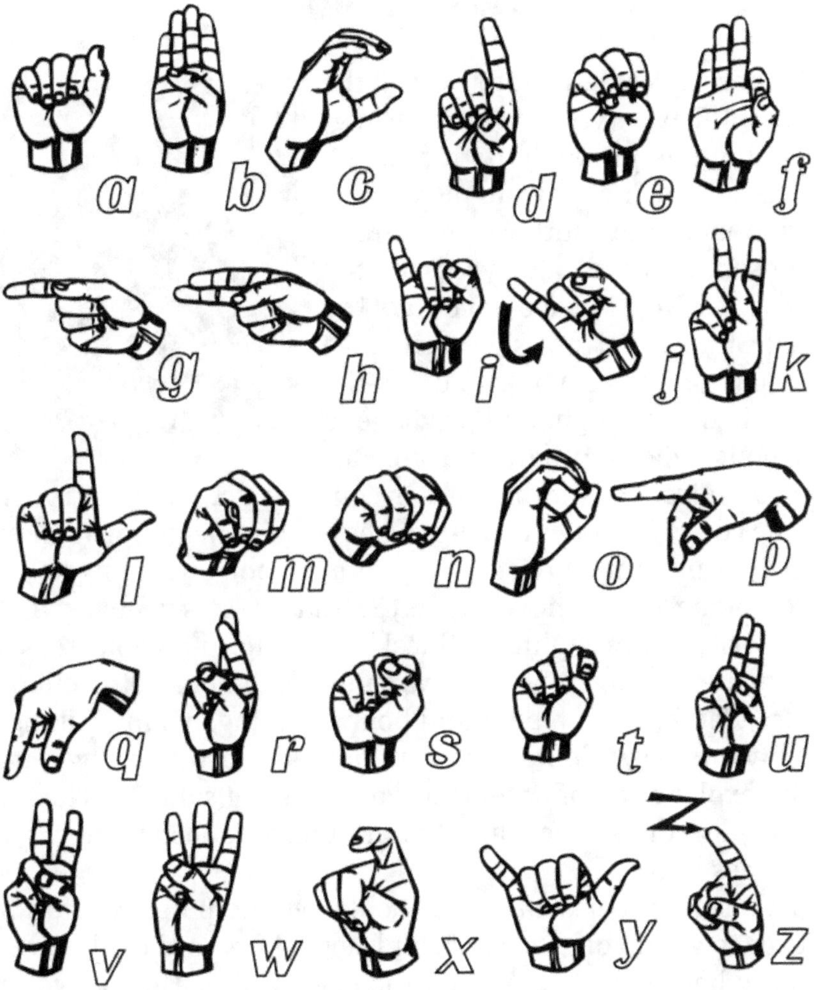

a b c d e f

g h i j k

l m n o p

q r s t u

v w x y z

Author Bio

Catherine Gruben Smith lives in the middle of Texas, which she begrudgingly admits is probably better than a magical tower. She grew up mostly in a dusty town in the southern New Mexican desert and will always carry the quirks. (Yes, New Mexico is a part of the United States, and no, she was not a missionary, and yes, you can drink the water.) It is her delight and privilege to be a housewife, mother, and an Earl Gray connoisseur. Another of her constant activities is trying to keep her dogs from terrorizing the house and neighborhood with their determination to be always underfoot and hungry. (The work of a dog lover is never done.) She has always been fascinated by the written word, philosophical reasoning, and good stories of bravery and honor. When not writing, reading, chasing children or dogs, Catherine can be found board-gaming, baking, hiking, or possibly broad sword fighting with her older brother. If you want a fuller explanation of Catherine, go and read Psalm 30. The heart and purpose of her life can be found there, especially in the last two verses.

Catherine prays reading her books will help her readers find the urge to get up off the couch and serve. The Lord of all life calls us to the battlefield, to mop up the enemy after He has won the war. Don't sit on the side-lines. We have the tools to fix this broken world.

Where to find more information, or contact Catherine:
catherinegrubensmith.com
catherinegrubensmith@gmail.com
posttenebrasluxbooks.com

Books by Catherine Gruben Smith

Sojourners:
Ravens Ruins
Ravens Rescue
Ravens Return
Ravens Refuge
Ravens Raid
Ravens Rebirth

Dreaded King Saga:
A Son Rises
Reign Falls
Knight Duty
Heir Raising
Splitting Heirs

Knight Jobs Series:
Wail of the Wyrm

Parabaloni:
The Parabaloni
The Slingshot Effect
As the Eagle Flies
Solitaire
Adele Angst
Blind Leader
Gathering Shadows
Black Out

Faerytales of Deweot:
How to Unmake a Dragon
Faery Wings and Pirate Things